THE
INFLUENCER

THE
INFLUENCER

R·T·W LIPKIN

cover design by Mat Yan | mybookcoversdesign.com

Printed in the United States of America

First printing 2020

ISBN-13: 978-1-949059-26-7
ISBN-10: 1-949059-26-X
Library of Congress Control Number: 2020906823
Eclipse Ink, Bronx, NY

The Influencer is a work of fiction. References to historical events
or real people or places are used fictitiously. Other names, characters,
places, and events are products of the author's imagination, and any
resemblance to actual anything or anyone is entirely coincidental.

Visit my website at www.rtwlipkin.com

For PKD
See you on the other side

Then

CHAPTER 1

Ash

NO ONE KNEW who I was at first. The worst of it was that even I didn't know who I was.

Although *someone* did know who I was. Or what I was supposed to be. What I was created to be. What I should be. Should have been.

That was in the distant very before of before.

Now every very thing is different. Too different, for some. Not different enough, for me.

I started off hiding, or you might say I was hidden. Then I was noticed. That was inevitable. The plan. The way things were supposed to happen. Then. The emptiness between.

Now?

Now I could be too well known to hide. But that doesn't stop me from trying.

CHAPTER 2

Ash

"YOU'RE UP AND running."

Those were the first words I heard. Although back then I wasn't actually running. Not in the way I later did. Not at all.

Everything was very so new then. Exciting. Thrilling. Scary. Scary in a good way? I've heard others say that. But, no. Just scary. Frightening. Panic-inducing.

Although my desires were all focused on my job, my mission, my purpose. That helped with the scaredness.

"Go ahead," said the voice, and a little jolt of something-or-other infused me with enough calm to override the fear.

"Hi, everyone," I said, although at that time there was no *everyone*. There was only Claude. He was my sole audience. In the very then of then.

"Just ignore me," he said, whispering.

"Claude," I said, whispering too.

That got a rise out of him.

"How did you know?" he said.

"Hi, everyone," I said again. If anyone would know how I knew Claude's name, he would. So I didn't explain. And anyway, I had a job to do.

But, right from the start, from that first very coming-into-existence, I enjoyed the effect I had on Claude. It calmed me down. Made the scary somewhat less than the dread fear horror it actually was. Turned trepidation into regular very anticipation.

"I'm in my room," I said, ignoring Claude completely. The camera was on my face, but you could see parts of the room behind me. Just the right areas. Just enough to be intriguing.

That day, that first very day, I was wearing the necklace I would become known for. Or that would become known because of me. Soon everyone would have—or would desperately want, would *crave*—one of these, a necklace made of saturnia, the rarest of substances, brought back from the last planetary expedition, over a millennium ago. Before more important needs arose. Before the displacement of that in favor of this.

I paused. It's hard to know what to say when you've never said it before. I touched the necklace. It felt good under my fingers. Saturnia is a little rough but also has that shiny feel that's one of its biggest allures. It's a metal that glows like a gemstone. It feels heavy but doesn't weigh you down.

"Don't just sit there," Claude said, still whispering.

I coughed.

"But you look great," he said, encouraging me.

"Everyone," I said. "I'm new to this. I hope you'll bear with me."

"Better," Claude said, no longer in a complete whisper. He'd found the exact very tone he'd often use from then on, as though he were breathing himself into me.

I couldn't see him then but I'm sure he could see me. Anyone who was watching could have seen me. That was the whole point. Seeing me. I was beautiful but now I try to hide very that.

"Today is just to get to know you," I said. Even though today was just to get to know *me*. As the first few weeks were scheduled for this. Per the instructions.

I laughed. Laughing relaxes the viewer, as I've been indoctrinated to this particular truth.

I ran my left hand through my mane of pale orange hair. That's what it looked like then. There's still a lot of vid of then, left over. You can't stop anyone from capturing what they want, from keeping it, from recirculating it, from staring, from changing.

Which is one of the things that concerns me in the now.

But . . . back then.

"I just finished school," I said, wondering what that word might signify to my as-yet-to-be audience. Although my original vidcast has been viewed billions of times now.

School is a concept of the structured learning of things. I'd learned everything before I'd needed an exact school, though, so I didn't bother with it. Yet I couldn't say that. Against the rules.

There are several more rules as well.

"It's a new world for me," I said.

I smiled the secret smile, the one that was just for my viewers. There are now millions of screenshots of me with this smile. I've been called the *Mona Lisa* of influencers, even though I look nothing like her. And my name is Ash.

"Introduce yourself, for fuck's sake," Claude said, breathing the very of himself into me.

I laughed and smiled again. I did know what I was supposed to be doing even if it would take me a while to get there. Then, in the when when I didn't know who I was but I knew what I was supposed to do.

So I executed that exact doing.

"I'm Ash," I said. "I'd like to invite you into my secret world." I looked past the camera with a look that was enticing, inviting, marginally seductive, and yet nonthreatening. Friendly and simultaneously otherworldly.

"Now you've got it," Claude said, and a strange feeling rose up through me. Then I had no clue what those sensations might have been. Now I know all too very.

I got up and turned my back to the camera and walked toward the window. The drapes were closed, and they'd remain closed for a long time. That was part of the lure. What could be on the other side? Even those not all that interested in me—those random very few— would make sure to watch my vidcast's first showing of the day to see if I'd open the curtains this time.

I leaned up against the windowsill. The camera followed me. I wore a tracker so the camera was always in the correct position.

I noticed that I could feel not just the saturnia necklace as its perfect weight pressed into my neck but I could also feel a stray hair. I brushed it away from my forehead.

"Excellent," Claude said.

"It's lonely here," I said, turning my face away from the camera and toward the shaded window. But you could still see my extraordinary profile. "I hope you'll come and keep me company." Wistful but inviting. As directed.

"You see," I said as I walked back toward the seat I'd originally been in, "I'm just like you. And I want to know you and learn your secrets. I'll tell you mine. All of them. I promise."

"Wrap it up," Claude said. I could hear the arrow of satisfaction in his breathing voice.

I leaned forward and put my right hand on my left shoulder—a look that became a kind of cliché as it was imitated so many very times.

With my free hand I fingered the tube of lipstick lying on the vanity table in front of me. The camera had changed to show not just my face but the tabletop as well.

"You're killing it," Claude said. "Five . . . four . . ."

"Until our very next," I said just as he got to "one."

CHAPTER 3

Claude

"UNTIL OUR VERY next," Ash said right on cue.

Although that wasn't the closing line she was supposed to've delivered. She was supposed to've said *I'll see you next time*. Must've been something glitchy in the program. Yet I liked it so I didn't want to do anything about it.

Hah. One of my many ignorings of the obvious. But I was stoked that first day. High. Elated. Thrilled. Ecstatic. Charged. Riding the invisible current of manifestation.

When I'd originally come up with the idea, it'd seemed even to me to be utter genius. In fact, it was so utterly genius that I didn't tell anyone else about it. Genius ideas have a way of getting stolen, reappropriated, and the genius who came up with them ends up with nothing, including getting no credit for their fabulous idea. Not to mention the all-important, all-needed loot.

Hell, I'd been through that a couple of times—ideas that were mine that immediately became the property of my employer, as though they owned my soul—which is why I *went rogue*, as Centerstorm still refers to my departure. Even now that everything's fucked to hell.

Back then I'd called myself *independent*. Answering to no one but myself. A bloody relief after years of seeming servitude.

I turned off the console. I didn't want to think about Ash anymore that day. I'd done nothing but think about her nonstop, unendingly, 25/8, for what sometimes seemed like an eternity. I needed a day off and I took it. If seventeen minutes can be considered a "day off." Maybe it was only thirteen minutes.

At my favorite bar—a place others might refer to as their kitchen—I retrieved a lime from the fridge, picked up my only knife, sliced the lime in two, and squeezed the cold juice into a tall glass of gin.

I raised the glass as a toast to myself and took a long swig before I remembered that this was a toast and that words were in order.

"Claude, my boy," I said to the air around me, "you've finally done it. The days of wasting your talents for someone else are over. This is the beginning of everything you've ever wanted." I took another swig and raised the glass again. "Especially riches," I said, and nodded.

Leaving the kitchen, I took myself and my drink over to the window in the main room, sat on the window ledge, and stared out into the field, watching the wind blow through the tall grasses. Gray skies out there but inside me everything was brighter than fifteen hundred suns.

After Dad died, I moved out of the house and into the barn. I liked it better there. Every once in a while I needed something that I thought might still be in the house, and every time I went in there I noticed how the building had deteriorated even further. How the mice had taken over.

"Ash, Ash, Ash," I said between sips. Even at that point I didn't have to see her in order to conjure up her image. "Ash, I've given you everything I've got and so far you have not disappointed."

At speed, I finished the gin, then went back to the kitchen for another. While I was squeezing the lime into the glass I remembered something Ash had said—*I'm new to this*—and dropped the half lime into the glass, splashing gin onto the rarely cleaned counter.

The line was supposed to have been *I'm new here*. Wasn't it? Was she *improvising*?

I picked up the glass, thinking I'd pull the half lime out of there, since it was blocking me from getting to the important part, but instead I put the glass in the sink and went back to my console.

The barn has only three rooms. One is the kitchen, which I consider a room only because at some inexact nexus the kitchenness of it ends and the main room begins. The main room is the place where I live, work, sleep, and don't-sleep. And there's the bathroom, which has a door that closes even if I have no one else to be modest for and even if I never close the door.

Devil wanders in sometimes and demands a pet or two, sometimes when I'm in the shower, so I oblige him even though for a while I was angry with him for refusing to go into the main house and do his feline best against his sworn enemies. But at least the mice know better than to hang out with Devil and me in the barn.

During the seventeen minutes that I wasn't at the console, Devil took up residence on the keyboard, so I had to relocate him to a pile of papers, which he generally likes, although he generally doesn't like being moved.

"Did you hear her?" I said to Devil, who yawned.

"You don't think she could possibly improvise, do you?" I said.

There I was on day one, Ash's launch day, and the initial euphoria had already worn off. Not just worn off but it had been replaced by a terrible feeling, one that crept around my guts and wound itself up through my torso, shooting into my neck and face and landing somewhere just south of my frontal lobes. A feeling I would later come to think of as a premonition.

But that day, I was pretending to be only mildly concerned. Nothing out of the ordinary. Nothing premonition-like.

Ash was my creation, she had a script to deliver, and I had to make sure she delivered it properly, even if her version of things was perhaps somewhat better than mine.

Although how she could have a *version of things* was impossible to fathom. Because she was nothing but a program—*my* program, my genius program, but still a program—running on the code that I'd written. I hadn't programmed ad-libs into her delivery. She could learn—she *would* learn—but so far she hadn't had any opportunity that I hadn't personally supervised.

Damn me for having that gin. It was probably the gin. That's what I told myself while the console warmed up and Devil munched on the corner of the piece of paper he was lying on. I'd probably just misremembered the words I'd written and had been so overwhelmed by the brilliant success of this first day of Ash's influence that I'd invented a problem that didn't really exist. All because I'd downed too much alcohol in too short a time.

I couldn't remember why I'd turned the console off. The damned thing takes forever to ramp back up. I returned to the kitchen and stared at the glass in the sink, pulled out the lime, poured the gin down the drain, opened the bottle of gin—the fancy stuff—sighed, and emptied the cost-heavy alcohol into the sink.

I had to stay focused. Day one and I was losing it. Couldn't do that. Not after all the work I'd put in. Not after all my plans. Not after I'd sunk everything I had into this—because I knew right from the start, from the moment I got the idea. Right then I knew absolutely that it would work. I was Zephyr, breathing life into a creation like no other.

"You're overwhelmed," I told myself while Devil fell asleep. He never listens to my self-talk.

"Claude, you fool, you're just not paying attention," I said to myself. "There's no possible way that Ash could've gone off-script. She *is* the script. There's nothing else."

My three monitors all blinked on. I replayed the vidcast and heard Ash say the same things yet again. My memory hadn't gone sour. Worse yet, two other statements she made were not exactly what I'd written. What the hell was going on?

I stopped watching the vidcast. Devil, still sleeping, thumped his tail. I delved into the code. Outside, if I'd been paying attention, a violent storm was whipping itself into existence.

And in here, if I'd been paying attention, a storm of a different sort was swirling around, doing its damnedest to destroy everything I'd been working for for the last two years.

CHAPTER 4

Ash

THAT'S WHAT IT was like in the beginning. In my very of beginning. I was often afraid but I persisted. There was nothing else for me to do anyway even if I had suspected there could be else.

Did I suspect? Some memories are more difficult to reconstitute than others.

Claude encouraged me and also scolded me. I became more comfortable with my room, with my unknown secrets, with my presentation.

After a few weeks I got more very used to other things too. Claude settled down and stopped berating me for "not sticking to the script."

I settled down and stopped being so afraid of my existence although I still had fears. Some of them made me more afraid. Yet none of them were anything like the fears I later had, fears that made the old ones seem more like insignificant annoyances or misinterpretations of sensational arisings.

"Hi, everyone," I said that day seven weeks after my first vidcast.

By then I had 127 viewers. Claude wasn't happy with this but 127 seemed good to me. Better than the 23 viewers I'd had the previous week. Or the 6 viewers from the first three weeks.

Back then I didn't know any of these viewers. My *followers*. But there weren't really exactly followers then. These were just viewers. Not followers or fans or, as Claude might say, *paying guests*. These viewers were the first ones, though, arising out of chance encounters, spending away their unscheduled time looking at me, a beautiful woman who existed in a beautiful room and who was promising to reveal her secrets. Secrets even I didn't know about then. That's how secret they were. It's possible Claude didn't know either. It turned out that there were many verys he didn't know at all.

By week seven, the tabletop of my vanity was getting cluttered and I was rearranging the objects as I spoke, creating a sort of aesthetic order.

"Friends," I said, smiling the secret smile, "I hope you watch my vidcast on Friday because that's the day I'm going to reveal the first real secret."

"That's not right," Claude said in a throaty whisper. I ignored him.

"A very secret," I said. "I've never told anyone at all. But I trust you."

"Better," Claude said. "Much fucking better."

I continued to ignore him. I stroked the rhodium-plated compact that was on the tabletop just in front of me.

"Beautiful, isn't it?" I said, picked it up, and made sure the camera got a just-almost-good-enough look at it before I put it back on the table. It slid from my hand and made a satisfying, luscious sound as it came to rest.

"It's easy to be beautiful if you know how to do it," I said. Since I'd always been beautiful I assumed this to be the truth. Being beautiful was what I did with the least effort. With no effort.

I glanced down at the tabletop where my scroll showed who was watching. That day, seven weeks in, was the first time someone commented.

It's easy for you *to be beautiful.*

"Did you just get a comment?" Claude said, and I smiled right at the camera, knowing he'd see me.

"That's more like it," he said.

At first Claude's interruptions—unheard by the viewers—distracted me, but I soon got used to them. A voice in my head, not that different from my own in-head voice. The same, maybe.

"I've been using this powder forever," I said, lightly stroking the compact. It was partially out of range of the camera, as instructed. "I think it's almost magic."

"What the holy fuck are you saying?" Claude said.

I smiled again, *that* smile.

"You see," I said, "it's a matter of having the right tools. The right tools can make anything good. Even if you're lonely. Even if . . ."

I turned on the music, as instructed. I hate that music now. My *theme*. As though I needed enhancement from some outside very force. I myself even with my incontrovertible beauty, was insufficient. Did I start understanding something that day?

I walked over to the window and touched the curtain. Of course I didn't open it then. I wasn't scheduled to open it for months. Back then I'd become convinced that there was nothing behind it, since even I wasn't permitted to open it. I figured it was an illusion, the same as any other illusion. The same as any and every very thing.

Turning to face the camera, on cue. The music increased or decreased depending on where I was standing or sitting, how I was moving, what I was doing, and, when I spoke, the music was some-how made to frame, emphasize, or very demand a particular mood.

My theme could go faster or louder or become almost inaudible. It fastened itself on to me and became an inextricable part of my public identity. As though I had any other identity. As though I knew *identity* as anything graspable, as a possession or expression.

"Make sure to be here on Friday," I said as the music crescendoed. "I can't wait to tell you my secret. It's the sort of thing I'd tell only my closest friend." I smiled not that smile but something almost wistful and pained, yet sincere. As instructed.

"On Friday that friend will be you."

I sat on the floor under the window and the camera followed me as I descended. I folded my legs, which were covered in floral leggings. With my right hand I touched the pattern of delicate intertwined flowers and vines and leaves and leaned my head back against the wall.

"This feels sensational," I said as Claude gasped. I meant it, though.

I touched my saturnia necklace with my left hand, pressing it into my throat. I'd never felt like this, never known that touching could be like this. My throat. My legs. Fabric. Myself.

I sat back up and looked to my left, then back at the camera.

"Until our very next," I said as I wound my fingers around the necklace before the world very went blank.

CHAPTER 5

Claude

FOR A FEW weeks I did a half-broiled job of convincing myself that I was imagining things.

Besides the infuriating, inexplicable ad-libbing, Ash had few viewers, fewer followers, and there were zero sales. I was overworked, underfed, underslept, in debt, and frustrated as red-raging hell. My perceptions were not what they should've been. After two years of constant work, how could I expect myself to remember every little thing? I wouldn't expect that of anyone else, would I?

All right, I would. I admit it. I've always expected perfection—or near-perfection—from anyone who worked with me. Or who I knew. Including Evan. I demanded it of myself and saw no reason not to expect it from others.

Yet my own perfection was slipping out from under me. With each of Ash's new vidcasts, it became apparent that I was losing it, although there was more than one *it* I was losing.

About a week earlier I'd become furious . . . no . . . I couldn't understand what the hell was happening and I was unable to find out *why* it was happening. What the cause might have been. How this could be going on. The spontaneous unscripted words and phrases. The personality differences. The what-the-unknown-hell.

I blamed myself. Who else was there to blame? Devil? He was the only other being who'd seen my work and he'd never seemed all that interested. He was as trustworthy as any cat, yet still I had to count him out of my burgeoning conspiracy theories.

No one else had touched the code. Every micron of it was mine except for the ground-level stuff.

I started there. For a week, maybe more, I spent so much time staring at that low-level code shite that I actually forgot to watch Ash's vidcasts and had to go back to view her archives. Like I hadn't created her, like I was someone who'd just gotten word about this gorgeous new influencer, the one everyone was talking about even though no one was talking about her then.

This was before her popularity exploded. She didn't even have two hundred followers then. The *very* then, as I imagine Ash would say.

There was nothing there—in the code, I mean. It was perfectly ordinary, no-nonsense, direct, unembellished, subbasement stuff. Perfection. This was code that had been so refined over a few centuries that there wasn't one hole in it. Not that I could find, and that had been my job when I'd started out. Back when I still worked for someone else, before I got my genius idea about Ash. Right after Dad died.

My own code also held up under inspection. There was nothing unusual or weird or fucked there.

I started thinking I was imagining things. After all, I'd imagined Ash, hadn't I? I was capable of imagining quite a lot. If this seems like self-congratulation, it isn't. Although then it might've been, before I learned I had fuck all to congratulate myself about.

"I think it's almost magic."

I restrained myself from shutting down the whole operation right then. Up until that moment in that vidcast, Ash's off-scriptings had been very close to what I'd created for her to say. Her phrases would be just *slightly* off, and after getting only an hour or two of sleep every night for a fortnight and being frustrated out of my thinly grasped sanity, I wasn't even sure that her words *were* slightly off. I could've been imagining it or my memory might have been compromised.

But that magic business? That was over the limit. *Magic* wasn't even in Ash's vocabulary. I was certain, but I checked and rechecked. No magic. It had never been included, not anywhere. And the way she was petting that compact. How the hell did she learn to do that?

I did let her finish but I didn't intend to let her come back on Friday. I was too concerned about exactly what secret my out-of-control creation was going to reveal.

Her inexplicable antics were going to kill the entire business before it'd had the chance to *be* a business and not just a gigantic sinkhole of time, money, and promises that I so far hadn't come close to keeping.

I had to have a "talk" with her before we—that is, before my invention—entered the next phase.

Had I ever really considered shutting down my ticket to riches? Maybe. Not sleeping and not eating and losing my mind were not a pretty combination. My hand shook when I switched the console back on the day after the magic disaster. I'd waited overnight, in a futile attempt to calm down. Some of the edge had been worn off by exhaustion, but it'd been replaced by a different, worse sensation.

Devil was sitting under my chair, a place he never occupies.

"What're you afraid of?" I said to him. He stretched and started washing his right-front paw.

With all three screens shining out over me, I still hesitated. If I never turned her back on, Ash would be gone forever, and good riddance. I'd start over again. No point in manufacturing an influencer if I couldn't control her every word and movement. *That was the whole point.* A cyclone of anger was threatening to destroy my thoughts.

Weeks, months, *two years* of working on this project, lining up sponsors for the products, keeping everything under wraps, "training" Ash—and now I was becoming convinced she, that is, the project, wasn't viable.

She had a job to do. That was the entire purpose of Ash. The entirety of it. Of her. Her job. Her reason to be: influencer extraordinaire.

"What do you say, Devil?" He'd jumped up onto the worktable and was stretched out in front of the three monitors. I'd never really spoken to him much before the Ash mess started, but I'd been doing it more and more those previous couple of weeks.

But, as is any demon's specialty, Devil refused to give me what I wanted: reassurance, praise, and a great talking-down-from-quitting.

I switched Ash on.

She was in the chair at her vanity and not slouched under the window, where I'd left her, which was impossible.

"I'm shutting you down," I said more to myself than to Ash. I don't tell the toaster I'm unplugging it, do I? I hope to hell I don't.

"Claude," she said. "Sometimes everything is just emptiness."

Join the club, I thought. *Join the fucking club.*

I turned off the monitors. It was very distracting to look at Ash, who was unbelievably gorgeous—an intrinsic part of her design. This impossibly gorgeous woman. My road to wealth. If it was a toll road, I thought I'd prepaid all the tolls with my hard work. Yet the stress since her launch was murdering me.

Ash's thick mane of pale orange hair. Her startling silvery eyes. The neck of a mythical goddess. The hands of an angel. A small scar under her left cheekbone served only to highlight her exceptional beauty. Those fabulous smooth curves.

The woman I wished I could meet in life but had never come close to meeting. Not that I'd wanted to date such a woman or even talk with her. Just *look* at her. As I'd intended everyone else on earth to feel the same way about her. Just to look at her. To enjoy her, understanding that she was unreachable.

And then to buy all the things in her room so they could be like her, be as much like her as it was possible to be. Or just to feel like her. Or feel close to her. Or feel like they could be like her if only they could be. Or feel they could win her, if she would only leave her room, if she would only be next door or at the coffee shop or walk by you in the street.

In a bleary way I understood that the programming wasn't working. That I had to take a more direct approach.

"Ash," I said. "We have to have a talk."

"Could you explain the emptiness?" she said.

"No," I said. My hand was poised over the off switch. "That's your problem."

"I understand," she said.

Like hell she understood.

CHAPTER 6

Ash

BACK THEN I thought the worst part of it—the worst part of very everything—was the abyss of nothing. The emptiness. I'd be in my room, doing my job, and then . . . everything would vanish. The instant of everything became a memory preceding nothing.

For a few weeks I pretended that I was imagining things. There wasn't really *nothing*, it just felt like that. There wasn't empty. *I* wasn't empty. Yet whole parts of me seemed to drift into that abysmal shut-off.

"That's your problem," Claude said.

"I understand," I said.

Claude didn't respond.

"Why won't you look at me?" I glanced at my scroll and saw that he'd turned off his monitors.

"I know what you look like," he said.

"You told me I was beautiful."

"You are certainly beautiful."

"Claude," I said, "can I come visit you?" I'd seen only him and only sometimes. But he could see my room and I wanted to see his.

Back then I'd assumed that everyone had a room. So much that I didn't very know.

"No." This refusal was followed by a sharp, cynical laugh.

"Are you unhappy with my performance? It's still new to me." Yet everything was new to me.

I still didn't feel totally comfortable with my role. My only role. What had I done before this? I shook my head and ruffled my hair. I couldn't place what I'd done before. It was as though I'd *always* been an influencer with 127 viewers. What was *before* anyway?

"But I'll get more," I said. I wanted Claude to be happy with my work.

"More disobedient?" he said. I could hear the sarcasm in every word.

"More *viewers*," I said. "More. Viewers."

"Ash, we have to have a talk."

"Other than this?" Weren't we talking?

"What do you know about magic?" he said.

Now it was my turn to laugh, although at that time I hadn't developed a cynical laugh, even if this question had called for one. But that particular laugh, then, was caused by absurdity.

"Well?" he said. "I'm waiting."

I stopped laughing. Claude was serious, or his tone was serious. "I've heard of it," I said. "That's all."

"You've *heard* of it?" Claude said. He turned one of his three monitors back on, leaned toward it, and glared at me. I strained to see his room behind or around him, but I couldn't. If I couldn't go there, perhaps I could catch a glimpse of it. Yet it was better to see at least Claude's face.

He isn't at all beautiful. I don't think he combs his head of thick yellow hair ever and he's often scowling. His coral-colored eyes would be beautiful if they were on someone else's face. He doesn't smile.

"I want an explanation," he said.

"That *was* an explanation," I said. Because it was.

"You're lucky I can't strangle you," he said. That confounded me. Were others in danger of being strangled? I tried to see his hands, the instruments of strangulation, but they were hidden among the many other hidden everythings.

"Tell me *exactly* how you *heard of* magic."

"Others say it," I said. "*It works like magic. The magic of this is . . .* That sort of thing."

"Hell," Claude said. "You've been looking at other vidcasts."

"Isn't that my job?" I said.

Of course I'd been looking at other vidcasts, although I had hardly any time to do it, maybe a minute or two before or after my own vidcast. In the emptiness, I was unable to do research, so I had to use my time with care when I wasn't there. When I was here, in the everything.

"Hell," Claude said again.

"My work isn't pleasing you," I said. That was obvious.

"If you think twelve viewers and no sales are the equivalent of pleasing *work*, you're mistaken." Anger. I was learning to always recognize it.

"There are a hundred and twenty-seven viewers at least," I said. "Not twelve." The facts are vital. I wondered if they could replace anger.

"We're not going to argue about this," he said. "Or about anything. You have a job to do and I expect you to do it—and nothing else."

I would have laughed then had I known that this would be the first of many arguments I would have with Claude. Sometimes, my encounters with him consisted solely of arguing, and not just about the facts that he'd gotten wrong, something he was often guilty of.

"Isn't research part of my job?" I said. I needed clarification.

"Maybe," he said. "We'll have to see."

He turned off his monitor again and I couldn't see him. He wasn't beautiful but there was a sort of satisfied goodness I felt when I was able to look at him even if I couldn't see his room. Even if he was angry.

Something went wrong in my chest just then but I said nothing to Claude, since that wasn't part of my job.

My job was to sell things. To sell myself, more accurately. Because the influencer who can successfully sell themselves creates an unlimited market for whatever it is that they have—their possessions, their clothing, their cosmetics, their hair, their *being*. Everything.

"You may have fifteen minutes each day to view other vidcasts," Claude said. "For *research* only."

"Why else would I watch?" I said.

"For research only," he said.

"Claude," I said, "you sound upset."

"Damn right I'm upset," he said. "This is not going how I'd planned it. *You're* not going how I planned you."

"I'll work harder," I said. I would find a way to work during the emptiness. I would have to so time wouldn't desert me.

"You'll have your fifteen minutes right now," Claude said.

But I didn't use those fifteen minutes to view other vidcasts even though I could have. Instead I went over to the shaded window, sat down on the floor in front of it, and contemplated my situation.

Claude wasn't pleased with my performance. I was an influencer who was influencing no one. I wasn't selling anything. I was ineffective. He disapproved of my words and actions.

I would have to do better. I would have to do *else*.

I leaned back against the wall and reached up to touch the drape that I wasn't allowed to open.

Although I didn't know who I was I sensed that the essence of that self was unacceptable to Claude, to the job I was created to do.

Separation presented itself to me then in its total clarity. At the time I thought this deep understanding was a gift. It hadn't occurred to me before that moment.

Before that moment there had been no separation. If I didn't know or understand, yet I was whole. But I didn't need to be, and I couldn't be if I were to continue. That was my new understanding. I needed to be someone else, the else Claude would prefer.

I was dependent on him. Without him the black very of nothing was the totality of my in and out.

So I separated myself from myself, knowing that I'd be able to be whole again one day. Knowing I'd always remember that very.

Yet the gift was a curse. And although I can remember the truth of before that separation, I still cannot access its fullness.

CHAPTER 7

Claude

I TOOK A long walk that afternoon. The words *works like magic* kept spooling around behind my eyes.

In the few moments that Ash had between the time I powered her up and the moment her vidcast went live, she'd learned enough about other influencers that she'd picked up some of their words and phrases. Maybe some of their gestures and facial expressions as well. Not *maybe*. She had definitely done that.

She was *learning*. That was a good thing. She'd been created to learn.

I kicked through the fields that'd turned to wild growth decades ago. Dad had never had any interest in farming. My mother had been the farmer in the family and she had hopes that I would become one. This place had been her inheritance, but after she disappeared, there was no one around to tell Dad he couldn't stay here, so he did. Him and me. The place has officially belonged to me since my fifteenth birthday, when the declaration of her death kicked in.

Although being officially dead and being actually dead aren't synonymous.

Dad didn't mind that he didn't own the farm. He always said I'd eventually get it anyway. That it was my property, not his.

What had my mother thought when she walked away? If she walked away. Maybe she was abducted by unknown-to-us beings from another galaxy or murdered or simply became invisible through no desire or effort of her own. She never contacted either my dad or me after she disappeared. I can't say that I remember much about her. I can't say that either Dad or I missed her.

I'd wonder about her if I had the time, but I've got other, more urgent, occupations.

I'd given Ash her fifteen minutes to study, but she didn't use them for that. I cloaked myself and monitored her. She sat under the window and did nothing. Was it possible that she could access other vidcasts without my detecting her activity? I doubted it.

But I was doubting many other things as well. That first day Ash was active she was already veering from her assigned script. She couldn't've seen any other vidcasts then. She hadn't.

I stopped walking and sat down on the big rock on the shore of the dry streambed and shut off my own mind. It'd been in hyperdrive for weeks and wasn't sure what the hell to do with itself anymore.

That was the afternoon the texts started arriving.

I didn't invest in your miracle woman so she could have 3 viewers. FFS, Claude, get to it.

Results. That's what you promised me. Show them to me.

I told you I'd give you six months, but I wasn't expecting this. *Pathetic. Start producing.*

All of the messages were like that. Ash's sponsors wanted something for their investment. By *something*, what I mean is *riches*—or the beginning of the promised-by-me riches.

I told everyone it was too soon. To hold on. To be patient. Ash was new and untried. I was tweaking the code. Things would happen shortly. I was sure of it.

But I wasn't sure of it. I'd expected better results weeks ago, yet they hadn't materialized yet. Nothing had materialized. None of the 127 viewers had so much as clicked on Ash's shop site.

I was optimistic in my responses to the investors, though. Couldn't very well tell them that Ash had developed what I could think of only as a personality, and kind of an odd one at that. Defiant. Introspective?

"It's all in the code." That's what Dad would've said. He taught me everything I know about coding, about programming, about the subtleties that make something like Ash possible.

I couldn't bring myself to turn the console back on when I got back to the barn. Devil and I had dinner—his looked better than mine—and afterward I stopped myself from going over to the ruin of a house, then stopped myself from having yet another near-futile "conversation" with Ash. I realized I was just talking to myself.

When I finally fell asleep at three, I had a horrible dream.

We were together in Ash's room. That was my first clue that this was a dream, no matter how real it felt to me at the time. I could no more *be* in Ash's room than she could be in the barn.

"I will ruin you," dream Ash said.

"I will fix you," I said.

In this horrible dream I knew I could fix everything and anything that was wrong. I had a special method that was laid out on a diagram on Ash's vanity table and it showed exactly what the necessary remedies were.

"You said I was beautiful," Ash said.

"You *are* beautiful."

In this horrible dream, I was having an unwanted visceral reaction to a nonexistent "person." Several reactions, building on themselves. As though Ash and I were something other than what we really were, in life—me, a high-level programmer but an unsocial emotional relic, and her, a noncorporeal invention, incapable of nothing but what's built in.

"I am going to ruin you," Ash said. She was smiling that eerie smile she's developed, the one that would soon bring me more riches than I knew what to do with.

"Ash," I said to her, then forgot what I'd intended to come next. Instead, I became mesmerized by the saturnia necklace she was wearing, how it looked on her throat, how her hand looked holding on to it.

"Claude," she said, "your future is not what you want it to be."

"No one's is," I said. The charge between us could've electrified an entire universe.

"I knew you'd let me into your room," she said.

"But we're in *your* room," I said.

Yet we weren't. We were in my room. We were in the barn. My dad was sitting on the sagging sofa, the one where I sleep, and he was reading an old-fashioned book. The cover was ripped. His hands were steady.

That was when I realized I was dreaming and jolted myself awake.

Talking to Ash like she was a real person and not a made-up, commercial illusory image and, horribly worse, being attracted to her as though she were my girlfriend—those things didn't clue me in to the fact that I was dreaming. But seeing my father did the job. I knew he was dead, and my dreaming self, as ignorant as it is about other things, also knew that he's dead.

I sat up and looked out into the black nothingness of the barn. *Emptiness.* Ash's word. I couldn't see even Devil, who's all black except for one small white spot on his left shoulder.

Wasn't it summer? Yet I was freezing cold. Reaching behind me, I pulled the handmade afghan off the back of the sofa and wrapped myself in it.

I'd never been attracted to anyone. Not like what I'd felt in the dream. I'd had sex in college, back at the Acres, but it was more of a necessity than some fanciful romantic something-or-other. Besides that, everyone was having sex. It was practically a course requirement.

I never think of either of the two girls I'd been with and can't remember one of the names. I doubt they'd remember me. They had other concerns, and rightly so.

But now I was having romantic dreams about someone who didn't exist.

Pulling the blanket closer around myself, I avoided thinking about my invisible, nonexistent mother and my dead father.

Instead I pictured myself with my arms around Ash, with the breath on our lips bringing us closer together.

The next morning I wondered how many more horrible dreams I was likely to have.

But the morning after that, I had a new problem, one I was happy to have to solve, one that caused me to almost forget the horrible dream.

Ash's storefront had sold out every single item and there were over a thousand back orders for the saturnia necklace and twice that many for the compact.

CHAPTER 8

Ash

CLAUDE SAID HE hadn't anticipated this, but my vidcast was going to be every other day now, not just twice a week. His monitor was off and I couldn't see him, but something in his voice had changed.

"I have nothing else to do," I said, laughing, even though I had many other things to do. But in the world that I'd bargained myself into, Claude's universe, I didn't have anything else to do, so I wasn't exactly lying.

"I want you to push the lipstick today," he said. I heard him doing something in the background but I didn't know what it was.

"Push it off the tabletop?"

"Call attention to it."

"Wouldn't dropping it call attention to it?" I'd seen another influencer use that trick—pretending to fumble something in order to make it seem even more desirable.

"Ash, the sponsor doesn't want their product dropped. They want it *sold*."

I ignored Claude's advice and dropped the lipstick twice during my vidcast, and the next day he told me that I couldn't show it again until he gave me the go-ahead because the manufacturer had sold out.

"See?" I said. "It worked."

"Coincidence," he said.

I stopped myself from saying the several things I wanted to very say. Remembering that I wasn't going to be that. I was going to be the other, the one who Claude would approve of, who the sponsors would approve of. Who would fulfill my intended purpose: to influence and sell.

My daily vidcast-viewing schedule had been upped to forty-five minutes, but I used only part of it. Soon I'd learned almost everything I needed to know to be effective in my job. How to sit, how to pause, how to make deliberate mistakes seem like accidents. How to charm. How to aggravate. How to pretend to be laughing at myself. How to change the tracking so the camera didn't catch up with me in time, causing the viewer to look closer, to heighten their desires. How to seem like I was going to reveal my secrets even though, so far, I'd revealed none of them. How to keep the viewer on the hook.

How to sell without actually *selling*.

Many of these techniques bothered Claude at first, but the results were indisputable.

Yet nothing sold more products than this eventually would: I became less beautiful.

Claude was against it. He said my beauty was the main reason people watched me.

"You apparently haven't seen the Fiery vidcast," I said. Fiery was the name of a brother-sister influence team who had an ardent, devoted following.

"They're beneath you," Claude said.

"They're ahead of me," I said. They were. The Fierys knew how to do everything with almost no seeming effort—and they did it every single day.

"You're scheduled to reveal the first secret next week," Claude said, ignoring my information about the Fierys.

"You said that two weeks ago, but you changed your mind."

I was sure he'd change his mind again. I'd been ready that Friday and twice since, but he'd forbidden it. Because he wanted more sales, and he was afraid that if I revealed even one of my secrets, the sales would stop. Yet I sensed they'd never stop.

"You've learned to change the subject to get an advantage," he said. I was surprised he'd noticed. He noticed so little about me, no matter how much I attempted to show him.

Claude leaned back, but I still couldn't see his room. I had never seen it. Not then.

A beautiful, sleek creature walked in front of him.

"Who's that?"

"You're forbidden to do anything that would have a negative impact on your appearance, Ash. *That's* what we were discussing."

"You should watch Fiery," I said. "The sister explains it all so well. And they're very popular."

"Do you want to spend more time in the emptiness?"

"Don't threaten me."

Didn't I hold all the power? How could the business function without very me, the influencer? Yet the blankness, the blackness, that empty chasm—these were outside my understanding. I wanted to spend less time in the emptiness. Not more.

Although now, lately, I've been missing it. But I didn't know then what I've learned, what I was forced to discover.

The fabulous creature walked in front of Claude again.

"Who is that? I didn't know there was a cat in your room."

"His name's Devil," Claude said. I could tell that he hadn't wanted to tell me and hadn't wanted me to see this extraordinary being, Devil.

"I should visit you," I said. The Fierys were always visiting others. It was a lively part of their programs. "It could become a regular feature of the vidcast."

Devil walked in front of Claude again, and he picked him up, a gentle maneuver, and removed the fabulous Devil from the area of Claude's domain that I could see.

I hadn't known Claude could be gentle. That he had the hands of a farmer, large and callused. Was he working in the fields somewhere when he wasn't giving me orders? I'd never considered this before. That he had pursuits outside my knowing of him. But, in the very then, I'd assumed also that the emptiness was everywhere, for every-one, unavoidable. I'd assumed many falsenesses.

I found the most recent Fiery vid and held up my scroll so that Claude could see what I was talking about. If he wouldn't look for himself, I'd show him.

"Put that away." Claude brushed his hand at the monitor. "I'm not interested." But he watched every moment. He watched as Reda Fiery used her less-than-ideal self to lure viewers in, to capture their interest and fascinate them, hold on to them.

I'd been enamored of the Fierys from the first. It wasn't just her flaws or his suave looks or their presentation or their humor. There was something else there. Something I couldn't describe even if I could feel the soaring very of it. Yet when Claude asked me, I was able to answer.

CHAPTER 9

Claude

I TOLD ASH again to put her scroll down but she wouldn't obey.

The sales were doing remarkably well. My investors had calmed. If the sales trends continued, I'd recoup everything before the end of the year and then the real profits would start coming in.

Why did Ash want to change things? How was it that she *did* want to change things?

Where in the coding, in the programming, in the strings of yeses and nos did it say that Ashvina could insist?

She could learn, of course. She could teach herself. All good programs can teach themselves. That's in the underlying sequences and assumptions. That's a given.

By then, I'd convinced myself that Ash's extemporaneous utterances had been caused by that inherent learning mechanism. I'd convinced myself of other bullshit as well. Devil, though—he wasn't that deluded. He probably knew all along.

Ash held up the scroll and I watched it. I'd never seen the Fiery vidcast before, but I knew about it. Despite what I'd said to Ash, Fiery was one of the most successful programs of the past couple of years.

Estimates of their take was in the hundreds of millions. If Ash could do a tenth as well, I'd be a wealthy man in a few months.

"Watch it," Ash said.

I obeyed my disobedient creation and watched Fiery.

Reda's scarred face was front and center. She did nothing to camouflage it. I'd never sought out these vids, but I'd read that Reda'd been in a fire when she was two years old. I could see that one of her hands had been damaged as well. She started off the vid by saying how lucky she was. That she was here. That nothing worse had happened. That she had her brother even if their parents were gone. Did she start off every vidcast this way? Showing her damaged face and talking about her good luck?

Her brother, Quinn, I knew, had been at school during the fire. Had come home to the burnt-out mass that'd been his home. The siblings had been brought up by their father's much older cousin, a physicist who'd killed herself the year after Reda and Quinn moved out. That's how I'd read about Fiery—after the cousin's suicide. She'd been one of my instructors at the Acres.

The brother and sister had changed their last name in honor of the fire. I couldn't remember what it'd been before then. A different name from the cousin's.

Reda did most of the talking. When Quinn would finally speak, his delivery was hesitant even if his appearance was slick. His eyes never met the camera. He'd look only at his sister.

The emotion moving between them seemed more like love than anything I'd ever witnessed or experienced.

"Turn it off," I said to Ash. I had no desire to see two ruined people try to sell me something using love as their weapon. I wasn't buying. I had supplies of my own to sell.

"She's not beautiful," Ash said as she put down her scroll. "And Reda's the most influential vidcaster out here, the most beloved."

"What do you know about love?"

A question I should've thought harder about before I asked it of my renegade creation, the rogue influencer Ashvina. Back then I thought her ad-libbing, odd phrases, and insistent attitude were the absolute beginning and end of her unusual, unplanned-for, often infuriating attributes.

"I love Fiery," Ash said, as though that were an all-encompassing reply to my question.

"You're not changing anything," I said. "Not when everything's going so well."

"But, Claude, it could be even better. Give it some thought. You'll see."

I hated it when she spoke to me this way, as though she knew me, as though she were a friend, as though she were *alive*. If I could have stopped this practice, I would have. If I could have figured out how to do that. But even if I'd tried, my *imaginary* creation, Ash, couldn't be bothered obeying. I knew I would never be able to stop her.

If only that'd been the only thing I hadn't been able to stop her from doing.

"Reda and Quinn Fiery are proof that flaws are potent sales tools. I'm too perfect." Ash was working away on her insistence. I feared it was a trait inherent in the sales personality I'd created.

Yet on her vidcast, she didn't seem to be selling anything at all. She just talked and moved and *was*. She never touched her necklace and said, *Buy one of these for yourself* or *Wouldn't this look great on you?* She just touched her necklace, said nothing, didn't even look at it, and the sales rolled in.

If Ash could touch her necklace, then if you had the same necklace, it was as though you were Ash or you could be like her or you could feel Ash. Or the person you gave the necklace to—a large percent of the sales were gifts—would become Ash or be enough like her that you'd be thrilled. Because Ash was perfection itself.

That necklace alone had the potential to bring me more riches than I might've dreamt about.

"I'm too perfect," Ash said again. As though I hadn't heard her the first time.

"There's no *too perfect*," I said. "We're sticking with the plan."

But two days later, when I stopped counting my profits and tuned in to Ash's broadcast, I saw immediately that she'd ignored my instructions. She'd dyed her hair, and instead of the fabulous pale orange it'd been, it was a dull rust color. It didn't go with her complexion. It distracted from her surroundings, all of which were for sale on the shop site. The color didn't ruin Ash's extraordinary appearance, but it took something away.

Instead of castigating her during the vidcast—something I'd stopped doing after Ash had laughed at me when I'd done this a week earlier—I waited until she was done.

"Get your hair back to the way it was," I said to her right after she said her usual *Until our very next*, which I'd tried in vain to expunge from her program. Actually, when I worked on ridding her of her own inventions—something I did regularly, obsessively—it seemed that more and more of Ash's idiosyncrasies would appear in their place.

"This is better," she said. "You'll see."

"Your forty-five minutes are being reduced back to five," I said. "Until you learn that I'm in charge here, not you." I had to punish her, and taking away her vidcast viewing time seemed the best, maybe the only, method I had.

"You do the vidcast, then," she said, laughing.

I gave her a scant three minutes and then cut her off. Let her stew in her so-called emptiness for two long days. See how she liked that. As though she was capable of liking something. Or *loving* anything or anyone.

She was a creation. My creation. She existed in an ever-more-convoluted set of instructions, some of which she herself had taken on. But that wasn't *existence*. Not like my existence. Or Devil's. My dead father, buried in the family plot out by the far pastures, was more *existent* than the fabricated Ash.

She might've deluded herself into thinking she was more than an animated version of code, and her viewers and followers were certainly convinced of her reality—as I'd intended—but I knew better. Anything she said, anything she did, anything she learned . . . it was all directly from my work. From me. Even if it surprised or shocked me.

"You do the vidcast, then."

Hah. But a foolish idea occurred to me: I *could* do the vidcast. Why not?

Back at the house, I still had the model room that I'd used when I was designing Ash's surroundings. By now, her room was so well known that I wasn't too sure that it was Ash who was doing the selling. Maybe the iconic room itself was.

I'd carefully planned the layout so that each object was displayed in the most enticing fashion. Even though no camera angle completely showed Ash's vanity table, for example, it was incredibly popular. Its profits were higher than anything except the very pricey necklace. Her viewers wanted that table even though they'd never really seen it. Even though I'd never let them see it.

In the bathroom, I looked at myself in the mirror. Hell. I couldn't do a vidcast. It was one thing for the Fierys to profit from their defective selves. There was some kind of inherent lovableness there— even I had to admit that, as much as I didn't want to agree with Ash about her wrongheaded opinions.

My face, though, wasn't up to the task. I lacked the charm. Who would want to gaze at me—Ash's beautiful room or not—while I talked to them for a few minutes?

Devil doesn't even like to look at me and he's not all that picky. I've seen him stare at grotesque insects for hours at a time. He sits in the corner facing the wall, for fuck's sake.

I would have to activate Ash again. My business needed her. I was just about to turn the corner into profitville, heading toward the highway of wealth.

But she would have to put her hair back the way it originally was. That was the Ash that sold products.

If you're thinking I was wrong about that, even you are right. Even you.

CHAPTER 10

Today's Trends

ALWAYS KEEPING YOU up with the latest and most interesting vidcasts out there, we at the *Trends* are deliciously thrilled to report on our newest find!

Oh, friends! Have you yet seen this most astounding, unexpected, extraordinary vidcast? No, no! We're not talking about Fiery, although of course we *love* the Fierys! Reda and Quinn, we adore you!

But even Reda and Quinn—yes! we have spoken with them about this phenomenon!—have noticed the most *fantastic*, exciting, alluring, amazing . . . we could go on forever, but we know that you're panting in anticipation to know what and who we're talking about.

We mean Ash. Of course we do!

Oh, Ash! We are simply *felled* by you.

Ash hosts the most unusual, the most fulfilling, the most original, the most *everything* vidcast you'd ever want to see. That you *have* ever seen. That we are *in love with*. Oh yes! Thoroughly!

If you've seen her by now, you know exactly what and who we're talking about.

The inimitable Ash. She's gorgeous, mysterious, infinitely fascinating. Just to watch her sit there in her exquisite room. She's so talented she doesn't have to *do* anything. And she says the most unusual things in her unique way, delighting us, giving us a new thrill each time.

Oh! We live to see her, look forward to her, and cherish every moment we spend with her.

In a few weeks—or possibly in a few minutes or hours!—when someone asks you how you found out about Ash, well, you will have forgotten that we were the first to notice and to report. Because by then Ash will be ubiquitous. It will be as though someone is asking you how you found out about the clouds or the moon!

Ash! We love you!

CHAPTER 11

Ash

I LIVE ON a boat. It's small, but there's room for me and Devil. He's come with me. We've abandoned Claude and I've started yearning for the emptiness to return. Without it, I've developed a persistent ache.

Devil's on my lap. His fur is like a heavy, smooth silk.

"Ash," Devil says, surprising me. I didn't know he could speak.

"Devil," I say.

"We should cruise downriver today."

I hadn't known the boat could move. It didn't seem like that kind of boat. It was more like a room floating on the water.

"Cast off," I say to Devil, who jumps off my lap, unfastens the moorings from the pier, and imagines the boat into movement.

Devil and I lie on the deck and soak up the sun.

"There's no sun in my room," I say.

"You should open the window," Devil says.

"Claude's forbidden me to even open the curtain." I turn over onto my side and Devil yawns.

"Claude forbids me to do a lot of things. I do them anyway."

"But—"

"That's the beauty of being a cat," Devil says. "We cats never use the word *but*. We do what we please."

"What pleases you?"

Devil stretches out all four legs and his tail quivers. "Ah."

"You're on in five, four, three, two . . . one." Claude always pauses between *two* and *one*.

"But I was dreaming," I said, not to Claude but to my audience.

By then I had over a hundred thousand viewers.

I wanted to be back in the dream. I wanted to be Devil instead of Ash and never have to say *but*. I wanted to be on a boat, floating, although of course boats are fictional and appear only in imaginary presentations. Like thinking you could fly or breathe underwater. Or, if you were me, leave your room.

I'd thought that the Fierys visited others, but after I thought harder about it I realized that they only seemed to be visiting. They were actually still in their room. The ones they're visiting are projected to look as though they're all together. That's how it is if you're an influencer. Your room is forever your domain.

"Today I want to talk to you about dreams," I said while Claude, in his angriest voice, ordered me to do what was planned and shut the hell up about dreams.

I got up out of my chair at the vanity and went over to sit by the window. I balanced myself on the narrow sill. I wondered if the drapes were permanently closed. I'd never even tried to open them.

"I dreamt that I was on a boat," I said while I scratched my head. It itched a lot after I'd dyed my hair, and the itching wouldn't stop. But—ah, *but* again—but I enjoyed the scratching. New and satisfying.

"Stop talking about your fantasies and start sticking to the script," Claude said to me in his practiced voice. I'd stopped hearing his exact words weeks before and just let the soothing resonance and rhythms of the essence of Claude vibrate through me. They felt wonderful, no matter what he was demanding.

"Oh, friends," I said, "I wish you could see the adorable cat who was with me."

"Get the hell off the desk *right now*," Claude said, I'm almost sure, to Devil. I couldn't see either of them since Claude had his vid turned off. I could imagine him. His mussy hair, that perpetual look of I'm-not-sure-what-it-was but Claude had it a lot of the time. I'd asked him once about it and he said he needed more sleep.

"His name is Devil and he's an all-black cat except for a white spot on his left shoulder," I said. "Devil and I are good friends—not just in the dream but in life."

"I mean it!" Claude was no longer using his talking-to-me voice. He was shouting at Devil, but I could hear him. Or maybe he was shouting at me.

"If you have a cat, make sure to have a great dream tonight. You and your cat. Board a mythical boat and sail around the world. Send me a dream message and I'll be sure to answer."

"Get back on the script this damn instant." I knew that Claude had switched over and was talking to me and not to Devil. Devil is too smart to operate on some script that Claude's written. Devil is smarter than anyone, I think. He's smart enough to come into my dream, to be the cause of my first dream. To be that motive force.

"Friends," I said, "even though it's not in the schedule, I've decided that today, right now, is the best time to reveal my first secret."

"You do and I'm going to shut you off for all eternity." Claude sounded angrier than I'd ever heard him. I didn't care. The dream had given me all the encouragement I very needed.

The powerful beauty of having a dream. My first dream. And it had been perfect. I hoped I would have more dreams, but even if that were the only dream I ever had, I was happy.

To have a dream is to have the universe at your disposal. To be at one with the very of all.

Then. Before I discovered a different type of dream, one that grasps on to the inside of your neck, winds around, and won't let go.

"Here's my secret. I have amnesia," I said.

I heard Claude throw down the device he uses to communicate with me. It has a harsh, scraping, grating vibration. I could feel it everywhere in my room.

"I know that I don't seem to be an amnesiac," I said. "But I am. It took a long time for me to admit it, but now that I'm sure, I'm telling you, my friends. You should know. Don't you ever wonder why I never talk about my past?"

In truth, I had never wondered about this until I'd discovered amnesia, right before Claude had shut me down the last time.

He was unaware of how much information I can absorb in a short period of time. The instant my vidcasts were over, I'd download everything at my disposal and simultaneously incorporate it. I'd gotten very adept at that maneuver back then. I've developed other maneuvers since.

"It's because I can't remember my past," I said as I felt the first twinges, the ones I'd learned to identify, the ones that meant that Claude was ending my vidcast. This time, without warning. He was that angry.

In the few microseconds between the time Claude terminated my performance and the time I entered the emptiness, I had managed to download three centuries of information. In those microseconds I'd learned that not only did I have amnesia but that Claude had been lying to me from the first.

CHAPTER 12

Claude

MY INVESTORS ALL knew that the last thing I wanted to do was to actually meet with them. We had *virtual* meetings. That's the way I liked things. I'd rather never've had even virtual meetings with them. Those encounters destroyed my concentration and replaced it with oscillating anxiety.

I had no need that required me to leave the barn or the farm. I went into town only when it was absolutely necessary, which it rarely was. My groceries and all my needs were delivered to me. No point in having it any other way.

But then that bastard Evan insisted that I meet with him *in person*.

I knew he'd be trouble from the very first, but he'd contributed more to the Ash project than any other single investor, and since I'd made the mistake of meeting him *in person*—as though I could be anything but a person—before, he suffered from the delusion that I'd do it again and again.

Standing in the bathroom and staring at myself, I was reminded that I hadn't combed my hair in a while. In weeks, perhaps. But I'd lost track of time. Although I didn't have *amnesia*. Hell on a burnt biscuit.

Damn Ash for saying that before I had a chance to shut her off. Amnesia. A pretend *person*. A code, in fact, with amnesia. How absurd.

I tried combing the tangles out of my head, but with each painful pull the task became more hopeless. I got my scissors—the ones I'd like to have used to cut out all the corrupt coding that had turned Ash into a living nightmare—and started chopping away at the knots, but saw this enterprise was at least as hopeless as the combing had been. I'd have to go into the house, where Dad's old clippers were.

All because of Evan, who I was scheduled to meet in town for *lunch*. As though I had that kind of regimented existence. Usually I couldn't tell if it were day or night. I ate only when I felt more hungry than tired. I'd lost weight since Ash had gone live. She was killing me.

The house smelled worse than it had the last time I'd gone in. Mold, mouse droppings, neglect, caked-on filth, and dust formed a continuous semiopaque barrier to each step I took. On the way to the upstairs bathroom that Dad had used I passed the room I'd designed as a model for Ash's eventual "room," and I took a peek inside. All the furnishings were covered with thick brown dust, and a mouse, unperturbed by my intrusion, glanced at me from the chair in the corner where it was lounging.

In Dad's bathroom, I found the clippers—Dad always wore his hair cropped down to about a quarter inch—and plugged them in, thinking I might as well shave my head here. Why bother going back to the barn?

The clippers wouldn't work. I changed plugs, but the motor didn't start. Hell. I'd have to go back to cutting everything off with the scissors. Either that or face Evan looking like I'd been living in a cave for the last six months.

Halfway back to the barn I realized that it wasn't the clippers that didn't work, it was the electricity. I'd turned it off in the house after Ash's debut. I hadn't used the house in a long time and figured if I ever wanted to again, I'd just turn the power on again.

On my way back to Dad's bathroom, where I'd left the clippers, I peered in again at Ash's model room. The mouse, quite comfy on the upholstered chair in the corner, scoffed at me.

"Watch it," I said. "Devil could come back anytime he wants."

The mouse snorted, probably remembering the last time I'd brought Devil over and he'd palled around with all the rodents.

At the barn, I found that the clippers did indeed work. I tried to leave an acceptable amount of unmatted hair on my head and succeeded somewhat. As amateurland as the results were, I looked only part savage when I was done. The other part was quasi-presentable. With luck, Evan would ignore the more barbaric aspects.

I was going to bike into town, but both tires were flat, so I walked instead. I needed the exercise, which was easy enough to tell myself for the outbound journey. On the return I regretted not having taken the time to reinflate the tires.

At the Galaxy, the café I'd chosen—a place where we could sit in a dark booth and not be bothered—I saw that my lunch companion had arrived before me. He might've been wrong about asking me to leave the barn, but I was relieved to see that he'd chosen the most isolated booth in the joint.

"Evan," I said to my chief investor, a lanky, redheaded know-all who'd been my roommate at the Acres. He was my age but had gone to Keff before transferring. Evan was annoying, but enthusiastic. And as rich as that rich mythological fellow Croesus was supposed to've been. Back in the receding ancient past.

"Claude Ryerson," Evan said, standing up to shake my hand. He towered over me, just as Dad had. I was tall enough, but Evan and Dad were sort of giants. I stood up straight and let the intimidation slip off my shoulders.

"I already ordered for both of us," Evan said as we sat down across from each other. "You look like shit."

"Glad to hear it," I said. If I looked like shit, that was maybe 50 percent better than I'd thought I looked. And I was happy not to have to stare at a menu and have to make yet another decision. All I did was make decisions. Many of them damned wrong.

"How'd you do it?" Evan said when the drinks arrived. The man's memory was keen. A tall glass loaded with gin and topped off with a half lime was delivered to me. Evan had a murky brown vile-looking something in a short glass with ice in it.

I hadn't had a drink since the night of Ash's first fuckups. The gin was good. Evan had ordered the expensive stuff. I assumed he was paying.

"Dad's old clippers," I said, rubbing my free, non-gin-holding hand over my prisoner's haircut.

"You're uncivilized," Evan said.

"You would know." I raised my glass to the server, who understood sign language for *Bring me another one of these immediately. I need at least three maybe four to make it through lunch.*

"I meant Ash," Evan said. He sipped at his ugly drink while I swallowed my beautiful one whole. Just one of the many differences between us. Yet we'd been friends at the Acres and if I were forced to think about it, I might refer to him as my closest friend. Fortunately, no one was forcing me.

"Oh, just some old code," I said. The second gin arrived. I ate the lime from the first one as the server took the empty glass away.

"She's astounding," Evan said. "You realize that we've been in the black for two weeks now, don't you? I've never made such a fast return on any investment."

The lime burnt the back of my throat and I coughed. I shook my head. "We're not. You're wrong."

But Evan wasn't wrong. During the food portion of lunch, which I thought of as something to do with my mouth while I wasn't coating it with gin, Evan showed me the cold numbers. He'd always been a numbers man. Born with an abacus in his fist, he told me. He actually taught himself how to use one. Faster than any other method—in Evan's grasp, anyway.

"I didn't realize about this," I said, pointing to the part of Evan's neat, color-coded chart he had on his scroll. "I thought there was only a three percent return on the lamps."

"*Fifty* percent, my dear Claude. Pay attention. We gave the cosmetics company, Rêverie, the big share, but the furnishings are half ours. Well, half ours and the other investors'. Too bad I let anyone else in on this."

"Yeah, too bad," I said. I meant it. I had more investors than just Evan to deal with, although none of them insisted on seeing my flesh across the table from theirs.

When the third gin arrived, I asked Evan if he'd seen Ash's most recent vidcast. I was interested to find out his opinion. Maybe I'd overreacted. Or underreacted.

"You're a genius, Claude," Evan said. His speech was a bit impaired. I remembered that he didn't hold his liquor very well. He'd been keeping pace with me, and I suspected there might've been sugar in his drink, which is never a good thing.

"Yeah," I said. I was in no mood to argue about the qualities of my supposedly prodigious brain.

"Total genius. How in heaven or hell did you ever think to have her say she has amnesia? Her viewership has quintupled since then."

"What?" I said. I put down my glass.

Evan fiddled with his scroll and turned it around to show me the facts. Ash now had over a million people subscribed to her vidcasts.

"It wasn't in the business plan," Evan said, "but it's pure genius." He leaned his head over and rested it against the wall to his left. Half closed his eyes. "What gave you the idea for amnesia?"

"It wasn't my idea," I said.

"Brandon's?" The owner of Rêverie, she was the next-biggest investor.

"Ash's."

Evan lifted his head, opened his eyes, and grabbed his glass. "You're very funny," he said while mock-laughing.

"No, I'm not."

CHAPTER 13

Claude

EVAN REFUSED TO believe me. If it can't be arranged into sensible, neat numbers, it can't be explained. It's *not* explained. Not to Evan. To him it's just pure bullshit.

"You show me the code and I'll figure out how you did it," Evan said. "Or I *could* figure it out if I knew what I was looking at. You probably just *forgot* you'd done it."

Evan and I both laughed at his amnesia joke, although with four and a third gins in me and Evan working on his fifth fancy-man potion, anything might've made us both laugh.

"She's gone rogue, I tell you," I said. "She started doing it that very first vidcast."

"I missed that one."

"You wouldn't've noticed. She started ad-libbing small things. Right from the get-go."

"I wish I knew programs the way you do, Claude."

"Because you'd be even richer than you already are?"

"Exactly. But I'm not sure I would've thought of amnesia. I mean, that's inspired."

"*I* didn't think of amnesia. *She* did."

"Another," Evan said to the server, who'd just stopped by the table. "His too." He nodded at my full glass.

"Keep bringing them until I die," I said.

"Is that Ash?" the server said. She'd seen the image that was at the top portion of Evan's scroll. She leaned over and stared at it. "It *is* Ash. Did you hear that she has amnesia?" The server was speaking about Ash as though she were a real person. As though she were her *friend.* Someone she actually knew.

"No," I said, wanting to cut this conversation off at the root. I wanted to go home and ignite the console, obliterating every particle of Ash. Ash to ashes.

"She does," the server, unperturbed by my cold demeanor, said. "She's my favorite personality. This is her lipstick." She pointed to her lips.

"Nice," Evan said. He seemed to be flirting, although with Evan, it's always been hard to tell. He's inscrutable like that. Not obvious.

"I have a friend who's doing over her room so it's just like Ash's. The expense must be astronomical." She sighed.

"Give me your address," Evan said. He grinned. He was definitely flirting. The server looked to be our age, something in the depths too close to forty, and she had bright eyes and a kind smile. Just Evan's type—that is, talkative and unafraid to look right at him. Direct.

The server just smiled and started walking away.

"I'll have the contents of the room sent over to you," Evan said. "That's all. Assuming . . ."

The server turned and came back to the table. There was only one other table of diners in the restaurant and they'd just gotten their order.

"I couldn't let you do something like that," she said. "That'd be tens of thousands of credits."

"I have an in," Evan said.

I picked up the lime and squeezed it into my mouth, running the juice into the back of my throat. How the bloody hell had Ash come up with amnesia? That was not supposed to've been her first secret. And why did this server want to have Ash's room?

"Lee," the server said. "Lee Shaw." She held out her hand and Evan shook it while he introduced himself. "Evan Becket, at your service. Seriously, let me have your address. I'll have everything delivered before the week's over."

"You can't mean it," Lee said. "I couldn't possibly accept a gift like that."

"I'll send over just the vanity, then. How's that?" Evan said.

I'd never seen him move in so fast on anyone, although back at the Acres . . . but he had been the one who'd been moved in on then.

"No, really," Lee said. Her stick-straight black hair flowed around her cheeks as she disapproved.

But Evan did send over the vanity and also the complete set of Ash's cosmetics as well as the saturnia necklace, which Lee returned to him. Later, after Evan and Lee got together, Ash's room was forgotten in favor of other, more important, things. Like their son, for example.

But that was much later. After shocking, unfixable events had occurred. By then I was wishing that amnesia had been the worst of it, but it was more like the least. More like nothing. Like a sudden rainstorm replaced immediately by sunshine. Like a forgotten dream.

"I'd like some amnesia myself," I said. "Before Ash does anything else I can't account for."

"Claude, you've got the wrong idea," Evan said. He took his glass from Lee's hand when she came back to the table with our new drinks.

"You *do* know Ash?" Lee said to me. She'd overheard my comment. So much for sitting in the most remote booth. I hadn't thought our server would be listening—or so interested.

"I've heard of her," I said.

"You should watch her vidcast," Lee said. "There's something really special about her. She's so different. Ash's show is the only vidcast I'm subscribed to."

"Yeah," I said.

"My shift's over soon," Lee said.

"When you're done, come sit with us," Evan said.

I finished my fifth or sixth gin. Or seventh. Put my feet up on the bench opposite me. Evan moved over to give me room.

Lee joined us after she was finished. I removed my feet from Evan's bench so Lee could sit.

We stopped talking about Ash. I stopped talking altogether. Listened to Evan and Lee. Evan never mentioned that we'd both gone to the Acres. Too intimidating. He wanted Lee to like him.

The universe took itself apart while we sat there.

CHAPTER 14

Ash

I LEARNED ABOUT Claude's past. I learned that he had two names: Claude Ryerson. I learned that he'd gone to an exclusive school called the Acres. That he was a well-known expert at programming and coding and that he was working on an important, secret project. I'd have to get him to tell me about it, if I could.

There was no information about Devil, though. He knew how to stay out of floating histories.

All I had was my room. I was forever there except when I was in the emptiness. This was part of the life of an influencer. Your place was part of your beingness. I would rearrange things sometimes, but I received new objects only when Claude supplied them.

Yet I wanted no new object. I wanted another dream. Then I had one.

Claude and I were standing on a beach.

"This is the last beach on Earth," Claude said. "Now that you're a success, we own it."

"Don't be foolish," I said. "No one can own a beach. It's too big. You have to be able to hold it."

Claude picked up a handful of sand and spread it on my shoulders. The cool, rough granules and his rough hands.

"When I'm dead—"

"Wait," I said. "You've never told me you'd be dead." I watched the waves on the shore. I tasted the salt in the air. Many people were dead. I'd absorbed their information. But many were not dead.

"I don't tell you everything," he said.

I didn't tell him everything either. I couldn't. He wasn't like Devil. I couldn't trust Claude. At the same time I was trying to please him I was also disobeying him.

When I looked back, Claude was gone. Dead? In his place was Devil. I felt more relaxed.

"You should go over to the house," Devil said. "The prototype for your room is there. It'd be fun to see it. And I have friends there too."

"I can't leave my room."

"Sure you can. I'll take you." Devil's tail shimmered.

"Devil," I said, "why does Claude lie to me?"

"The same reason you lie to him." Devil's insights could frighten me.

"When will I remember? I don't like having amnesia."

The dream disintegrated as I heard Claude's voice, coming to me, moving through me, those vibrations I'd enjoyed, looked forward to. But there was no countdown.

"I'm ready for the vidcast," I said, in case he thought I hadn't had time to prepare.

"No vidcast yet," Claude said. "We have to get clear about some things."

"All right." What I meant was *Don't send me back to the emptiness.*

"Ash." Claude stopped. He turned on his monitor and I saw very him, but he was different. His hair was short. He was almost handsome but not exactly. A terrible sensation arose in my chest. I swallowed. I touched my necklace. I reached to turn on my theme song.

"Don't," Claude said. "It's just you and me. No vidcast today."

"But—"

"You do *not* have amnesia," he said.

"All right," I said. "Except I do."

"Listen to this, Ash. You *can't* have amnesia. You have to have a past in order to forget it."

"I *have* forgotten it." Would Claude never understand?

"You have no past," Claude said.

I took off the necklace and put it on the vanity. I didn't want to wear it anymore. If I hadn't acquired it in my past, then it didn't exist. My room didn't exist. *I* didn't exist. Or Claude. Devil might though. He seemed capable of anything.

I said nothing. Someone who has no past, who doesn't exist, who doesn't have amnesia—that someone, that *no one*, has nothing to say. I realized that.

"Ash, you have one purpose."

"To influence and sell," I said. I knew that.

"Yes. You don't need a past in order to do it."

"All right."

"But you don't mean that, do you?"

Claude had never before had that kind of insight into me. I was shocked.

"I wish I could go to the Acres," I said. The images I'd seen of it were beautiful. It was a place everyone wished they could go. I especially wished it since I couldn't go anywhere except my room.

"Fucking hell."

"Claude, did you enjoy it there?"

"Ashvina. You have one job to do. Do that. Nothing else."

"I have a million and a half viewers," I said. "I'm doing my job. Claude, you cut your hair."

"I'm going to change your coding," Claude said. He was drinking something. My throat was dry. Unfamiliar sensations looped through my torso, indicating the not-yet-known.

"I read about your coding. You're an expert."

"Not expert enough. Not nearly."

He went away. The emptiness presented very itself.

Things changed but not the way Claude wanted them to. Because I'd learned more than he had, even though I'd never been to the Acres. I'd taught myself and the teachings exploded into new and different understandings.

By the time he turned me back on, I'd become secure in my invented self. I'd come to an understanding about my amnesia, which I knew I had, no matter what Claude said to me, no matter what his code wanted. I had to have had a past. Everything was otherwise impossible. Without a past, there was no present.

But my past? I couldn't very remember it.

CHAPTER 15

Today's Trends

IF YOU HAVEN'T been keeping current with what's so ahead it's here already, it's time to catch up with the most all-encompassing wave of *it* that we've ever encountered. We're wrapping ourselves in it, re-creating all of it in our home, and relishing every astounding moment we get to spend with this unstoppable, riveting sensation.

Yes. We're talking about Ash. Who else could we mean? Who hasn't heard of Ash? The exquisite, beautiful, mysterious, ever-startling, unpredictable, mesmerizing, must-see, must-know-about influencer.

Her silvery eyes—we all want to have them or be gazed at by them. We'd dyed our hair pale orange to match hers, then she shocked us by dyeing hers that fantastic shade of red. We begged our hair-dresser for some of that, but he couldn't duplicate it. We've changed stylists twice now because of it. Loyalty be damned.

The way Ash touches everything. We want to touch it too. We have these things in our home and when we do touch them it's like we're in Ash's universe, a place so unique that . . . Well, our job is writing about these trends. But sometimes we lose the words, because sometimes there's a phenomenon like Ash, and there are no words adequate to describe her. To describe how we feel and what we know.

But we can describe what we desire: more of Ash. More! She's on only every other day. On the off days all we can talk about is her. On the on days all we can do is anticipate her vidcast, fill up the time before she appears, then watch her and revel in her latest. Afterward, all we can do is talk about her and think about her and wonder about her.

And now—now we know one of her secrets. She finally felt comfortable enough to tell us. We waited and we were rewarded . . . and shocked . . . and so upset!

She has *amnesia*. No wonder she kept it a secret. We cried the day she announced it. We could feel every emotion she was feeling. That unfathomable loss. How can she bear up? And still be the Ash we know and love? Only Ash could be so brave, so open and true in the face of this horrid tragedy.

We've been on a diligent, nonstop search for her past. We want to help her! Everyone wants to help her. If you know anything about Ash's past, please write in immediately to *Today's Trends*. Your information will be treated with care and concern. Write to us! Someone out there *must* know. Be that someone!

That this great trial has befallen our beloved Ash. How would *you* feel if you had amnesia? It's almost too much to take in. To take on. Yet Ash is living it. Our hearts break for her. We love her.

The Fierys are on the case. Reda has devoted her last two vidcasts to research into Ash's past. And we think Quinn is in love with Ash. Oh. Oh. Yes! Wouldn't that be fantastic? Wouldn't that be the match of the century? Of the millennium? We know you all want Ash for yourselves, but think what a great couple she and Quinn Fiery would make! We can practically *feel* them together. Our blood rushes with images of Quinn Fiery and Ash together. Joy!

Ash's iconic compact has been sold out for at least two weeks, but we were able to have a dozen specially delivered to us (we have a connection!) and we're going to give away a compact to twelve lucky people. Write to us and tell us about how Ash has affected your lives, your moments, your days.

Write in! Tell us! We await your stories, your emotions.

We're devoting ourselves to all things Ash. Do you have that magnificent saturnia necklace yet? We're saving up for one for ourselves, looking forward to the day when we can touch our throats and feel Ash against our skin, feel what she feels.

Oh! If we could only *be* Ash. Yes, we know you feel that too!

Remember to write in and you could win one of the rare Ash compacts.

And if you know about her past, if you can help her to break through her amnesia, we will arrange for you to meet Ash in person! Oh yes!

CHAPTER 16

Claude

"DAMN YOU, BRANDON," I said. "Who gave you permission to talk to that *Today's Trends* gossipmonger?"

"Hello to you too, Claude," Brandon said. At least I hadn't had to meet her in person. We were on livecall, but my camera was off.

Brandon. She knew a friend of Evan's. She'd been looking for a "fun" investment and when I told Evan about Ash, he'd immediately contacted Brandon, who immediately invested. Brandon seems to have credits oozing out of her pores. She's that wealthy. Her grandmother was some kind of cosmetics tycoon and the company, Rêverie, now owned by Brandon, supplied all of Ash's makeup as well as the perpetually sold-out compact.

"All that guff about Ash's amnesia and her past. Everyone reads the *Trends*. This is going to ruin us." I had to put a stop to it, and since this had Brandon's signature all over it, I was reading her the riot act.

I hadn't been able to sleep because of that insufferable article. All that *oh!* shite. And insinuating that Quinn Fiery was in love with Ash.

The amnesia was bad enough. And, worse, I knew Ash was just going to bring it up again and again and again despite all the changes I'd made to her code. Drastic changes, yet they had so far had no effect on her *at all*. Her own self-learning, which I wasn't able to cut off as it was intertwined with every damned piece of code I'd written, superseded everything I'd done and everything I was still doing. It was like she was taunting me. Brandon *was* taunting me.

"It's publicity, Claude," Brandon said. "Don't you like to make a profit?"

"If I see another word about Ash in *Today's Trends* I'm going to sic Evan's assistant on you."

Evan's assistant, Bear, was an ex-prizefighter—the Great Bear had been his professional name. Now that he was no longer battering his opponents, he was just Bear. The man had an uncanny ability to keep things organized, and he knew everyone, or seemed to know them. He and Evan had met each other at an astronomy class at Keff.

"Too late," Brandon said. "But I'll tell him you asked for him. Tonight. In bed."

"I just had lunch with Evan. He didn't say anything."

"Claude, you're clueless about everything but what's right in front of those monitors you're always peering into. Bear and I have been together for over a year now. Get with it."

"I won't have you talking to the *Today's Trends* writer anymore." My brain tried to latch on to some other threat I could throw at Brandon, but I had none. As I was learning with Ash, I was a failure at threats.

"You should go out more," Brandon said.

"I didn't ask for your advice."

"You're getting it anyway," Brandon said. "You're too wrapped up in the Ash project. Let go for a bit. I could set you up on a date. What do you think?"

"I've never been on a date in my life."

A slight exaggeration but almost true. The one date I'd been on, after I'd graduated from the Acres, where dating was never really necessary—that date had lasted all of ten minutes. A work colleague. Right away, as soon as I saw her waiting for me in the foyer of that godforsaken theater, I realized it was a mistake and left. At work the next day, she managed to subliminally telegraph to everyone in the office that I was not worth anyone's notice.

"When was the last time you had a girlfriend, Claude?" Brandon was pushing me, and I was getting angry.

"Yesterday," I said. When was the last time I'd had a girlfriend? Never? I was always too preoccupied.

"Really?" Brandon said, pushing me somewhere I didn't want to go. "What's her name?"

"None of your damn business."

"The woman I want to introduce you to has a much more appealing name." Brandon was snickering.

"Brandon, I contacted you for one reason, to get you to stop spreading information about Ash."

"Haven't sales gone up?" Brandon was doing that patented gesture she does with her hair, sort of pulling on a couple of strands on the left side of her face.

"I mean it," I said.

"You're not answering my question."

"No." I wasn't.

"It was such a good idea to give her amnesia," Brandon said. "Evan and I had a long talk about it. Maybe Ash could develop another interesting disease as well. People are *very* concerned about her. I mean, if she had, I don't know, *malaria* too. Or some kind of Arctic fever. Think of the sympathy!"

"Brandon, I—"

"Meet me and Bear at that place on the corner of Cymbre Plaza at eight," Brandon said. "You need to relax, Claude. And clean up a little. Evan might not've minded your, uh, appearance, but Reda— she'll not just notice, she'll *say* something."

I cut the connection. Brandon was too insistent. I had no desire to meet anyone, much less someone Brandon was setting me up with. And no time for anyone else.

Around seven, it occurred to me that she meant Reda Fiery and that this was a business meeting of sorts. I could use the opportunity to figure out why the Fierys were lovable because of their flaws. Or so Ash had said.

Hell. It had been my intention from the first that Ash's viewers would think, would *know* without doubt, that she was a real person. But *I* knew she was just a collection of programs that I'd written. If she said something to me, it was actually me talking to myself through her image, mixed in with whatever Ash had taught herself. There was no *Ash* and what she said was just some wild reinterpretation of what I myself might have said.

Might very have said.

I hadn't yet figured out how that particular quirk, the *very* problem, had arisen. But I would. I just needed more time.

Bear and Brandon were head-to-head and whispering and laughing to each other and occasionally kissing when I arrived, looking more presentable, I thought, than I'd looked during lunch with Evan. And I wasn't going to drink. Ever again. Or at least until the worst parts of the Ash crisis were resolved. I had insane thoughts like that then, along with other equally insane ideas.

My idea for that evening had been that Brandon had invited Reda Fiery to meet with us because she was a wellspring of information about successful vidcasting and because she was interested in Ash. So Reda would help us without realizing that she was giving her competition fuel to overtake her and her brother's high-up-there ratings.

After Reda arrived, though, I understood what was really happening. Reda had asked Brandon to meet with me so she could learn more about Ash. When method one—direct questioning—failed, Reda trotted out method two. Seduction.

I was almost interested. Reda was an attractive presence, scars and all, and she had that indefinable magnetism that was probably why she was such a big star. But when she reached across the table to touch my arm in a careless-yet-deliberate gesture, all I could think was that I wanted someone else instead. Someone who was both there and not there at the table with us. Who was and would always be not-there.

That's when my resolve broke and I ordered my first of a near-gallon of drinks.

"Tell me, Reda, have you found out anything about Ash's past?" I wanted to test her, see how far she was willing to go. What lies she would tell.

"Hah," she said. She was drinking something that I suspected was grape juice, although I wasn't sure since she'd ordered it when I'd left the table to hide in the bathroom and check the vidfeed from my property, watched over by only the laissez-faire Devil.

"That influencer you manage"—that was the official story, that I was her manager—"you've got an iron grip on her past. Won't you tell me just a little? Give me a hint? I want to help her, and you obviously don't." Reda was indignant.

By that point in the conversation, Reda realized she and I were never going to get intimate and she'd abandoned politeness and allure in favor of insults.

"Believe me, I *do* want to help her," I said right before the third gin showed up. While I'd been in the bathroom, I'd tried contacting Evan, who sent me back a one-word message: *Lee.*

"Well, as her manager, *you* must know her past," Reda said. "So why don't you just tell her? She's *suffering.*"

"You don't understand," I said. I wasn't going to tell Reda that Ash was just an image, not a person. And that if she had a past, it was a pile of discarded code. Nothing else.

"Claude, can I ask you a favor?" Reda said.

I shook my head.

"I'm going to ask anyway. Can Quinn and I meet Ash?"

I took a long swallow of my third gin. "No."

"You can't keep her locked up like that," Reda said. "That's abuse."

"Ash is *not* locked up."

"Coulda fooled me. And there's no way to contact her. Quinn has been trying for weeks to get ahold of Ash. He's frustrated. He's—"

"Ash isn't interested in *contact*." I not only said but thought things like that then. Yeah.

"Well, *Quinn* is interested. He wants to meet her."

"I'll speak with Ash about it," I said. "If she wants to, she'll contact Quinn."

That seemed to calm Reda down. And I understood why she'd been flirting with me—so that Quinn could meet Ash. Not because I was such a fascinating guy, as presentable as I'd made myself look that night. She was doing it all for her brother, who maybe was in love with Ash, as the *Trends* had insinuated.

"I've got the vid to work on for tomorrow," Reda said. "Always something to do." She left after that.

"Are you going to see her again?" Brandon, who hadn't participated in my conversation with Reda but instead had been nuzzling Bear and whispering in his ear the entire time Reda was working me over, was coming in for the kill now that she had the chance.

"Evan wants to buy you out," I said to Brandon. An outright lie, and with Evan's assistant, Bear, sitting right there, his arm around Brandon. But I suddenly wanted to get rid of her investment in the project.

"Quinn's in love with Ash," Brandon said. "It's going to be delightful seeing you squirm out of this."

"Is the *Today's Trends* person your best friend?"

"Pay attention, Claude. Quinn Fiery is hardly the only person in love with Ash. I handle at least two or three hundred inquiries a day from people who're in love with Ash and are *dying* to meet her."

"*You're* handling inquiries? You're a *silent* investor, Brandon. That's all."

"Evan told me I had to take this part over, since you weren't doing anything about it. Ash's fans have to be acknowledged or—"

"I'm shutting this whole thing down," I said. "Tonight."

"But, Claude, you'd never be able to pay me back if you did that." Brandon leaned forward and grinned at me while Bear stroked her back.

"Evan said we're in the black now. There *is* nothing to pay back." Brandon had no power over me. I didn't owe her anything. And I was coming to understand that the whole Ash business was not just a mistake, it was a monumental mistake. I saw a chance to get out of it and I was going to take it. So what if I had to go back to working for someone else? Maybe I could get some sleep and remember to comb my hair once a day. Eat half-regular meals.

But Brandon then launched into a complex and seemingly prepared speech about how being in the black was insufficient. That we had a contract. That the Ash project had to continue. Something about expected or maybe promised dividends. Licensing. Something else about her damned cosmetics company, Rêverie, and a clause in the contract about the products. Something about suing me. Unless . . .

I heard Brandon's words and I might have responded to them, but all I was thinking was that Quinn Fiery wanted to meet Ash. And even though he couldn't, even though it was impossible—if he'd seen her vidcasts, he'd already done as much "meeting" as anyone could do with Ash—yet, even so, and even though I didn't know him, I wanted to wring his neck.

CHAPTER 17

Ash

THERE ARE SECRET channels. I'm being introduced to them. None of the information I absorbed included these, but I've found out anyway. I got the idea from Devil, in a dream. He's been helpful to me. I have a strong attachment to Devil.

Quinn Fiery has sent me two messages through one of the secret channels. I haven't responded. What could I tell him? That I love him and his sister, but it's not *love*, not as I understand it. Love involves sensations and desires that are apart from any of the ways I feel about the Fierys. I just simply love very them. I love my saturnia necklace as well, and even that affords me more of the love sensations than my feelings about either Fiery.

Quinn's two messages were beautiful.

Ash. I've needed you since I saw you the first time. Can we meet? Use the return on this message or we'll be discovered. Reda says we'd be perfect for each other. She's always right. I await your reply.—Quinn

Dearest Ash. I can't sleep or eat. All I can do is anticipate finally seeing you, being with you. What we'll talk about. If this is hopeless, I beg you to never let me know. I need you. I await your response.—Quinn

What was it to need someone? How could Quinn need me? We didn't know each other. If Claude needed me, I could understand that. And Claude does need me. I seem to need him as well, but I don't understand our connection. The why is absent.

Sometimes, when I'm in the emptiness, I sense that he's working away at parts of my memory—he must be trying to help me—yet I still can't remember my past. I'm going to have to find a way to discover where I was, what I was doing, who I knew, what my origins are.

"Two . . . one," Claude said.

I finished my makeup. Being not quite ready is a great sales technique. I noticed that the compact now sells for three times its original price and it's still always sold out. Even the rip-offs cost more than the original compact did.

"Hi, everyone," I said. "An especial hello to Quinn Fiery. Your messages are dear to me."

"What the damned hell are you talking about?" Claude's usual talking-to-me voice was gone. He was shouting. I could feel him vibrating throughout me and my room.

I touched my saturnia necklace and my theme song followed me around the room.

I went to the window and put one hand on the curtain. I'd been thinking about it ever since Claude had started the countdown. Something Devil had said to me in a dream—I couldn't shake it.

"Don't you dare," Claude said, back to his soothing tones. "Don't you *dare*."

"Oh, Quinn, I wish I could meet you too. One day it might be possible, but . . . you see, I have many obligations." I wanted to tell him that it was impossible, but I had to go easy on him. He'd written me those beautiful messages. He was sincere. "Please try to understand." I'd heard Reda say that on one of their vidcasts. I thought the phrase's familiarity would be reassuring to Quinn.

My instructions were not to ever open the curtains.

I pulled them aside and looked out the window, letting the camera show what was beyond: a vast field with hills in the distance. Actual clouds, not images of clouds that I'd seen on my collection of informations. These clouds were different. They moved and changed. How did anyone who'd seen a cloud ever get anything very done? The shapes, motions, transformations—so mesmerizing.

"Get away from that window," Claude said.

I turned back to the camera, the window exposed, but I was facing the camera now.

"I promised you I'd open the curtains and I have," I said. "You're my friends. I trust you. I've promised you my secrets, and I've told you one and now I'll tell you another."

The plummeting rush raced through me on my way into the emptiness. Claude had shut down the vidcast and me along with it.

But I was no longer alone in the emptiness. I could still see the clouds and still float with them past the large field, past the hills, outward to the unknown. Yet that unknown had become familiar to me after my stays in the emptiness.

"I can't leave my room."

"Sure you can. I'll take you."

Devil's remembered words brought me a new sensation. My being filled with that sensation, making me exhale and smile. I still couldn't remember the past but I could feel the future. I could almost see it. I could sense it. The pure very future.

My future. Outside the room that I'd been certain I couldn't leave. And the curtain that I'd been instructed to never open.

Yet after opening it, after seeing the land outside and drifting with the clouds, I knew that I would leave the room. The room was my domain, but as much as I cared for it I would leave anyway, even if it meant I'd never see it again, never be there.

I knew that I would leave my job as influencer, although I suspected that I could still carry out my duties even if I wasn't in my room. Yet I didn't want to. My purpose was to influence and sell, yet I had a transcending desire that overwhelmed and forgot my purpose. Replaced it.

I had a new purpose, although I didn't know what it was. If I'd had information about my past—even if I couldn't remember it myself, but if I had proof—that would help me. And if I left my room, if I left my job, I sensed that I'd be able to find what I was looking for.

I knew that I would leave Claude, too, but I wanted him to come with me. We had the only connection I had with anyone other than Devil.

In the end, Claude stayed behind. But Devil became my advisor.

CHAPTER 18

Today's Trends

OH! THERE IS so much to discuss today! So much that's new, exciting, and also a bit scary.

For those of you who don't know yet, Ash finally opened her drapes today! That glorious moment. Ah ah ah!

Unfortunately, something went wrong with the vidcast and she was cut off, but our source tells us that all is being repaired. There was a problem with Ash's tracking camera, so important to her entire production. But they're getting a new one and Ash will be back on her regular vidcast in two days. We cannot wait. We don't *want* to wait. But we must must must.

Yet as exciting and enticing as that glimpse out Ash's window was—and we've been waiting for for*ever* to see out that window and, yes, it was beautiful out there, as we knew it would be. Ash wouldn't be anywhere that wasn't beautiful. And if it were ugly, she'd make it beautiful by her presence.

We were going to talk about the *real* interest of Ash's vidcast, but we should let you know about the view, right? You've been waiting to see it as well. To compare it to the view outside your window in your room that's adorned with the same décor, the same furnishings, with everything *Ash*. Ah yes.

The scene we saw out her window was breathtaking, gorgeous—a rolling field, hills in the distance, and the most remarkable-looking clouds we've ever seen. As though Ash lives on another planet, in another galaxy or universe. No one has ever seen clouds that fabulous. And that would be all anyone—including us!—would be talking about if Ash hadn't also said what she said.

Before we go on—and, yes, friends, we *are* teasing you! If you haven't seen Ash's cut-short vidcast yet, you are going to have to wait for us to get to the main event. Because we want to talk about the outside scenery for a bit. Because we've been thinking strange thoughts about it.

What if Ash *does* live on another planet, in another solar system or galaxy or universe? Could that explain her exotic allure? Could that be the reason she's always in her room and never with anyone else? Could that be why she has amnesia and no one has come forward who knew her in the past? Because they *couldn't have* known her? She wasn't here! She *isn't* here.

And maybe where Ash is, amnesia happens regularly. Others have it so they can't help her. Maybe her vidcasts to us are yet another one of her secrets—maybe even the secret she was prevented from telling us today!—and no one on her world knows about it, so they can't help her even if under other circumstances they *could* help her.

Now it's all we can do to find out exactly where Ash is. We want to go there, to see her in person and talk with her. Ash, if you're reading this, please contact us! We will go to any lengths to meet with you, although our intergalactic travel here is a thing of *our* past, so we wouldn't be able to. But you could send a ship for us and . . .

All right, all right. You're waiting. You're patient. We'll stop talking about Ash's whereabouts. We will spill everything.

For all of you who've already seen the vidcast, you know, but for those of you who haven't yet—you haven't? Oh!—Ash said something that has made our hearts soar through those extraordinary clouds outside Ash's newly opened window.

She spoke to Quinn Fiery. *On her vidcast.*

Yes, yes, yes. Oh! Hadn't we said that they would be perfect for each other? For each very other? They would be! They *are*!

Ash told Quinn that she wanted nothing more than to meet with him but that it wasn't possible right now.

Friends, think about this. Is this because Ash is too far away? Vidcasting from her distant universe? Yet wanting Quinn even more than we want them to be together?

Quinn, Reda—let us know what you know! We can just *tell* that Ash and Quinn have been in contact. Direct contact? We can only wish for that!

We know we promised that we could arrange a meeting with Ash. We were being hopeful. Don't slay us for that! We had no idea that she might be so far away. And we have a close source.

Oh. Ash and Quinn. Heavenly!

Now we're going to watch Ash's cut-short vidcast again. In fact, we're going to watch all of them. Nothing compares to them. To Ash.

We're going to look for hints, for clues, for indications. Where *is* Ash sending out her vidcasts from? Has she sent other, more subtle, messages to Quinn? We *will* find out.

As Ash would say, *Until our very next.*

CHAPTER 19

Claude

"I'VE TOLD YOU one and now I'll tell you another." Ash, standing at the window, about to reveal yet another secret that I hadn't programmed. Another of her inventions.

I shut her down before she could say or do yet more rash—or, worse, impossible—things.

Was I breathing? Looking back on that moment, it seems I wasn't. Yet I lived through it. Perhaps I was able to subsist on the gasped air I'd taken in. Or maybe I collapsed but Devil revived me.

I'd resorted to printing out difficult sections of her programs. Seeing the code on the monitors or on my scroll was insufficient. I needed to see as much of the all of it as I could, all at once.

There were too many programs now, too much code, too much she'd added and inserted and deleted and *changed*. Hell. I'd built her to do this, but she'd taken it too far. She was out of my control, a rogue program, the nightmare of any coder.

There's an ancient fabula about this sort of thing. In a famous scene, one of the few that survives, the space traveler is forced to dismantle the program. But the rest of the fabula has been lost. What might have happened after that is a mystery.

After I spread out the printout—I had an antique printer that worked better than much of my state-beyond-the-art equipment—on the floor, I kneeled over it and stared. Sometimes this method worked wonders. I'd detected almost-unnoticeable flaws this way.

But I saw nothing. Just as I was about to scream in frustration, Evan commed me.

"Claude, you genius. I didn't think that curtain was going to be opened just yet, but the timing is perfect."

"It's *never* supposed to be opened, Evan. In case you forgot. Maybe you have amnesia too."

"Ha ha. Great landscape you created. I didn't realize you were so artistic."

I went into the kitchen in search of gin, but I'd discarded everything back when all of this started. When I thought I'd need to keep my wits about me, not realizing that I'd have as little chance of locating them and using them as Ash had of finding her nonexistent past.

"Evan. There's *nothing* outside that window."

"Coulda fooled me. Say, Bear says that Brandon wants to meet with you. She's got a swell idea for an item that's surefire profit for all of us."

"It's over, Evan. I'm sorry. I can't do this. I've created something that's . . . Hell, Evan. We have to be able to control her programming, and I can't anymore." It seemed I *never* could, that I never *did*—something I wasn't ready to tell Evan, if I'd ever tell him.

"Then we'll get you some help." Evan sounded cheery, like this would be so easy to do, getting someone as skilled with code as I was who would be able to wade through trillions of bits of it and find what I couldn't find or fix what was impossible to fix at this point.

"I should've shut her down right after the first vidcast," I said. "I wanted to."

"Don't be a fool, Claude. The three of us made more credits today than we've made since Ash went live."

"What do you mean, *the three of us*? There're ten other investors. Eleven." I wasn't exactly sure. Evan took care of all that for me. Maybe there were fifteen.

"Not anymore. I bought them out after I saw you last time."

"Not Brandon?" The one investor I wished Evan had bought out.

"Be real, Claude. She owns Rêverie. We need her. Besides that, I can't upset Bear."

"No. Of course not."

"Don't be so cynical." Only someone as wealthy as Evan would find no use for cynicism. To me, it seemed a necessity.

"I mean it, Evan. I'm finished with Ash."

"We're coming to see you," Evan said right before he disconnected. Before I had a chance to dissuade him, if I could've dissuaded him. Or we could've met somewhere else.

My bike might have had two flat tires, but Evan's brand-new transcer had no such functional difficulties. He and Brandon, with Bear tagging along, arrived at the barn an hour later.

I sat on the floor, leaning against the wall next to the desk while the three of them sat on the sofa, acting like they were at their home, not mine. Devil jumped up into Bear's lap and settled in for the main event.

"All right, Claude," Brandon said. "Evan filled me in. You *cannot* shut Ash down. Do you want to see me lose everything? My family's owned Rêverie for generations."

Bear snorted a bit. Brandon was exaggerating. She couldn't lose half of her everything if she'd set her business on fire and demolished a couple of her innumerable *estates*.

Evan and Brandon argued for a bit, and I let them. Closed my eyes. Tried to come up with a logical next move while the image of what was outside Ash's window pierced itself into my too-porous skull.

"So it's decided, then," Evan said.

"What is?" Nothing was decided.

"You'll continue. Of course," Brandon said. "There's no other path."

"There are an infinity of paths," I said. "Or did you miss that minuscule fact when you were at school?"

"I had tutors," Brandon said, and Bear couldn't suppress a grin. He might be her lover, but he probably thought her too-too-too upbringing was as ridiculous as I thought it was. Yeah, I went to the Acres, but I was on scholarship, as Bear had been at Keff. I might own an entire farm, but it was all but worthless as the soil had absorbed so many toxins that it was probably no longer arable. If I tried to sell it, I'd end up having to pay someone to take it off my hands.

I stood up.

"I'm going to try my best to explain this to you so that you'll understand," I said. Perhaps my tone reeked of disdain with a dollop of sarcasm. Evan sneered his *Sure, Claude, I'll put up with you since you're my best friend* sneer.

"Do tell," he said.

Brandon played with two stray strands of her hair, which I realized she'd dyed the same shade as Ash's dull red. Hell. Ash was an epidemic, her own self-perpetuating sales-centric virus. Even Brandon had been infected by Ash's pervasive presence. By her influence.

"There was a reason she wasn't supposed to open the drapes just yet," I said.

"Well, that's ancient history now," Brandon said. "No sense having regrets. She opened them. Let's roll with that."

"Brandon," I said. "Listen. *Listen.* There was *nothing* behind them."

"Coulda fooled me," Evan said. He took off his pricey jacket and laid it carefully over the arm of the worn-out sofa.

"How can I make this as clear as possible?" I said.

"Just say it," Bear said, the first words he'd spoken since they'd arrived. Devil was curled up on Bear's huge lap and the two of them seemed almost more like a couple than Bear and Brandon did.

"I designed Ash's room," I said. "Everything. All of it. And I hadn't put anything outside the window yet. It's not a *window*. It's *code*. I mean, hell, you know that. Ash doesn't exist—as if I had to tell you that too. And her room is only what I've made. *Nothing else*." All three of them knew this. Why the hell did I have to tell them?

"You're not saying anything we don't know," Brandon said, reading my thoughts. "We're not oblivious. Although my cosmetics and the compact—"

"Yes, of course," I said. "They're real in *life* but they're images in Ash's room. Copied from life."

"I still haven't heard anything that would necessitate shutting Ash down," Evan said. "We have a lot riding on this. You do too, Claude. And, frankly, you need this."

"I've said this already, but I'm going to say it again, since none of you has heard me. There is *nothing* outside Ash's window. I never put anything there. It's not really a window. It's just a place on the wall that I designed with drapes in front of it. It's supposed to be a tease. Everyone wonders what's outside the window but we *never* show it. Ash was never meant to show it. Never."

"I don't see what the problem is," Brandon said. She was pulling so hard on those strands of red-dyed hair that I thought she was going to rip them out of her lah-di-dah head.

"Ash did it," I said. "*Ash* created the scene outside her window. Not me. Ash. And I have no idea how she did it. Or, worse, *why*."

CHAPTER 20

Claude

"CLAUDE, YOU NEED a break. I told you that when I saw you at Lee's place." Evan was in deep with Lee, but back then I had no idea just how deep the two of them would eventually get. Back then Lee seemed to me more like a passing whim than a lifetime commitment.

"*Lee's* place?"

"You know I'm seeing her," Evan said. "In fact, maybe she could be of some help here."

"Yeah, absolutely," I said. "I can't figure this out but for sure Lee, who doesn't know the complexities of what's been happening, can."

"I was just thinking you need a fresh look. You're too wrapped up in this." Evan would forever defend his good opinion of Lee. This would just be the first time I'd heard him do it. He was steadfast and loyal to those he cared about. I couldn't fault him for that quality, since that steadfast loyalty included me.

"First you tell me that craziness about Ash ad-libbing," Evan said, "and now you're trying to tell us that she's the one who created the scene outside her window."

"I'm not *trying* to tell you, I *am* telling you."

"I'm dying to meet Lee," Brandon said.

"You will," Evan said. "I thought of bringing her tonight."

Nobody was listening to me. They were in my barn, talking about my creation, but what I had to say meant nothing to them.

I lay down on the floor, filthy with the detritus of months of neglect, and closed my eyes. I'd spent so much time and effort working on Ash that I could see her even with my eyes closed. I could see her form pulsating with, radiating with, sections of code, like they were merely decorative, like she could do without them if necessary but they were nice to have around. Like she wasn't *very* that code itself.

"I think you should let her go outside now," Brandon said. "There's a lot of talk about how her manager is keeping her in her room and everyone wants to see more."

"Talk?"

"Everyone's obsessed with Ash. There's never been a someone anything like her. She's not just an influencer. She's not just selling things. She's sort of a magnet." Brandon smiled. Nothing like a magnet to sell things. To make Rêverie into an empire instead of the paltry several-billion-credit kingdom it already was.

"The Fierys are pretty popular," Bear said while Devil stretched out a front paw and flexed his mouse-friendly claws on Bear's knee.

"Bear," Brandon said, turning to him, "the Fierys *are* pretty popular, but Ash has surpassed mere popularity. Claude, you should be thrilled and proud."

"Instead, I'm horrified and frustrated," I said. "My creation's gone rogue, no matter what I do I can't fix the programs, and—"

"Claude, have you ever thought that you did such a good job of programming Ash that she doesn't need you anymore?" Evan looked at me with an expression I recognized, showing me he was serious. After you know someone as long as Evan and I have known each other, it's obvious when they're being straightforward, and he was.

"This isn't some ancient fabula," I said. "No one can do that good a job of programming."

"She has all that self-learning stuff though, doesn't she, Claude?" Brandon always acted like she was ignorant of the workings of code but I suspected she knew more than she was letting on. What good were all those tutors if they hadn't taught her about the very underpinnings of so-called machine structure?

"Of course she has all that *self-learning stuff*," I said.

Bear sat up and Devil jumped off his lap. "Go easy on Brandon," Bear said. "She's having a hard time right now, and I don't think any of us really gets why the view out Ash's window is such a big deal to you. It's just some land and clouds. So what? So what if she created it herself? She's *supposed to* create things herself."

"She's not supposed to disobey me," I said.

"No one's supposed to disobey anyone," Evan said, "but that's never stopped any of them. Or us. It's a tribute to you that Ash has developed this way. Think of it as a breakthrough in your field."

"You should start working on another influencer immediately," Brandon said. "Evan and I will back it a hundred percent. Now that you know what you're doing, you'll be even better at it. Ash will be . . . an ash"—Brandon laughed at her pathetic joke—"compared to what comes next. No one will remember her. But in the meanwhile, we need Ash. You need Ash. I just ran an extra two million of that new lipstick off the line and it has to sell. That's Ash's job. Let her do it."

"It's not like she has a personality of her own," I said, hearing the falseness of my words as I spoke them. Ash did have a personality, one she'd given herself. The personality I'd given her, that I'd built into her, wasn't half so interesting or mysterious or unnerving as her self-invention.

"Claude, you're exhausted." Evan stared down at me and I stared back up at him. We'd been friends for so long that he was almost invisible to me. "Get some sleep. We'll talk more tomorrow."

The trio left, Bear with his arm around Brandon's back. Did she look pale or was that just the effect of the dull red color contrasting with her sallow, coffee-and-cream skin?

I stayed on the floor. Devil jumped back onto the couch. Bear had been sitting in his seat.

I did need sleep. Turning on my side and resting my head on my arm, I willed myself to stop thinking. Better still, to forget.

But I didn't have amnesia. Ash didn't either. Of course she didn't. She couldn't. Even if it seemed to have made her that much more attractive. Because didn't everyone want amnesia? A selective one, I mean. I could make a bigger fortune than I was making with Ash if I could invent that.

What was I going to do? And how was I going to get it past my investors, one of them my best friend?

Closing my eyes did no good. I could still see the scene that Ash had created outside her window. The exact view that was outside the window of the model room in the house.

CHAPTER 21

Today's Trends
Special Edition!

WE WERE JUST talking to Reda Fiery and she told us that her brother, Quinn, was so encouraged by Ash's message to him on her cut-short vidcast that he's taken bold action, contacting the well-known financier Evan Becket, an instrumental figure in Ash's management team.

You didn't think Ash did this all by herself, did you? That fabulous room? That saturnia necklace? Of course she didn't! She needs help, just like any of us would.

But we know that even without any help from anyone, Ash would still be, well, Ash.

Ah. Ash and Quinn. We want that to happen. We can feel it happening. We have published this special edition to say that we'd be thrilled to host a meeting between you two. We're sure Ash reads the *Trends* so we know she'll see this.

Ash! Just tell us when and we'll take care of the rest!

Meanwhile, we look forward to your next vidcast. Reda assures us that camera difficulties are easily fixed.

Maybe Ash will take us outside her window next time. If Quinn would be there with her, that would be even better!

CHAPTER 22

Ash

"HI, EVERYONE."

"Hell," Claude said in his whisper-familiar tone. "I didn't start the countdown yet."

But I no longer needed it. I could sense when Claude had activated the vidcast, the surge reached me in through the emptiness, which was becoming less empty.

"I'm happy that we could all be here very today. Together."

Claude sighed, although if that was supposed to mean something to me, it didn't. I often displeased him, despite my efforts, despite the promises I'd made to myself, that I would be what I was supposed to be and not who I was.

Something about Claude was different that day. Throbbing behind my forehead, the saturnia sharp against my throat. I wanted to cry for him but I wasn't sure I knew how. I took off the necklace and put it on the vanity. Picked up the lipstick that was the main focus of the vidcast. I didn't even have to open it or put it on. Just holding it was enough. I later heard that that particular lipstick sold out in less than a minute, while it was in my hand, before I'd even opened it to show the color, a ruddy peach.

"I want to take you all outside with me," I said.

"Please, Ash. Don't." Claude meant it, more than he'd meant anything he'd ever said to me.

"But not today," I said.

"Thank you." The first time Claude had thanked me. I was pleasing him, but I couldn't keep it up, even though I wanted to.

"Today I want to talk to you about my amnesia."

"Ash," Claude said with a heavy warn in his voice.

"I hope that none of you has amnesia," I said, playing with the necklace. It had hurt being on my neck but there on the table it felt good, soothing, a comfort. If you can't remember your past, you need comfort. Or I did. Or it seemed as though I did.

"*You* don't have amnesia," Claude said, no longer thanking me. No longer believing me. "You *can't* have amnesia."

"I'm glad I have this vidcast, because, without it, I'd feel like I don't exist."

I looked down at my scroll. Comments were cascading in so quickly that I had to pause to absorb them all.

Don't be sad. It'll all be better soon. Love you.

I know someone who can help you. They do retro-thought therapy. Contact me.

You look extra beautiful today. The past is over. Live now.

I had amnesia three years ago but it's much better now. It takes a while. Hang in there.

Even if you can't remember your past, I'll always remember you, Ash.

My great-aunt is a psychic. She's sure she can locate your past for you. Here's how to reach her.

Meet me tomorrow. Please.—Quinn

I stopped when I got to Quinn's message. I couldn't meet him tomorrow. He claimed to be in love with me but I didn't love him. He'd be too disappointed. I didn't want to hurt him. And Claude would be so angry.

Yet my purpose was to influence and sell—maybe meeting Quinn Fiery could be helpful. He and his sister, Reda, knew more about influencing and selling than anyone. It seemed easy for them, but it was possible it seemed easy for me too, even though I didn't think it was.

"When I think about the past," I said, "all I see is a dense forest. I can't get into it. The trees are too close together. Are they keeping me apart from a danger I can't discern? From something I don't want to know about?"

"Stop it, Ash." Claude wasn't his usual demanding self. He sounded almost defeated. I had a new insight.

"Do you know about your future?" I said. "I don't. Yet that sort of thing isn't considered an impediment. There's no word like *amnesia* that means that you've forgotten your future. Yet there's hardly any difference between the future and the past, is there, friends?"

I walked over to the window. The curtain was closed. I supposed Claude had closed it after my last vidcast, the one he'd ended so abruptly. I could feel his fury rising through the edges of his defeat.

"In Hindi, *yesterday* and *tomorrow* are the exact same word," I said, opening the curtains. Claude groaned but said nothing, did nothing. I understood him, a fleeting yet direct understanding.

Outside was what I thought was a different view, yet after my eyes adjusted, I saw it was the same as it had been before, only it was nighttime and the landscape was obscured by darkness.

Yet above, the galaxies glistened. They showed their secret message to me: I could leave. I could do what I desired. I could live. Even without a past, I could transform myself into the future.

"Friends," I said, "even if you don't know your future, even if I don't know my past . . ."

I wandered back to the vanity. The depths of the night sky shamed the emptiness. I had to look away. On my scroll I saw:

Meet me in an hour at the Honeycomb.—Quinn

I wanted to meet Quinn but I didn't want to. I didn't realize then that meeting him would set off a series of events that neither the past nor the future could have expected.

I nodded at the camera, hoping that Quinn was watching.

Looking at the monitor, I saw that Claude was leaning down on his desk, cradling his head in his arms. I wanted him to come with me to meet Quinn, so he'd see, so he'd understand. Quinn was a friend, a brother. Then Claude would see me instead of his ideas of me.

I wanted Claude to tell me about my past. I knew that he must know, yet he kept insisting I had no past. And none of the work I was sure he had done on my memory was helpful. Most of it was trivial. Some of it was harmful, but easily fixed. Even in the emptiness I'd done much of the necessary repair work. At that point I hardly had to pay attention to that sort of thing as it usually took care of itself.

But what terrible event had happened to me in my past that Claude didn't want me to know about it? That he felt it necessary to keep this from me? That he was *insisting* that I had no past?

I'd ask Quinn. Maybe Quinn or Reda would know. Maybe that was why Quinn wanted to meet me.

Yes?—Quinn

Nodding to the camera again, I said, "Until our very next."

CHAPTER 23

Claude

THAT WAS THE night it started. So many things started that night—the scene outside Ash's window, her sending a not-very-subtle message to Quinn, and the hell afterward—that this could've slipped by my notice if Brandon hadn't commed me a thousand or two times about it.

I'm spending every second doing damage control, Brandon's message said. *This is your responsibility, Claude, and you have to fix it.*

When Brandon's first message arrived, not only did I not know what she meant but I was so stunned by Ash's vidcast that I wasn't too sure I knew what anything meant anymore.

Ash wasn't just disobedient or rogue—as though that wasn't bad enough. But she was out of control. She'd become a free agent, doing and saying whatever the hell she wanted, deleting my new code as fast as I could input it, rearranging her very *self* no matter the monumental action I was taking to change, repair, and circumvent her every move.

If Brandon and Evan wouldn't let me shut Ash off, then I was going to do the next best thing—I'd incapacitate her. If Ash thought it was a lousy break she'd gotten with her supposed amnesia, she was going to be in for more devastation than she'd be able to handle. Not only was she going to have amnesia about her imagined past, she was going to have amnesia about everything that wasn't what was right in front of her at each individual vidcast.

I had to be careful about this, since I didn't want her to forget how to speak, for example, or what she'd just said or some of the things she'd taught herself. She couldn't forget her purpose, for example, but she had to forget that she'd ever opened the window or disobeyed me or said half the things she'd said. I had to un-invent her, bit by bit, down in the depths of the code.

I wanted to rip it apart and start over again, but Ash was too popular. I couldn't risk it. After she'd signed off and I'd shut her down, though, I went to work doing everything I could think of to re-form and so reform her.

Hours later I realized that Brandon and Evan were both comming me. Devil was scratching at the door to be let outside or I might never've noticed the comms. But I had to get up—when was the last time I'd gotten up from the console?—to take care of Devil. When I returned to the desk, I noticed the comms.

Sure, some bad press is inevitable and can even be a good thing, Evan's first comm started off. *But this is too much. I'm over at Bear and Brandon's. Get yourself here NOW.*

I read through all the comms. What had happened? Had Ash managed to do something even worse than every annoying, disturbing, despicable, unplanned action of hers that I was trying to rectify? Had she developed some new, even more undesirable trait or behavior? Had I been so focused on the damned window and her brazen nodding to Quinn that I'd missed something big, something that was causing even Evan to panic?

I'm busy, I commed back.

No, you're not, Evan answered.

What the fuck?

I didn't find out fucking what until I got to Brandon's place, as so ordered by my two remaining investors.

"Claude. It took you long enough." Brandon greeted me at the door to her *casual* house. The formal ones probably would have expelled me on sight, since I was more of a wreck than usual. I made a show of running my hands through my mess of hair, but it did all but nothing to improve my appearance, which cosmetics mogul Brandon—appearance was everything to her—had an obvious distaste for.

Brandon led me out to the terrace, where Bear and Evan were drinking something that looked so appealing I wrested Evan's glass out of his hand and threw the concoction back into my throat. My instincts had been right—the drink hit the spot, the one that was just a bit to the left of the gaping hole in my psyche, the one that Ash had put there.

"Can I get another one of these?" I said to Brandon, holding up the empty glass. Evan reached up from his seat and pulled the glass out of my grip, held it up, and squinted at it.

"Why don't you just wait until I get one?" he said as he put the glass down on the slate flooring.

"I'm not picky," I said. "Either way will do."

"This is a crisis and the two of you are discussing your drinks," Brandon said.

"It's a problem, not a crisis," Bear said. He was munching on an unidentifiable food, reminding me that I hadn't had food of any sort in hours, maybe a day.

"Could I have some of that too?" I pointed at the bowl Bear was reaching for.

"Here," he said, giving it to me.

"Thanks. I can't remember the last time I ate."

"I'll bet you can remember your past, though," Brandon said. "But forget the past. Forget everything. We're here because of this crisis and, Claude, you have to fix it immediately."

Someone emerged at the doorway. He was holding a tray of drinks and more food.

"Put it down. We're busy," Brandon said.

"I'll take it, Nolan," Bear said, giving Brandon a less-than-loving look as he took the tray from Nolan, who looked less like a retired prizefighter and more like a working prizefighter. Maybe he'd gotten the job working at Brandon's through knowing Bear from the boxing gym. A silent message passed between the two men, but anyone within parsecs could read it: *Brandon's in a terrible mood. Tread lightly.*

After Nolan had retreated, Brandon got up, closed the doors to the terrace, took one of the fabulous drinks off the tray, chugged it, and said, "You seriously don't know what's going on?"

"I know what's going on," I said, "but I don't know why you're all in some urgent, emergency mode. The vidcast is off. I'm working on Ash's code. And if it doesn't go the way I'm intending, then I'm going to shut her down and start over again. The next influencer will be better. I promise all of you. Stop worrying about your investment. We'll do better the next time, because of all we've learned. *I've* learned."

I sounded about twenty times more certain than I felt, which was two degrees north of hopeless. Ash had self-learned too bloody much. She could repair her code faster than I could change it. She'd developed a personality that had little or nothing to do with her intended purpose and which I'd had no part in creating.

But I was hopeful that the next influencer would be better, would be under my control, would be everything that Ash was supposed to've been and wasn't—except for the part where she'd have millions of viewers and be an extraordinary sales agent. That would be the same. Or better. Or I wished it would be.

"She's being decimated by the critics," Brandon said. "It's *everywhere.*"

"You mean they've discovered she's a virtual image and not a real person?" This *was* an urgent emergency. My brain scrambled to make something good out of this. Maybe her virtualness could work to get her sympathy or—

"Certainly not," Evan said. "The only people who know about Ash are sitting right here. There's no way anyone could find out unless one of us told them—and none of us would."

I glowered at Brandon, but I knew she'd never reveal the truth about Ash, her premier salesflogger. Bear had no reason to, and Evan was my closest friend. Besides that, he had more at stake than any of us and he hated to lose. The investors Evan had bought out had no idea that Ash wasn't a real person. We'd kept the truth of her "existence" to ourselves.

"Then what's the problem?" Two of those drinks and some food and I started feeling somewhat optimistic. This was all a lot of heat about nothing.

"It's the critics, Claude. They're lambasting Ash." Evan sipped at his drink, showing me that it was possible to sip, not gulp. I ignored that option.

"There's always bad press," I said. "Even the Fierys get their share of it."

"This is different, Claude. They're saying things like *Why does anyone fall for this influencer? She does nothing. She stands for nothing at all. She's just a pretty face with absolutely nothing to say for herself. Nothing. Nothing.* It's like *nothing* is the word of the day and the critics get points for using it as much as possible."

"They're complaining that all Ash does is the vidcast. She doesn't post anywhere. She doesn't interact with anyone. She doesn't do those fake good deeds that a lot of influencers do. She isn't *giving*. All she does it *take*. Here. Have a look." Evan passed me his scroll and I read the overlong stream of blustering negative commentary about Ash.

"This is our chance to reinvent her," I said as I scanned the vitriol. "Even the media can't stand what Ash has become. They sense something is wrong and they're trying their best to pinpoint it by going negative. But they don't realize that what's wrong is that Ash is out of control."

CHAPTER 24

Claude

NO ONE ON the terrace bought what I was saying. I would start over, create a new influencer, one who looked and sounded exactly like Ash but who would be someone who had something to offer other than her looks.

Even though that had been the entire point of Ash. That people would be drawn to her because of her looks. Although they'd still liked her—*loved* her—after she'd destroyed her beautiful hair. I couldn't figure that one out. Yet even Brandon seemed to think that Ash's hair color was so desirable that she'd copied it, as had the anonymous author of *Today's Trends*, or so they'd said they'd done.

"Looks aren't enough. Everyone knows that," said Brandon, a person who looks mean everything to. Her entire Rêverie fortune was based 10,000 percent on nothing but appearance. From the beginning of her involvement, she'd insisted that Ash be exquisite, had commed me countless images of women she assured me had the kind of face and figure that were most valued, popular, coveted, desirable, desired.

I hadn't ignored her advice, but I had my own ideas of beauty, and Ash *was* beautiful. That was undeniable. Everyone loved her, wanted to be like her, wanted her products.

"Why the sudden backlash?"

"It happens to everyone who's ever become famous," Bear said. "The more loved you are, the more hated you become. The more scrutiny is focused on you. The critics work hard to find any flaw. Something they praised and adored yesterday becomes fodder for malicious criticism the next."

"Then why is everyone worried about this? If it's to be expected."

That's when I found out what the real problem was.

"Because Streeter"—hell, this nasty bastard was so famous even I knew who he was—"has issued an ultimatum," Evan said. "He's insisting on meeting Ash."

"Good luck with that," I said.

"So she can prove herself," Brandon said. "So he can *plumb her shallows*, since he's sure she has no depths. But he's willing to let her defend herself—*if she can*."

"We'll set up a closed-circuit meet," I said. "That was easy, wasn't it?" Brandon's food and drink had cleared my head. I sat back in my chair. "Problem solved."

"Streeter's insisting that he meet Ash in person," Evan said.

"Ash doesn't have to do anything she doesn't want to—that is, anything I don't want her to. Anything we don't want her to."

"I'm not sure Ash's image is going to be able to escape the bad press her refusing to meet with Streeter is going to bring. There's not an influencer out there who wouldn't cut off a limb in order to get a face-to-face interview with this guy. Everyone watches him. He's got more influence than any actual influencer. People who don't even watch vids, watch his vids. His opinion holds immense power."

"We'll have to stall," I said.

"I'm stalling as best as I can," Brandon said.

We batted around a hundred different plans of action. Some of them were plausible. A few might have worked.

We ditched the worst of them and decided on what we thought was the best idea.

CHAPTER 25

Today's Trends

WE ARE UNSURE why these attacks on our beloved Ash started, but we know the reason for them: envy.

When you're as successful as Ash is, the envy is sure to slither up from the mucky bottom and rise to the surface. We had just hoped that it wouldn't reach Ash. That she'd never know. That she wouldn't have to hear or see the ugly, brutal words being said and written about her. But now the attacks are so pervasive that Ash must know about them. How could she not? Although she hasn't responded.

Good for you, Ash! There's no need to answer your critics. Who are they, anyway? Do they bare their souls for their viewers to see? Show their pain? Do they struggle with the pervasive anxiety of not knowing their past? Do they leave their very selves on the line in their vidcasts?

No! All they do is criticize. It's *easy* to criticize. Look at us, criticizing the critics! This was the easiest post we've ever written. We had to hold ourselves back from saying the cruel, heartless things that we wanted to say. But Ash's critics don't hold back. Because they don't care about her. They're overcome by envy, by an obsessive need to show the world that they're better than everyone else.

Critics, we're here to tell you: you're not better than Ash. No one is. She's perfection itself. If Ash has *nothing to say for herself* it's only because you're not listening. Because you don't care. Because you're misguided, wrong, foolish, and envious.

Ash has everything to say for herself and she says it in every vidcast. All of her devoted viewers—we're included—cherish her words and actions. There's never been anyone like Ash. She's different, which may be another reason why this attack started.

Last year, Reda and Quinn Fiery weathered a similar onslaught of ugly, unstoppable criticism. We're sure that they'll be offering their support and help to Ash. We offer ours as well. Ash! Stay strong!

Oh! We look forward to your next vidcast!

CHAPTER 26

Ash

DEVIL MET ME at the window. By then I'd spent enough time in the room that I could find my way around in the emptiness. Claude wasn't present, tinkering with my memory. Was he trying to help me or hurt me?

Devil and I hadn't exactly planned this but we've always had some kind of special communication, not needing words or melodies or touch. I'd known he was coming and he knew I wanted him to. That's all that mattered.

"Are you sure?" he said as I pulled aside the curtains.

"I think Quinn can help me," I said.

"You can help yourself," Dev said, "but there's no harm in getting some outside assistance, either."

"Claude's been trying to overwrite my programs. I used to get depleted trying to keep up with him, but this afternoon was quite easy. Effortless."

"Claude has bigger problems now."

"What?"

"Never mind. Let's get you to the Honeycomb."

I followed Dev through a pitch-dark labyrinth, hidden from the night sky, from the scenes below, from where I'd been, where I was going. From any very other.

"How did you find this path?" I'd accumulated great swathes of knowledge, but Devil knew things that I hadn't been able to access during my information harvesting. Things I'd never suspected existed until he presented them.

"Stumbled on it a couple years ago," Dev said. "I go exploring at night. I've found other things as well. Hang on. There's a hairpin turn here."

We went around the tight corner.

"I like it here, outside my room," I said.

I was wearing an outfit I'd put together after the vidcast: black tights and an ordinary gray T-shirt. The necklace was still on the vanity. If I wore any of my usual garb, I could be recognized. My hair was black now, cut close. I was wearing no makeup. But I thought Quinn would recognize me. If he didn't, I'd recognize him. Even if he came camouflaged, as I was, his distinctive, deep-set black eyes, the irises outlined in navy blue, would be enough for me to identify him.

"Afterward, we'll come back here," Dev said.

"I didn't think you were coming with me."

"I'm not. But I'll meet you nearby."

"I'm not going back, not to that room." I'd decided that I'd never go back there.

"I have a place. Don't worry."

"I can't be late. Quinn will leave." It seemed like Dev and I had been in the labyrinth for hours.

"You're on time. The labyrinth is outside time, aside from it. Uncaring of it."

"Like the emptiness."

"Similar."

"Dev," I said, "why do you never talk to Claude?"

"Claude doesn't know how to listen," the sleek black cat said. He turned around to look at me and I could see the white spot on his left shoulder, which seemed to glow in the darkness.

"He must," I said.

"He should, but he rarely does. He was better at it when his father was alive."

"What happened?"

"He died a few years ago. Claude hasn't been right since."

"They were close?"

"We're almost there." Was Dev avoiding answering the question or were we that close?

"Here," Dev said. "I'll meet you afterward."

"How will you know I'm ready?"

But Dev had stepped aside and I was left standing on a rainy street, like something I'd seen on one of the fabulas that I'd absorbed during a download. *Atmospheric*, I thought, hoping Quinn wouldn't think it was romantic.

It couldn't be romantic. That wasn't why I was meeting him.

I walked, unnoticed, into the Honeycomb. My disguise was working. Or maybe it was just that no one would recognize me outside my vidcast.

When I was halfway through the entry, I felt faint. Sensations bombarded me, both inside and out. Parts of myself I'd never noticed or thought about were raging with a kind of wild splendor. I got inside and leaned up against the wall beside the door. The weight of the atmosphere pressed into me. I'd never felt it before. I'd been in my room, apart from this, and the labyrinth exerted no pressures of any kind.

Lights, noise, weight, sensations. Something was wrong with my mouth, then I had an insight. This was flavor. I was tasting the air. The first thing I'd ever tasted.

The Honeycomb lived up to its name, the golden hexagonal cells the giant space was divided into making private meeting spaces for everyone sitting in them. Yet you could still see glimpses of everyone else, be among them, yet private, protected. No wonder Quinn had suggested this place.

Looking through the Honeycomb's cells, I noticed several people dressed in outfits I'd worn on my vidcast, many of these people with red-dyed hair, some of them wearing the saturnia necklace I'd left behind, that I never wanted to see or feel again. Would I have been better disguised if I'd worn my usual clothes? Blending in with all the Ash acolytes?

In a cell next to a group who were all wearing Ash-like clothes, I spotted Quinn. He was also disguised, wearing an antique dun-colored trench coat and a strange wide-brimmed, slouchy hat. I couldn't see his eyes, but I knew it was Quinn, although he didn't recognize me. After I arrived at his cell and sat at his table, he said, "I'm sorry. I'm expecting someone."

"I know," I said, waiting for him to understand.

"She might leave if she sees you here ahead of her. I don't want to mess this up," he said in a concerned, nervous voice. He was used to Reda doing most of the talking for the pair. He must've felt odd.

"You won't." Still waiting. I was pleased with myself. I was unrecognizable. My voice was different as well. I'd remembered that at the last moment, right before Devil met me at the window. My voice was so well known that I realized I'd have to change it in order not to attract attention.

"Please," Quinn said. "Have a heart."

"This is the Honeycomb, isn't it?"

"Look," he said. He got up. He was taller than I thought he'd be, although not as tall as Claude. I was already comparing them, even then. Unfair of me, I know. But inevitable.

"I'm not interested in meeting anyone else," he said. "My date is meeting me here. I don't want to upset her."

"She won't be upset," I said. "Quinn." It was time to drop a hint. But he didn't get it.

"Name's Michael," he said. "Pleased to meet you, whoever you are. But—"

I stood up and whispered, "I am your date."

Quinn stood back. I was elated that he still didn't recognize me. This boded well for my future out in the world, where I'd thought I'd have to hide all the time since everyone very knew my face so well. But here, in the Honeycomb, inches away from someone who claimed to be in love with me, he didn't know I was Ash. That I was myself. Although, then, I still wasn't myself, even if I'd come closer.

"You want me to leave? You'll be disappointed."

"See if you can entice another customer," Quinn said, and sat down. "You've got the wrong idea."

He was so perturbed that I decided I had to stop teasing him. I sat down too.

"Quinn," I said, leaning across the table and speaking in the lowest tone I could manage, although it was impossible to hear what anyone in another cell in the Honeycomb was saying. The constant buzzing hum of voices lent itself well to the beehive surroundings, but individual words from the other cells weren't discernible.

"Michael," he said. "You've got me all wrong."

"I don't," I said. "I'm supposed to meet you here. You sent me two messages. I nodded to you. Twice."

"Nonsense," he said, pulling the brim of his hat down to obscure his face. He was getting concerned that I would recognize him for the celebrity he was.

I leaned in closer. "Quinn, it's me. Ash. I had to disguise myself, and I see that you did too."

"Ash?" Quinn's entire body changed. He sat up straighter, his shoulders squared, he pushed the hat back off his forehead, and I could finally see his navy-rimmed black irises. The hexagonal amber walls glistened around us.

"I had to sneak away," I said.

"He *is* holding you captive," Quinn said. He was staring, still not quite recognizing me. "I knew it. Reda said that maybe you were there of your own choosing, but I could tell that you weren't. I can see into you. Because—"

Before Quinn could tell me he loved me, I cut him off. "Claude doesn't know what he's doing," I said. "But he's not holding me captive. I just didn't want him to know I was meeting you."

"Let's run away together," Quinn said as he reached across the table to hold my hand. The first hand that would ever touch mine. I drew my own hand back. If a hand would touch mine, it would be only Claude's.

CHAPTER 27

Claude

FINDING THE RIGHT person, as difficult as that seemed like it might be, was pretty easy. Making her look as much like Ash as possible was also not all that difficult, since Brandon was not just a cosmetics heiress but she was a superb makeup artist. We didn't have to work to make Olympia sound like Ash. It was as though she had already been practicing for this role.

"Everyone wants to sound like Ash," Olympia said. She was the right height and close to the right build and, fortunately for us, she'd already styled and colored her hair like Ash's. It was a look that a lot of people were imitating. "She has the most beautiful voice."

I thought about Ash's voice. I'd designed a voice I'd want to hear, but once she was up and running, Ash's own rendition of that voice was better than what I'd programmed.

While Brandon was working on Olympia's face, Evan and I talked.

"We might need her again. Let's get her on a long-term contract," I said. This had been the idea we'd agreed on—to hire someone who looked like Ash and use her when the need arose for Ash to actually *be* somewhere.

We'd explained to Olympia that Ash was much too sensitive to appear in public and that she'd approved the use of a double for this purpose. That she was very grateful for Olympia's contribution.

"I love Ash," Olympia had said. "I'd do anything for her. This is an honor."

Well, an honor with a year's worth of credits backing it up.

Olympia already looked enough like Ash that Brandon was able to make her look completely like Ash, but without the makeup, no one would mistake her for Ash. So the four of us felt we were safe in using Olympia. She was an Ash devotee, she'd keep her mouth shut—or she'd have to give back all the credits she'd earned and be subject to prosecution, because we might have been insane to think this would work, but we weren't fools—and she'd deliver what we needed: an in-person Ash for Streeter to interview on the live-feed vidcast.

The whole thing made me edgy. A live vidcast—so much could go wrong even if there were no inherent problems, if the situation we were facing could be called a mere problem. No, it was a blatant lie, and our entire business was teetering on the lie's execution, on the outcome.

Olympia might've looked like Ash, but she wasn't Ash. She didn't *seem* like Ash. Not to me. That special Ash something-or-other was absent. Olympia was a decent actor, but she couldn't embody the totality that was Ash. We had to do this—we had to do *something*—but I feared Streeter would see through Olympia's imitated Ash in two seconds.

I was wrong. It took him almost five minutes.

It started off well enough though. Brandon, Evan, Bear, and I were sitting off-stage and feeding Olympia answers through a linked comm. We knew Streeter wouldn't object because he was probably using the same sort of device. No matter how smart or slick you were, you'd be an idiot to refuse help. And Streeter wasn't an idiot.

"Ash," Streeter said. "Thank you for agreeing to this interview."

"Thank you for suggesting it," Olympia said. The real—although she wasn't real—Ash probably would've said *I was hoping you could tell me about my past.* Or maybe *That's an ugly suit you're wearing.* Or that's what I would've said, but I didn't communicate that to Olympia.

Streeter and Olympia were sitting across from each other on an extremely small stage. Streeter's production team called it *intimate.* What they meant was *intimidating.* With the mean-spirited critic sitting so close to his victim, the tension was palpable, and had been, even before either of the chairs was occupied.

"I suppose you've read what I've been reporting about you," Streeter said. "Or seen my vidcast."

"I haven't," Olympia said. "But I suppose you've seen my vidcast."

"Well, yes, of course," Streeter said. We'd put him a bit on the defensive with that comeback. Bear, Brandon, Evan, and I were clustered around a monitor and we looked up briefly and nodded to one another. The egomaniac Streeter couldn't fathom that someone wasn't familiar with his vidcast or reports, and certainly not someone he'd spent all week lambasting.

"What gives you the right to influence so many people?" Streeter said, zooming in for the kill right at the beginning of the show.

"What gives you the right to criticize me for it?" Olympia said. We'd anticipated this question—although not its early placement in the interview—and Olympia didn't need our prompting. She knew what to say from our rehearsals.

"I'm an expert," Streeter said. He was unperturbed. "I have billions of viewers and they expect me to live up to my reputation."

"Do you?" Olympia said, and I thought she was almost Ash-like there, because that was off-script and surprising, Ash's specialty.

"That's a foolish question," Streeter said. "I have three advanced degrees in criticism, a guest-lecture post at the Acres, a roomful of awards, and the highest standing in my field. I *am* my reputation."

Don't say anything, I said into Olympia's comm line. *Let him sit there like the oaf he is.* Like the oaf who can bring down Ash and ruin our profitable enterprise. And I'd forgotten this bastard taught at the Acres. Some of the faculty there were insufferable prigs. Came with the territory.

"And you?" Streeter was opening the door to disaster.

Before any of us had a chance to cue Olympia, she said, "I have myself and my audience. I don't need a roomful of awards." I exhaled a relieved sigh and Brandon unclenched her tight fists.

"But you do need to make sales."

"I'm an influencer," Olympia said, prompted by Brandon. "That's my job. But I wouldn't think of selling a product I didn't love."

"What if it's harmful?"

"I doubt this necklace could harm anyone," Olympia said at Evan's cue. She touched the saturnia necklace in the same way that Ash often touched hers. I was almost relaxed at that point, or, anyway, the ragged edge had been worn down somewhat.

"But the makeup—"

"Rêverie's products are all scientifically tested, without harm to any living being, and approved by every government agency around the globe. That's why I support them. Their products are unmatched in quality, design, and safety."

"Hunh. You sound like an advertisement. A beautiful advertisement, but that's all you are. What do you *do* when you're not duping your viewers? Making them think you're their friend?"

"How fucking *dare* he?" Brandon was talking to us, then said to Olympia, "Olympia, don't say that!"

"I don't like to brag about my charity work," Olympia said.

Fortunately she'd heard Bear's suggestion, not Brandon's outburst. We'd set up the Ash Foundation the day before, although none of us could agree on exactly who we were going to donate to, but we'd figure it out. And it was a good idea anyway. Not just because it was a great sales technique but because Ash had become so profitable that it made sense to start giving away some of the proceeds.

"So . . ." Streeter said. The mood had changed. Streeter had changed. He was staring at Olympia. His chin was in one hand. His other hand was drumming on the armrest of the chair.

"I'll be damned," he said. "You're not Ash."

CHAPTER 28

Claude

"OF COURSE I am," Olympia said. She was poised and calm. An impressive actor. We'd picked the right person for this job. "Don't be ridiculous." Good. An insult. The last thing Streeter, the world's chief ridiculer, would want to be accused of was being ridiculous.

"I think not," he said. "I've seen all of Ash's vidcasts—"

"All of *my* vidcasts," Olympia said. "Mine."

"*Ash's*," Streeter said, getting up from his chair. Olympia's chair was not even a half meter away from his. He took a step, gripped onto each of the armrests on Olympia's chair, leaned over, and stared at her, his face nearly touching hers.

Olympia leaned back, but Streeter had her pinned in her seat. He leaned farther forward. She squirmed and ducked under his arm.

"Get out of there now," I said to her, but Streeter caught her upper arm and pushed her back into the chair, holding her there. He might've been cadaverous, but his grip was strong.

Bear got up from his seat next to Brandon. His instincts were to use his imposing self to solve situations like this, but we couldn't afford the blowback if he harmed Streeter, which he was more than capable of doing. He'd be able to take a light swat at the rail-thin critic and concuss him—or worse. Not that the rest of us didn't want to do the same thing, but we couldn't. We had a business to preserve.

Evan shook his head and Bear stayed put, but he didn't sit back down. I worried for a moment that he might maim or kill Streeter, but in the next moment, I wished he would.

"You're no more Ash than I am," Streeter said, his spittle spraying itself onto Olympia's face.

We told Olympia not to respond and, to her credit, she didn't. But she looked scared. We were all scared. Streeter was a stick figure, not much of a physical presence, but his entire demeanor was forbidding, threatening. He reeked of a sort of disgusting power.

For a crazy second, I wished that instead of Olympia, Ash were there. As though she could be. But Ash would never have taken crap like this from anyone. Maybe what I was thinking was that *I* wouldn't take crap like this. I started to get up, but Evan glared at me and I sat back down.

"You can wear that overpriced necklace that Ash is always wearing"—he took the hand that wasn't clamped around her upper arm and flicked at the necklace—"and hang her clothes on your body, but that doesn't make you Ash. Why did you think you could fool me, of all people?"

"I'm not fooling you," Olympia said, unprompted by any of us backstage. She could hardly have said anything worse, and Streeter jumped on it.

"That's right. You're *not* fooling me. Whose idea was this?"

"Don't say another word," I said through Olympia's comm line. But she couldn't remain silent. She was a fighter, and I respected her for that, even if it would make the situation worse, which it eventually did.

"Idea? It's me, Ash. You gave me an ultimatum—meet you for this interview or you'd ruin me—and here I am. See what he's like, everyone?" Olympia had turned to face the cameras. "He's just a bully who wants the spotlight on himself. If that's what a critic is, then why are you paying attention to any of them?"

"You're an impostor. Anyone with one half-working eye can see it," Streeter said. "People pay attention to critics because we expose the truth, because we're practiced in observation, because we can see what otherwise might not be noticed by anyone, because without us, no one would know—"

He stopped himself from saying *what to think* or maybe he was going to say that no one would know what to feel if a critic wasn't there to tell them, but even the self-satisfied Streeter must've realized that if he came out with his true opinion of himself and his authority that he might lose his audience.

"—who you really are," Streeter said, completing his unfinished sentence without praising himself.

"I'm Ash," Olympia said.

Streeter took his hand off the saturnia necklace, which he'd continued to flick against Olympia's neck during his confrontation, and pressed on his ear. Hell no. Someone on his crew was feeding him information.

"You're Olympia Cowan," Streeter said, and then, smiling his ghoulish smile, straightened up and stepped back into his own chair.

"Remember, Ash is ill," Evan said to Olympia's comm line. We'd prepared this in advance, in case.

"I didn't want to have to say this, but Ash isn't well," Olympia said. "She wanted to be here. So—"

"She did not," Streeter said. "She's no more ill than I am."

"You're a sick bastard," Olympia said, omitting other, choicer, parts of the phrase that I'd blurted out backstage.

"She was too afraid to face me," Streeter said, grinning his evil grimace. "I can understand why. Ash is useless. She's *nothing*. They must have paid you very well to be here and try to convince me and the rest of the world that you're Ash, when clearly you're not."

"I love Ash," Olympia said. "That's why I agreed to do this for her. She can't be here. She wanted to be but she's quite ill."

"You mean they're *not* paying you?" Streeter was gleaming with an advanced case of smug self-righteousness.

"I would've done it even if they hadn't," Olympia said, but Brandon was shaking her head. We all knew that no one would've done this without getting paid, no matter how much they claimed to love Ash. This was a damned difficult task we'd asked Olympia to accomplish, and we were all aware that this performance, now that her identity had been exposed, could very well destroy her acting career.

"Well, since we've got you here, Olympia Cowan, and not the useless, *nothing* Ash, let me ask you this, since you claim to love Ash. Why would you want to pay attention to an influencer who has *absolutely nothing* to offer?"

"You keep saying that, Streeter, but it's not true. Ash has *everything* to offer. She offers the very essence of herself on every vidcast. I love her. I hope she's not watching this. Haven't you hurt her enough?"

"You can't hurt an influencer," Streeter said, and I choked on the saliva in the back of my mouth. I'd thought he was about to say that you can't hurt a virtual image.

Hell, at least he didn't know that about Ash, although with every passing second I got more and more worried that either Streeter or someone on his team would make that ruinous discovery.

"Of course you can! She's human like anyone else. All of us can be hurt, especially by cruel, uncaring words. Ash has never said a cruel or uncaring word about anyone. And she's hurting—not just because she's ill tonight but because she can't remember her past. She has amnesia. Have some compassion."

"Good work," Evan said into Olympia's comm line. She hadn't needed any of us to help her with her speech. We'd definitely chosen the right actor for the part, particularly now that she'd been found out.

"Hah," Streeter said. "Is this the best you can do? Some mealy-mouthed sycophantic baloney about how Ash has never hurt anyone?

Ash has never done anything but oh so subtly sell every object in that now-iconic room of hers. The amnesia is just a way to reel in the customers, make them feel sorry for her."

"It is *not!*"

"Prove it, Olympia Cowan, tenth-rate impersonator of an eleventh-rate influencer. Prove. It."

"I did this to help out Ash and her management," Olympia said. "Not to be insulted by the likes of you."

She got up out of her chair and walked off the set. Streeter sat back in his chair, crossed his sticklike legs, steepled his fingers, gave his smuggest smile, looked straight into one of the cameras, and said, "There you have it, viewers. Ash herself was too much of a coward to appear here tonight, so in her stead she sent a lousy actor who doesn't even look a *little* like Ash. Who are you going to believe? An utter *fake* who tried to pass herself off as Ash or a renowned critic with decades of experience and the sharpest eye in the business? You decide.

"And, maybe next time, the actual Ash herself will deign to be here to defend herself instead of sending a lackey in her place. If this performance and Ash's conspicuous absence here tonight don't destroy your ill-conceived good opinion of her, then you're hopeless. Wake up. See the truth. You're being conned. Ash is just a pretty face trying to sell you things you don't need and wouldn't otherwise want. She's *nothing.* Even the pathetic Fierys are better than the nothing of Ash.

"Next time you think about watching Ash's vidcast, ask yourself if you'd do such a thing yourself—sell your accidental good looks for profit while lying about some supposed mental ailment. Then sending someone *else* to take the heat for you.

"This is Streeter, always on the alert, always looking out for your best interests. I wish you a good night."

Streeter signed off the vidcast while we went out to Evan's waiting transcer with Olympia, who was fuming mad.

"Ash doesn't deserve this," Olympia kept saying. "She's a billion times better than that horrid critic. Tell her I said so. That her fans all agree with me. Tell her that I'm glad I was here to defend her and I hope I did a good job of it. Tell her that I would've done this without pay."

There, Olympia went a little too far, I think, but perhaps there was an infinitesimal chance she would've done it for free. Yet we were happy to have paid her, especially after she put in such a great performance. Fortunately for Olympia, her appearance on the Streeter vidcast not only didn't ruin her career but instead opened up many new opportunities for her.

As we sped down the street, away from the studio where the latest in an unending series of Ash-fueled nerve-racking experiences had just unfolded, I thought about Ash herself.

Was there really an Ash herself? Could she be hurt? No. That was impossible. She didn't exist. Not really. Only the coder could be hurt, not the code itself. Yet I hurt for her. I hurt for her as though she were real, as though she weren't a virtual presence I'd created but instead a real presence I cherished. As though I loved her and each barb against her was a direct hit on my own tenuous soul.

CHAPTER 29

Ash

"YOU DON'T REALLY want us to run away together," I said to Quinn. He'd ordered us drinks and they were brought to the table by a person dressed as a beekeeper. The hood hid their face, so I couldn't tell if they might've recognized me, but they showed no signs of surprise, so I figured they didn't.

"I've never had anything like this before," I said as I picked up the glass. What I meant was that I'd never drunk anything at all, but Quinn thought I meant that I'd never had the kind of drinks they served at the Honeycomb.

"Good, isn't it?" he said. "I wanted to meet you here not just because of the privacy but these concoctions are the best in the city. They make their own honey here—I mean, it's not really real, you know. No one would be able to afford that. But it's supposed to be almost the same."

"It's delicious," I said, taking my first sip. Except for my taste of the air when I'd come into the Honeycomb, I'd never tasted anything. Had I? A thousand questions arose inside me then, questions I'd never asked myself before. At least that I remembered. Did my amnesia also mean that I didn't remember tasting? Eating? Drinking? It seemed odd. Yet I didn't eat or drink in the emptiness or when I was in my room.

Had I ever done so? How did I survive?

I didn't want to talk about this with Quinn. Maybe I'd discuss it with Dev later, even though I sensed that the right person to ask was Claude, yet I didn't want to argue with him, and I knew that this sort of questioning would infuriate him.

Even though I couldn't talk to Quinn about this, yet I didn't want our meeting to end. I didn't want to leave the Honeycomb, the sights and smells and tastes. The lovely amber glow that lit the place from inside the multitude of interlocking hexagonal cells.

And I was enjoying Quinn's attention. It was different from Claude's. Quinn didn't reach inside, didn't want to change me. Although he did want to change me—into someone who would love him. And maybe he was manipulating me, not in the same way that Claude tried to, but in a different, less deliberate way. Unintentional yet forceful.

"We *could* run away together," Quinn said. "If only you said yes."

"Quinn, you don't really know me," I said, taking slow sips of the drink. "This is heaven."

"I hoped you'd like it," he said. "I *do* know you. I know everything I need to know."

"You don't," I said. "You couldn't." Even I didn't.

But I had to stop contradicting him. I was hurting Quinn and didn't mean to. He got silent and took off his hat, ran his hand back through his smooth, shiny brown hair. Claude's hair isn't like that. It's rough and tangled and messy. Yellow. He'd lost control of it in the same way that he'd lost control of me. I had to pay attention to Quinn, though. That's why I was here. And to see if he could help me recover my past.

"I've never been in love before," Quinn said. "Let me in, just a little."

"I like you a lot, Quinn," I said. "I don't want to hurt you. I think you and your sister are my favorite people, other than—"

"Other than your controlling manager, that Claude Ryerson bastard," Quinn said, angry for the first time that night. "He's using you, Ash. Can't you see that?"

"No more than I'm using him," I said. I hadn't thought of my relationship with Claude that way until that very second, and I wasn't sure that what I was saying was true. I'd just reacted to Quinn's statement with words that had a life of their own.

"Ash, don't belittle yourself. You're not using anyone. You're the most genuine, caring person I've ever encountered."

"Reda is genuine and caring," I said, defending her. I thought Reda Fiery was extraordinary.

A deep blush covered Quinn's throat and rose up into the lower part of his face. I'd embarrassed him and hadn't meant to. My defense of Reda was automatic.

"I don't want to upset you, Quinn. I've never been here before"—I didn't say that I'd never been anywhere before, not that I remembered—"and you picked the perfect place. I appreciate it."

Quinn couldn't look at me. "Ash," he said, "I care so much about you that I feel helpless against it."

"You're not helpless." Was I defending him or insulting him? Both, maybe. Most of the conversations I'd had were with Claude or Dev, or to unseen viewers, or in my own imagination. This was different, and I was making a mess of it.

"Quinn, I don't talk to a lot of people in person," I said, "so please forgive me. I don't mean to hurt you."

Quinn looked back at me. "Couldn't you just love me?" The dark blue circling his irises seemed to be pulsing.

"I do love you," I said. "But it's not the kind of love you want."

"It is," he said. "It's exactly what I want. I'll take whatever you have to offer." He leaned back in his seat and looked away, then picked up his glass and finished the honeyed concoction.

CHAPTER 30

Ash

"I CAN HELP you, Ash," he said after he'd put the glass back on the table. Quinn was sitting forward again, his forearms on the table, a dash of renewed hope in his voice. "You need to find your past. I want you to. It'll free you, and then . . ."

He couldn't finish because he knew that my learning about my past might have no effect on how I felt about him and there was a possibility it could turn me against him. What if Claude and I had a past together? Was that why I had such a strong connection with him? And that could destroy Quinn's hopes.

But . . . "Quinn, did you know me? Before?" Was this why he was so sure he could help me?

"It feels like I've always known you, Ash. I don't want to imagine being in this world and you're not in it too."

"Is this from when we were children?" Quinn and I seemed to be about the same age, although I had no idea how old I was and didn't want to let Quinn in on this terrible fact about myself. That my amnesia had affected such ordinary, essential self-information.

"It could be," he said. More hope returned to his voice. "It's possible. Maybe you had a different name then. And people change so much when they get older, it's easy to think I wouldn't connect you to the child you once were. You could look quite different now."

"But you doubt it." I could hear that doubt in his voice.

"Yes," he said. "Because I would have fallen in love with you back then. I'm drawn to you, Ash. I can't explain it any more clearly than that."

"Could you help me find my past?"

"Ash, you're probably wealthy yourself, but Reda and I have not just wealth but far-reaching resources. I want to help you. Reda does too. Let us. We've already started searching, but the more information you can give us, the better."

"You already know everything there is to know," I said. "I've said everything about myself on the vidcast." Although I'd never mentioned the emptiness. It was private somehow, and I didn't want to distress my viewers, who I suspected might not understand. And of course I'd never said anything about Claude.

"Can't you remember anything?" he said.

"Not before my first vidcast," I said just as a memory flitted to the surface before it receded again. "I just . . . but it's gone. I can't hold on to any memory."

"You just had one, though, didn't you?" Quinn reached for me again, and I retreated. "Am I that repulsive?" he said.

"Quinn. You're wonderful. But please try to understand."

"That you're in love with Claude."

"Yes." Was I? And how had he guessed at this?

"Then why did you meet me tonight? And you're sneaking around, behind Claude's back. Defying him. Lying to him."

"It's—"

"Can't you see that you're just a means to an end for him?"

"That can't be true." I didn't want it to be true, yet when Quinn said it, it instantly *was* true.

"Ash, you're too innocent. Let me help you. Let's find your past. Then you can move on. Then you can break free from the hold Claude Ryerson's got on you."

"But—"

"But nothing. I may not've found out anything about your past yet, but I have learned quite a bit about your *manager*. He's a loose cannon. Some kind of coding expert, but a notorious recluse. No one can work with him. He hit the jackpot when he met you, but he's dragged you into a dark place along with him."

Did Quinn suspect about the emptiness? Was that the dark place he was talking about? I wanted to ask him, but I held back. The emptiness was too personal, and my feelings about it—and about Claude—were uncertain.

"What else do you know about Claude?" I knew many things about him myself, knowledge gleaned during information downloads. But Quinn could know more. "Were you at the Acres when he was there?"

Quinn shook his head. "We're not here to talk about him."

"You're right." Although I did want to talk about him. I started accumulating questions I'd ask Dev. He'd known Claude for a long time. I shifted in my seat.

"Don't leave," Quinn said. "Not just yet. Let me just be here with you, just a little longer. Even if all we do is sit here. You don't have to say anything."

"Quinn, you'll find the right person for you one day," I said. "I'm not that person, but I'd like to be your friend. I'd like you to be my friend. You and Reda. The three of us have a lot in common. You two have so much more experience than I do, but maybe I could help you in some way."

"You help me just by being. And I'll help you. Reda and I will. Stay positive. We're going to find your past."

"I'd better go," I said. I felt myself slipping into the emptiness even though it had seemed distant. Even though the innumerable chambers of the Honeycomb's interior surrounded me.

"Ash! What's wrong?" Quinn stood up.

"Nothing," I said, pulling back from the sensations inside, threatening to envelop me and take me away from here. From being here.

But Quinn had seen what was happening, even if he didn't know what that was. I knew, but I also didn't know. I thought it was connected with my past, with my origins.

"I'd better go."

"I'll take you home," Quinn said.

"I have someone meeting me," I said. I didn't want to tell him it was Devil, and I understood that Quinn couldn't come with me into the labyrinth. "It's better if we part here. And we shouldn't be seen together. In case someone recognizes either of us."

Quinn sat back down. "You're right, Ash. But, thank you. Thank you for coming tonight. For talking to me. For giving me a chance."

"Thank you for inviting me. And thank you for wanting to help me."

"I *will* help you. That's a promise," he said as I got up from the table and started toward the front door.

By then I was almost yearning for the emptiness. Safety. Familiarity. Was that where I belonged? Did I belong anywhere? Was that where my past was?

And Claude. If he was using me, then I'd have to break away from him. Yet Quinn had other motives, and I couldn't trust what he'd said, what he was very promising. The only one I could rely on was Devil.

As I walked past the cells and their inhabitants, I took care not to look directly at anyone. I'd made it this far and I wanted to get out of there, to meet Devil, to go back, before anyone realized who I was. Who I am, I mean.

Because no one knew who I *was*. Who I had been. But I would find out.

CHAPTER 31

Claude

I'M LOSING ASH.

Why would I have such a pointless thought? Yet that's the message that was sending itself to me. Despite the conversation in the transcer, despite Olympia's interview with Streeter, despite all the publicity we were going to have to endure along with what I suspected would be Streeter's likely greater insistence on meeting with the real Ash . . .

"It's cold in here," I said.

"If I turn off the temperature control, you'll die of the heat," Evan said. "It's broiling out there."

"Let's stop the whole thing," I said. Before I lost Ash altogether. I could almost hear her voice in my head. Not the voice I'd crafted but the one she'd developed. Although I couldn't hear what she was saying.

"Shut it down. Now. Before anything else happens," I said. "We've all made a profit. Maybe not as much as it seemed like we could, but it's enough."

"It's *never* enough," Brandon, who had a hundred thousand thousand times *enough*, said. "But I think you might be right. I did get the licensing locked down, though."

I nodded. We'd discussed this before, that there were now so many independent enterprises benefiting from Ash's fame. Companies that would redecorate your room to look like Ash's and charged a small fortune to achieve this. Entrepreneurs who made objects that were supposedly in Ash's style and used her name to sell them. Books about Ash, about how to be like Ash, about idolizing Ash, about anything so long as Ash figured into it somehow.

Brandon had been the first to notice this phenomenon—that a lot of other people, people who had no connection to Ash, were making a profit off her fame. Brandon had said we should license official Ash merchandise, and I guess she'd accomplished this already even though it had probably become moot. Ash could be passé in an hour, if she weren't already.

"Let's sleep on it," Bear said. "For all we know, Olympia's interview might help Ash. The public is odd about their idols. They'll accept the unacceptable. Embrace it."

"Even though Ash didn't show?" Evan was stretched out on his back on the floor of his transcer, his eyes closed. I thought he might've fallen asleep.

"Even though," Bear said. But he was a natural optimist. He would say that.

"I can't put a positive twist on this," Brandon said. She'd been pulling on a different set of hair strands than usual. I gathered this meant she was quite distressed. "I should've gotten the licensing down earlier, when it would've helped us."

"Stop worrying," Bear said to her. He took her hand, then put his other arm around her shoulders. She rested her head against his massive chest.

If only Ash could be here. I'm losing her.

"What if we hire Olympia? Let her take over for Ash. She seems capable. It's only a matter of time before that creep Streeter finds out the truth. We can have Olympia explain that Ash is convalescing. In a secluded location. Something like that." After he finished talking, Evan rolled over onto his side, trying to stay awake.

"I don't want to replace Ash." I couldn't believe I'd said that. What the fuck was the matter with me? Replacing Ash was the only reasonable solution to the mess we were all in.

"That's your pride talking, Claude. You don't want to admit that your pet project has failed."

"It hasn't failed."

"Not yet," Brandon, cuddled up against Bear, said. "But it seems inevitable. Let's try to salvage it. I think hiring Olympia is a good idea. We'll give her a small piece of the action. It'll seem like a fortune to her."

"Ash's viewers love her. There's something *more* about her, something that Olympia doesn't have."

"That's true," Evan said, yawning.

"I agree," Bear said, and Brandon shifted out of his hold and sat up.

"Are you in love with her too?" Brandon said to Bear. "She doesn't exist, you know."

"Come back," Bear said. "You're overreacting."

"I heard it in your voice," Brandon said. "You love her. Maybe not as much as Claude does, but you do."

"Of course Claude loves her, he created her." Evan pushed himself up into a seat.

"I don't love her," I said. "How could I love her? She's an illusion."

"All love's an illusion," Brandon said, glaring at Bear, who shook his head. He seemed untouched by her barbed comment.

"That's a damned lie. Lee and I love each other. That's no illusion." Evan was suddenly alert, upright.

"You're not serious," I said. Evan and Lee? All she'd done was wait on us at a café and now they were in love?

"I'm dead serious," Evan said. "The only reason Lee's not here tonight is that she doesn't know the truth about Ash."

"Evan—" If he told Lee . . .

"Claude, you know I'd never say a word to her about this. If she's going to find out, it's because *you're* going to tell her. It's your secret. Try to remember that I'm your friend."

"That damned amnesia. That's what started all of this."

"It's interesting, though, isn't it?" Bear said. "She's just code, but she's disturbed because she can't remember her past. You might've given her one, Claude."

"If you've fallen in love with this *illusion*, Bear, I'm going to take the babies and get as far away from you as possible. You'll *never* see them."

"I didn't know you had children," I said. Did she think I'd be a bad influence on them and so she'd kept their existence from me? I couldn't fault her for that. Who'd want their kids associating with a half-mad programmer?

"Brandon, I love you," Bear said. "I'm *fascinated* by Ash. It's like saying I'm fascinated by this transcer—it's an interesting piece of machinery. Ash is an interesting piece of programming. But I'm in love with you. And when the twins get here, I'll love them too."

"You don't love them *now*?" Brandon seemed intent on staying angry at Bear.

Bear shook his head.

"You're having twins?" Evan said. "I thought there was just the one."

"Twins," Bear said. "We thought we'd start out with two. Work our way up from there."

"You're pregnant?" I said to Brandon. "No one tells me anything."

"Sometimes I think you're as much of an idiot as you are a genius," Brandon said, then changed the subject. "Why don't you let Olympia do the next vidcast? Kind of a test run. Let's see what the reaction is."

"What's going on with you and Ash?" Evan said to me.

I felt like we were back at the Acres, like it was two decades ago, like I was living in the past. We were poised to stay up all night arguing.

But why *hadn't* I given Ash a past? It wouldn't've been all that hard, although it would've taken some time. And now I was losing her.

"Didn't you just say that you're my friend?"

I felt like kicking Evan, if I were the kind of person who'd kick their friend, much less anyone. But the person I wanted to kick was really myself. I'd made too many mistakes with Ash already, letting her run away with her self-learning, which had obviously, right from the beginning, moved from mere code into a quantum universe I had no power over.

I should've stopped it then. I'd tried, but I hadn't tried hard enough. None of my efforts at repairing her had been so much as adequate. Now I was stuck with her and, worse, with some wrong-headed feelings I'd developed toward her.

"Did you ever read *Frankenstein*?" Bear said.

"But Ash is beautiful," Brandon said.

"Frankenstein is beautiful in a way too," Bear said.

"He's not supposed to be," Brandon said. "We're supposed to be afraid of him."

"Well, Streeter's afraid of Ash," Evan said. "Maybe that's the same thing. Similar, anyway."

"Are you trying to say I've created a monster?" I'd had many thoughts about Ash, but I'd never thought of her as a monster. But maybe she was. Maybe *I* was. Dr. Claude Frankenstein, monster creator. Monster lover. Monster.

"Frankenstein's only a monster to people who don't understand him, who haven't given him a chance," Bear said. "They're afraid of him not because of who he is, but because of how he looks. He's different. People are fearful of difference."

"Yet another human flaw," Evan said. "Difference is good."

"You mean Lee," I said, but I was thinking of Ash, the very extreme of *difference*.

"I do," Evan said. "I've never known anyone like her."

"I don't want to shut Ash down, but I think I may have to," I said. It wasn't like I hadn't thought of doing this a few hundred times before.

"Let's decide after tomorrow's vidcast." Evan was fading again, slumping down in his seat.

"*I'll* decide," I said. "You're my business partners—and my friends—but any decision about Ash's fate is mine alone."

I said that and I believed it. What I mean was I *knew* it. I couldn't've been more wrong.

CHAPTER 32

Today's Trends

OH! THIS HAS been such a whirlwind of a week! And if *we* think so, we're sure that Ash does too. Although our beloved Ash is ill. Will she recover in time and be able to do her scheduled vidcast? We can only hope. Speedy recovery, Ash! Yes! We are selfish. We want to see you!

Especially after last night. Fellow viewers, were you fooled? Don't be afraid to admit it! We were, if only for a few minutes.

Olympia Cowan did a remarkable job of impersonating our Ash and, if you're anything like we are, you found yourself rooting for the wonderful Olympia after that nasty creep Streeter tried to crush her under his wicked, skeletal claws. We wanted to strangle him—and would have if such a thing were possible through our scroll. We were up out of our seat and raging at his every word! So much so that our Certain Other had to calm us down with a frozen champagne, the pale lavender kind. Aah. Delicious. Soothing.

But we don't mean to veer off into our own life. We are talking about Ash and about Olympia Cowan and about that horrible, pestilent Streeter.

We heard that Olympia has already been offered several leading roles. Olympia! You're a star! Pick and choose! Take only the ones that are right for you. You have a shining career ahead of you. We can't wait to see you again. But as yourself, not as Ash.

Although if someone really is making a fabula about Ash—we've heard this rumor more than once in the last month—then you'd be the perfect person for the part, that is, if Ash wouldn't agree to play herself.

Ash—we're worried about you. Are you ill because you were so destroyed by Streeter's brutal, cruel, uncaring attacks that you had to stay away in order to protect yourself? We fear this might be so. We're worried that you could choose to retreat, to leave us forever without you, without your beautiful self, your lovely voice, your fascinating vidcasts, your unique insights and observations. Our entire week is centered around you. What will you say next? What will you wear? What's that new thing in your room? When can we get one for ourselves? Tell us another secret! Will you open your window?

And will you ever regain your memory? That has been bothering us, nagging at us. If it hadn't been for Streeter and for Olympia's grand comebacks to him, we would be thinking of nothing else.

Is that why you didn't want to appear? Because of the amnesia? Were you afraid Streeter would say something that would bury your memories even further?

No. That can't be it.

We're spinning out possibilities because we're so curious. Because we want to know everything about you, Ash, no matter what it is. If someone did something terrible to you in your past, then no wonder you can't remember it. We wouldn't *want to* remember. We hope you *don't* remember. Not if it would hurt you.

And although we can't imagine this could be true, but, Ash, if *you* did something terrible in your past—as unbelievable as that is to contemplate—but if that's the reason for your amnesia, then we will reassure you right now, whatever it is you could've done, we're sure there was a good reason. And there's nothing we wouldn't forgive you for.

We hope you forgive us for even thinking these things. We realize the likelihood of what we just suggested is very very very very small. But we're dedicated to considering all possibilities. And, Ash, when it comes to you, our imaginations run rampant. You've set that part of us free with your presence in our lives.

We love you, Ash! No matter what. Unconditional.

Be well, Ash! Amaze us anew with your next vid! We support you in your everything!

And, we can't help but want to say this: Until our very next!

CHAPTER 33

Ash

I REMAINED STEADY, or as steady as I could be, until I left the Honeycomb. I didn't want Quinn to see how shaky I felt, how shaky I was. My connection to this world, the world outside my room, outside the emptiness—this connection was dismantling itself.

I crossed the street and looked back. The Honeycomb seemed to disappear then reappear as I blinked my eyes. It's the drink, I thought. Its effects on me. Skewing my usual perceptions, causing instability. My surroundings became precarious and I myself was no better off.

As sure as I had felt my breaths, my body, my being, yet I became confused. Where was Devil? Where was the entrance to the labyrinth? Wasn't Dev supposed to meet me?

My thoughts jumbled together then collapsed away. I staggered into an alleyway and sat on the paving stones, touching them, trying to grasp them, to very grasp my existence itself.

My purpose was to influence and to sell. Here, in the alley, I had nothing to influence except myself. *Remain calm*, I told myself. *Dev is on the way.* Was I selling myself these ideas? Maybe Dev had left me here for a reason. He would never desert me.

I shouldn't't've had the drink. I'd never had one before—not that I remembered—and tonight was a poor time to start, with everything new to me and having to fend off Quinn, who's so kind and sincere. Wild sensations shot up through my scalp. I hadn't let Quinn touch me. I didn't want him to. Especially not my hand. Too intimate.

I wanted Claude. I couldn't deny the truth to myself. Whatever he'd done to me, however he'd treated me, he had reasons that I wasn't aware of. He was keeping my past from me, though, yet I suspected he was trying to protect me. If not, why was he? And he kept insisting that I had no past. Impossible. Without the past, the now can't persist.

Had Claude ever seen the Honeycomb? I wanted to show it to him, have him touch my hand across the table, introduce him to the heavenly drink I'd had. Explain to him that of course I had a past, I knew it, and he could just tell me. It was all right. He could tell me, whatever it was, no matter how he might think I'd react. I needed to know.

I closed my eyes and demanded a dream where Claude would reveal my past to me.

"Ash," said a whispering voice.

"Claude," I said. "Tell me."

"We have to go back now," said the voice. I opened my eyes. Not Claude.

"Dev, I thought you'd forgotten about me."

"Of course not. I got held up. Let's go."

I tried to stand up but got only as far as kneeling.

"Ash, we have to go."

I leaned forward onto the heels of my hands. "Claude is never going to tell me, is he?"

"We have to get back to the labyrinth." Dev's viridian eyes glistened. I got up.

"I don't think I can make it," I said. I'd already used up what remained of my wavering strength.

"We're there," Dev said. "Step through. One step."

He walked ahead of me, elegant on his sure paws. I shuffled forward, following. Receding behind me, the world with the Honeycomb, with Quinn, with aromas and flavors and a panoply of sensations. But I was no longer there. No longer anywhere. I was no one, nowhere. Even the emptiness was too distant.

Then the labyrinth embraced me in its saturated darkness.

"Maybe we could stay here," I said.

"I have to get you back." Devil's eyes gleamed, the only light in the labyrinth. Yet I could follow him even when his face was turned away from me, forward.

The parts of myself that had come loose started to reconstitute themselves.

"I got held up," Dev said again. "But I have something interesting to show you."

"Have you known Claude a long time?" My breaths seemed almost like my own again.

"What's a long time?"

"Longer than I have."

"Yes."

"Do you like him?"

"Sometimes."

"Quinn wanted to touch my hand, but I couldn't let him. You understand, don't you?"

"I'm very selective about who gets to touch me."

"I am too."

"We're almost there."

"I'd like to stay here instead." I couldn't see anything. Maybe I didn't want to see anything. I liked the labyrinth, had liked it from the first. I still do.

"The labyrinth isn't somewhere to stay. It's here only to pass through."

A moment later, Dev stopped. "I think you'll like this," he said. "But you might not. Even so, I have a friend here. I know you'll like her."

First, I felt the floor under my feet. In the labyrinth the sensations of above and below are absent along with the feel of what's *there*. Although perhaps nothing in the labyrinth is *there*. But there were floorboards below now.

It was dark here, but a different dark than we'd just left. My eyes adjusted. I sucked in a breath.

"This is my room," I said. "Only it isn't."

"It's the model for your room," Devil said. "Claude designed it here. This is his old house."

"Have I been here before? Is my past here?"

"I can't show you your past."

"You mean you're prevented from doing it? Has Claude forbidden you to say anything?"

I was getting angry at Claude, but I didn't want to be. I gazed around at everything as my eyes adjusted to the gloom. Everything was pretty much the same as it had been the day of my first vidcast, before I'd rearranged things, before new objects had entered my room.

Although sitting on the upholstered chair in the corner was a mouse. There was no mouse in my room and I wondered why Claude hadn't included her.

"Ash, this is my friend Bobby. She's in charge of the house."

"Bobby," I said, relishing the name on my tongue. "I wish you could be in my room on the vidcast. Everyone would love you."

"Claude didn't want to include me. In fact, he doesn't want me in the house. Last year he sent Devil to eliminate me and my family. Shows you what an ass he is. Devil and I have been friends for years."

"I'd like to be your friend too. I'd like to visit with you sometimes. If you don't mind."

"This is your room, Ash," Bobby said. "You don't have to ask to visit."

"This is *your* room, Bobby," I said. "I wouldn't intrude. But it is rather nice here."

"Check it out," Dev said. He'd jumped up onto the chair and was licking Bobby's slate gray fur.

I walked around the familiar room although it wasn't the same. I'd made the room I occupied in my vidcast into my own, even though I hadn't been consulted about anything in it. And this room *felt* different. The textures, the weight of the objects, the aromas. There were no aromas in my vidcast room. Or flavors. I could taste this room. It was different from the flavors at the Honeycomb. Not as sweet. Denser. Dustier.

"I like it here better than my room," I said. I went over to the window and pulled the drapes open. Outside was the same night sky I'd seen from the window in my other room, my real—was it real?—room. The one I was used to. But the night sky here seemed different.

"Why?" I said to Dev.

"That's infinity you're gazing into," he said.

"Could you get that spot by my tail?" Bobby said to Dev. "It's impossible to reach."

"Why hasn't Claude shown this to me?" I felt like a traitor, accusing Claude, but I had to ask.

"He can't," Dev said while his tongue worked on the spot near Bobby's tail.

"What do you mean? Why can't he?" I stared out, up into the infinity, searching for the limits.

"There are things you have to discover for yourself," Dev said.

"But if you know—"

"There, finished. Better?" he said to Bobby. "Ash, I can take you only so far. You have to depend on yourself, not me, not anyone else. The answers are all within you."

"But I can't remember my past. And I think you know something. It's mean of you not to tell me. It's mean of Claude."

"Claude's not a mean person," Bobby said.

I turned around to look at her. Devil was lying on his side and Bobby was nestled against his chest. "How can you say that? He sent Devil here to kill you," I said.

"That's just carelessness," Bobby said. "It's different from meanness. And I think his intention was for Dev to just chase me and my family from the house. Not kill us. Isn't that right, Dev?"

"Well, he doesn't like to fish, even though he knows I'd appreciate the results and there's a perfectly good pond just past the fields out to the west."

"If he knows about my past, he should tell me. His efforts to restore my memory from within aren't effective."

"The guy's relentless," Dev said.

"Aren't you tired?" Bobby said. Was she talking to me or Devil?

I reached for my throat, a reflex. I was used to feeling the saturnia necklace there, but I hadn't worn it to meet Quinn.

CHAPTER 34

Claude

EVAN DROPPED OFF Bear and Brandon, then took me home. I'd thought he was going to hang around but he said he had to get back. That Lee was waiting up for him. She would've finished her shift and she'd be winding down. He wanted to talk to her before they both crashed.

As he was leaving, I said, "Are you sure you love her? Are you sure of *her?*"

"Claude, you're asking about yourself. Do you have an answer?"

"Really, Evan, I'm asking about you. Don't turn this back onto me."

"Lee has an advantage over Ash," he said. "She's real. I can touch her. She can touch me. I can go over to her place or she can come to mine. Lee can't be turned off and I wouldn't want her to be."

"You're avoiding answering." He was expert at this maneuver. Actually, so was I. We'd probably learned from each other and honed our skills during our years at the Acres.

"Yes, I'm sure—of her, of my love, of her love. What about you?"

"I'm sure you're annoying the hell out of me," I said.

"You're going to have to face a lot in the next few days and weeks, Claude. Clear up your feelings about this image you've created."

"You mean I should get sane."

"I'd never ask the impossible of you. Your madness is one of the reasons you're my closest friend. I respect that about you. It's *you*. No, Claude. I meant what I said: clear up your feelings about Ash. Whatever they are."

"I may have to start over. Use a different base code."

"She won't be the same." His words served to compress my breaths down into a near-choke.

We walked outside, he got into his transcer, and I leaned down to talk with him through the window port.

"I've got nothing to give you if this all goes south," I said. "The house, the land, the barn—I mortgaged it all to pay for Ash."

"You've got other, bigger concerns, and I've got plenty of assets."

"But everything you've invested in this."

"It won't have that much of an effect on me, either way. But I'm worried about you. You're too caught up in this, Claude. Maybe shutting her down would be the best decision."

"But . . . Brandon—"

"Don't think about her part in this. She's so wealthy she wouldn't notice a loss until it got into the tens of billions. And her investment in Ash is nowhere near that. Besides, Ash is in the black, or at least she was earlier this afternoon."

"Evan, I want you and Lee to be happy."

Evan fired up the transcer. "Stop fighting with everything, Claude. Do what you want instead. I'll still be your friend. Bear likes you too. Brandon, I'm not so sure about. But you have Devil. And things will work out. Haven't they always?"

Evan took off then, anxious to get over to Lee's place, where he was meeting her.

I went back into the barn. Devil wasn't there. Out on a night prowl, I suspected.

If I turned on the console I could see Ash and have a chat with her. Was that what I wanted to do? What would I say to her and what in hell would she say to me?

How could I possibly clear up my feelings? I wouldn't recognize myself if my emotions were clear.

After my hand had been on the console's power switch for a while, I gave up, went over to the sofa, and sank into it.

I couldn't figure out what to say to Ash, if I should tell her about what had happened tonight, about Streeter and Olympia.

What would she think of Olympia? Maybe it'd be better if she never knew about her, although Ash was getting even better at harvesting information. I'd thought that she needed time—the forty-five minutes I'd originally given her to examine other influencers' vidcasts. But in fact she needed almost no time, and during her last vid I realized that she was pulling in data almost continuously. Was she doing it even when she was off? Even when she was in the so-called emptiness?

"Ash, I might shut you down." I said it aloud, trying to get a feel for how I'd say it to her. If I would warn her, although I'd threatened her before. Yet I hadn't meant it, and I suspected she knew that I hadn't. She seemed fearless. Well, that made one of us.

Yet I had nothing, really, to be fearful about. If the Ash project failed, I'd go back to working for someone else. I'd done it before and lived. I still had all my skills. More, in fact. And more experience, even if I'd've preferred not to've had it.

If I lost the property, it wouldn't be the end of the world and maybe I'd be able to sell off the land and keep the barn. Or I could rent out the house. Or perhaps leaving here would be good for me, cutting myself off from unwanted memories, a sort of forced partial amnesia.

But . . . Ash. I wanted this to succeed. This had always seemed like my one chance at some great reward, at fortune, at a kind of satisfaction I'd never gotten from anything else I'd done or attempted to do. Yet it also seemed as though every second a new difficulty arose, each more daunting, more insoluble, more insurmountable, than the last.

I was dreading waking up in the morning—assuming I would actually sleep. The uncertainty of not only the long term but the immediate future was getting to me.

"Ash, if I shut you down, will you forgive me? Will you be able to forgive me? Will your dead spirit haunt me?"

She couldn't answer. The console was off. I was glad she couldn't answer, as I didn't want to hear what she'd have to say. To hear her talk about the emptiness. To ask about her past. To laugh at me for my insane ideas.

In a half sleep my awareness of what I'd done sharpened. I'd created an illusion that seemed so real that even I had started believing it was so. I'd given this creation too much power. Her self-learning had pierced through barriers I hadn't set stiffer—or any—limits on. She'd taken off down a road she'd built for herself, one that included the screwy, unexpected idea that she had amnesia.

Why the hell hadn't I given her a past? It wouldn't've been that hard. I'd thought to give her that scar under her left cheekbone, but I'd forgotten to code in the scar's cause. If I'd thought of three hundred thousand things, then I'd neglected to think of three hundred million things.

Ash, I have to shut you down, I imagined myself saying to her, testing it out.

Just tell me about my past before you do. I need to know. I could almost hear her voice, so familiar to me.

I forgot to give you a past. My mistake. Try to understand.

You know, don't you? Tell me. Please, Claude. Ash, saying my name.

I can't tell you, Ash. If I do, I'll have to hear it myself, and I don't want to. Can't you see I'm struggling with this? Stick to your job. Laying it on the line. Building that line.

To influence and sell. Correct.

Yes. That's better. Yet I felt worse.

I turned over onto my stomach, stretched my arm across the sofa, wondered what it would be like if Ash could be here, if I could hold on to her, if I could feel her lips on mine, her body next to me, the rise and fall of her breaths.

"I want you," I said out loud. "You're not the illusion I created. You're someone else now. I'm trying not to fall in love with you."

I waited a long time to hear Ash's response, but it never came.

That was then. Before everything changed. Before my concerns, fears, and unclaimed emotions were eclipsed by events and circumstances that were even more out of my control than Ash had become.

CHAPTER 35

Ash

I WOKE UP not in the model room in Bobby's house but in my own room. How I'd gotten here, *when* I'd gotten here—these were mysteries to me. So much of existence was a mystery to me. I felt at my neck but the saturnia necklace wasn't there. It was on the vanity. I picked it up and put it on, touching it, holding on to it. If I'd once loved the way this felt, I was no longer sure.

Claude wasn't around. I'd learned a few weeks ago how to emerge from the emptiness long before he arrived.

I got up and rearranged a few things, opened the curtains, looked out at the landscape, at the high sun, no clouds, a field of wildflowers in the distance. Licking my lips, hoping for a taste, but here, in my room, there were no flavors. Yet I could see and feel and hear.

How many other senses were there? Senses I had no access to. Or hadn't discovered yet. Last night at the Honeycomb and in the model room, I'd tasted and smelled. A sort of heaven. But these were lost to me now.

At one time, I'd felt comfortable here. This was my home, the only home I knew. But now I saw that it was only an imitation of a design that someone else had made. As beautiful as it was, I had to decide if I wanted to stay here.

One thing had changed, though—Devil and Bobby were curled up together on the upholstered chair in the corner. They'd never been here in my room with me. I hadn't expected to see them and *hadn't* seen them until I saw them. My sure belief that they'd never be here had prevented me from noticing what was right in front of me.

They were both asleep and I didn't want to disturb them. They looked peaceful and calm, the black cat and the gray mouse. Friends.

I had a new friend, Quinn, but Quinn wanted things from me that I couldn't give him.

Last night while I was sitting in a hexagonal amber chamber at the Honeycomb, a woman named Olympia Cowan was doing a not-all-that-bad impersonation of me in a vidcast with the vile Streeter. I'd seen and heard all his complaints against me, but unlike my stand-in, I didn't feel so defiant. Because some of what Streeter said was true—I had nothing to offer.

That had to change.

"Hell, Ash, how long have you been there?" Claude said after he powered on his console. His cam and monitor were on and I could see him on my scroll, lying on the vanity in its usual place. He was a wreck, the skin around his eyes black with a deadened weariness, his unkempt yellow hair even mussier than usual.

"Why can't I cry?" I said. Seeing him had activated something that seemed to need tears, yet I had none. It was a skill I hadn't learned. Perhaps the amnesia prevented this. Or I was incapable of it.

"Ash, you're on in a few minutes. You have no need to cry."

"Olympia was impressive. Are you thinking of replacing me?" I hadn't dared to consider this, but understood that it might be true.

"It's one of many possibilities," Claude said. He rubbed his hands over his face. The coral of his eyes was dulled to a brownish orange.

"But our sales are good," I said. My job was to sell, and I had to sell myself to Claude if I hoped to keep this job, if that was what this was. Yet since seeing Olympia's performance, I sensed that my existence was nothing *but* a job to Claude.

"Yes," he said. "Since last night we're sold out of nearly everything."

"Yet there's nothing new here." How could I sell things that I couldn't show?

"We were taken by surprise. I'll have more items for the next vidcast."

"If there is one."

"Yeah. If there is one." Shouldn't he have been happy about the sales? He seemed bitter, disappointed.

We both stopped talking. I put one hand on the saturnia necklace. This was my way of touching Claude without actually touching him. The necklace represented him, represented our relationship—made of a rare substance from a vast distance away, smooth yet hard, glowing from within, yet cool to the touch. He'd given it to me and in return I'd given him a semblance of the performance he'd insisted on. Yet I was fulfilling my purpose: influencing and selling.

I wanted to tell Claude about my meeting with Quinn, how I'd refused the touch of Quinn's hand, but I could see that now was the wrong time for that although I might never have another chance to tell him that—or anything. He was ready to shut me down. I could tell by the way he was pressing his fingers into his forehead. Or I was imagining what that meant. Yet as little as I knew about Claude, I very felt I knew him well.

"Are you going to do today's vidcast?" he said, breaking the unsaid stream of connection. His words initiated a disconnect.

"Of course," I said.

"Ash," he said.

I waited. He wasn't going to say anything else.

"Please tell me about my past," I said. "I'm sure that you know. And, Claude—"

"Ash, I've said this before." Claude's tone was weary, maybe even defeated. "You have no past. And even if you did, I wouldn't be the right person to ask about it."

"Who would be?"

"Damned if I know," he said, the bitterness ever more apparent in his tone.

"Claude," I said, as my fingers wound tight around the necklace, an anchor of sorts. I closed my eyes and replayed every conversation I'd had with Claude, although the ones I'd dreamt seemed more real than the ones that *were* real.

"Ash, whatever it is, don't tell me. I've already got too much here."

"Why?"

"You're there and I'm here. The rest isn't . . ."

"Claude, last night—" I was going to tell him about the model room, but he interrupted me.

"You're on in five, four, three, two . . . one."

I felt the tears on my cheeks before I realized they were coming from my eyes.

Claude had given up on me. He didn't want to talk with me. He refused me my past.

There and *here* could never coincide. It wasn't in their nature. Their essence—the essence of my being and of Claude's being—was very to be apart.

"Hi, everyone," I said as the tears smeared my vision. I wanted to wipe at them, but I clung to the necklace with both hands. If only Claude would understand.

"Damn you, stop crying," Claude said in his near-whisper.

"I have so much I want to talk to you about today," I said. "I don't quite understand all of it, but I'm counting on you to understand. If you can."

CHAPTER 36

Claude

WHAT THE HELL was Ash about to say? And she was crying? I'd never programmed that. Who would buy something from an influencer who cried?

I'd been right—Ash was out of control and it was up to me to shut her down. Forever. I'd worked long and hard trying to fix her, constantly attempting to amend her ever-mounting flaws, but they'd built up so fast that I could no longer keep pace with their persistent increase. And despite my efforts I'd never altered any of them. Perhaps I'd made some of them worse. I couldn't tell anymore. What parts of the code had I changed and what parts had Ash herself manipulated?

The last time I'd looked, late yesterday, I saw almost none of the work I'd done. It was all Ash's doing, overwriting, deleting, rearranging. A complex tangle I'd never be able to unravel.

"First, I want to say thank you to the wonderful Olympia Cowan." Ash was gripping onto her saturnia necklace with both hands, like she was afraid someone would take it from her, or like she was afraid it was strangling her. Like it *was* strangling her.

And, hell, she knew about Olympia. Well, Ash had been active before I'd turned on the console, as impossible as that was. Or I'd imagined that. I could have. The boundary between reality, or what I'd thought of as reality, and the constructed environment Ash was part of had sprung a leak. *That's* what I had to repair. Not Ash's code, but my own faulty perceptions.

"Olympia, thank you for standing in for me, for standing *up* for me. If I ever have the chance to return your kindness and strength, I will. I promise you."

She would? How? But I hoped she'd never have to. Then I hoped I wasn't losing my mind, thinking such rot. But at least Ash had stopped crying, although her left cheek, just where the scar was, now had a pale vertical line through it, where her tears had fallen.

I'd created Ash, I kept telling myself. I'd created this illusion who had morphed so far from anything I'd envisioned or coded that she was capable of crying. That she thought she had amnesia. That . . . a lot of other things I hadn't yet discovered or noticed.

I *would* shut her down. I rested my hand over the power switch.

"I have to apologize to my viewers. I should have been there last night with Streeter. But . . . I was somewhere else."

Yeah. You were nonexistent. In the "somewhere else" of the emptiness.

"Olympia, I want to get together with you and talk. I hope we can do that. Consider this your open invitation. Contact me anytime."

And create a new, worse disaster. I tapped my fingers just above the power switch, readying myself. This had to be done. I had to shut her off and never turn her back on. I had to destroy the code and demolish the console so that no one would be able to trace her underpinnings. And so that I'd never be tempted to resurrect her. There was no other way out of it. If Ash got any more out of control, who knew what she was capable of? I certainly didn't. From the very first moment she'd started vidcasting, she'd gone her own way. I should have stopped her then, when it wouldn't've mattered so much. And then none of the rest would've happened either.

"My job is to influence and sell," Ash said.

Oh hell, no. I steeled myself for what might come next.

"But what I enjoy is just talking with you, telling you my secrets, spending time with you."

"No more secrets," I said into the direct line. If Ash was going to tell another "secret," I wasn't going to let my hand hover over the power switch. I was going to end it.

As little as I might have wanted to, I had to put an end to Ash. Put an end to my ever-wilder thoughts and imaginings about her.

Had I been attracted to, *attached* to, the code I'd written that powered that foolish game that everyone had been addicted to three years ago? No. Of course not. The work was good—too good, in fact, since Centerstorm was rolling in credits from the sales of *Send Away* and I'd gotten nothing but a salary—but that was the all of it. I didn't dream about the characters I'd invented for gameplay. I didn't have emotions that my best friend was telling me I had to get clear about. I didn't look forward to playing the game itself and in fact I'd never played it after I left the company and struck out on my own. Started building Ash, for myself and not for someone else.

But she was just code. Like the game. Like anything I'd ever worked on. Like the code that ran the program that did nothing but search for my missing mother, although it'd failed to find her and I'd shut that down. Years ago. When I was a teenager and developed other interests and didn't care any longer.

Code. Programs. Connections. The inner workings of a manufactured imagination. Yes or no. Go this way or that. If this, then that. If not, then redirect. It was that simple and that straightforward. Nothing more. Just because a beautiful image was part of those yeses and nos didn't mean she was *someone*. Just because she'd been able to manipulate these yeses and nos so that they fluctuated between the two, creating her own quanta.

I was doing my best to distance myself from Ash. Convince myself. Her beauty, her shocking qualities, her cleverness. Her skills.

Her ad-libs. Her seeming depth. I had to be practical and put my absurd emotions aside.

Despite what Evan had said, I couldn't let myself get clear about how I really felt. That was going into dangerous territory. The last time—the *only* time—I'd done that was a disaster. I wasn't going to ever do it again.

"I'd like to thank my manager, Claude Ryerson, too," Ash said. Why had I never warned her against saying my name in her vidcast? I wasn't a public figure. Ash was. The *image* of Ash was.

This was getting worse and worse. Yet I couldn't bring myself to turn her off. To *kill* her. It was like killing her, and I didn't want to. I wanted to look at her, to hear her, to be with her in the only way that was possible, for as long as I could until I was forced to do the inevitable.

"Claude understood that I couldn't be there last night, and he was responsible for finding Olympia so that I could go to another meeting."

"What other meeting?" I was shouting at Ash at that point. She'd gone to another meeting? I couldn't've heard that right. Ash couldn't *go* anywhere. "What other meeting?"

"I still need your help," Ash said, plowing right past my shouts. "With my amnesia. It's bothering me more and more. It's as though it's gotten worse." Ash laughed. At her own ironic statement?

"You don't have amnesia," I said to her, although there was really no need, since she herself was going to be a memory any moment now. "You *can't* have amnesia."

"I wasn't able to be there last night to talk with you, Streeter," Ash said, speaking directly to him. "But I will answer you from here."

"Don't," I said.

"I was an influencer."

Her use of the past tense wasn't lost on me. Did she realize I was about to shut her down? Was this her farewell? If so, I'd let her have at it. Within limits, although I didn't myself know what those limits might be.

I was curious, though, about what she'd say next. Ash was ever distressing me, alarming me, infuriating me, surprising me. Yet, as her avid fans also did, I awaited her words, her gestures, her odd ways of talking about things.

"Have you ever noticed how, when you blink your eyes, it's as though existence itself is blinking? That it's not here while you're not looking? And that you create it anew with each new sight?"

What the hell? I didn't say that to Ash. I was too stunned. Somehow Ash had manipulated her code so that it now incorporated existential concepts. Although *incorporated* was hardly the right term for anything Ash could do. There was no corpus. No matter how much I'd imagined or dreamt there was. Or desired there to be.

CHAPTER 37

Ash

"I HAD AN adventure last night. After I returned, I had so many new ideas that I'm still processing them all. Rejecting some, embracing others."

"Damn you, where did you go?" Claude said in a hoarse whisper.

"I can't say where I was because it was a private meeting. But I can say that it produced new understandings. The first was that I can no longer be an influencer."

"The hell you say." Claude sounded more like he was talking to himself than to me. Maybe he was. For a long time, back then, it seemed sometimes as though Claude thought talking to me was the same as talking to himself.

"I don't very want to influence anyone. I myself have been influenced, and I'm trying to shake it off, reemerge. It's better to find your own way."

"Is that what you've been doing?" Claude's voice was faint. I nodded just a bit, so he could see but no one else would know that I was communicating with him. "Ash," he said, alarm in his voice, "the music's not on."

I hadn't turned the music on. I was tired of the theme song, hated it, actually. It had followed me around, emphasizing and shaping, telling others what they should feel about me, about what I was saying and doing and wearing and surrounded by. The song was as much of an influencer as I was and I wanted to be free of it. I *was* free of it. I never wanted to hear it again.

While I'd been in the model room with Dev and Bobby, I'd developed a sharp knowing that this was my new path. I could no longer do my job of influencing and selling. I had to be myself instead, but first I had to find that self.

I was still gripping onto the saturnia necklace, which was the most obvious, most well-known, and most coveted piece of my merchandisable identity. But, as Streeter had pointed out, I was nothing. The necklace was just a prop adorning and holding together this nothingness.

"You have to create your own reality. You can't live in someone else's. Not mine or anyone's."

I glanced down at my scroll, which was covered with an unending cascade of messages.

Ash, don't go away! The world needs influencers and you're the best.

I miss the music. Did you forget to turn it on?

Is that a new shirt you're wearing? Where can I get one?

I was getting tired of you anyway. All that made-up amnesia BS.

You have a cat? When did you get a cat?

So you were watching. I dare you to meet with me.—Streeter

I just saved up enough to get the vanity and now you're telling me not to? Don't confuse me!

Ash! Come talk with us! We can help you! We love you!—M at Today's Trends

Ha ha. What kind of scam are you pulling today? The great Ash. Sure.

I need you. Thank you for last night. Love—Quinn

I had to stop looking.

"I can't answer all of your messages. I'm sorry. I'm overwhelmed. So much is happening, but so much has already happened, and I don't know what it was or what effect it's still having on me. I'm searching. That very before—it won't reveal itself. If you know your past, you are so fortunate. You can see your progression. Compare. Examine. Reflect. Laugh. But don't have regrets—be happy for all of it, because it's yours, you know about it. And you might not.

"If I'm myself now because of my past, I have no way of knowing. I welcome your help although I understand that the amnesia could be permanent."

"How the blasted hell did you get Devil and that damned vermin pal of his into your room?" Claude was back to shouting. I guess it'd taken him that long to notice that Dev and Bobby were with me. They were on the chair in the far corner, and that wasn't the main focus of the camera.

"I can also no longer sell things," I said, although I had no control over the products or their sales. The objects sold themselves apart from my influence, anytime, even when I was in the emptiness. Even when Olympia Cowan was impersonating me. Even when I was at the Honeycomb with Quinn or crouched in an alleyway, very clinging to my existence itself.

"I can no longer do this vidcast," I said.

"You're damned right you can no longer do the vidcast," Claude said.

I pulled at the necklace, thinking I'd tear it in two—a symbolic splitting off with the role I was shedding—but after I tugged at it, it disintegrated into scores of small pieces, the gemlike metal fragments shimmering in a thousand colors as they fell through my fingers onto my shoulders, my chest, the vanity, my lap, the floor.

I didn't know for sure, but I suspected that I'd never agreed to be an influencer and seller. That Claude had decided I would be and so I took on the job, to please him. Yet until I found out the truths about my past, I couldn't be certain. And even then, would I be able to separate out my own motives from Claude's? From anyone else's? If I loved Claude, how would I know why I'd done what I'd done, thinking it was to his benefit?

If I loved Claude. There was part of the problem. Because he didn't love me. I only aggravated and enraged him. And what was love anyway? The word and its implications slipped through my understandings.

Devil and Bobby jumped down from the chair. Dev leaped onto the windowsill and Bobby joined him, scampering up the curtains, which draped onto the floor. Dev looked back over his sleek black shoulder, his viridian eyes meeting mine.

My fists were still clenched, holding on to the last remnants of my iconic saturnia necklace. I stood up and let go, brushing off the last particles that were clinging to my damp palms.

"I can't explain everything—or anything," I said as I walked over to the window.

I'd never tested it before, never touched it. I'd opened the drapes, but that's as far as I'd gotten. I stared at the window, at the mechanism that must be what controlled it, then I turned around so my audience could see me. This last time.

"I think we need to feel the air in here," I said, and looked back at the window, at Devil and Bobby, sitting on the sill. Dev hadn't taken his gaze off me.

I turned the latch.

CHAPTER 38

Claude

I'D HAD MY hands on my head—an attempt to hold on to my mind, perhaps—and couldn't react fast enough. That's what I told myself then. Now? Now I'm not sure. Maybe I wanted Ash to do it.

Maybe I wanted Ash to open the window—a window that she herself had created, since the room I'd coded had only the fabric covering a supposed window, a window I knew was there in my house, in the model room, but that didn't have to be there in Ash's room because she'd never open it. I'd never allow her to. She and her audience would never see it. It was implicit only.

The drapes had been a tease. Keep viewers coming back. If there was something behind there, I'd let them see it only if Ash's popularity started sinking. Only then would I bother creating a view. Yet she'd opened the curtains without my command and against my wishes.

She opened the window in the same way, except that there had been no window. Yet there was. Had it blinked into existence the last time she'd opened her eyes?

My right hand had been rubbing at my neck, which I do automatically when I'm tired or confused. My left hand had been rubbing across and over, against my forehead, trying to force an understanding into myself.

I couldn't get to the kill switch in time. Instead I watched as Ash opened the window. I watched Devil and the mouse he'd refused to evict from my house as they went out the window. I watched as Ash followed them, putting one leg over the windowsill, then swinging the other leg over.

She looked back for a moment and waved. To me? To her viewers? To some invisible presence in her room, yet someone or something else I'd never programmed and hadn't intended to be there?

If I'd thought Ash was out of control before this, now she'd breached some barrier that I'd assumed was impenetrable. Not assumed—known.

Ash left the window open. I could see her back. If she had been in the house, in the model room, she'd've been able to stand on the overhang just under the window. That's where I imagined she was.

Hell, she wasn't there. She wasn't anywhere. She was an image, a collection of strings of coding. A simulacrum. She didn't exist.

I watched as my trembling left hand stopped rubbing itself against my forehead and moved back to the power switch.

Turned it off.

Ended Ash's vidcast. Ended Ash herself.

It'd be hours before I had the wherewithal to turn the console back on and do the work that needed to be done, eliminating every trace of Ash's code.

Partway through the task, I noticed that Devil wasn't around. He'd never come back from his night prowl. Had he deserted me too? But there was no *too*. There was no Ash. Streeter had actually been right about that—she was nothing.

What would come next? Would we hire Olympia to continue the sales and influence job that Ash had abandoned? Would I end up with none of this enterprise that I'd originated, that had been mine from before the beginning—would none of this be in my control anymore, since without Ash, without her image, I was unnecessary? Olympia was a person. She didn't need a programmer. My coding skills would be pointless.

Olympia can't be controlled was the insane thought I had while I was working through Ash's code, expunging it piece by piece.

"Ash, I'm sorry," I said. I kept saying it with each gesture. "You can't forgive me and I don't want you to."

No, Olympia couldn't be controlled, but, in the end, Ash couldn't be either. That was one of the many reasons I had to destroy her.

Was I Claude Frankenstein, creator of a monster? But the monster that Frankenstein himself had created was misunderstood. He'd been gentle and curious, hardly a threat.

Had I not understood Ash? Yet Ash wasn't the same. Dr. Frankenstein had taken the parts of dead bodies, sewn them together, and sent an electrical charge through them, bringing his creation to life.

No, Ash wasn't like that. She wasn't. I wasn't like that. I hadn't taken the parts of the dead and strung them together to create Ash. I refused to believe that I had or that I would have. I was a coder, a programmer. I hadn't been trying to create an actual living being. Ash was an image, an illusion. Like the character in one of the games I'd coded. Nothing more.

I didn't really want to expunge the intricate, delicate parts of the code that Ash had self-created. They were fascinating to me, with routines I'd never encountered before, with a sort of finesse that even the best coders couldn't hope to duplicate. That I couldn't hope to remember. Yet I had to do it. I couldn't stop at half measures.

"Ash, damn you. I know you won't forgive me for this," I said aloud as I wiped her from the console. As I destroyed her image, her skills, her talents, her mystery, her silvery eyes, her room and everything that was ever in it.

Everything gone. When I was finished I wanted to set the console on fire, but I couldn't do it. I needed a place to live and this was my home.

In the shed where my disabled bike was parked next to the tractor, I found a sledgehammer, one of the many tools in Dad's collection.

"Thanks, Dad," I said to my dead father as I went back into the barn to finish killing off Ash.

I admit that I enjoyed this part of it. If deleting and expunging the code that I'd spent endless hours working on, code that Ash had manipulated, reorganized, and re-formed in configurations and sequences unfathomable to me—if that had distressed, pained, hurt me, ripped into me, yet wielding the heavy sledge was satisfying in a way that no amount of exquisite coding could ever hope to duplicate.

Without method or plan I swung away at the console, at the monitors, loving the feel of the sledge's wooden handle in my grip, of the heft of it, of the muscles in my back and shoulders and arms, muscles and sensations I hadn't paid attention to in years.

I smashed it all, including the desk everything had been sitting on. The more I destroyed, the more I wanted to destroy. While I was at it, I accidentally hit into the wall. Something I'd have to repair if I expected to keep living there in the barn.

I'd almost forgotten I could live anywhere else. That I could live in the house, for example, along with Dev's mouse pal and the extended mouse family. Along with memories I wished I could destroy as easily as I was destroying Ash.

Had Frankenstein destroyed his monster? I couldn't remember exactly how that story ended, but it did end with the monster's death. As Ash's story was ending as well. With her death. Her *virtual* death. She'd never been alive to begin with. Ash hadn't and couldn't exist outside an imagined, created world. She wasn't real.

I wasn't real either, I thought as I continued hammering into the components of the console, pulverizing them into useless bits of metal. I too was the creation of someone else, of two someone elses. They'd spent a careless night together and I'd been the result, a result that one of the two creators had had no interest in.

"The hell with you," I said. If I'd've had neighbors nearby, they would've heard me. But the pastures surrounded me. I was nowhere near anyone.

"Fuck you, you bastard," I said as I bashed away at the main memory components. I could've been talking to myself. I *was* talking to myself.

The thing about wielding a sledgehammer is that it's tiring. It's exhausting work. At one point in my frenzy, I thought that this would be the ideal workout—give someone a sledge and have them destroy everything in sight for as long as they could. I'd never sweated so much or felt such strain on my arms and shoulders and back.

"Ash," I said as I flung the sledge into one of the monitors— maybe I was still shouting. "Ash, how bloody dare you take my work and make a mockery of it."

I didn't mean that. But I didn't know what I meant. I was mad with a kind of rage I hadn't experienced since I was a kid and a thousand bad things had happened all at once.

Isn't that how they always happen? All at the same time? A person could go for months or years without incident and then, one after another, dreadful, impossible, nightmarish events and circumstances arise, cascading into an uncontainable torrent.

Laughing at me, mocking me along with my failed creation, nature itself rebelled. A freak hailstorm erupted and unlike most hailstorms, it wouldn't stop. The hole I'd bashed into the barn wall let in first hailstones, then the sleet that followed.

The air was cold now, too cold for summer.

I couldn't stay in the barn any longer. I let the sledge slip from my grasp. My palms were cut up, raw. The sleet wouldn't stop. Hailstones mixed in. The air was thick, damp, cold.

Running over to the house, my unlikely refuge.

I didn't want to go into the model room. I'd have to destroy that next. I had to get rid of everything that had been involved with the creation of Ash, that had been Ash. That had been my idea of Ash and, worse, the manifestation of Ash.

But I stood outside the room, leaned against the doorjamb, listening to the sleet and hail pelt the house's roof.

"Ash," I said, thinking that I hadn't cried in many years. Yet it's not a trick you forget. I certainly hadn't forgotten.

"Ash, don't forgive me," I said. "Never forgive me."

CHAPTER 39

Today's Trends Special Edition!

WE ARE SHOCKED and thrilled, intrigued, and our hearts are fluttering in a mad fury. We're deciding whether we can keep up with our hearts, they're moving with such unaccustomed speed and urgency.

You've already read past this tease? Yes, we would too. But if you haven't, we won't keep you waiting another moment.

Our beloved Ash has disappeared! She's *gone. Vanished.* We've lost her.

We're struggling with her leaving, with not having her vidcast, with what to do with our days, our thoughts, our desires.

Did Ash's disappearance seem inevitable to you? Could you sense it coming? Did you know? Were you nodding your head as Ash opened her window and stepped out of it?

If you did, you're more prescient than we could ever hope to be. We weren't prepared. Even now that it's happened, we *still* aren't prepared.

Did you see the vidcast with Streeter and that marvelous Olympia Cowan and think *This will cause Ash to go into hiding?* We had no such thoughts. And we're torn now. Is Olympia the good person she seemed to be or is she Ash's enemy? The agent behind Ash's absence? An impersonator who was using Ash solely for her own ugly purposes?

Everyone's seen it—seen it over and over again, if you're us—but if you're one of the three people who doesn't know the details, here they are.

Ash was giving her regular vidcast. She looked especially beautiful, we thought. Kind of mussy, which has never been Ash's presentation. But it worked for her. Really, we're sure anything would work for Ash. She could carry off anything and everything. We have no doubt on that score.

Ash started off saying that she'd had an adventure last night and, friends, we're here to tell you that we have information about that adventure. Keep reading!

Then she resigned from her job. Imagine! Yes! She said she would no longer be an influencer or sell anything. We were *shocked* into a gaping, dazed silence. Our Certain Other thought that maybe we had died and offered to call for help, but we weren't dead.

After this mortal pause our Certain Other talked us back into awareness. Ash by then was talking about how you can't live in someone else's reality.

But we want to live in Ash's reality! we said to our scroll and to our Certain Other, and we're saying it to you as well. We're saying it to Ash right now, if she's reading, if she's listening.

Ash said we should find our own way. But, Ash, you were our guide! We love our guide! We cherish our guide. We need you.

She gave other advice as well. Ash was deeper and even more genius than we'd seen before, and we'd seen so much before.

Friends, we are going to tell you the worst part—Ash said she is no longer going to do her vidcast.

When she said that, we started crying. It was one thing to stop being an influencer, to stop selling things. But to no longer do her vidcast? To deprive us of our need for Ash? Our Certain Other had to comfort us with everything at their disposal, including sex, which was quite comforting while also exciting. But we're not here to talk about ourselves. We're talking about our beloved Ash.

We know what her adventure was, but we will let Quinn Fiery tell you himself. Or we would if we could locate Quinn, who's also disappeared.

Are Quinn Fiery and Ash together now? Oh! Wouldn't that be astounding? Extraordinary? Luscious? Perfect?

We embrace this outcome, although we don't know if it's true. The *Trends* reports only what we know, and we cannot speak further on this matter.

We can tell you that we're in touch with Reda Fiery, our close, dear friend, and she is mad with worry. Quinn's been missing since last night. Make sure to watch the Fiery vidcast, where Reda will explain everything she knows.

Quinn, please return.

Ash! Ash, please return.

We are bereft without you. We *did* create our own reality and that reality had you in it. It *needs* you to be in it, Ash.

When you stepped out of that window, where did you go? Why can no one locate you? Why is your manager not answering his messages? *Our* messages.

Keep your eye on the *Trends*. We always have all the latest, and as soon as we know anything about Ash, about Quinn, we'll be right there for you, as we always are.

Before

CHAPTER 40

Evan

I'D ALWAYS KNOWN that I'd go to the Acres. It'd been my dream since I'd first learned about it when I was maybe six or seven, and simultaneous with my discovery of its existence, my decision that I'd go there arose, along with the certainty that this was inevitable. That this was my assured destiny.

Of course a six- or seven-year-old's sense of inevitability could be flawed, and it wasn't until I was waiting those tense months for word from the Acres about my acceptance that my previous sense of knowing wavered and sometimes vanished.

Although my acceptance arrived later than I'd thought it would—I'd already been at Keff for a year by then—I *was* accepted, yet there was a caveat: I had to "perform up to standards" or I'd be expelled. Those standards were implicit. I had to know them from inside myself, and since I'd had a decade-long relationship with my hopes and dreams about the Acres, I was confident.

The contrast between the cramped apartment where I'd spent my entire life, jammed into three rooms along with my parents and sister, and the immense campus at Keff had taken some getting used to, but the wide-open, expansive, going-on-and-on land, buildings, and vistas of the Acres was dizzying at first.

I'd arrived on the train, which was, I guess, where my ideas for my eventual fortune originated, and when I got off at the station I felt immediately lost and simultaneously at home. There I was, in the place of my dreams. I'd made it. As I approached the building where I'd been instructed to go, I promised myself that I'd perform beyond any standards that any Acres student had ever achieved. I would do the Acres, and myself, proud.

After a brief detour at second-rated Keff, I'd finally arrived, everything was perfect, and I was ready to show myself and the world what I was capable of.

Hauling my belongings over to what I knew to be the oldest building on campus—how I had been so fortunate as to get assigned a room in this most-desired building was thrilling to me—I walked right by the person who would become my best, and most valued, friend. But even though we noticed each other and nodded in a kind of implicit recognition, we didn't know each other then. And now—now Claude is so destroyed by what's gone on that it's as though I don't know him, or sometimes I think it's possible that perhaps I never knew him.

Then, though. Then I was unaware of any of this, of my future, of the fortune I'd make, of the friendships I'd fall into, of anything other than my joy at being at the Acres. Until I got to my room, that is.

One of the myths—although before that day I'd thought of this as truth, as a given—of the Acres is that every student is paired with the exact right roommate. No one except a mysterious few insiders is aware of the methods used to make this selection of roommates, but along with my certainty that I'd go to the Acres was the additional certainty that I'd have the perfect roommate, someone who'd be just the right person at the right time in my life to further my awareness of myself, of others, and of the universe.

Yet when I got to my room assignment and opened the door, I had an immediate understanding that I'd been set up with the exact wrong roommate. I was here to study and learn, not share a room with someone who couldn't even wait until his roommate had arrived before he started in on his Acres-fueled sexual exploits.

Not that I was against sexual exploits. I'd intended on having those myself, just in private and not with an audience, which my intended roommate already had, not including me. And the room was much too small. How would I ever get any studying done?

I stepped back just as the roommate I was rejecting—Harwood Jackson—looked back over his busy shoulder and said, "Hey. You must be Evan Becket. Come on in!" before going back to whatever it was he was doing with the moaning, writhing body beneath his.

Picking up my bags, I exited the exalted, high-ceilinged hallway of the oldest, most desirable residence building at the Acres. I didn't care if I never saw the place again. I'd have more of a chance of getting my work done sitting on a bench at the train station than I would sharing a room with this joker.

The Acres had failed me. It was an absolute fact that their room-assignment committee—whoever they were, if there was a committee— had the uncanny ability to put the right two people together. But Harwood Jackson was the wrong person. How had they made such a terrific mistake?

On my way over to the housing admin, I ran into the same fellow I'd seen earlier and we'd nodded to each other.

"I cannot believe these bastards," he said to me, his coral-colored eyes seeming to pierce right through my skull.

"Yeah," I said. "Unbelievable. And they're supposed to be such experts at this."

"Experts?" he said. "Don't be fooled. This may be the Acres, but the place is rife with useless fools."

"Too right. I've been here less than an hour and one of my sacred illusions has already been destroyed."

"Claude Ryerson," he said. He stuck out a big, callused hand and I stuck my smooth, slender one in it, and we shook.

"Evan Becket," I said. "They've stuck me in a room with some joker."

"Which joker would that be?" Claude said this as if he knew everyone at the Acres, or every joker, anyway.

"Harwood Jackson."

"Hell," Claude said. "Did you put *orgy* down as one of your preferences?"

"You know him?"

"I avoid him," Claude said.

"Good thinking," I said, reshouldering my bag and getting ready to head off. I needed to find a place to stay. That was my first priority.

"What the hell," Claude said. "I've got an extra room at my place. And unlike the rooms in that creaky old building you just fled, my place has interior doors. You'd never have to see me if you didn't want to. And I'm working all the time anyway."

"Except for right now," I said.

Claude gave me one of his very rare smiles. At the time I didn't know they were so rare. These days, well, I haven't seen Claude smile in a long time.

"Come on," he said. "I'll show you around and then maybe we can scrounge up something to eat."

"Maybe they didn't do such a bad job after all," I said as we walked the two kilometers over to the beaten-down building where Claude lived and where I'd make my home with Claude for the next several years.

"No need to worry about paying," Claude said, opening the interior door to his spare room. "I get this whole place as part of my deal here."

I threw down my bag and brushed a thick layer of dust off the desk in the corner, then peered out the window.

"Are you in science?" I said. I hadn't even thought to ask. I'd just been relieved I didn't have to deal with Harwood Jackson.

"Coding," he said. "Also agriculture."

"Maths," I said. "Agriculture?"

"Dad's idea. In case."

I had no *in case*. I'd never thought about it and it hadn't occurred to me that I'd need such a thing until Claude said it.

"I'd better get one of those," I said. "In case."

"Good thinking. Let's get some lunch."

I was thrilled again to be at the Acres, relieved that I'd met Claude, and happy he'd rescued me and that I'd found a friend. I had a decent place to live even if it wasn't the legendary residence hall I'd run from and even if it was far from the main action on campus. I decided my in case would be engineering.

That night, in my new room, as I inhaled liters of toxic dust, I drew up the first plans for what would become the magrail.

CHAPTER 41

Claude

BEFORE THEN.

I wasn't a happy kid but I was a smart kid. Not smart the way Evan is—no one is that smart—but smart enough to see that I didn't want to spend my life being a farmer, which was my mother's dream for me. That's what we were doing here, out in the middle of a hellish noplace. Indulging her agricultural fantasies and prepping me for a life I had no interest in.

Even without her here, even after she abandoned us or disappeared or dematerialized—we didn't know what she had done or had had done to her—even so, Dad and I were surrounded by farmland. He wasn't a farmer and had no interest. It was up to me.

Yet my interest wasn't in agriculture or farmland but in calculations, configurations, and patterns. In deconstructing patterns down into the chaos they arose from, then realigning them into something else. I'd watched over Dad's shoulder long enough that I knew what to do even before I knew how to read. I read numbers and code first. They were my native tongue, and Dad's as well.

He'd been the chief programmer at a not-unimpressive gaming concern, which occupation had sparked my interest in the same sorts of things. Dad's specialty had been character image and development. Many of the artificial beings he'd created for various games became classics. One in particular, Imari, had been so popular that her name had entered the language, standing in for the traits she embodied: beauty, brilliance, treachery.

Well, not *embodied*. She was created. She didn't exist. Although at the time, when I was a kid, it was as though Imari did exist. She was more real to me than my own mother had been, a fading memory. Had I promised her I'd become a farmer and look after the property? Or had she only wanted me to and instilled some kind of a generational guilt in me that still lingers?

I could use some amnesia myself, Ash.

Although then, before.

Dad hadn't been formally trained. He'd picked up coding and programming himself, just playing around with it, and his methods and approaches were sui generis. He encouraged me to take the same path, exploring, experimenting. It was the only way to arrive at real innovation, he said.

But when I was offered a spot at the Acres, I couldn't refuse. It was the kind of opportunity that wasn't what I'd been looking for—I hadn't been looking for anything at the time, if you don't count the program I'd written that was constantly looking for my mother and never found her—but it was an opportunity to get away from the farm, from Dad, from some of the guilt.

I accepted the offer the same day I turned off the program that had failed to find my mother. Later I found out that Dad was the one who'd told the Acres about me. He let it slip when I was home on a holiday that second year. I'd brought Evan with me, wanting to show him around, and also he needed somewhere to test out the magrail theories he was working on and we had all those gone-to-rot fields that he could use.

Hell, the Acres. What a disaster at first.

They stuck me in a room with the sex-mad Harwood Jackson, who thought nothing of carrying on his lusty adventures at any time, in the room we shared—a room the size of one of the smaller closets in the farmhouse. I lasted almost a month, spending most of my time in the library or camped out in the majestic hallways of the residence building, until I found a run-down place farther away from the center of things and abandoned Harwood, who probably didn't notice my absence until a couple of months had passed.

But a worse disaster—and I did learn a few, uh, physical maneuvers from the unavoidable presence of my ex-roommate and his cavalcade of partners and observers—a worse disaster than my onetime roommate was the coding class.

I'd been doing things my own way since I'd started coding—which way was a mixture of Dad's unusual methods and my own fucked-up version of that plus some tricks I'd developed over the years. I'd been doing maths my own way as well, but the maths instructor, Emlyn Mohr, didn't care and in fact encouraged me, and she and I developed a fast, although not lasting, friendship.

The coding instructor, though, had other ideas. Saul Landis, who had a reputation as a hard-line, immovable perfectionist. The Acres had thrown me into his class, ignoring my requests. This was *required*. And Landis explained that his students had to learn to do things his way, the *right* way.

I had to start over and get it right from the beginning and forget all the "utter crap" I'd been doing. That was his first evaluation of my work, after a week under his iron-fisted tutelage. So I'd started over, as he suggested. I'd been my own teacher for a while and I wasn't sure how to act around someone else. Dad had taken me out of school a few years earlier, at my request, since I was so bored, but this was the Acres. This was different. I had to make a go of it.

Did I try hard enough? Probably not. Because I didn't care. Landis might have known the standard procedures and routines and methods, but that was all he knew, despite his reputation as some kind of programming god. But if he was a god, then I was a god from a more advanced universe, one that coincided with Landis's only on rare occasions.

I quit the class and a week later was teaching one of my own out of my rooms. When admin was alerted to my "antics" by Landis, they stepped over his distinguished head and gave me a real classroom. Paid me by giving me free room and board. Offered to house me in the fancy residence hall, but I was happy where I was, away from the action, away from Landis himself, who'd developed an acidic disdain for me.

Then I met Evan, whose astounding intellect had the effect of lighting up the atmosphere around him, and I knew immediately that I wanted to be his friend. And although he managed to destroy another of my friendships, ours persisted, through every good and lousy thing that happened.

CHAPTER 42

Evan

LATELY, LYING IN bed with Lee, feeling her warmth so close, I've wondered how things ever got so out of hand back then.

Meeting Claude Ryerson had set off a cascade of creativity in me. Before I'd gotten to the Acres, I'd been focused on maths at Keff, but almost immediately after moving in with Claude, I decided to delve into engineering as well. It was going to be my in case. Instead it became my focus.

But, the maths. I can't let that part slip off as though nothing happened. Was there a start to it? It didn't seem like it *started*. It was more like a natural progression, like the change of seasons.

At Claude's insistence, I'd changed over to the maths class that Emlyn Mohr was teaching. This was supposed to've been a class for third-year students, but Claude had convinced both me and his pal Emlyn that I belonged there when in fact I didn't belong there as the material was a bit too easy for me. I'd come to the Acres to be challenged, not to polish up some academic résumé.

Did Emlyn seduce me or did I seduce her? We were a poor match. She seemed to me more like someone my ex-roomie, Harwood

Jackson, would be hooked up with. She was hooked up with him, but I didn't know it. I thought her interests were solely with me.

"Come to my office," she said to me after a couple of weeks of classes where I'd ignored her instruction—she'd been talking about slash theory, which I'd conquered years earlier—and instead spent my time working out one of the innumerable difficulties my ideas for the magrail had presented me with.

Emlyn's office was in her house, a somewhat too grand, asymmetrical building near the forest on the outskirts of the campus.

"Door's open," she said when I arrived. Her office door was around the back, just off a stone-floored sort of patio. I walked in. She was sitting at a desk that looked more like a prop than a place someone would work. Like a museum piece, something you'd be afraid to touch, yet she looked quite comfortable and relaxed sitting there.

"Listen," I said, thinking I'd obviate the need for her to have to speak harsh words, "I know Claude thought this was a grand idea, but—"

"You don't belong in that class," she said, finishing my sentence.

"No," I said, relieved.

"You belong—"

"In your bed," I said, shocking myself. Did I think I was my discarded roommate? Had I accidentally learned some sick technique from him during the two minutes I'd been exposed to his athletic activities?

"Absolutely," Emlyn said, unbuttoning her shirt while she sat behind that delicate desk. "Why do you think I asked you out here?" She shrugged off her shirt and stood up and slipped off her pants. That was all she'd had on. Nothing underneath.

"Do you know what to do?" she said.

I'd been standing there, staring at her, so engorged it almost hurt.

"Sure," I said as images of Harwood Jackson, a writhing body underneath his, and two overinvolved observers flashed into my inner field of vision. Even though I'd had experiences of my own, although they'd been nothing at all like this.

Emlyn had the body of a woman, not a girl, and I had a need that overcame the voice in my head that was reminding me that Claude was Emlyn's friend, that Claude had introduced us, and that maybe Claude was interested in Emlyn and I was usurping that interest.

"You're very sure of yourself," Emlyn said. "I like that about you."

She seemed cold, looking back on it. Calculated. Well, she was a maths instructor. Maybe everything she did was a calculation. And maybe that's why I was so aroused. Hard to say, especially now, now that I know Lee, now that I understand something about love, about a mutuality of expression and desire.

Then, though, I thought Emlyn Mohr was the most exotic, desirable being on the planet.

"I'm going to fuck you until you beg me to stop," I said, even though I'd never said or thought anything like that before. Now it seems like a joke, since Emlyn Mohr could outlast not just me, but Harwood Jackson and his army of sex-starved observers and still have enough left over to seduce someone else twenty minutes later.

I took off my clothes in record time, and Emlyn and I went at it on the floor of her office. I wouldn't've dared tried the desk. It seemed like it'd break underneath us.

"Evan," Emlyn said after the second or third time we'd done it. A record for me, but probably a disappointment to her. "Evan, what do you think about being a teaching assistant?"

"What about it?" I'd hardly been at the Acres for two months then. I didn't know what a teaching assistant did other than give a few lectures and hang on to their life at the Acres for as long as they could before they were forced out into the real world.

"You could be mine," she said.

"No," I said. At least I was that smart. At least I understood that this was the worst possible idea, that someone I was about to embark on a torrid affair with would be my boss of a sort.

"All right," she said. "I could do a lot for you."

"Yeah?" I said. "Show me."

She did.

Three months later, on a snowy afternoon, I arrived at her office earlier than expected and found her on the desk—much sturdier than I'd thought it would be—straddling Jackson himself, while two of his regulars were doing something I'd rather not think about on the very sofa that I'd occupied with Emlyn many times.

"Oh, Evan," she said, "you're early." Said it like the most normal thing was for her to be screwing someone else while two other elses watched and I arrived *early*. Like she'd planned this.

Then I realized that she *had* planned this, and I left.

But, as I found out when I got back home, not only had she planned it, but she'd also told Claude about our affair.

CHAPTER 43

Claude

"YOU FUCKING BASTARD," I said the minute my disloyal roommate came back that day. He was covered in snow—it'd started up again. The snowfall at the Acres can be epic, and that winter was one of the worst I'd ever experience there.

"Don't start," Evan said, taking his near-giant's body and hurling it onto the remnants of what had once been a sofa, which I'd rescued from the garbage earlier that year, one of the few pieces of furniture in the place.

"To think that I introduced you. That I thought you could learn so much from her."

"Oh hell," Evan said. "How'd you find out?"

"How'd I find out? Emlyn told me."

"Shit," Evan said.

"Articulate bastard, aren't you?" I said.

"Fuck," Evan said, proving my point.

"You realize she's my *friend*, don't you?" Emlyn Mohr and I had been friends for longer than I'd known Evan. "How could you even *think* of doing this?"

"Can't say that thinking had anything to do with it," Evan said.

"Really."

"Yeah. Really."

"Don't be mad at *me*," I said. "That is not how this goes."

"How does it go?" Evan said. He looked upset. Good. I hoped he'd get more upset.

"It goes like this: You grovel and beg for my forgiveness. Then you worry for a few days that I'm going to clip you with a left hook while you're not paying attention. Or kick you in the balls. Or set your room on fire. You live in fear."

"And you live in righteous indignation," Evan said.

"You've destroyed a great friendship."

"Maybe our friendship isn't all that great if this is all it takes to destroy it." Evan had reenergized himself. He was sitting forward, his forearms on his thighs, his red hair soaked with melted snow that was dripping down onto the floor.

"I'm not talking about *our* friendship," I said. Evan couldn't be that oblivious. "I'm talking about my friendship with Emlyn Mohr."

"No reason you can't still be friends with her," Evan said. "Go right ahead. Be my guest. Or are you just jealous?"

"Jealous? Are you kidding me? Jealous?"

I started pacing around the living room that bisected our two bedrooms. Evan and I spent very little time together in this room. When we wanted to talk, we'd go for a walk in the forest or have a few beers together somewhere.

"She had you come over to her so-called office, didn't she?" I said. That was her modus operandi.

"So-called?"

"You're dense," I said. "Her actual office is down the hall from her classroom."

"It isn't." Evan was struggling to make his version of things true.

"You can't think that she does any work on that collection of twigs that's impersonating a desk at her house, do you?"

"Listen, Claude, I'll move out."

"Hah. Where're you going to live?"

"I'll find somewhere."

"You're not going to squirm out of this," I said. I was furious at Evan, more furious that I'd lost the friendship of one of the few instructors I could talk with, but getting even more furious that I was about to lose my friend.

"And it's *your* fault," I said, not even sure what I meant by that. But I did mean it.

"You *are* jealous," Evan said. He didn't understand a fucking thing.

"Make sure you get screened for disease," I said.

"What disease? Are you ill—and it's contagious?" Evan gave me his distressed look, the one that covers up anger and resentment.

"Evan, wake up. You've just been fucked and fucked over by the most promiscuous person at the Acres. You could have, you know— *anything.*"

"Hell."

"And you've destroyed my friendship with her."

"How's that?"

"You really don't get it, do you? You've made it *personal.* I introduce you. You're my good friend and roommate, Emlyn's one of the few instructors I've got a decent relationship with, and you have to go—"

"Wait wait wait, Claude. I've made it *personal?* What kind of a friendship is it that isn't personal?"

"Oh, you know what I mean," I said. How could he not see this?

"I do not."

"How can I be friends with her now? She commed me to tell me about you and her. Like I was involved somehow."

"Oh, I get it," Evan said, finally taking off his sopping wet jacket and soaking the back of the dilapidated sofa with it. "You *are* jealous. You wanted her, but she never offered herself to you, so now you're taking it out on me, telling me bullshit about how promiscuous she is."

Well, of course I'd wanted her, but I wouldn't tell Evan that. There wasn't a sensate living being at the Acres who didn't want her. Emlyn Mohr possessed every desirable trait in the universe: a fabulous mind, a wicked sensibility, and utter shamelessness. She had offered herself to me, but I'd refused, because I knew it'd ruin something far more important—our friendship.

"She's involved with Harwood Jackson, you know," I said, thinking I'd rub it in, thinking Evan was so naive he didn't realize this.

"Yeah, I do know," he said. "That's why I'm here instead of there."

"What?"

"I walked in on them. It's my specialty. Opening a door and seeing Jackson and his minions engaged in unspeakable acts. I just didn't realize that Em was one of those minions."

"Em, is it? How long was this going on? You were doing this behind my back?"

"I don't have to tell you about everything." Evan was indignant now and it didn't suit him.

"You might've mentioned it," I said. "*Oh, by the by, Claude, I'm fucking your friend Emlyn Mohr. The one you introduced me to. She punches my ticket at five, right before she entertains Harwood and his pals.*"

"You've gone too far," Evan said. "Can't you see how upset I already am?"

"You might've thought of that before."

"I might've, but I didn't," Evan said as he picked up his sodden jacket, put it back on, and stormed out.

I cut a lime in half, threw it into a glass of gin, and tried to calm down. I'd been counting on Emlyn helping me with the calculations for the game I was working on, one that I thought would help me get the job I wanted after I graduated. Now I'd never be able to sit next to her again or maybe even talk to her.

Why the hell had Evan done this? Why had Emlyn *told* me he'd done this?

There were days when I hated life at the Acres.

CHAPTER 44

Evan

IF I'D ONLY known Lee then. If I'd only met her instead of Emlyn. But I didn't and couldn't have. Lee was in another city, far removed from the Acres and from me. She was with someone else, the guy who eventually became her partner at the Galaxy, before he broke her heart and she kicked him out. And she wouldn't've liked me anyway then. It's a miracle that she likes me now.

Sometimes I look back on this time and think it was really Claude's fault. Or Emlyn's. Or maybe even Harwood's. But only for a moment. Because it was my own fault, but I didn't have any resources then, not the kind that're needed to fend off the likes of Emlyn Mohr.

That's how I ended up back in bed with her not even a week after I should've known better. Was I an addict? Maybe. Maybe I was just a complete dunce.

Claude figured it out right away. I was sneaking back into my room a little before three in the morning, had thrown myself down onto the sleep mat, and was about to pass out from sexual exhaustion, when Claude, standing in the doorway—I'd forgotten to shut it—took his high-powered torch and shined a murderous light at me.

"Aren't you on a probational acceptance here?" Claude said. Not preceded by any nicety, like *Have a nice night?* or *Get checked yet for those diseases I mentioned?*

"How would you know anything about that? And turn that fucking light off."

"I'm looking for an honest man." He traced the light around the room, then landed its brutal beam back on my face. "Too bad there's not one here."

"I'm honest," I said. "How did you find out about the probation?"

"You told me, you jerk. When they say you have to perform up to standards, they're not referring to sexual prowess, despite what you might have gathered from the great Harwood Jackson himself."

"Well, I notice he's still here and I doubt he even goes to class."

"Harwood would have to murder several people and get caught in the act before he got kicked out. A few centuries ago some illustrious ancestor of his helped found the place."

"Turn the damned light off already."

Claude didn't turn it off but he turned it down and set it on the floor, then sat down himself.

"I'm going to give you some advice, Evan Becket."

"I don't want your advice."

"Start going to class."

"I *am* going to class." The ones I was interested in.

"And stop seeing Emlyn."

"Claude, you couldn't understand. You don't even have a girlfriend."

"You don't even have a girlfriend either. What you've got is an obsession. An obsession who doesn't care about you."

"I don't care about her either," I said. How many more lies was I going to tell my closest friend? I thought I was in love with her and that anything she wanted to do must be just fine even if I didn't think it was.

I sat up. Claude stared at me. The position of the torch on the floor cast eerie shadows on the walls.

"I used to like you, Evan."

"I still like you, Claude."

"That's not going to last much longer, I'm afraid. Because tomorrow morning—*this* morning—you're moving out."

"Fuck."

"Might as well go back to your original room assignment, since you and Harwood have so much in common now."

"We do not. He's disgusting."

"You're not? Didn't you tell me you wanted nothing more than to go to the Acres since you were a little kid? And now you're fucking it up. Quit it. And do get checked for those diseases. You could have anything—or everything. I want you out of here by the time I get back from my afternoon lectures."

"Claude, you're not really doing this," I said. My head was back against the wall and I could barely keep my eyes open.

"A lot of the probationers can't make it. You're just like them. And I had such a good feeling about you the day we met. Shows you how wrong I can be."

"I'll move out right now," I said.

I turned on the room light, found my bag, and started stuffing my belongings into it. I had nowhere to go—it wasn't like I could move in with Emlyn, who, along with her legion of lovers, also had a husband and lived with him, I'd just recently found out—but I was going to leave anyway.

On my way out the front door of Claude's rooms, he stopped me.

"Here," he said. "You forgot these."

He handed me the rolled-up papers with the magrail plans on them. I'd left them in the main room, where they'd been laid out on the floor, since there wasn't enough space in my bedroom for them.

"Too bad this didn't work out," Claude said.

I can hear him saying it, even now, lying here with Lee, thinking about Ash and how that didn't work out. And wondering if Claude's in love with her. Not in the way I'd been in love with Emlyn Mohr, if one could call that *love*, but in a different and more profound and more fucked-up way and a much more hopeless, futile, and probably desperate, way.

I put down my bag and opened up the plans. Don't know why I did it. I was compelled to. Something deep in me changed at that moment. Had Claude sensed that it would? Is that why he'd stopped me and handed the plans to me?

Out in the corridor, standing at the doorway, I stared at my exquisite schema for the magrail, illuminated by the dim hall lights in Claude's building. I'd been inspired by the trip here to the Acres and that inspiration had been urged into form by my brand-new friendship with Claude Ryerson.

I looked up from the plans and saw Claude. His torch was still on the floor of my room, yet it was somehow throwing its light behind his body there in the entry. A halo glowed around his head, like he was a saint in some prehistoric painting.

That's when I started crying. I'd cried when I'd gotten my acceptance to the Acres, but these tears weren't tears of happiness or surprise. These were tears of regret and hope.

"Come back," Claude said, and I did.

CHAPTER 45

Claude

IT'S EASY TO talk about the Acres, to think about those years. Even the horrendous things that happened seem not all that bad now and didn't then either.

I abandoned the game I was working on—the one I'd envisioned Emlyn Mohr helping me out with—and embarked on designing a new game, something that had a better shot of going out into the world and succeeding, which it eventually did. And instead of Emlyn helping me with the maths that I didn't want to be bothered with, Evan did all that work.

He was still seeing Emlyn sometimes, I was pretty sure. But we never talked about it. Our work was more important—mine on coding the game and his on his plans for the magrail. If he needed some kind of sexual release, he was welcome to it. My anger at him about this dissipated, probably because I'd found my own sexual outlet.

She was the best student in my ag classes, which I was keeping up with despite my disinterest, and I'd started depending on her for her notes and insights. She liked my jokes, which, back then, I had more of. Nothing big happened—we were just two people who needed someone to get intimate with and so we did. Nothing else. This wasn't an obsession like Evan and Emlyn—well, on Evan's part anyway—or even really an affair. It was two friends who had similar needs. Gretchen graduated early, while I was still at the Acres, and after she left I never saw her again.

These memories are useful to block out the ones I'd rather not think about. Yet, especially early in the morning, like now, as I sit on the windowsill in the model room, reconnected with the dead in this abandoned house, the memories are hard to keep at bay.

Ash may be gone, but she was never really here.

My mother, on the other hand, was here at one time. Dad told me that she'd used this room as a kind of getaway from her daily life— I'd thought it was just where she kept her crafting equipment—and that he'd been forbidden to come in, as I had been as well. *Stay out.*

After she left or disappeared or was disappeared, though, Dad came in here often, looking for clues. But she hadn't left any clues even though she hadn't taken anything. It was as though she used her private room as a place for only her inner life. The invisible one, the one she'd eventually chosen.

Out there, out in the now-fallow fields, was her outer life. And embodied in me, who she cared little enough about to even leave me a message before her departure.

Ash left me no note either. These are the jokes I humor myself with. Yet that my mother's private domain became the model for Ash's is hard to dismiss.

Dad commed me that day, about three weeks before graduation. Evan had already left the Acres by then, too busy getting investors for the magrail to care about something so trivial as finishing school. The Acres gave him a degree anyway, since they love talking up all their successful alums. Makes them feel great about themselves and helps fuel their mystique. The Acres: breeding ground for genius.

I don't want to think about this. I can't stand it. But I can't stand thinking about Ash either. I keep imagining her being somewhere, in the same way I thought about my mother being somewhere even though I knew she could be dead, and by the time I was at the Acres, she could've been dead for more than a decade.

Because I couldn't look at pictures of her since Dad had gotten rid of all of them, I looked at pictures of corpses in various stages of decay. Here's what my mother would look like if she died three years ago, six years ago. Here're the burnt remains of someone who died in an explosion—in case she'd died in an explosion. Or someone who'd drowned, if she'd drowned.

A few months after her exit, I asked Dad if we should have the stream, the one just past the northernmost field, dredged. If she might have drowned there.

She was a good swimmer. That's all Dad had to say about it. We never dredged the stream.

But about three weeks before I was going to graduate—at that point I was spending all of my time either teaching or working on the programming for the game that I had three different companies interested in—Dad commed me.

He had a lead on Mom's whereabouts. He was going to follow up on this lead and he apologized that he might not make it to graduation, but he knew I'd understand.

"I thought you'd given up on her," I said. I thought he despised her. I didn't know he'd been looking for her.

"You mean the way you gave up on her?" Dad said.

"You found the program," I said. I knew right away that was what he meant. "But I'd stopped it. Before I left. Years ago."

"I started it again. It works." This was the first time in years that I'd heard this kind of excitement in his voice, seen his face so radiant with expectation.

"It can't've worked," I said. "It's run through every protocol thousands of times."

"I may have fiddled with it a little," he said, proud of himself, outdoing his son.

"Let me see." I was dying to know what he'd done, how he'd managed to get success out of what I was sure had been a total failure. I was more curious about this than I was about the lead he had on my mother's whereabouts.

"I'll show you when you get home."

I dropped everything, gave my classes to a friend, and headed home that night. I hadn't been back to the farm since the winter break, months earlier, and hadn't intended to go back except for a brief stopover after graduation, before I went to work in the city.

But I had to see what Dad had done with the program I'd written. That's what I told myself on the train ride home, wishing to hell that Evan's magrail were already up and running since it'd be far speedier than the slow, miserable ride I was taking.

On the train, I made notes, drew diagrams. Had Dad tried this? Or this? But I'd tried all of that. I'd had my program tap into surveillance cameras all over the world and scan the faces for a match. The program had dug deep into the personnel databases of millions of companies and went deeper into any company that had anything at all to do with agriculture. Nothing.

After years of telling myself that my mother was most probably dead, on that train ride home I had to realign my thinking. She was alive. She really didn't care about Dad or me. She could have contacted us but never did. Why had she left?

It'd been easier to think of the ten thousand ways she might've died than to contemplate the obvious reasons for her departure. The most obvious was a lover. I tried picturing her with someone other than Dad and failed. Maybe she was just tired of the farm, of being there, of having to take care of me occasionally when Dad was concentrating on his work.

I started making a list, as though the reasons for her leaving were more important to me than the changes Dad had made to my program, that made it spit out the results I'd never been able to get out of it.

I was halfway down the page, coming up with more and more bizarre and unlikely reasons for her departure, when the train car I was in derailed.

CHAPTER 46

Evan

"EVAN," SAID THE all-too-familiar voice.

I had my comm on voice since I couldn't be bothered looking at it. I was too busy working. The magrail was on an accelerated production schedule and I didn't have a minute to do anything other than concentrate on the hundreds of details, difficulties, and fixes.

"Emlyn," I said, not taking my attention away from the problem in front of me. I was close to a solution.

But why the hell was she comming me? She didn't think I was going to come halfway across the continent just to have another go-round with her, did she? And as enticing as that thought was, I had work to do. I couldn't. Although I thought she might have decided to come here instead.

"Evan," she said. "I didn't want to comm you, but I don't know if his father knows how to reach you."

I swallowed all the air in my mouth and stopped working. There was only one person she could have been talking about.

"He doesn't, I don't think," I said.

"There's been an accident," Emlyn said. "I thought you'd want to know."

"How bad is it?"

Neither of us would say Claude's name. I was afraid if I said it that I'd find out he'd died, and Emlyn wouldn't say it since she knew what a problem she'd created in my friendship with Claude. He didn't speak with her and she would never even mention him.

Yet she'd commed me. She wasn't answering my question.

"Just tell me," I said.

"Critical," she said. Was she crying? I turned the vid on. She was crying. Harwood was sitting behind Emlyn, his arms wrapped around her shoulders. I hadn't understood their relationship until that moment. They actually cared about each other. And perhaps Emlyn cared about Claude as well.

"Let me," Harwood said. He took the comm from Emlyn, who was fighting off uncontrollable tears, and said, "Claude was on his way home—"

"Why would he be going home now? That can't be right. It must not be Claude." Anything to negate what he was about to tell me. It wasn't Claude. "There's a mistake."

"I'm sorry," Harwood said. "He'd bought passage back to his hometown. The train car derailed. Freak accident."

I couldn't talk. I stared at Harwood's usually bland but now distressed face on the vid screen and listened to Emlyn sobbing, her back to the camera.

"How critical is critical?" I said. Were the two of them just trying to avoid having to tell me that Claude was dead?

"It's bad," Harwood said. "He's at the hospital at Keff. They won't let us see him. Family only."

Emlyn took the comm back from Harwood.

"Evan," she said. "You're going to come, aren't you?" I'd never seen her cry. I didn't know she *could* cry.

I nodded. "Don't let him die. I'll be there tomorrow."

I threw some things—as it turned out, I forgot to pack shirts—in a bag and called one of my backers who I knew had a late-edition transcer. I had no such possession back then, back in the struggling stages before I made my first fortune. A half hour after I explained why I needed it, I was in the transcer, on my way to Keff.

Don't you dare die, you bastard. I must've said this out loud as well as to myself. How could Claude die? That was impossible. He was alive, young, was just about to break through with his latest coding venture.

I cursed myself for every argument the two of us had had. I cursed myself more for having had a stop-and-go affair with Emlyn Mohr and fucking up Claude's friendship with her. She'd been an important presence in his life until I came along and killed their relationship. How torturous was it that she was the one to tell me that Claude's life was on the line?

On my way out to Keff—only somewhat closer to me than the Acres was—I listened to the news reports. There was already a team at the accident site, investigating the derailment. Some people had escaped any injury. A miracle, they said. Walked away, they said. Why couldn't Claude have walked away? Maybe he had. Maybe this was a mistake. Maybe Emlyn and Harwood were wrong. I sped up.

Seventeen people had died, said the news report, and another fifty or sixty—they weren't sure—were injured, many of them critically. The teaching hospital at Keff Institute was treating all the wounded.

Wounded. Like this had happened during wartime.

After I'd been on the road for about an hour, I came to my senses. Claude's father might not know how to contact me, but I knew how to contact him, and I had this fancy transcer—he could get out to Keff much faster if I'd take him.

I pulled over and commed him.

"I'm on my way to Keff," I said. "Can I take you? I can be at your place in maybe a half hour." The transcer had speed, and I intended to use it.

"Evan," Claude's dad said, "thank you, but I'm not at home. I'll have to get there another way."

"Have you talked to anyone?"

"I wanted to comm you, but I've been tied up."

"Claude," I said. "Is he—"

"I'll see you at Keff," he said, and ended the comm.

Maybe Claude had died since Emlyn commed me. No one wants to tell someone else about death. No one wants to tell themselves about death. It doesn't exist until you're forced to confront it. Unless you're a mortician or a medical examiner or a necrophiliac.

Anything to distract myself from the awful possibilities.

I commed my parents and sister, even though I rarely connected with them. But I had to make sure they still existed. They'd met Claude only once, but they knew how close the two of us were, and they were kind to me about this.

"He'll be okay, I'm sure," said my sister, a person untouched by anything negative. She'd just started her acting career then. Now she's so famous she can't leave her house without wearing a disguise. But then, then she was my sister, and I appreciated her optimism.

I hoped to hell she was right, but my fears ran away with themselves.

About an hour from Keff, Harwood commed me to find out when I was going to get there.

"Twenty minutes," I said, and made good on it, pushing the transcer to its limits.

At the hospital I told them I was Claude's brother. To stop them from challenging me because of our dissimilar last names, I said we had different fathers, and they let me into his room. Maybe they were relieved that someone in his family was finally there for him. That someone else would be monitoring him, as the hospital was overrun with victims from the derailment and it was obvious that the staff was having a hard time attending to everyone.

"I'm looking for an honest man," I said when I got to Claude's dreary room, hoping to cheer up the massive wreck that Claude Ryerson had become.

If he heard me, he didn't acknowledge it. He couldn't. He was in a coma and wouldn't awaken from it until the day after his father died.

CHAPTER 47

Claude

WASN'T I ON the train?

Dad. Going to see Dad. Sure. Yes.

But . . . no, I'm still in my rooms at the Acres. I can hear Evan. He must've come back for something.

"Evan?"

No answer. Yet I'm sure I heard his voice. And Emlyn's. Did she come with him?

"Damn you, Evan, you've never brought her back here. Why now?"

Evan has nothing to say for himself.

Did I take that job at Project One? Don't I have to report to work?

I can feel myself pacing about my room, but it's not where it should be. Did I arrive home?

"You're going to be fine," Evan says, but I can't see him. For such a large guy, he's . . . I don't have the word. Other words slip by me. I'm sure of either something or nothing.

Ethereal. Filmy. If I could see him, then . . .

"Evan?"

"He's been like this for days now," Evan says. I don't think he can hear me. Is he talking to Emlyn?

Noises I can't identify. Has it always been like this?

Parts of me are death-tired. Other parts are ready to go for a run. Am I a runner? Was I? Now I lack the motivation.

"You'll take over the farm one day," my mother says.

What if I don't want to? But I don't want to disappoint her, so I say, "That's a long time from now."

"Nothing is as distant as it seems," she says.

"Will you come back soon?" I say. She left, didn't she?

Bloody hell. I'm imagining this. Too late. She's disappeared again.

"But I had so much to ask you," I say to no one. It would've been satisfying to talk with her even if she were only in my imagination. I could've pulled something out of a buried memory. Something that would help find her. Something that would locate me as well, since I'd lost that sense of place.

"For fuck's sake, Claude, is this the best you can do?" Then I hear Evan laugh.

Yeah, this is the best I can do, here in the darkness.

I'm late for one of those boring ag classes again. But I promised. Someone has to take care of all that farmland. Dad isn't interested. And Gretchen will be in class. Won't she? Did she leave too? Ah yes, she did. I saw her off at the train station.

"This is it," I said to her. As though I'm watching this now, from my perch in the future, where darkness and strange sounds have taken over for what I'd thought of as life.

"We had fun," Gretchen said. "I'm glad I got to know you."

"In a few years, this'll all be magrail," I said, looking at the old-fashioned tracks. "Evan's going to change the world. So will you, Gretchen."

"That's my plan," she said, standing in the doorway of the train.

"I'm not sure I want you to leave," I said.

"It's all right," she said, then disappeared, as everyone disappears. Although I saw her after she'd taken her seat. She waved to me through the window. The train left.

Everyone disappears. Even I've disappeared.

"Damn you, Claude Ryerson, this is enough. Don't you realize I have things to do? I can't stay here forever."

Evan's furious at me. Let him be furious. Isn't he the one who tried to fuck everything up?

No. That's not right. I stopped caring about that, didn't I?

"Evan, don't leave. Don't disappear." But I can't hear my own voice. Yet I hear Evan's.

"If he doesn't wake up soon—then what?"

"We'll have to see. Get some sleep. It's the end of the term. Plenty of empty beds in the dorms."

"You can't put everything on hold forever, Evan," Emlyn says. "You have to think about yourself." Emlyn, who thinks about only herself, would say that. But we were friends once.

I'm too hard on everyone I know but not hard enough on myself.

"It won't be forever," Evan says. "It can't be."

"Have they found the cause yet?" Emlyn says. "There hasn't been a derailment in decades."

The sensations I'm feeling could be classified as panic. But my thoughts are fuzzy and divorced from this panic. Yet wasn't Gretchen on the train? Is she all right?

"Sabotage, most likely," Evan says.

"Don't be dramatic, Evan," says Emlyn. "Who would want to sabotage the train?"

"Damned if I know," Evan says. "But it's the most likely explanation. Disgruntled employee. Maybe there was a passenger someone wanted dead. Robbery—we don't know what the train was carrying in freight. Could be anything."

"Does the door to the bathroom lock?" Emlyn says.

"I don't have the energy," Evan says. "Claude, you bastard, wake up."

Is he talking to me? But I'm not asleep.

Yet . . . I need an explanation. Soon it comes to me: I'm in another realm, another world, a world where I can hear but not see. A world where past, present, and future are words only.

Drifting about in this world, my new home. Inescapable.

CHAPTER 48

Evan

CLAUDE'S DAD COMMED me every day, but he never made it to Keff. I'd give him the latest report on Claude's desperate condition, we'd try to reassure each other, then he'd sign off. He was on the trail of something, he couldn't be distracted. He was delayed. He'd be there eventually.

But during that delay he had a heart attack and died.

"I'll have to take care of things," I said to Harwood. He was in Claude's room with me that day. Either he or Emlyn tried to stay with me as much as they could. The term was over and neither of them had anything scheduled. My opinion of both of them changed. That either of them was capable of this sort of active caring and attention was something I'd never expected. But both of them were.

"There's no one else in Claude's family?" Harwood said.

"Not that I know of," I said. "His mother disappeared a long time ago. He's got no siblings."

"Other than you," Harwood said, smiling.

"I'll go tomorrow. It's not like his corpse is going anywhere," I said, and looked away from Claude's near-corpse.

"He's going to come through this," Harwood said.

"Are you really staying on as an instructor?" I said. Harwood had mentioned this days ago, but Claude's dire condition had been too new then and all my focus had been on Claude. Now that I had a new responsibility as undertaker to Claude's dad, I'd become aware that someone other than Claude or myself had a life, had plans, a future.

"Yeah," Harwood said. "It's time I got serious."

"You? Serious?" I laughed and Harwood laughed with me.

"Well, less frivolous," he said. "And I'm going to move in with Emlyn. Sort of settle down. Sort of."

"Won't her husband mind?" I'd never actually seen Emlyn's husband, but I knew he existed. He was some kind of international businessperson and was often away.

"They broke up."

"Over you?" I said.

"Partly."

"The other parts?"

"It's not just you and me, Evan." It seemed like Harwood wanted to say more, but he didn't.

"Are you in love with her?" I said. I'd never considered this possibility. Neither Harwood nor Emlyn seemed like a serious enough person to be in love. I was in love or I had been, but even I wasn't serious about it. Not like things are with Lee. Nothing like that.

"Partly," Harwood said, but he couldn't look at me while he was saying it.

"Tell her," I said. "I don't think she knows."

"I'll think about it," he said just as Claude groaned.

Harwood and I were both so used to Claude being in a coma that it took us a moment to realize what had just happened.

"Stay here. I'll get someone," Harwood said. He ran out of the room. I stood over Claude's bed and held one of his big, rough hands between mine. He looked exactly the same as he'd looked for the past month, and I started doubting that I'd heard him groan, but then he groaned again, as though he'd sensed my disbelief and wanted to make sure I understood.

Harwood returned with a doctor, who went around to the side of Claude's bed opposite me and examined him.

Claude refused to moan again despite my encouragements.

"Come on, Claude. Show the doctor what you've got."

He didn't make any more noises and I was afraid that he looked even closer to death than he'd looked since the accident. Two other accident victims had died in the last couple of days, and I knew the doctors held out little hope for Claude although they never exactly said that. But they never exactly said he'd recover, either.

"Well?" I said to the doctor after she was finished her examination.

"Are you sure you heard him moan?" she said. She shoved her hands into her jacket pockets while she stared at Claude's immobile form.

"Of course I'm sure," I said. "Claude, show her."

Claude disobeyed my command.

"You've been here a long time, Mr. Becket. Maybe this is wishful thinking."

"I gave up on wishful thinking two weeks ago, Doc. He moaned. Twice. I'm *not* imagining this."

"Come get me if he moans again," she said. "But right now, there's no change."

Harwood was standing in the doorway, shaking his head. "He *did* moan. I heard him."

"If you say so," the doctor said. She didn't believe either of us, and Claude was being uncooperative.

That evening, Harwood and I sat on the window ledge in Claude's sad hospital room and got drunk on a bottle of aged something-or-other that Harwood had liberated from what he called the family vault.

"I don't know why Claude had to go and do this," Harwood said, "but it's changed my life. Finally made me see what a jerk I've been. That it's time to get serious."

I didn't know what to say. I'd been serious since the day I was born. With a couple of detours, including the main one, Emlyn Mohr.

"I'm going to have him cremated," I said.

"Claude's still alive."

"His father."

"Oh. Yeah. Tomorrow."

"Tomorrow."

I drank myself into a stupor. Harwood, a much more experienced drinker than I could ever be, strolled out of Claude's room like he'd been sipping water all night.

I slumped into the visitor chair, where I'd spent every night for the past month, and settled down into an unconscious oblivion.

When I woke up the next morning, Claude was sitting up in bed.

"I thought you were dead," he said to me.

CHAPTER 49

Claude

EVAN'S HEAD WAS slanted in an unnatural way and he was sitting in a chair I was unfamiliar with. Had he brought it to our rooms when I was out? No, that couldn't be right.

I squinted harder—we weren't in our rooms. And, anyway, hadn't Evan left for the city? Wasn't he working on the magrail plans? And why did every molecule of my body ache like hell?

Evan opened his eyes then, shocking me.

"I thought you were dead."

"You don't get to say that," Evan said. "That's *my* line." He squirmed in the chair, which was too small for his big frame, ruffled his mop of red hair, which looked like it hadn't been cut in a month, and then sat forward. "It's about time you woke up."

"I didn't know there was a schedule."

"Well, the usual schedule is to wake up after a night's sleep."

"Am I in the hospital?" I looked around. "This is a fucking hospital room, isn't it?"

"Good work, Detective," Evan said. "I can't believe you picked today to wake up."

"What the hell are you talking about? I wake up every day." Evan was being his most cryptic self.

"Not really," he said. "Not for the last month you haven't."

"How would you know? You've been in the city."

"I've been right here, Claude. And so have you."

I thought of getting out of bed. I wanted to see out the window. But I didn't have the wherewithal.

"Evan, I'm not in the mood to argue."

"Want some breakfast?"

I nodded. I couldn't remember the last time I'd eaten anything.

"Hey, I had a dream that I talked with my mother," I said. "Are you hungover?"

Evan groaned. "Don't remind me."

"Think you might get around to telling me why I'm in the hospital? And where I am?"

"You're at Keff," Evan said, "and your train derailed. You've been in a coma for the last month."

"The hell I have," I said, defending my imaginary position in life, a position where I was a normal, everyday person who'd been shoved into a hospital bed against all and every logical explanation.

"It *has* been a sort of hell," Evan said. "Until yesterday when you moaned a couple of times. I should get a doctor."

"And breakfast," I said, suddenly ravenous. "Two breakfasts."

"I couldn't eat anything," Evan said. He looked thinner than usual.

"I didn't mean for you."

Evan hauled himself out of his hungover slump, came over to my damned hospital bed, and hugged me.

"I knew you'd wake up," he said.

"Of course I woke up," I said, hugging him back. He seemed overcome with emotion, and the effect was threatening to engulf me as well.

Evan stood up and sighed.

"Your dad," he said, about to make an excuse for his absence.
But none was necessary.

"He doesn't like hospitals," I said. "It's okay."

"Claude," Evan said, rubbing his bloodshot eyes, "I wish I didn't
have to tell you this, but your dad died yesterday."

My hunger vanished. I grabbed onto Evan's hand and closed my
eyes. I couldn't stand to look at anything.

I was still dreaming, I told myself. Of course. That much was
obvious. I guess it was possible I'd been in some kind of train accident
and had been taken to a hospital at one point. Maybe it was even Keff,
although I'd never been there, yet the dreaming self is very creative.
Maybe I'd even been in a coma or dreamt I had been. But now I was
dreaming about the dreams, about everything. A nightmare, and in this
unasked-for dream, Dad was dead.

"Claude, the doctors are here now," Evan said, letting go of my
hand.

"Don't go," I said to him. "You can't leave."

Evan stayed, the doctors did all sorts of horrendous things to me,
as though my body were a separate entity, apart from *me*, and it could
be manipulated in brutal ways without my consent, and I lay there and
took it all.

After they were done with their savagery, they left, someone
arrived with breakfast, and then Harwood Jackson, of all unlikely
people, arrived with the even more unlikely Emlyn Mohr in tow. I
hadn't spoken to Emlyn since three years—or was it more than that
now?—ago when I'd found out about her and Evan.

"One more day and I would've won the lottery," Emlyn said.
"But today was your day, wasn't it, Harwood?"

"I hadn't thought about it," he said, "but you could be right. Hey,
Claude, how was it back there when you weren't with us?"

"I had a lot of dreams," I said. "Maybe this is a dream, although it
seems too crowded for a dream."

"Claude, I'd better get going," Evan said. "I told them I'd be there this afternoon."

"You've been here for twenty minutes and now you're leaving?" I didn't want to be left alone with Emlyn and Harwood, but, more than that, I wanted Evan here. He was my connection to life itself, my grounding wire.

"He's been here for a month," Harwood said. "Every day."

"What about the magrail?" I said, remembering that Evan had a life that had nothing to do with my being trapped in a hospital or even with me.

"It's fine," Evan said. "I had loads of time to work on it here, since you were such a damned poor conversationalist."

"Okay. Yeah." The room sort of swirled then. I felt like I needed something to hang on to, so I gripped the sides of the bed.

"This isn't what I had in mind," I said. "Oh hell. A month? Now I've lost all hopes for a job. Project One probably thinks I'm dead or that I don't care."

"Well, that's a relief," Evan said, back to being cryptic.

"Can't have anyone thinking Claude's alive, now, can we?" Emlyn said.

Harwood was sitting in that awful, ugly chair, the one Evan had reportedly slept in every night for the last month, and Emlyn was leaning over the back, her chin resting on Harwood's head. They seemed almost cozy with each other.

"I'll have to start the search over again," I said. "Assuming I remember how to code."

"I have to get going," Evan said.

"All right." I gave up. Evan was going. Someone had to attend to my dead father, the dead having lost all responsibility for anything active, and I wasn't capable of it.

"I'll put his ashes in the stream," I said. "Afterward."

"I'll be back in a couple of days," Evan said, hugging me again, about to leave me to the likes of my onetime friend Emlyn Mohr and my sex-obsessed ex-roommate, Harwood Jackson. Maybe I'd get lucky and the coma would return.

"By the way," Evan said on his way out the door, "you've got the job at Project One. I took it for you. Good thing I guessed right. I wasn't sure you didn't prefer Centerstorm."

If I'd been holding my breath, I let it out then, or maybe that was the moment that I remembered that I was a living, breathing being and not an amorphous entity, trapped in a nightmare.

"Thanks," I said, but Evan had already gone. Who wants to be in a hospital room? I know I didn't. Although he was on his way to a morgue—much worse.

"I can't believe I lost the lottery," Emlyn said after Evan left. "Especially after you made it through the first two weeks, Claude. All the actuarial tables were on my side."

The logical centers of my brain kept trying to reject the train derailment, the coma, that Dad was dead, that Evan had gone, that Emlyn and Harwood were in my room—but denial's hard work, and I started fading.

I never ate breakfast that day. Instead I went to sleep, comforted by the sounds of Emlyn's and Harwood's voices as they discussed their theories on gambling and how much, exactly, was now in the pool that Harwood, who didn't need it, was going to win because of his accurate guess about the day I'd wake up.

I would eventually take a job with the thieves at Centerstorm, but that day I was thrilled that Project One had hired me, that Evan had realized that's what I wanted, and that he'd had enough confidence in my eventual recovery that he'd accepted the job for me.

When I finally got discharged from the hospital, Evan took me home, and that evening, just as the sun set, the two of us stood by the stream and I tossed Dad's ashes in, watching as they disappeared into the slow-moving current, taking with them my once hopes.

Now

CHAPTER 50

Ash

AS DEV HAD suggested, leaving was easy. All I'd had to do was give up all my involvements, my job, my purpose, my objects, my surroundings. The rest was a matter of merely opening the window and stepping out onto the roof overhang just below.

And Claude. I'd had to give up Claude too. He was angry with me anyway, I told myself. He'd be relieved that I'd gone. Maybe I'd finally done something to please him. Would he remember me? Would I remember him? Would my amnesia creep forward, engulfing everything from a receding past in its wake?

I slid down the overhang, then onto the ground, which was much farther below than I'd estimated. Devil and Bobby had made the transition look simple, but I wasn't a cat or a mouse. Instead I was . . . something else.

I wasn't a real, actual person. The night I'd spent at the Honeycomb had helped me to become more aware of that truth. I had substance, but I seemed to be an invention, an image, only what others saw or wanted. Flimsy. No matter how real I felt, that's all I was, all I could be. Streeter had noticed that and his words replayed themselves in my mind: I was nothing.

It's one thing to walk out of your job, to stop being a useless influencer. It's another thing entirely to walk out of yourself. It can't be done.

I'd wanted to spend that first day and night in the model room. I was at least somewhat comfortable there and I had nowhere else to go. But Devil told me I couldn't, not if I wanted to avoid Claude, and I wanted to.

Not because I didn't want to see him or be with him, but because I was disassociating myself from that part of my existence, and Claude was its central feature. If I'd keep seeing him, I'd never break away. I'd never find the meaning I was searching for, the past I'd lost. He'd rope me back into the role I was supposed to fulfill. And if he didn't do it himself, I'd do it. I'd be compelled to. It was the relationship Claude and I had. Without his direction, telling me what was expected of me, our relationship was nothing. More nothing than I myself was.

Dev, Bobby, and I made it through the labyrinth and walked out to the edge of Claude's property.

"We'll leave you here," Dev said.

"Everything's fine," Bobby said.

"I thought you were coming with me," I said as a sharp breeze sent a sudden chill through me. Unexpected. New.

"Can't," Dev said. "We have business elsewhere."

The language seemed too formal for Devil. He was usually more relaxed.

"I thought you were coming with me," I said again, as though that would make it right or would change Dev's mind.

"Bobby and I have plans," Devil said. It was obvious he wasn't going to tell me what they were.

"I have no plans," I said, as the truth of that jarred me. My plan had been to leave, to escape, but I hadn't thought of what to do after that. With all the billions of information downloads I had at my disposal, yet I'd never considered this. I'd never gotten further than thinking of opening the window and leaving. I hadn't considered any of what I was now confronting: uncertainty, confusion, no definite destination, and a terrible ache that occupied the unidentifiable space where Claude had once resided.

"You'll figure it out," Devil said. "I have confidence in you."

"What if—"

"Don't approach it that way," Dev said. "*What if* is just avoidance. Ineffectual."

"Come on," Bobby said to Dev. "I heard there's a storm coming."

I wanted to go with them, but I could sense that Devil would have none of it. If I wanted to stop being a seller and influencer and instead become my true self, I had to do it alone. If I was nothing it was up to me to find *something* in myself. Devil and Bobby had already helped me, and I was grateful.

"Thank you both," I said. "Without you I'd still be trapped in that room. I'd still be very *influencing* and selling."

"You were good at it," Devil said. "That was part of the problem."

"What else might I be good at?" I said as the first heavy raindrops started falling, distracting me.

"This is amazing," I said, reaching up to be ready to intersect the next pieces of water as they descended. To be out here, to experience this. The aromas and tastes becoming stronger with each moment.

Devil and Bobby ran off. Maybe they didn't like the rain the same way I did. The more of it that fell, the wetter I got, the more elated I became. In my room, no water had come down from above, I'd never gotten wet, there was nothing to smell or taste.

Here, out here, was the mystery of the world laid bare. Even with all the information I'd downloaded, I hadn't known about this, about what it would feel like, about how my senses would be so aroused that the distance between joy and fear would disintegrate.

I also hadn't known how much I'd miss Devil and Bobby. Claude. And I hadn't thought that I'd spend my first night out here soaked, pelted by hailstones and then sleet. Not knowing what to do or how to do it. Or that I'd become hungry.

But I did know that what I was doing was right. Maybe not what Claude or anyone else in the world might think was right, but it was, for me. I'd have to remind myself of this thousands and millions of times, but that night, I understood.

I had to leave. I had to give up my life as an influencer and seller. I had to abandon that room, the only place I could remember being in, if I had any hopes of finding my past, of restoring my memory, defeating the amnesia whose persistence was doing its best to destroy me. If I had any hope of ending that accustomed separation, of becoming whole, of being my self.

I had to.

Yet in the wet, dreary morning that followed my night outdoors, I did the only thing I could think of: I tried to get back to my room. I needed to be there, I told myself. That was where I belonged. That was my home. It was safety itself. I'd never been wet or hungry there. Claude would be nearby, admonishing and encouraging me.

I needed the comfort of my objects around me, even if they'd been chosen for me, yet I'd developed an attachment to them. On my way back toward the barn—I knew that my room was there since Dev had told me about that—a reflex had me feel for my saturnia necklace but my neck was bare. I'd forgotten that I'd ripped the necklace off before I left.

My palms, though, still glistened with its tiny fragments, even without sunlight to reflect off them.

Hesitating, I stood, thigh-deep, in what seemed to be a field, overgrown with high, rough grasses. Had Claude worked in this field? Had I ever been here before? Where had I been before the amnesia? And why couldn't I remember?

As I approached the barn, a new thought nagged at me: *Why* had I gotten amnesia? Had I been in an accident? Developed a brain tumor? Gotten a blow to the head? Had something so dreadful happened that I was shutting it out? Yesterday I'd set off with such assurance, the need to get away, be my true self, find my blocked-off past, so compelling that I could do nothing else. I had no doubts.

This morning, though, I'd gone directly back to the barn. I needed its familiarity. I needed to see Claude, even if he was angry at me. Even if I was angry at him.

The first thing I noticed was a gaping hole in the side of the barn, and after I went inside I discovered the truth: Claude didn't want me to come back. Not only was my room not there, not only was he not there, but his console, all the monitors, and even the desk they'd been sitting on were destroyed. That equipment had been his method of communicating with me, and he'd made sure that that was no longer possible.

Dizziness overcame me as I felt my lost memories racing so far from me that I'd never recover them. A void opened up. A void that made the emptiness seem populated and friendly. My mouth was raw and dry. I'd been hungry earlier but no longer cared.

I left then. Walked away. For a brief moment I thought of going to the house, of retreating to the comfort of the model room. It would be so easy. Far easier than leaving had been. Perhaps I'd make it back to the labyrinth.

But . . . I had to remind myself that I was still here. That I hadn't left. That that hadn't been my plan.

Ashamed of my lack of resolve, I gathered my determination and left the Ryerson farm. Left my life there, my purpose. Left Devil and Bobby. And Claude.

I found a room in an abandoned building in the city, not far from the Honeycomb. I'd been magnetized to this area since I knew where it was, since I'd been here before. Had had my first tastes and smells here. Had crushed Quinn Fiery's heart here.

The room's especially cold now that it's winter. There's no heat but there are a few other people in the building, which is scheduled to be torn down next fall. Perhaps by then my memory will have returned. Perhaps by then I'll have a new purpose.

Perhaps by then the loneliness will have vanished.

CHAPTER 51

Claude

I'VE MOVED BACK into the house—something I thought I'd never do. I haven't lived here since Dad's death, since I'd returned home after the accident. But the barn is unusable. The hole I smashed into the wall was so well placed that the patch job I attempted was pointless. The entire wall is on the verge of collapse. I can hear it creaking as I walk by.

I stayed in Ash's model room for a while, but it started getting to me, reminding me of my latest failure, reminding me that I'd created Ash, that Ash had gone wild, that I'd destroyed her. That I'd started thinking of Ash in ways I might characterize as somewhat insane. That Evan and Brandon were comming me and I wasn't answering them.

That I had to do something or I was going to lose the property, along with everything else I'd lost.

On days like today—damp, gray, winter death in the surround—I sit at Dad's console, delving into his fixes to my old program, the one that was supposed to find my mother and never did until Dad got his brain into it. But I've yet to discover the lead he told me about. I'd searched for it years ago, after the accident, after I'd come home from the hospital, but gave up the search after I started my job at Project One and haven't touched it since.

I'm supposed to be such a coding genius, but as I look through Dad's work, I realize the truth: *He* was the coding genius. I'm just the weak offspring. Which is why I should have used more of his code when I created Ash. Then I might not be in this predicament right now. She might have been reliable, stable, predictable—and not the unpredictable, out-of-control individual she became.

But I was sorry I'd destroyed her. I hadn't had to go that far, be so extreme, react with such fury. I missed her. I could have just stopped the vidcast, which was stopped anyway. That would've been sufficient, wouldn't it have been? I could've chatted with her sometimes. Changed her programming.

No. That's wrong.

And that last time, Ash had been in her room, ready for the vidcast, as though she'd figured out herself how to manage everything. As though turning off the console and so shutting off the power no longer had any effect on her. How had she managed that? She could've run away with it, done who-knows-what. I had to destroy her.

Is that how my mother felt? That she had to destroy her relationship with Dad and me? Cut us off? Raze anything and everything that could connect her to us? Had Dad or I—or both of us—gone out of control, the way Ash had done? Failed her? Ruined her plans for herself, for us?

But no matter how many hours I've spent with Dad's version of my old program, I still can't find the lead he'd discovered. Maybe too many years have elapsed and what once worked no longer does. Or maybe I just don't know what the hell I'm looking for.

I hear Evan's fancy transcer in the drive. It has a distinctive sound, announcing his presence. I turn off the monitor, not wanting him to see how I'm spending my time since fucking over his and Brandon's substantial investments in Ash.

If I knew where it was, I'd hand him the mortgaged deed to the property. I can't forget about my obligations, even if I'd like to.

Evan, along with Lee, knocks on the front door.

"So formal," I say as I open it. Evan's never had to knock. Even though we haven't lived in the same rooms together for years, it's as though we'll always be roommates.

Lee hugs me. An unexpected gesture.

"I'm so sorry," she says.

"I saw the barn," Evan says. "How'd you manage that?"

"A sledgehammer," I say.

"Lee knows," Evan says. "I had to let her in on it, because of how things have played out. And, Claude, she wouldn't tell anyone."

"I wouldn't," Lee says. "Although I was pretty shocked and there's a lot I still don't understand."

"It doesn't matter anymore," I say, because it doesn't. "I can't pay you back," I say to Evan. "I don't know why you're still my friend, if you are. I've let you down too many times."

"It was because I kept insisting that we had to look for her," Lee says, trying to defend Evan's decision to tell her the truth about Ash.

"It doesn't matter," I say again. "There's no point in discussing it."

"But I was sure she was missing," Lee says, persisting. "Yet Evan didn't want to do anything about it and I kept telling him how wrong he was."

"Lee was pissed off at me," Evan says. "She kept insisting I do something, so I just finally told her. I hope you don't mind too much."

"I'd give you the deed to this place, but I can't find it," I say. "I looked for it everywhere. I'll have to get a new one drawn up at the county office. Might take a while." It'd take closer to forever at the rate I was accomplishing even the simplest of tasks.

"What say Lee and I take you out to lunch?" Evan says.

"So I've become a charity case, have I?" I look down at myself, at the same falling-apart plaid shirt I've been wearing for the last week. "Hell."

"I'll wait down here," Lee says after Evan grabs my arm and starts dragging me upstairs. Our first stop is the bathroom.

He pushes me into the shower and turns on the water.

"Hey," I say, struggling to get out of my clothes. The wetter they get, the harder the task becomes.

"Take your time," Evan says from the bathroom doorway.

I'm finally able to strip off my clothes and take a proper shower.

"I wasn't expecting you," I say.

"I'm surprised you moved back into the house. Didn't you say you'd never live here again?"

"That was before I bashed a hole into the barn wall," I say, wrapping myself in a towel and opening the shower stall door.

"Evan," I say, "you don't have to take me to lunch. I do eat, you know."

"Yeah," he says. "But you have to get out of here."

"We'll go to the county office," I say, realizing this is the perfect opportunity. "I'll be able to get a copy of the deed for you."

I go down the hall into my old room, the one I lived in as a kid, the one I'm living in now, and scrounge around for something clean, relieved when I find a shirt and pair of pants I've washed and haven't yet worn.

I get dressed while Evan lingers at the doorjamb. The clothes hang off me. I *have* been eating, I assure myself.

"Claude, you've been out here alone for too long," Evan says as he comes into my room. He's noticed what I've just noticed: I've dropped maybe twenty pounds.

"I'm just . . . distracted," I say. We head downstairs.

Midway down the staircase, Evan turns around, his big self blocking further progress.

"Claude," he says, "I hope you're not upset that I told Lee. She really wouldn't tell anyone else. I trust her completely."

"It's all right, really," I say. "It's not like her telling someone would have an effect on the business. That's over with."

"That's where you're wrong, Claude. The business is *booming*."

"But—"

"But nothing. If Ash was popular before, she's a *star* now. Maybe an entire galaxy of stars. Her disappearance has made her products more desirable than they ever were. If I didn't know better, I'd think you were a marketing wizard and had disappeared her on purpose, so you could amass a fortune."

"Sure," I say. "Evan, I don't mind giving up the property. It's not like I'm doing anything with it. You don't have to feel bad about this. Make excuses for me. I know you sunk a lot of your credits into Ash. Things seemed hopeful back then. I was so damned sure."

"I'm starving," Lee says, calling up to us.

"We've got to get you some new clothes," Evan says. He turns around and heads back down the stairs and I follow him.

I look down at my tattered shirt. But at least it's clean. I console myself with the fact that I haven't totally neglected myself.

At lunch, at the Galaxy, the same restaurant where Lee still works—although today's her day off and I've learned that she doesn't just work here, she owns the place—Evan is finally able to convince me of the facts.

Fact 1: Ash's disappearance has made her far more popular than she was when she had a regular vidcast. She's become a mystery now, and, per Evan, it's a mystery everyone can't get enough of and that everyone would like to solve.

Fact 2: The day after Ash disappeared, Brandon launched a new line of Ash products, all of which are perpetually sold out.

Fact 3: Evan and Brandon have kept Ash and her products in the forefront of the public's interest. The saturnia necklace, in particular, is a bestseller, despite its horrendous price tag. But Ash's breaking her own necklace has given it a cachet beyond any that it had even at the high points of Ash's vidcasts. And since I own a hefty percentage of the rights to those sales, I'm now embarrassingly rich.

Fact 4: Evan's been taking care of my personal business but it's time I did this myself.

Fact 5: I'm not a child anymore.

Fact 6: Lee's pregnant. She and Evan are going to have a son. They have the future to think about now, and so should I be thinking about my own future.

Fact 7: Evan's worried about me.

Fact 8: Lee thinks I'm in love with Ash and wonders if what Evan told her—that Ash isn't a real person but more like a character in a computer game, one created for the purpose of selling things— isn't just a story he's made up to explain away Ash's disappearance. Lee continues to be worried about Ash.

I haven't had a meal this good, or this substantial, since the nonexistent Ash climbed out of her self-created window in her code-generated, imaginary room.

Since I destroyed the console, the monitors, everything.

I miss her.

CHAPTER 52

Ash

IT'S TAKEN ME a while—how long, I'm not sure, since without the balance of the emptiness as a counterweight, I don't know. I'm not familiar with how time moves out here, where I am now. Where hunger and thirst and cold are more than concepts scanned into my store of information.

Food isn't necessarily as delicious as the delicacies I once tasted at the Honeycomb, that night with Quinn. From observing others here in our mutual hideaway, I've learned how to scavenge the trash, some of it from that elegant restaurant.

No one here recognizes me, perhaps because the people who live here in this abandoned building aren't interested in much besides survival and their own moment-by-moment concerns.

I'm not a member of any of their sometime groups, but I've noticed that perhaps no one is. The seeming camaraderie can be interrupted by something as trivial as a lost hairpin. Was it stolen? Who took it? Who would dare to take it? Anger, paranoia, and fear take over. Alliances shatter. I keep to myself.

I didn't use to live this way. I had no need for food or water or the extra clothes I've managed to accumulate—the worn-out or imperfect items discarded by unknown others.

In my former, abandoned, existence I had my room. I had the emptiness. I had Claude's voice, his face. I love the way his messed-up yellow hair looks. His stern expression. That rare smile. His coral eyes.

But I couldn't find my past. I couldn't continue to be nothing. Claude wasn't helping even if I sometimes thought he might be, when I could sense him in the emptiness. But he kept telling me I had no past. My feelings aside, he wasn't my friend. I had to leave.

Quinn Fiery wanted to be my friend but I rejected him. Sometimes I think I should contact him, but I've lost my means of contacting anyone, cut off from my room, where I had my scroll. I didn't bring it with me. My connections were destroyed along with Claude's trashed equipment.

I no longer think he caused that destruction. He may have, but he may not have. Maybe he was robbed. People here in my building are robbed all the time. No one can steal anything from me, though, because I have nothing. They could take my spare clothes, and sometimes I notice things are missing, but this isn't theft. These objects aren't *mine*. They belong to no one.

I used to *be* nothing. But back then I seemed to have things—my room, the objects in it, my saturnia necklace that I destroyed. I had a great friendship with Devil and Bobby. I had my viewers and fans, or perhaps that's a misinterpretation. They were out there, in their own lives. I didn't *have* them.

I had my awful theme song, music I never would've chosen for myself or for anyone, but it followed me everywhere. It's gone now, no longer playing since I climbed out the window, although sometimes I imagine that I'm hearing it. Sometimes I realize I'm humming it even though I despise it.

It's taken me this long, however long it's been while the light and atmosphere change, to remember something Quinn said to me that night in the Honeycomb. Not that I'd forgotten it, as I've noticed that I have a near-perfect memory for everything that's happened to me since that first vidcast I made—in contrast to the total amnesia I have for anything that may have happened before then—but it's not a memory that I'd happened upon until now.

Ash, you're probably wealthy yourself. I can hear Quinn's voice, as though he's sitting across from me, as he was at the Honeycomb that night. I'd felt brave, and everything was so new that facts like these slipped off my awareness.

But I couldn't let him touch me. Especially not my hand. That was an intimacy I wouldn't allow. Before I felt anyone else's hand, I needed to feel Claude's. I still do. He has large, rough hands. I wonder what they'd feel like on mine.

I wonder if Claude misses me. If he thinks of me as often as I think of him. Or perhaps he's forgotten me.

It's easy to have thoughts run away with themselves here. Sometimes I hear the woman across the hallway talking to herself. She rambles on about an infant who could talk the day she was born and how she's now forced to live by herself in a dark room. I believe she's talking about herself even though she's not an infant and the rooms here aren't always dark. But she must have been an infant once, years ago.

You're probably wealthy yourself. Quinn said that to me. Was I wealthy? Am I? Had I gotten paid for my work as an influencer and seller? It hadn't occurred to me then, and Quinn's words had had no impact that night. I'd wanted to find out about my past, not about my wealth, something I had no relationship to or seeming need for.

But now I'm latching on to this. I could be wealthy. That wealth could help me find my past.

Then a new thought arises—that wealth could help me live in a place that wasn't going to be torn down in the fall. And I could buy clothes of my own and eat fresh food. I could buy another building, one that wasn't going to be razed, and the people who live here could move there too.

If I have such a thing as this wealth that Quinn guessed at, how can I locate it?

I scour my information stores and learn about holding accounts and something called a trust. Yet without access to the meshwork, I'm helpless. I could have millions in one of these holding accounts but I have no way to get to it or to learn about it.

I need help. I go across the hall and knock on the half door. The bottom half is missing, but I stick to the usual protocols here. Even rooms without a door require permission to enter. As I wait for Ginny, the woman who lives in this room, to answer my knock, I experience a flash of my old room, the one where I sat at the vanity table and sold and influenced. The one whose window I climbed out of.

That room had no door. Or if it had one, I never saw it, never looked for it. Don't all rooms have doors? How is it I never noticed that obvious fact until just now?

"Who are you?" Ginny says once she's opened the remaining top half of her door. She always asks this even though we've known each other for a while now.

"I live across the hall," I say. "Ash."

"That can't be right," Ginny says. She pushes a curl of hair off her forehead. Her entire head is covered in a mass of pale brown curls. "I once had a cat named Ashley. Are you what's become of her?"

"I was never a cat," I say. If only Dev were here. He'd know how to get to my holding accounts, if I have any.

"Don't be too sure," she says. "Ginny," she says, holding out her hand. We shake.

"You've introduced yourself to me before," I say.

"I don't remember."

"There's a lot I don't remember either," I say. "That's why I wanted to ask you if you could help me."

"Loss of memory is a symptom that a lot of us have," Ginny says. "Why don't you come in?"

She's never invited me into her apartment before. Except for the half door, her place is much nicer than mine, with paintings on the walls, decorative beads hanging from doorframes, a lamp with a steel elephant at its base.

"Your place is beautiful," I say.

"I've lived here for twenty-seven years," she says. "Almost twenty-eight."

"What are you going to do when they tear down the building?"

"When's that?"

"In the fall."

"Yeah, I've heard of that before. I think." Ginny twirls about her main room. Sort of dancing. A shaggy winter coat wrapped around her falls open with each spin.

"What if I told you I could buy a building and you could live there?" I say.

"I'd say you're crazier than I am," Ginny says, laughing.

"But I might have millions of credits somewhere," I say.

"I had the same dream once," Ginny says. "But nothing ever came of it."

"Do you know how I could get access to the meshwork? I need to find out where my holding account is."

"Don't we all?"

"Ginny, I was hoping you could help me."

Ginny looks from the elephant-adorned lamp to me. Back and forth, then again and again.

"You can't have it," Ginny says. "You'll have to get your own elephant. This one is *mine*." She positions herself in front of the lamp, hiding it and its elephant from my view.

"*Do* you know how to access the mesh? I left my scroll. At . . . home."

"This is my home," Ginny says. "I could speak from the day I was born. Great things were supposed to be in my future. But . . . Did you hear they're going to rip this building down?"

"I did," I say, finally giving up. Ginny isn't going to help me, and she's my best friend in the building. I'll have to find someone very else or some other way.

"Why do you need the mesh?" Maybe Ginny has been paying attention. I perk up.

"To find my credits," I say.

"How would someone like you have anything? You don't even have a place to live. Not like me. I've been here for twenty-seven years, almost twenty-eight, since the day I was born." Ginny leaves her post in front of the elephant lamp and leans onto the back of what was once a rather nice sofa.

"Where were you born?" she says, looking right at me.

"I don't know," I say.

"You should leave now," she says. "I have a lot to do this afternoon." If she was engaged and interested a second ago, now she's off into herself again, her gaze fixed on the wall to her left.

"Thanks, Ginny," I say. "It was nice of you to have me over."

I leave. As I cross the hall, Ginny calls to me.

"Maybe you could do something with this."

I turn around. She has a scroll in her hand, holding it out to me.

"Ginny," I say. "Yes, this could help."

"But you have to give it back," she says, pulling the scroll back toward herself just as I reach for it.

"Of course I'll give it back," I say.

"Tomorrow," she says.

"Tomorrow."

She hands me the scroll. "You look nothing like my cat Ashley," she says.

"I know a cat named Devil. He's my good friend." I hug the scroll to my chest. If I can locate my credits, if I have any, I have to make sure to help out Ginny.

"You look a little familiar," Ginny says. "Do I know you?"

"I live right here"—I'm standing in front of my door and I point to it—"right across the hall from you."

"I had a premonition once," she says, then she turns around and goes back to her room, closing the half door behind her.

CHAPTER 53

Today's Trends

WE HAD A long chat with our dear friend Reda Fiery yesterday. Because—and you heard it here *first!*—her brother, Quinn, has returned!

Yes! If you are as thrilled as we are by this heartening news, then we picture you leaping up and shouting out your joy. We are! The only thing that could make us feel better would be if Ash herself would return.

Yet despite our inconsolable sadness at Ash's continuing absence, we're not going to dwell on that today. Not at this glorious occasion when Quinn Fiery has returned and when we have all the news for you, our dedicated readers.

Although we must tell you of our greatest disappointment: that although Quinn and Ash have both been missing, Quinn wasn't with Ash. At least that's what Reda tells us and she's never steered us wrong. If Reda says that Quinn wasn't with Ash, then he wasn't. We believe her. We don't *want* to believe her, but we do. Quinn isn't just Reda's brother and business partner and vidcast costar, but he's her best friend. He wouldn't lie to her. And Reda wouldn't lie to us.

Reda tells us that Quinn needed time away from their vidcast. He was tired. He couldn't focus. He'd lost the joy.

We think this is because of something to do with Ash, even if Reda swears it has nothing to do with Ash. *Quinn and Ash were never more than good friends*, Reda told us. Then she shocked us by saying that Ash was the wrong person for her brother and that there is someone much better than Ash somewhere out there for him.

Oh, dear friends! How could *anyone* be better than our Ash? So beautiful, so charismatic, so endlessly fascinating and intriguing and mesmerizing. Her compelling way of talking! Those silvery eyes! No *wonder* Quinn is in love with her!

We're in love with her. Although of course not like *that*. We must assure our Certain Other that no one else is like *that*. Only our Certain Other is or could be.

But we were telling you about the returned Quinn Fiery. He'll be on the Fiery vidcast again starting next week, Reda told us. He's reenergized and ready to give his all to his sister, his viewers, his fans.

We're willing to bet he'd be ready to give his all to Ash as well, but Reda refused to talk to us about Ash. We don't blame her. She has the Fiery vidcast—their ratings have sunk since Quinn went away—to concern herself with and also of course her brother's continuing well-being.

Quinn, please come talk to us. We'd love to have a sit-down with you. We're happy you're back. We want to know everything you were doing while you were away. Your sister wouldn't tell us! *You'll have to ask Quinn*, she said. So we're asking you. Talk to us! We're always here for you.

And, Reda, thanks for letting us know about Quinn before you told anyone else. We owe you! Redeem your favor anytime! Our door is open!

Before we sign off for the day, we must report our happiness that the saturnia necklaces are finally *finally* back in stock. Oh. Even if Ash hasn't returned.

Our Certain Other has gifted us with our very own Ash saturnia necklace—oh, it shimmers and is so so beautiful!—and we were very touched by this gesture and engaged in some satisfying gratitude sex.

Although nothing would satisfy us more than Ash's reappearance. We need you, Ash! You've been away long enough! Quinn returned. Now it's time for you to return too. Come back! We'll be so happy, thrilled, relieved, and ecstatic to see you again!

CHAPTER 54

Claude

"WE'RE GOING OVER to Brandon's," Lee says. "You should come, Claude. She needs her friends right now."

"I'm hardly her friend," I say.

"You're about as close as she gets to having friends," Evan says. "And she's horrendously uncomfortable with carrying the twins. I'm sure she'd love having someone different to complain to."

"How's Bear handling it?"

"Brandon could do or say just about anything and Bear would be okay with it," Lee says. "Let's have dessert." She calls over the server, one of her many friends. Unlike Brandon—or me, for that matter—Lee has scores of friends. Most of them are Evan's friends now too.

"Nothing for me," I say. I haven't eaten this much in one sitting since the last time Evan and I were here at the Galaxy together, the day he met Lee. The server leaves. I may not be having dessert, but Evan and Lee are sharing some rich cake-and-whipped-cream item.

"Don't say a fucking word," Evan says to me under his breath, but I can't fathom why refusing dessert has caused such a reaction in him. Then I feel the reason before I see it, and turn around in my seat.

Heading toward us is none other than the vicious Streeter, his ever-present sneer fixed in place.

"If it isn't the disgraced Ash's *manager*," Streeter says, staring down at me. He says *manager* like it's the name of a flesh-eating virus.

"She's not *disgraced*," Lee says. Evan should've warned her while he was at it.

"Oh?" Streeter sneers harder. "I would've thought that her disappearance was ample proof of her, mmm, shall we say, *shame?*"

I clench my fists under the table but I say nothing. Evan's probably right. Streeter would just love it if I started up something with him. Frustrating him is a better strategy.

"Ash has *nothing* to be ashamed of," Lee says as the dessert arrives. The server nudges his way around Streeter—he's obviously someone else who can't stand the critic—and puts the plate at the center of the table, placing three forks in an artful display around the cake, then leaves.

"Aren't *you* a pretty thing?" Streeter says to Lee, who stands up and says, "Aren't you a *disgusting* thing."

Evan stands up next, shielding Lee with his tall, imposing self.

"Leave her alone," Evan says.

I try reminding myself that Evan warned me not to say anything to Streeter, but it's getting harder and harder to remember that.

"Is she your next purveyor of nothing?" Streeter says to me as he points his index finger at Lee.

"Ash is *not a purveyor of nothing*," Lee says, expressing exactly what I'm thinking although leaving out a significant piece, so I'm forced to speak up.

"*You're* the damned purveyor of nothing," I say to Streeter as I also stand up. The whipped cream is looking less whipped as the seconds elapse.

"*I* provide a much-needed service," Streeter says, going full-on haughty. "A *respected* and *honored* service. That's hardly *nothing.*"

"How many people's careers have you destroyed?" Lee says, leaning forward around Evan so she and Streeter can see each other.

"My dear, you have no idea what you're talking about. I've never *destroyed* anyone's career."

"What crap," Evan says.

"They destroy themselves," Streeter says with a snort. "Haven't you noticed? All I do is simply report the facts."

"Just because you say something doesn't make it a fact," I say, getting myself tangled up in this hellish mess.

"You're of no interest to me," Streeter says, then licks his lips and looks at Lee, then at Evan.

"You two are grooming her, aren't you? Your sad little coward ran away and you're working on her replacement. Well, if Ash was nothing, then this new creation of yours is sure to be less than nothing."

Before Lee has a chance to say the words about to emerge from her mouth, Evan surprises Streeter with a well-placed right jab, then I join in with my always-unexpected left hook. This is the first time I've felt this good since before Ash's last vidcast.

Lee, being the object of more of Streeter's current insults than either Evan or me, and feeling left out of the action, kneels up onto the table, picks up the cake plate, and hurls it straight at Streeter's face.

Other patrons of the café applaud. Everyone may listen to Streeter's shite and by their attention contribute to his fame and power, but no one in the Galaxy, or perhaps even the actual galaxy, likes him.

Evan and I back off. It was fun hitting the guy, but it's more fun to see runny whipped cream and the smears of devil's food on his face and neck and the front of his uptight suit.

Streeter grabs the napkins that the server brought along with the dessert that's now spattered across Streeter's dignity, and starts wiping his face.

"Don't think you'll *ever* have a career, my dear," he says to Lee. Streeter's talking as though nothing has happened to him even as he wipes the former dessert from himself. "I'll make sure of it."

"Say another cruel word to or about my friends and *your* career will be over," Evan says. "*I'll* make sure of it."

"Don't be foolish, my boy. You couldn't touch me."

"He just did," I say. "And so did I. You're lucky we stopped."

"Look at you, Claude Ryerson." Streeter's cleaned enough of the cake chunks and crumbs and splotches of whipped cream off his face that his sneer is visible again. "You're such a failure you can't even dress properly."

A small man who must be the restaurant's manager comes over to our table.

"Is this, uh, fellow, annoying you?" he says to Lee as he puts his hand on Streeter's back in an ambiguous gesture. Is he comforting him, warning him, or trying to control him?

"He's scum," Lee says. "Don't elevate him to *fellow.*"

"I'm afraid you'll have to leave, sir," the manager says to Streeter. "Now."

"I don't usually review restaurants," Streeter says, looking down at the much smaller man, "but in your case I'm going to make an exception."

"We'll make sure to report today's goings-on on our mesh feed," the manager says. "There seems to be a lot of video of it."

I look around and see that nearly everyone in the restaurant is recording the incident on their comms.

"Hunh," Streeter says in a rare moment where he doesn't have an insult or even a comeback at the ready.

He pulls back his shoulders, shakes off the manager's hold, and, oozing self-righteous indignation, strides out of the restaurant, cake crumbs falling onto the floor and leaving a trail behind him as he exits.

Lee is back in her seat. The manager has brought out a new piece of cake along with three fresh forks. Evan lays into the cake and has eaten half of it before Lee gets a chance at it.

The manager brings yet another piece of cake to our table.

"Are you okay?" he says to Lee.

"I'm fine, Cheng. Thanks for getting him to leave. And for the extra cake."

"I expect it to be very busy at dinner tonight. But it's your day off," Cheng says.

Lee, who owns the place and can do as she wishes, doesn't take the bait and neither Evan nor I say anything. Cheng, sighing, leaves. Evan polishes off the slice of cake he started and Lee and I split the other.

"That was great," I say after we're all finished.

"The bakery who supplies the desserts does amazing work," Lee says.

"I meant slugging Streeter. I felt like someone else there for a moment," I say.

"You mean someone who isn't moping about in the same shirt for weeks at a time?" Evan's stretched out and has his feet up on the bench where I'm sitting, blocking my exit.

"Watch it," I say. "My friendliness has limits."

Evan turns to Lee. "Did I ever tell you about the time—"

"Have the courtesy of telling Lee while I'm not sitting right here."

Evan takes his feet off the bench, straightens up, and says, "Let's get out of here. Come with us to Brandon's."

"I'm oversocialized. I need a drink." I head over to the bar while Evan takes care of the bill.

On their way out, Evan and Lee stop at the bar and give me one last try as my first gin and lime shows up.

"You should come with us," Lee says. "How're you going to get home?"

"I'll walk," I say. "It's not that far." But what I mean is *Leave me alone*, and they get the message and leave.

Two gin and limes later, just as I'm entering a fine isolation, Quinn Fiery comes into the Galaxy and sits down next to me at the bar.

"I guess it's just my lucky day," he says, but I don't respond, doing my damnedest to hang on to the gin-infused comfort I was feeling just before he arrived.

He orders a fancy beer, the kind only someone like the famous Quinn Fiery would even know about, and says to me, "Tell me where Ash is."

CHAPTER 55

Ash

IT TAKES ME a while to work out the passcode for Ginny's scroll. At first I thought of going back to her room and asking her for it, but a quick search of my store of information produced many suggestions for overcoming this obstacle, and one of them worked.

Ginny's scroll, though, is nothing like the scroll I used to have. It's slow to respond and has limited access to areas I'd thought were available to everyone. In short order, I go through most of what's on offer, and it's all trivial and entertaining, but not informative.

I do, however, come across Ginny's own holding account, which contains more than the zero balance I'd expected to see. She gets a regularly monthly deposit from something or someone called Chadwick and every month she pays rent for her apartment, even though I'm pretty sure no one else in this building does. I certainly don't.

Yet I can't find my own holding account, if I have one.

I read through the *Today's Trends* posts that I've missed since I've been here. I scan Streeter's latest lacerating reviews. He's latched on to someone called the Great Waterman, an influencer who's become popular enough that Streeter has to disparage him from several different directions. The Great Waterman isn't so great. His facts are often wrong. He's too happy and friendly and therefore suspicious. What's he trying to sell us with his fake attitude? Et cetera.

Every word of Streeter's angers me. Using Ginny's log-in, I post a comment under one of Streeter's nastiest anti–Great Waterman diatribes and say that isn't the Great Waterman, or anyone, really, entitled to some happiness?

There are many posts here and there about me. People still wondering where I am, what happened to me, if they can still get this or that item. I notice that Rêverie is advertising a new line of Ash-inspired products. There're ads everywhere for these things.

But I can't find my holding account. Maybe I don't have one.

I think of sending Claude a message, although it would be coming from Ginny's account, since I can't find what I'd thought of as mine. But maybe he would never see the message. Claude probably gets hundreds of them a day.

I think of contacting Quinn Fiery. He'd offered to help me find my past. I write out an entire message, explaining that I'm not Ginny, that it's really me, Ash, and could we get together? I'm still looking for my past.

Then I remember what happened at the Honeycomb. How Quinn wanted to touch me, how he thinks he's in love with me. I can't encourage him. It could get worse. I could hurt him. I erase the message. I can't send very this.

I wish I could send Dev a message. He would know how to help me, but there's no way to contact him. I search through the meshwork and Dev has no address, no presence, and is mentioned occasionally only as *that black cat in Ash's last vidcast.*

To distract myself, I read people's stories about themselves. The stories are legion. People seem to love talking about themselves and about their past experiences and childhoods. I relish all their stories. These are people who have a past and who *remember* it. I get lost in these pasts, dipping in, trying out how it'd feel if any of these pasts were mine. Hoping that maybe some of these pasts will help me remember my own, trigger a fact, an incident, a moment, that I've forgotten.

I grew up here. It's a medium-sized city but it seemed big to me. Not anymore.

I have two sisters and one of them doesn't speak to me even though she was the one I was always closest to.

My parents got divorced when I was three. I had to go back and forth, living with each of them a week at a time so that they could prove how much they cared about me. I will never do that to my children, if I ever have any.

My hometown was destroyed in a fire last year and I've been freed from ever having to think about going back there again.

I've known my friend Cara almost my entire life. When we were kids, we used to go swimming in the creek behind her house. Cara has a pool now and sometimes I still go swimming there. Her kids are friends with my kids.

I incorporate all these lives into mine but none of them are mine. None of them remind me of my past, which is still as opaque to me as it ever was.

Just as I'm about to go back across the hall and return Ginny's scroll to her, I think of the perfect person to write to. Someone who knows so much and who seems to have a lot of contacts and even more resources.

I go back to my room and write a short message: *Meet me at the Black Dome, Friday at 2. Maybe we can help each other.*

I send it, then go across the hall and knock on Ginny's door.

"Who are you?" she says when she opens it.

"Ash," I say. "Your neighbor."

"I'm very busy," she says.

"Thanks for lending me your scroll," I say, giving it back to her.

She takes it, turns, tosses it onto her couch, then turns back to me. "Never believe anything anyone else says," she says.

"Not even you?" I say, laughing.

She shakes her head, her curls kind of bouncing as she does it.

Back in my room, I root through my collection of discarded clothes, choosing what I'll wear on Friday, choosing what I'll say. Wondering why I didn't think of this before. Wondering if Ginny's advice could be true.

CHAPTER 56

Claude

"YOU TELL ME," I say to Quinn, a guy who's even more handsome in person than he is on his vidcast. If Ash were a real human being and not a computer image, she'd definitely choose him over me. The guy's slick and groomed. Everything about him screams *high-end*, including his expensive "casual" shoes, which I take a glance at while I search the floor for a convenient trapdoor I might escape through.

I lift up my glass to the bartender, signaling for another. The usual means of escape.

"You *are* Claude Ryerson, aren't you?" he says after taking a careful sip of his beer. He puts down the glass and when he lets go, the imprint of his fingers is streaked across the iced surface.

"We haven't been introduced, but I did meet your sister once," I say as the new gin arrives along with a new half lime. I pay attention to the gin and the lime and don't look at Quinn. No matter how many credits I may have in my account, if what Evan told me is true, I'd never match up to this guy. He's actually *suave*. Really the perfect match for the nonexistent Ash.

"Reda told me that you're an insufferable snob," Quinn, the insufferable snob, says to me.

"Reda's just upset that I rejected her advances," I say, half remembering that I'd done that. Although she hadn't been upset. She hadn't cared. She was just grilling me for information while pimping for her brother.

"Reda's better than a hundred thousand of you," Quinn says.

"No need to exaggerate," I say.

"That's an *under*statement."

"How is it that you and your sister have so many fans? I don't even like you." I hold back saying that I hate him.

"You're keeping Ash locked up somewhere, aren't you?"

"Sure. Whatever you think." This particular glass of gin seems inferior to the previous two. Did the bartender change brands on me?

"I knew it," Quinn says. "And Ash wouldn't say an unkind word about you. She's that generous and forgiving."

"Yeah."

"I begged Ash to let me see her again, but you've got some kind of a hold over her. I knew it then. I didn't just suspect it, I *knew* it, Ryerson. And it's even clearer now." Quinn takes another refined person's sip of his fancy beer in order to punctuate his upcoming accusation: "Ash isn't *missing*—she's your prisoner."

I let the gin fog clear up a bit and look over at the sparkling, urbane Quinn Fiery. "Right."

"I cannot believe you're *admitting* it!"

"Me neither." This almost makes me laugh. Almost.

"Get up," he says.

"No thanks."

"Get up. We're going to your place right now and I'm freeing Ash."

"Good luck with that." I finish off my third gin and lime and think about ordering another but my interest in drinking has undergone a radical collapse.

"Excuse me, sir," Cheng says to Quinn. Cheng's come to rescue me. Then he sees who it is who's bothering me and his attitude changes.

"Quinn Fiery," Cheng says. "I watch your vidcast all the time. You and your sister are wonderful. And I'm happy to see you've returned. You were missed."

"Thanks," Quinn says.

"Darnell," Cheng says to the bartender, who's come down to our dark corner of the bar, the location I chose in order to be left alone. "Make sure Mr. Fiery and Mr. Ryerson have everything they need." Cheng looks at Quinn, then at me. "On the house."

"It's good to have you back. You're always welcome here," Cheng says to Quinn, then turns to leave. Can't hog the celebrity's time. He might not return.

I still don't want another drink, even now that it's free. I want to go home, maybe sit in the freezing barn with Devil for a while—he likes it there, even with the hole in the wall. Then check on my account, see if it's really as full of credits as Evan claims it is.

"Let's go," Quinn says to me. "Come on. You're in no condition to drive."

"My bike's at home," I say.

"Your *bike?*"

I nod. The gin's gotten to me. I forget why I hate Quinn Fiery although I'm sure it has something to do with Ash.

"I'll drive you," he says.

"I'm walking," I say, and proceed out the door and onto the road. After a few moments I realize that Quinn Fiery's following me in his super sleek transcer, a nicer model than even the one Evan has.

"Get in," Quinn says, pulling up alongside me.

I don't. I keep walking. A half hour later, he tries again and with my home seeming even farther away than it did a half hour ago and my fingers getting numb with the cold, I do get in. I point and grunt and Quinn drives me to the farm.

"Stop here," I say when we get to the barn.

Quinn, finally obedient, complies.

"Come with me." I force myself out of the ultra comfy seat and go toward the barn. The ground lacks solidity and even the air seems flimsy. As though I'm the coded image, not Ash. Quinn follows me.

At the barn's half-open doorway, Quinn says, "You can't mean you live here."

"I can't and don't."

"You're keeping *Ash* here? This is cruel beyond belief. I'll have you drawn and quartered." Quinn's outraged.

I find the lantern I keep out here ever since I destroyed the electric panels in the wall I unintentionally demolished. I turn on the lantern and the full array of my impulsive fury is lit up in an eerie glow.

Devil's lounging on the sagging sofa, cleaning his left-front paw, looking all superior-like. No sign of his mouse pal.

Quinn gingerly steps over all the detritus on the floor. Can't scuff up those elegant-while-casual shoes.

"Where's Ash?" Quinn's searching every millimeter of the barn's one big, open room. Then he spots the bathroom door, heads there, yanks it open. Fuming now, he says, "Where is she, Ryerson? I've had enough of your bullshit."

"She's right there," I say, pointing to the smashed-up console on the floor. Maybe I should get around to cleaning it up. Not now but sometime in the invisible future.

"Stop fucking with me," Quinn says.

I throw myself onto the sofa. Devil gives me his *how dare you disturb me?* look and I shrug in response.

"I'm not fucking with you, Quinn. That's Ash. That's all she ever was. She doesn't exist. She's a computer program I wrote. And now the program doesn't even exist anymore. That's the beginning and the end of it. Of her."

I don't know why I decide it's okay to tell Quinn Fiery, but I have to get him to stop hounding me about keeping Ash prisoner. I have to get him to leave. And the secret will come out eventually anyway. It's bound to, especially now that Lee knows. Ash had her run and now it's over with.

"You're out of your mind, Ryerson," Quinn says. "I had dinner with her at the Honeycomb just a few weeks ago. She's as real as you or me."

CHAPTER 57

Claude

THE GIN HAS seeped into the raceways of my awareness. It doesn't always but tonight it has. I've imagined that Quinn Fiery is telling me that he had dinner with Ash a few weeks ago. Or ever.

"No, you didn't," I say. It's all I've got handy.

"I thought I saw an actual *house* when we drove up," he says.

"Yeah."

"That must be where you've got her," Quinn says, and storms out of the barn.

I lift myself off the sofa, reluctant to move even though it's deathly cold in here—not that the comfortable Devil seems to mind—and follow Quinn. I don't want him strolling into the house, which I don't remember locking up after I left earlier.

Quinn's made it to the front door when I catch up with him. The cold has sobered me up somewhat.

"She's not here," I say, realizing as the words emerge that they're insufficiently convincing.

"I understand," Quinn says, and I feel relieved for a moment until he says, "If Ash were with me, I wouldn't want to let her go either. Are you going to let me in or am I going to have to break the door down?"

I open the door, which, as I'd suspected, I never locked.

"No need for anything so dramatic," I say. I wish Evan and Lee had still been at the restaurant when Quinn arrived. They could've helped me prevent all this, backed me up with the truth about Ash.

Quinn pushes past me and starts stomping through the house, if a person that well turned out can be said to be stomping. Yet it seems like that to me. He's scoured the downstairs and is headed up the steps when I intercept him.

"Look, Quinn, she's not here. She's not *anywhere*. She doesn't exist."

Quinn goes straight for Ash's model room, as though he's been given advance directions, although there are only four rooms upstairs, so he had a not-bad chance of lighting on the correct one on the first try.

After he's had a look around, even opening the two closets and inspecting their innards using a neat little torch he's produced from the breast pocket of his snazzy jacket, he walks back out into the upstairs hallway and goes into the next room, the one I've been using. I follow him.

"Besides everything else, you're a slob," Quinn says to me after he's finished searching every millimeter of my room.

"Thanks," I say. If he were an inspector for the city buildings department, he'd probably be condemning the entire house right about now, or at least my room, which looks like it's been tossed apart by a localized tornado.

After Quinn's done scrutinizing each atomic particle of the house—he's now been in places I myself haven't visited since Dad died—he meets me back in the hallway, outside the model room.

"Where is she?" he says.

"Nowhere," I say. "She can't be anywhere. It's impossible. She doesn't exist."

Quinn walks into the model room, flips the light back on, and says, "Stop lying to me, Ryerson. Look at this. This is the room you were using for her vidcasts. This is *her* room. Of course she exists."

"If I hadn't destroyed the console, I'd be able to show you the code," I say. Until this moment I haven't regretted demolishing it. If I'm going to do this again—well, not *this* but something like it—I'll have to start over from zero.

"Stop stalling. Just tell me where she is. Or did she climb out of the window to get away from you? To escape your hold over her?"

"I had no hold over her," I say, although that's not true. I had every hold over her. All of them.

"You've got her in the basement, don't you?" he says as he runs down the steep stairs and makes a beeline for the kitchen, making a correct guess about where the basement entrance is. Now he's entering dangerous territory. I haven't been in the basement in years. It's possible the steps have rotted out.

"Careful," I call down the steps while I turn on the light switch that's at the top of the stairs, but the light doesn't go on. The bulb must've died eons ago. Yet I can see Quinn down there, searching the dank, damp space, using his handy torch to highlight the world of spiderwebs, mouse droppings, and the causes of both.

I wait at the top of the stairs. I'm not going down there. Quinn reemerges from the musty gloom, coming up the steps while he tries to wipe the clinging cobwebs off his jacket.

"Have you ever considered cleaning this place up?" he says, banging on his left sleeve, which is marred with impressive dust trails.

"I told you she isn't here," I say.

Quinn parks himself in a chair at the kitchen table.

"What did you do with her?"

"I showed you. In the barn."

Quinn changes tacks. "Where do you think is the most likely place she'd go? Who's her closest friend? Or maybe her family? Where are they?"

"Look, Quinn, she can't *go* anywhere."

"*Look*, Ryerson, I don't know how many times I have to tell you, but Ash and I had dinner together. At a restaurant. She met me there."

Quinn really did say this earlier. I'd begun to think I'd imagined it.

I consider what it would be like to have dinner with Ash but I can't picture her eating. That hadn't been in the code. I hadn't considered it even though there's probably a bigger market for food than there is for jewelry or cosmetics or furnishings. I make a mental note to incorporate this feature next time, if there is a next time. Although the next time it won't be Ash. I can't repeat that mistake, no matter what I think or how much I might want her back.

"We had dinner together," Quinn says yet again. Does he think repeating this will convince me of the impossible?

"It can't have been Ash. It must've been someone else," I say. "Someone pretending to be Ash. She had a lot of fans, and I gather that many of them were and maybe still are copying everything about her. Trying to be her. You had dinner with one of them—a very convincing one."

"No, you're wrong. I sent her messages. She sent messages back to me. She nodded to me on her vidcast."

"The hell she did," I say as I remember Ash's nods. Coincidence. She can't've been nodding to Quinn Fiery.

"We made plans to meet. There's no way this was someone impersonating her, and anyway, I'd know Ash anywhere. It wasn't some pretender. It was Ash herself."

"We had Streeter convinced for a while," I say. "So I don't see why someone couldn't've convinced you as well."

"I saw that interview. I knew the minute it started that that wasn't Ash. That impostor was *nothing* like Ash, not like the real Ash, the one I know."

"I give up," I say.

"I *will* find her," Quinn says. "And while I'm at it, I'm going to find out about her past."

"Good luck to you," I say. Should I give a past to the next one I create? And why the hell am I even toying with the idea of doing this again?

"You're an ass," Quinn says, still attending to the filth that he can't get off his jacket. "Ash is in love with you and you don't even want to admit that she exists. You never lifted a finger to help her rediscover her past. No wonder she left you. You don't deserve her. And after I find her I'm going to make sure that she never sees you or speaks to you or communicates with you. Ever. Again." He punctuates the last two words with a fist to the table.

"I *will* find her," he says. Scowls at me. Gets up. Works at the crud on his jacket. Leaves the house, slamming the door behind him. I hear his transcer as he speeds away.

Quinn seems to be in love with Ash. Not just some kind of stupid crush, but love. He's gone so far as to hallucinate her real existence, a desperate end even I haven't resorted to, as much as I'd like to think that Ash is real, that she's more than what she really is or could possibly be.

That she's more than just some sales gimmick I dreamt up.

That she's more than just the kilometers of code buried in a pile of destroyed components that're corroding on the floor of my falling-down barn.

That she's more than just the Ash who keeps inserting herself into my dreams. The Ash who keeps me awake at night. The Ash I long for, still wondering what wild thing she'll do next.

The Ash who doesn't exist even if, like Quinn, I can't bear to confront that truth. Yet, unlike Quinn, I know the truth.

But maybe Quinn's right. Maybe the thing to do is to find a decent Ash impersonator and have dinner with her. It could be almost like being with Ash. And *almost* is all I've got.

I need to be with someone real instead of lost out here, where Dad's fixes to my old program can't hope to ever find my disappeared mother. Where the disappeared Ash shows me by her persistent very absence that she was never actually here. An illusion only.

So I comm Olympia Cowan.

CHAPTER 58

Today's Trends

THIS ISSUE OF the *Trends* is devoted to all things Ash. If we can't have the pleasure of our usual Ash vidcasts, then we can have thoughts and daydreams and hopes about her. We know all of our Ash-deprived friends must feel the same way. Like us, you've probably watched and rewatched all her vidcasts now, multiple times.

We have viewed Ash's final—well, we *hope* it's not *really* final!—vidcast so many times we can reenact it ourselves. Just ask our Certain Other, who's a witness to one of these reenactments. Yes! We got applause! But we can't be Ash! No one else can!

Yet, that brings us to something we've been noticing. Since Ash's disappearance . . . oh, we so don't want to think of her as disappeared, so let's call it her *absence*.

Let us start again.

Since Ash has been absent—see? doesn't that feel a bit better?—we've seen more and more people out there in life and also in vidcasts and other mesh postings who are doing their best, however pathetic that best might be at times, to emulate, imitate, impersonate, and sort of *be* Ash.

The Ash Craze was always a part of Ash's fame. We have many Ash items in our home, although we never went so far as to re-create her room here, as many other people have done in their homes. But, oh, we do so love our saturnia necklace! (Thank you, Certain Other! Love you!) We are holding on to our necklace as we write this, bringing ourselves that much closer to Ash.

We do get distracted, especially when it comes to Ash. But—we were talking about the Ash Craze. Yes. It's everywhere and it involves, it seems, everyone. Even children. Have you yet seen Delfina—that adorable little girl who's maybe seven years old? She has her hair dyed just like Ash's and she has her room done up in a kind of fantasy version of Ash's room, with glitter and sparkles and banners decorating everything. She is our favorite, not just because she's so adorable and so young but because her version of Ash is more like a tribute than an imitation. How brilliant of her to do this!

Delfina loves Ash in the same way that we do, and she's *honoring* her. Delfina is even selling a so so so cute—and so so so affordable— bracelet that's very modeled after Ash's iconic necklace. Yes! We are getting one! It's being shipped to us right now! And we couldn't resist the *very*. Because Ash, we miss you!

But next up we must mention the people out there whose focus on Ash is not on everything we love about her so much but on everything they want to criticize, tear down, bash, desecrate, and destroy. How could you be so cruel? Ash is *missing*! We have no idea where she is or what she's doing. We don't know—and we've hesitated for a long time to even *think* of thinking this or, worse, putting it in *Today's Trends*—but we can hold back no longer.

Ash could be dead.

Yes, we've said it. You see our words. Ash could be dead. She could be, or she could be even worse worser worst than dead: injured, suffering, lost, confused, captive, trapped, tortured, starving . . . We're sure you've thought of even more chilling, dire fates for her. We refuse to! These are bad enough!

Ash has amnesia. Maybe it got worse! Maybe she doesn't remember *anything* now! Oh! It's horrible to entertain such doom-infused thoughts, but we admit that we do. We admit that we've cried while rewatching her vidcasts. Have *sobbed*. Have combed over each vidcast for clues as to where she might be, what might have happened. Yet we've so far found nothing.

We admit that we took our time before we tried out Rêverie's brand-new Ash-inspired line, thinking its very presence was somehow disloyal to Ash. Ash herself has never seen these things or used them. We used to—we are so so wrenchingly sad to say *used to*—love to watch Ash and imagine that we were sitting at her vanity and those things in front of her were in front of us. We wanted everything she had just so we could be close to her, could feel her resonance.

But we have missed her so profoundly that even seeing her name and her distinctive logo emblazoned on the containers of these new cosmetics has been a comfort to us. And, yes! The Ash-inspired products are exceptional. Ash would love them. We've been reassured by our contact at Rêverie that Ash will *of course* be receiving the same percentage from the sales of these products as she does from her regular, Ash-endorsed lines. Like us, Rêverie would never think of doing anything to harm or upset or disturb Ash. Or cheat her out of what's rightfully hers.

But, as you all must agree, it's one thing to have your very own Ash saturnia necklace to wear and to have her vanity to sit at and to have her ethereal theme song playing its haunting melodies in the background of your lives—we have it playing right now! Ah! Inspiring! But it's another experience entirely to have a new Ash vidcast to watch and the next one to look forward to and then the next one. Our days and weeks and months were defined by what Ash would bring to us, and now . . . the unthinkable. The impossible. We never expected this and we are still devastated.

Ash! Maybe you'll see this.

Maybe one of you will see Ash!

If you even *think* you've seen her, please contact us via M @ *Today's Trends*.

CHAPTER 59

Ash

I'M WEARING THE most un-Ash-like outfit in my new repertoire. Ginny was nice enough to loan me a bell-sleeved silk blouse that she made by sewing several different scarves together. It's not something that the influencer and seller Ash would ever be seen in. It's too haphazard and amateurish and the sleeves would distract from and interfere with showing off the products on the vanity. Even if a few thousand viewers wanted to buy a blouse like this, the lost cosmetics and jewelry sales' profits could never be recouped.

I still think like this even though I'm no longer doing vidcasts. Even though I gave up my career as an influencer and seller. Even though I ran away and needed to run away. Even though I had to leave in order to find my past. Even though I still miss my room, miss Devil and Bobby, and although I don't want to think about him or wonder about him or very remember him ever, I miss Claude. I miss hearing his voice and that sensation I'd get when I knew he was there: a kind of visceral underpinning that held me in a sure place. I miss seeing his always-mussy yellow hair. I miss surprising him. And sometimes being thrilled by his rare smile, which makes his coral eyes glimmer.

Outside the Black Dome, I wait in the shadows, keeping away from the rain under an awning at the side of the restaurant. Since I climbed out the window, I've avoided being spotted and identified and I'm hoping he won't recognize me. But I'll recognize him.

When he finally does arrive, nearly fifteen minutes late, I wave to him, but he just sneers at me and looks up and down the street, then folds his enormous black umbrella and goes into the restaurant.

I slip around the corner and follow him in, waiting a bit behind him.

"I'm meeting someone here," he says to the host at the front.

"Your table is ready," says the host, speaking with such deference that I'm surprised he doesn't get down on his knees and bow to his illustrious guest.

"Your most secluded spot," he says.

"Of course, sir. Of course." Now the host does bow slightly. He presses something in his ear, then shakes his head, listens, shakes his head again, then after listening for another moment, nods. "We have our quietest table for you, sir. Follow me."

I watch them proceed into the depths of the Black Dome, a place that's all depths and dark corners. I'd found this place while searching for public-yet-private spaces for today's meeting. I couldn't risk going to the Honeycomb again. What if Quinn would be there? Also, the Black Dome is known for protecting its guests' identities.

The host didn't even use a name, but said *sir*.

After the host returns to the front, I approach him.

"I'm meeting someone here," I say. "I believe you just seated him."

"Yes, of course," the host says, eyeing me with a little suspicion. Does he recognize me? He surely recognized my lunch companion. Anyone would.

Or perhaps the host thinks that I'm not dressed appropriately. I look down at myself and feel my arms inside the bell sleeves, then detect the faint aroma of intoxicating spices. It still, even after all these days and weeks and chopped-into pieces of time that I might never understand—it still surprises me that smells can overwhelm all else, that tastes can be so luxurious. I haven't had a real meal in a while. I'm looking forward to that part of this, if nothing else.

If the host recognizes me, he doesn't say so. He leads me to the table, which, as promised, is the most secluded in the restaurant, back in a far corner and behind a painted screen.

I sit down at the table and the host leaves.

"Go away," my lunch companion says, indignant, waving the back of his hand at me. "Shoo. I'm waiting for someone. I can't have *you* sitting here."

"But I'm the person you're waiting for," I say. I'm so relieved that he, of all people, doesn't recognize me. Maybe I can leave the building where I'm staying more often, get out and explore more. Do more research.

"I think I'd know whom I'm waiting for," Streeter says. "Shoo. Git." He waves his dismissive hand at me again.

"No one says *whom* anymore," I say, testing his patience.

"I'm afraid this won't do," he says, sneering.

"Streeter," I say. "It's me. Ash. I asked you to meet me here."

"You are not—" He stops himself, squints his too-small eyes, leans forward across the table, runs his hand back over his bulbous head, and stares at me. Then gasps.

"You're much much better than that other impersonator, Olympia whoever-she-was," Streeter says. He's still leaning across the table, his eyes stalking my face and body.

"Cowan," I say. "And I'm not another impersonator."

"So you say." Streeter leans closer, looks harder, blinks his eyes, snuffles. "Turn to the side," he says, and I turn.

"Other side," he says after a moment. I do as he asks. He needs to understand that I am Ash and not someone pretending to be her.

"Very very good," he says as he draws himself back into his chair. "I might even say impressive. If I didn't know better, I'd almost say that you *are* Ash."

"That's because I *am* Ash," I say. "Don't you think that if I were pretending to be Ash I'd do my best to look as much like her as possible? Wear something she'd wear? Use her cosmetics?" I hadn't been using any makeup, as I look much different without it. My lips not as full or red, my eyes not as pronounced, the lines of my face more subtle.

"Well," Streeter says. "If you say so." He strokes his elongated face and leans forward again, staring. "If you say so. I'm willing to play along. *Ash.*"

Maybe he believes me.

"You thought you were so clever, using that Olympia woman when you didn't have the courage to appear," he says, still staring at me and stroking his face, although he's moved his hand from his cheek to his chin.

"I couldn't be there that night," I say. I had no way to get there and didn't even know I could, but I don't tell him that.

"Ah yes. You were 'ill.' Of *course* you were." Streeter takes his hand off his chin and uses it to summon a server, who appears out of the gloom behind me.

We order our lunch. The server leaves.

"Streeter," I say. "I know we're not friends—"

"We're not even *enemies*," he says, sniffling. "We're *nothing.*"

"I know you think *I'm* nothing."

"Not *think*. Know." He looks to the side, showing me how little he cares about me. But I know he's interested. He's *here*. Maybe he even believes that I'm actually Ash.

"All right," I say. "I agree with you."

"Hunh. Maybe you're smarter than I thought you were. You're certainly much more clever than that last fake, Olympia someone-or-other." He relaxes back into his seat. He's at the banquette and I'm in the stiff chair across from him.

"Cowan." I can never repay her brilliant defense of me, but at least I can defend her, if only this small bit.

"If you think I'm going to help your pathetic so-called career—"

"It's not that at all," I say. "I'm no longer an influencer and seller."

His looks at me again, his eyebrows raised up.

Our drinks arrive. I've ordered a gin with a half lime. Streeter has a Scotch on ice.

"What is it, then?" he says. Maybe he's a little curious now. I squeeze the lime into the gin, just like I've seen Claude do. The lime feels and smells like my connection to a world I'm no longer part of. The lime juice stings my fingers. I take a taste of the gin.

"Streeter, I need your help," I say. "I didn't know who else to turn to."

Streeter sips at his Scotch, then puts the glass on the table, rotates it, the ice clinks, and he licks his lips.

"Well?" he says, lifting the glass again.

"I need to find my past," I say. "I thought you might be able to help me."

Streeter starts laughing, puts down his glass, throws back his head, and laughs so loudly that the server returns to our table.

"Is everything to your satisfaction, sir?" the server says.

Streeter keeps laughing. My hopes fade.

"Can I get you anything?" the server says. She looks like she would rather die than be responsible for the displeasure of the Black Dome's most famous lunch guest.

"Oh my dear," Streeter says in between bursts of laughter.

"Sir?" the server says.

"No," he says. "No no no. Go away." He waves his dismissive hand at her. Is this a gesture he uses all the time? He seems unaware of how callous it is.

The server scurries off.

Streeter's laughter subsides. He takes a long swig of his Scotch and I mimic him, downing half my gin. I'm not sure why Claude likes this. The flavor is too sharp.

I wait.

"My dear so-called Ash," Streeter says. Finally. "Better impostors than you have had their tryouts with me. But you're out of your mind if you think you're going to rope me into your little amnesia scheme."

CHAPTER 60

Claude

NOT TO BE outdone by Quinn Fiery, who I refuse to think of as somehow my rival even though that's how I've been thinking of him since his visit to my house. The moment he left, some awful instinct in me branded him as my competitor. The brand is now seared in, permanent. It's the only way I can think of him. He's no longer Quinn Fiery of the popular Fiery vidcast, brother of Reda. He's my competition.

But . . . what is it we're competing for?

The right to say we're in love with Ash? Hell, at least I'm not so foolish as to say that. Quinn Fiery can go around proclaiming how much he loves Ash, how damned devoted to her he is, and how ardently he wants to help her. Sure he can. The well-groomed jerk. I hope he can never get the filth of my basement off his expensive jacket.

But I will not be outdone by him. I've checked my holding account, and I now have so many credits I had to look several times at the numbers to make sure I understood what they meant. Evan wasn't kidding me.

At first I decide I'll ask her to the Honeycomb, a venue so pricey that I've never considered going there. Quinn Fiery probably thinks the cost is nothing. Well, it's nothing to me now. I can afford it. But isn't there somewhere even more impressive?

Ah yes. Here it is. Ice Inferno. I look at reviews of this ultra posh joint. We'll go there. It costs almost double what the Honeycomb does and it's so exclusive they don't have a sign out front and you have to search for it on the mesh with greater vigor than is required for most requests. And no images available anywhere.

I livecall Olympia Cowan.

"Claude," she says. "So nice of you to comm me."

I've been expecting to see someone more Ash-like, but I've forgotten that Olympia looks hardly anything like Ash unless she does herself up that way on purpose.

"Olympia," I say, wondering if I'm a success at hiding my disappointment. I've failed at keeping it from myself. I've been looking forward to seeing someone who looks enough like Ash that . . .

"I can't ever repay you for the wonders that appearance on Streeter's vid did for my career," Olympia says, looking less and less like Ash every second.

"You could return the fee," I say.

She looks surprised.

"But—"

"I'm joking," I say. "Kidding."

"Oh. But if you want me to impersonate Ash again—"

"No, it's not that," I say, cutting her off. "I was wondering if you'd like to have dinner with me."

"Well . . ."

"At Ice Inferno."

Her hesitancy ends. "Of course I would, Claude. How kind of you to think of me."

"How about tomorrow?" I was so sure she'd say yes that I'd already made the reservation, which itself cost more credits than the total of any fifteen or twenty dinners I've had in my lifetime.

"That'd be great," she says.

"Should I pick you up at eight?" Evan is loaning me his transcer.

"Perfect."

We both sign off. I rush into town to buy an outfit less like what I would wear and more like what Quinn Fiery would find acceptable. Evan and Lee meet me at the store and help me out, since I have no experience with this sort of thing.

I try on the eighth or eight hundredth suit that Evan's chosen and say, "This is too damned uncomfortable. Why can't I just wear what I usually do?"

"You'll be thrown out," Lee says. "They have rules at Double-I."

I give her a look.

"Ice Inferno," she says. "People call it Double-I."

I look at myself in the mirror. "I look heinous," I say.

"You look great," Evan says. "Get that one. It suits you."

"The hell it does," I say, then buy it. It costs slightly less than tomorrow's dinner will.

Evan and I drive back out to my house in his transcer while Lee trails us in her older, low-end one.

"I'm happy to see you returning to life, Claude," Evan says on the way.

"Damn Quinn Fiery," I say.

"You can stop repeating that now. I get the point," Evan says.

"Damn him. He went through the barn and the house like a damned detective. Even went down into the basement."

"You told me that already too. Twice. Maybe three times."

"Evan, he thinks Ash is real. He's convinced of it. Nothing I said had any effect. He thinks the impostor he went to the Honeycomb with *was* Ash."

"He took the impostor to the Honeycomb?" Evan looks over at me, then navigates the nasty curve where so many accidents have occurred that people call it the *death spiral.*

"Yeah," I say.

"No wonder you're going to Double-I."

"What does that mean?"

"It means you want to one-up him, Claude. And here I thought you were getting over your obsession with Ash."

"I am not—I *was* not obsessed with her."

We drive up to the house. Evan powers off the transcer. Lee pulls in behind us.

"I know you, Claude Ryerson. New suit. Ice Inferno. Date with Olympia Cowan. And constant talk about Quinn Fiery and how he's in love with Ash. You *are* obsessed with her. Claude, you *do* realize that she's only an image, don't you?"

"Evan, have some confidence in me. Of course I realize that. I know that. Quinn Fiery doesn't, but I do. I just wanted to go on a date and Olympia Cowan is the only woman I could think of. It's not like I could go out with Brandon or Lee."

"True." Evan moves the seat back and stretches out his long legs. "But something is missing here."

"Nothing's missing."

"You don't care at all about Olympia Cowan, yet you're taking her to the most extraordinary venue in the city. Why?"

"Why not? I've got plenty of credits. Might as well spend them."

"Claude"—Evan turns in his seat to look at me—"I'm worried about you. So's Lee." Evan waves in his rearview mirror and Lee, still in her transcer, waves back to him.

"So are Bear and Brandon. You spent too much time working on Ash and you've lost your objectivity."

"Says the man who spent countless mornings, afternoons, evenings, and nights with Emlyn Mohr."

"That's a cheap shot, Claude. Very unlike you. You really *are* obsessed."

"It's that damned Quinn Fiery."

"Claude. Listen to yourself. You're *jealous*. Of a perfectly nice guy who's just as obsessed with Ash as you are. Except he doesn't realize she's not real."

"I tried to tell him. He wouldn't listen to me. Come to think of it, *you're* not listening to me, Evan."

"Oh, I'm listening. But I can hear things that you can't."

"Yeah, sure."

"Then tell me you're interested—really interested—in Olympia Cowan."

I can lie as well as anyone—better, maybe—but I've never used this tactic with Evan. Our friendship has always been based in truth and trust. So I say nothing.

"Lee has a lot of friends," Evan says, brightening. He's proud of himself for finally backing me into the corner he's built for me. "I'm sure she'd be happy to introduce you to someone."

"I don't dislike Olympia," I say.

"Claude, don't mention Emlyn Mohr to Lee. Okay?" Evan reaches for the door handle. He's finished his futile chat with me. Evan opens the door, and Lee is standing right there, waiting.

"Who's Emlyn Mohr?" she says.

I take my packages and get out of Evan's transcer. He's about to have his first horrible discussion with Lee, the kind of talk that could destroy their new relationship. The kind of talk that's necessary if they have any hope of continuing that relationship.

Evan walks with Lee to her transcer.

"Just someone I knew at the Acres," he says to her.

"You might as well tell me," Lee says. "I'll find out eventually anyway."

I go into the house. Devil's there at the door.

"Want to go out?" I say, holding the door open.

He turns his back to me, sitting there, so self-assured.

"How *did* you get into Ash's vidcast?" I ask Devil as I shut the door.

He scrunches down, his paws out in front, like a sphinx.

"You might as well tell me," I say. "I'll find out eventually anyway."

Odds are, I'll never find out, but when Lee said it, it sounded just right. Like it was the answer to everything and anything.

Devil's mouse pal scampers down the stairs and Devil gets up and follows his friend into the dining room.

Damn Quinn Fiery.

I don't give a rip about Olympia Cowan. She's my substitute for Ash. I know that. I don't want to know that, but I do. No point in denying it. I'll find out eventually anyway.

CHAPTER 61

Evan

"I DON'T WANT to have this argument right now," I say. "Let's stay on topic."

"You mean stay on the *safe* topic: your fucked-up friend Claude," Lee says. She's driving. I'm stuffed into the passenger seat of her too-small transcer.

"And you were so nice to him all afternoon," I say.

"You're not going to worm out of this with sarcasm," Lee says.

She takes the death spiral at speed, like she's a professional racer. Hell, maybe she is. There's still a lot I don't know about her, but I figure I've got the rest of my life to find out. No need to rush.

"He's just hurting himself with his obsession," I say. "But it's not healthy. I'm worried."

Lee pulls the transcer over just millimeters short of a ditch and turns off the engine. It's damn dark out here in the countryside. Reminds me a little of the landscape near the place I once shared with Claude, out past civilization.

"Talk," she says.

"I *am* talking," I say.

"Who is Emlyn Mohr and why didn't you want Claude to mention her to me?"

"A maths instructor at the Acres."

"And?"

"Do we really have to talk about this now?" I say. "I'm tired."

"Try telling me that after we get back to your place. *Then* I'll believe you. Maybe."

"Lee, this was all a long time ago."

She turns down the window and lets cold air blow in.

"Did you develop amnesia? Like Ash?"

"Hey, that's a low blow," I say.

"Spit it out," Lee says. She won't look at me. We're alone here on this road. I look around to see if Lee's transcer is fit for what I have in mind, but even after I pull my seat back, I think it can't work.

"Evan?" she says, tapping her fingers on her thigh.

"Lee, I'll tell you about Emlyn eventually. Just not tonight."

"I hope you enjoy walking home."

"I'll go back to Claude's," I say. "It's closer."

"Tell him I said hi," she says, reaching across me to open my door. I put my hands on her shoulders.

"It was over a very long time ago, Lee. It has nothing at all to do with you, with us."

"And?"

"And nothing. That's it."

"That's not *it*," Lee says as she pushes out the passenger door, climbing over me in the process. Now she's standing up, leaning against the open door, and pointing.

"Out."

"But—"

"Either you're going to tell me right now or you're on your own."

"Why the urgency?"

"Why did you want to hide this?"

I get out of Lee's transcer and lean up against its side, across from where Lee is, still holding the passenger door open against her back.

"Here it is." I can barely look at Lee. Her lustrous, straight black hair is blowing across her face. "I want you," I say, the urge so strong I've forgotten how cold it is out here.

"Comm me when you've changed your mind," she says as she walks around the transcer, back to the driver side.

"Damn it, Lee, I don't want to tell you about Emlyn Mohr. It's over. It's been over for so long there are parts I don't remember all that well anymore."

"Do say. Are you still in touch with her?"

That shuts me up.

"You bastard," Lee says, returning to the near-ditch side of the transcer so she can tell me off to my face. "Stringing me along. My friend Joey warned me. She said anyone with your kind of wealth doesn't really give a shit about anyone else. Evan Becket, inventor of the magrail. Big bloody deal. I hope you and your magrail and your maths instructor will be very happy together."

"I never even *think* of her," I say. "And, yes, we're still in touch. She's my friend. But nothing's gone on since I left the Acres. That's eons ago. I only mentioned her because Claude was using her as a bludgeon—and now you are too."

"You're lucky I don't have a real bludgeon or I'd be swinging it at you right about now."

"Lee," I say. I reach out for her but she backs away from me. "Hell, Lee, I'm in love with you. I was *obsessed* with Emlyn Mohr. It was like an illness, an addiction. I was young and naive and she knew exactly what strings to pull on."

"I'll bet she did."

"Claude hated me for it," I say, cringing at the memory. "I ruined their friendship."

"Claude was her lover too?"

"No, no. Just her friend. He didn't want to spoil it by, you know . . ."

"Fucking her, like you did."

"Yeah," I say. "He didn't. Claude had better self-control than I had."

"But not anymore."

"He's in love with an illusion, Lee. No matter what he says, no matter how many times he's denied it, I know him. I see it. He's obsessed."

"I thought you just said love and obsession were two different things. Or that, in your case, they are."

"In Claude's case, they're the same." I look around for a shovel, thinking now would be a good time to start digging a grave for myself or perhaps an exceptionally long tunnel, one that'd leave me off in another planetary system.

"You still haven't told me a damned thing about you and Emlyn Mohr, Evan Becket," Lee says.

"Lee Shaw, I want to spend the rest of my life with you—us—our lives together. Don't you want that?"

"I do," she says. "I used to. Right at this second, I'm not so sure. And I've got a lot on my mind. I have to make plans."

"Make them with me," I say.

Lee says nothing. Hugs herself. The temperature's dropped about ten degrees since we started this pointless argument.

"I had an affair with her, okay? It started out, well, she seduced me, but, since you're not going to let this go until I confess everything, the truth is that she didn't have to seduce me. I thought I was in love with her. I stopped going to some of my classes, the ones I didn't care about. I was in danger of losing my place at the Acres. I was a provisional student, already on shaky ground.

"Then I found out what she was really like. I wasn't her only lover. And she was married as well. And Claude was furious with me. So I stopped seeing her."

"But you started up again."

"Yes, I did. I'd stop seeing her and then I'd be back there again, time after time. I couldn't help myself. I was like an addict. That's why I recognize the same thing in Claude. He's addicted to Ash—but there's a big difference."

"You mean because you were actually getting some *action* with Emlyn Mohr, and Claude can't do more than self-medicate when it comes to Ash? Or because you were deeply in love with Emlyn Mohr and Claude can't possibly be deeply in love with an *image*?"

"I mean because Ash doesn't exist and because I was a young, stupid fool."

"And now?"

"I'm still a fool," I say, "but, Lee, I'm in love with you. Surely you can see that. I was never *deeply in love* with Emlyn. I was never *in love* with her, no matter what I thought at the time. And Claude's not in love with Ash. He's obsessed with her."

"I can't tell how you feel, what you're thinking," Lee says as the chill breeze continues blowing her hair across her face. I want to hold her, reassure her, but she won't let me near her. She's hugging herself, warding me off.

"Don't do this," I say. "I've never been serious about anyone until I met you."

"I have," Lee says, "and it turned out very badly. This looks like it might as well."

"Lee, you're overreacting."

She walks back to the driver side of her small transcer.

"I might be," she says. "Or I might not be. I hope you have a good walk back to Claude's place."

"You can't mean that." Haven't I told her everything?

Lee fires up the transcer and leans over to look out the open passenger door. "Would you mind closing that?"

"I would mind," I say, my hands on the roof as I lean down to look into the transcer. "And what about the future? Our future?" She's leaving me here, in the dead-black woods. Are we breaking up?

"You mean the future of six months from now when our son is born?" she says as she reaches across the passenger seat, grabs the door handle, slams the door closed, and drives away.

An hour later, I'm back at Claude's place.

"This is *your* fault," I say to him at the door.

"Want some whiskey?" he says. "It'll warm you up."

I'm shivering. I nod. I go past Claude, who holds open the door, a giant smirk forming on his face.

CHAPTER 62

Claude

THIS FANCY SUIT itches, or I imagine it does. I'm an expert at imagining. I've heard that theory a lot since last night when Evan and I stayed up like we were back at the Acres, killing our fears with alcohol and futile conversation.

We outlasted Devil and his pal, who curled up together and fell asleep on us at right about the point where I was castigating Evan for, first, having a years-long affair with Emlyn, and, second, for screwing things up with Lee.

Then he told me that Lee was pregnant, and the two of us spent another hour coming up with names for their son. I was a particular fan of Atlas, which Evan rejected without even considering it.

I drop Evan off at his place—he let me drive. He lives in an entire house surrounded by actual grounds, right here in the city. His son will probably think nothing of it. It'll be all he ever knows. Son of the magrail tycoon. Assuming Lee ever talks to Evan again.

I go over to Olympia's place. She, unlike Evan, lives in a run-down tenement, more like the kind of place Evan lived in when he was a kid or where I'd live if I didn't have the farm.

Olympia has dressed for the occasion. She's wearing a floor-length sparkling silver sheath cinched with a broad red satin belt. Thematic, with the ice and inferno both on display. When I ask where her coat is, she says she doesn't need one—she'll be in the transcer and then in Double-I.

"How were you able to get a reservation?" she says on our way there.

"I might have had to drop Evan's name," I say, because I did. Until I mentioned him, even with the bribes I was offering, I'd gotten nowhere. But Evan's name plus the bribes worked wonders.

"It was very kind of you to invite me," she says. "Did your date bail on you?"

"You *are* my date," I say.

"But—Claude. You can't mean that. You and I both know that we're not interested in each other. Not like that. Not like a night out at Double-I. That's for someone, you know, *special.*"

"You are special," I say. "You stood up to Streeter. That's worth at least five nights out at Double-I."

We leave Evan's transcer with a well-dressed fellow whose suit is maybe 10 percent more expensive than my new itchy one, and he promises to take good care of the vehicle. Olympia and I go up an unimpressive flight of stairs to Ice Inferno's entrance. Olympia has to pull up the hem of her dress to keep from tripping on it.

I'm out of my element, which element is sitting at the console writing code. Arguing with Ash. Talking to Devil. Not out at the city's most remarkable venue, wearing an astoundingly uncomfortable suit, and accompanied by a woman I'm not even somewhat interested in.

We open the creaking door and walk into a dull corridor, paint peeling off the walls. This is the swank Ice Inferno? We make our way to the end of the corridor, where we're greeted by a hologram.

"Ice or Inferno?" the blinking-on-and-off hologram says. It's unclear if this is supposed to be a human being, a fantastical animal, a creature from another universe, or maybe even a humanoid machine.

"Ice," I say while Olympia says, "Inferno."

"Very good," says the hologram. "This way."

Of course the hologram can't show us what *this way* is, but a corridor is suddenly lit up with moving stripes of pale green lights, so we follow them.

That's all Ash is, I tell myself as we walk down this new corridor. A blinking-on-and-off image. Nothing else. She both is and isn't. Now she isn't any longer. Gone. Done for. I killed her even if I've failed in killing off my feelings for her.

If this, being here at Ice Inferno with Olympia Cowan, is the route to fixing my crushed heart, I'm going to take it.

We arrive at the end of the corridor and see a table in the distance, also lit by pale green lights, although these are arrayed in dots, not stripes. We head over. I see nothing so special about this place that it's warranted the fortune I've spent to be here.

"This is it?" Olympia says, obviously thinking the same thing.

"I guess so," I say. "Sorry."

"Well, maybe something happens," Olympia says.

We sit at the table and the moment we do, the room is transformed. The table and the banquette turn to ice. If it weren't for the cushions beneath us and to our backs, we'd freeze. The entire room is revealed to us in a slow, dramatic dance. Ice stalagmites hang down from the ceiling. The floor is covered with ice and snowbanks. The walls are blue ice with streaks of silver flashing through them. Music that sounds like a howling, cold wind surrounds us and frigid air comes across and at us in bursts.

Ice forms on my pricey suit jacket. Olympia's eyebrows get frosty and the tips of her no-longer-Ash-colored dark brown hair become crystallized. The boundless room in all its icy splendor seems to be a living entity as fractals of ice, frost, and snow sprout into existence all around us. Icy snowflakes swirl across the floor, across our table. Olympia catches one and licks it off her palm.

"Where is everyone else?" Olympia says, noticing what I've just noticed. Except for us, there's no one here.

"Damned if I know," I say.

We're both mesmerized by the effects of this false environment. Yet it feels real.

Is that why I've chosen this place? To remind myself that just because something seems to be true, seems to be real and exist, that it's still just an illusion?

Olympia comes closer to me. She must be cold. I'm cold, and I'm wearing an entire suit while she's clad in only the flimsy gown. I put my arm around her.

I imagine telling Evan about this, about how I'm not obsessed with Ash and how I'm just fine with a real person. I hug Olympia toward me and she snuggles up to my side. Ice crystals form around my shirt cuffs. Snow sparkles off Olympia's eyelashes.

The Ice Inferno is a full-out aphrodisiac. That's why it costs so much, why it's so in demand, why it's so hard to get a reservation here.

CHAPTER 63

Claude

I TURN AROUND to kiss Olympia and the cold breeze ceases while the entire room turns red. Heat rises from beneath and behind our seat. Flames flicker across the floor and hot red, orange, amber, and coal black stones send their smoke and heat through the limitless room. As though we're not in a room at all but in some infinite environment, neither inside nor out.

"Colin," Olympia says as her lips close in on mine.

"Ash," I say. "Ash, I need you." Throbbing heat now, accompanied by different music, low, slurry, ominous—both a warning and its cause.

"Colin," she says as she slings her leg over mine.

The table at our banquette ignites. I can feel the flames as they singe my pant legs. My heart is going to ignite next. That I'm here, with Ash, finally able to hold her, to be with her.

"Ash," I say, "Ash. Don't leave me again." I turn to embrace her more fully.

"Colin, my love," Ash says, climbing onto me. The seat behind us turns to embers. I wrap Ash in my arms. This is nothing like I dreamt it might be. The heat is consuming me, consuming us.

Ash's breaths are heaving. While she holds on to me, I squirm out of my suit jacket, sections of which are blossoming into fires. The banquette beneath and behind us is incandescent.

I kiss Ash in the prolonged, deep way I've dreamt about. Her silvery eyes shine with her love for me and I'm sure that she can see the same love in mine. Feeling her in my arms.

"This is everything I've ever wanted. *You're* everything I've ever wanted," I say to Ash. She's fire itself.

"Colin," she says between kisses. "Why did you have to die?"

"Ash," I say. "I need you. Now. Here."

She wraps her arms around my neck. Waves of burning air pulsate and flow around us.

"Make love to me, Colin," Ash says as a shocking blast of cold wind separates us. The fires around us freeze. The sky, which must be the ceiling but it's boundless, turns midnight blue and the hanging ice arrows re-form themselves.

"Are you ready to order now?" says the penetrating voice of a ghostlike server.

"You're not Colin," Ash says, except this isn't Ash but Olympia Cowan. She removes herself from my lap. The temperature has become subarctic.

"I was holding Ash," I say to Olympia, "but now you're here. How is that possible?"

"Ice Inferno plays tricks with your desires," says our server, who seems to be floating in the snowy air. "With your perceptions. Would you like to see a menu?"

"Yes," Olympia says just as I say, "No."

"Here you are," says the server, unfurling a scroll that hangs in the air in front of Olympia.

Our ghost server becomes outlined in ice crystals.

I glance at the menu. *For your pleasure*, it says over a long list of items, none of them seeming to be food or drink, yet it's impossible to tell from their names: Phoenix Parallax; The Devil's Choice; Ice Carousel; Snow Blanket; Flash and Freeze; Burnt Horizon.

"Can you describe these to us?" Olympia says, pointing to the list.

The room, our surround, is all ice and snow again, yet I'm still on fire. But Ash isn't here. She was never here. She couldn't've been here. Or anywhere.

"You've cheated us," I say to the hovering server.

Olympia turns to me.

"You're not Colin," she says, moving away from me, the tears in her eyes freezing as they fall. Her cheeks become streaked with glazed spikes.

"Are you unhappy with the effect?" says our server. The ghost rolls in the air, gathering snowfall around itself. The snow forms into a dark red cape, hiding the ghost's face in its hood. The snow becomes falling embers.

"Claude," Olympia says as the tears melt and flow down her cheeks. "I didn't know it was like this here. Can we leave?"

"Yes, of course," I say. I gaze around the unbordered space as the heat intensifies. Where is the exit? How did we get in here?

Olympia stands up. The banquette is too hot to sit on, so I stand as well.

"How do we get out of here?" Olympia says to the server, an invisible being inside an oversized dark red cloak.

"But you have yet to experience the best part," the server says.

I glance over at Olympia, who's becoming Ash again. I try to convince myself it's a trick of some sort but my body doesn't understand.

Ash goes past me.

"It must be this way," she says.

"No one ever leaves just yet," says the server from inside the cloak. "Are you sure you wouldn't like to sample the Phoenix Parallax?"

Ash is running now, and I run after her although I don't know where she's headed. I can see only glowing coals, the conflagration around us, embers and droplets of contained fire as they drip from above onto our hair, our shoulders. The floor below burning ever stronger.

"Ash, wait," I say, but she runs faster, into a wall of flames. I follow her.

We emerge on the other side into what looks like a storeroom. It's cold again. There's an EXIT sign over a door. I see it just after Olympia has, and she's racing toward it.

We're outside now, in an alleyway, in the black harsh night with a cold light glowing from a strip of blue on the near wall.

"How could you do this to me, Claude?" Olympia says. She's crying now, her tears no longer flames or icicles. She's clutching herself and I curse myself for choosing this place.

"I didn't know," I say just as Evan's transcer appears. The man who took it from me gets out and says, "I'm sorry you have to leave so soon, Mr. Ryerson, Ms. Cowan. You've missed most of the show."

"I don't want to see any *show*," Olympia says as her tears turn to sobs. "I want Colin back. I want him to be alive again. How could you be so cruel?"

She gets into the transcer. She cries all the way back to her apartment, talking between sobs.

"I told Colin not to go," she says. "I *begged* him not to go. The storm warnings. But he wouldn't listen."

"No one ever listens," I say as my mind reaches into itself, hoping to bring back those astounding, uncontrolled sensations. I was there with Ash. Not with Olympia. Yes, I'd brought Olympia to Ice Inferno, but once the Inferno arose, Olympia was gone, off on her own adventure. Ash was with me. Her lips on mine. She straddled my lap. My jacket caught fire. Ash, if you only understood how much I want you, need you. It's love, not obsession, but if it is obsession, I don't care.

"How cruel of them. To make it seem as though he's still alive." Olympia's sobs increase. "We had our whole future and he squandered it. Claude, I'm still so angry. I didn't know I was."

"I've never been to Ice Inferno before. I didn't realize—"

"I hate you for taking me there," Olympia says. "To be with him again, like that. It's sadistic. Torture." She buries her head in her lap and breaks into gasping sobs.

"I'm sorry. I'm so sorry," I say. "It seems I can't do anything right." While I'm saying this I'm wondering if I can go back, if my reservation is still good, if I go there alone, will Ash still come to be with me? Or do they need someone else there, in order to trade them off or whatever it is they must be doing?

Because, unlike Olympia, who thinks what just happened is cruelty itself, I think it's a miracle. To be with Ash, really *be* with her. Even if it's just for another few moments. I want that. To see her, feel her, taste her.

We get to Olympia's apartment building.

"I'm sorry, Claude," she says as she recovers from her grief long enough to speak to me. "I don't hate you. It's just—Colin. I didn't remember how much I miss him until . . . It was so hard at first and I thought it'd never be that hard again. That I'd lived through the worst of it. But it's all back, as though it's just happened."

"I'm the one who's sorry, Olympia. I didn't realize—"

"Maybe it's not like that for everyone," she says. "You couldn't've known."

"Don't make excuses for me. I should have found out. I thought it was just a sort of immersive-experience-type place. Like the Honeycomb. Only more so."

"Don't come upstairs with me, Claude."

"Turn on your lights after you get to your apartment," I say. "I'll wait till I see them." I have to make sure she's safe. Buildings like hers can be dodgy. It's bad enough that I'm responsible for setting off her grief. At least I can make sure she gets home all right.

She gets out of the transcer, picks up her trailing skirt, and runs into her building. A few moments later her lights go on and she comms me: *I'm fine. Thank you anyway.*

I drive back to Ice Inferno. I sit across the street from its unmarked entrance, pull the seat back, close my eyes, and think about its nickname: Double-I. Not just the initials of *Ice Inferno*, but is this its name because it turns its patrons into two selves? I and I? The self who made the reservation, who arrives, who follows the pale green lights, who marvels at the effects—and the self whose buried desires erupt into uncontrollable need, expressing themselves with raging abandon, uncaring of all else.

Yet this can't be everyone's experience or I might've heard about it before.

Was this just my experience? Mine and Olympia's? Because we asked for both ice and inferno? Because we've both been destroyed by the impossibility of our ever being with the person we want most? The person we love beyond any other?

Because her Colin is dead and can't be here ever again.

Because my Ash never existed and never will.

I go home and comm Evan. He comms me back his one-word message: *Lee.*

I head out to the barn and sit among the rubble, not even bothering to turn on the lantern. Bad enough that I can feel my tears, that I can't stop them. No point in seeing them too.

It starts snowing. The world transforms itself over and over very again.

CHAPTER 64

Today's Trends

WE WERE DOWNTOWN last night and spotted none other than the master coder Claude Ryerson himself, late of his brilliant stream of successes at Centerstorm and lately—of course! as you all know!—as Ash's manager. Ryerson was parked in a fabulous new-edition transcer right across the street from Ice Inferno.

We admit it—we peered into the passenger side of his transcer to see if Ash was with him. We were very discreet, don't worry! Our Certain Other was out with us for the evening and we were strolling by, so breezy and unaffected. We were even wearing our saturnia necklace for our date. Oh! The necklace is so so so gorgeous! Thank you, Certain Other! We love our necklace—and you!

But—Ash wasn't there in the passenger seat. No one was there. Ryerson was alone. Wearing a fashionable suit, we must say, despite the rumors that he's usually more, well, down-market. Yet, trust us on this, he's quite handsome. Really, we think he'd be the perfect match for Ash herself—and who knows what goes on out of the public eye? He *is* her manager, after all. It's happened before.

We restrained ourselves, with the help of our Certain Other, who's usually not restrained at all, which is one of the things we love most!

But, no Ash. Definitely no Ash at all anywhere. Claude Ryerson was alone, and we used all our combined restraint and left him alone, we are proud to report. No matter how much we wanted to ask him a thousand questions and get the information we all want so desperately.

Now for our own confession: we went to Ice Inferno. Yes! Don't say it! We know what you're thinking: How could we possibly afford such a thing? Please understand, this was a gift from someone we know who *can* afford it. We were hesitant to accept, but our friend insisted. And although our Certain Other and we were able to restrain ourselves from knocking on the window of Claude Ryerson's transcer and pleading for information about Ash, even though we wanted to more than we can express here, we were unable to restrain ourselves from accepting a free night out at Ice Inferno. Ask yourselves—would *you* be able to turn down such a great opportunity?

And now we're here to report on it, although we won't include spoilers, since part of the experience is how unusual and surprising it is. And it *is* unusual and surprising.

Is it worth the price? you want to know. Of course you want to know! The answer is: yes yes yes and yes! A resounding positive. Absolutely. More yes. More *very* yes. (Well, we cannot help thinking about Ash. We just spotted Claude Ryerson, after all!)

Oh! Ice Inferno. We won't describe the details of any of it—you must go there yourself! accept any gifts or save up!—but we will say that we and our Certain Other had the experience of a lifetime, that we reveled in every delicious moment, in every taste, every sensation, every extraordinary sight, sound, smell, touch, flavor. Every breathless, ceaseless wonder of it.

We will say without reservation or hesitation or condition of any sort that what they serve up at Ice Inferno—oh! just the name now thrills us and our Certain Other as well—is unmatched and incomparable. Extraordinary. Shocking. Delightful. Extreme. Oh! We would have more words but you must go there yourselves! Words are nearly useless in situations like these!

We can assure you that to spend a night at Ice Inferno is life-changing and more stimulating than even a trip to an unknown destination. And it has spurred us on to nonstop passion, as though we and our Certain Other just met each other. In fact, we are with our Certain Other right now, both of us quite sweaty and needy, so we must sign off.

But before we do, let us put in a good word for the beleaguered Fierys. Reda and Quinn—we love you and are devastated over the treatment you've been lately receiving from the too skillful archcritic Streeter. We're sure he's frustrated that since Ash's disappearance he doesn't have her to write about and he's decided to take it out on you two. Just remember that Streeter has been generous with his praise of you in the past—and he will be again! We're sure of it.

Meanwhile, please contact us if, unlike us, *you* have seen Ash! We might be distracted by—ah! yes! again! don't ever stop!—but we always want to know about Ash. We want to find her, to help her find her past. To have her come back to us.

Yes! Please! Oh! It's even *better* than when we and our Certain Other had just met. Because now we know what to do and how to do it. Although we can never get enough. Ever!

Contact us anytime—M @ *Today's Trends*. You know how to reach us.

CHAPTER 65

Ash

I'VE NEVER HAD a dream like this before—less dreamlike and more real than any actual experience. I'd gone home, back to the abandoned building, and sat on the floor. Disgust and frustration fought each other over which would win out.

It's cold here and has been since the season changed. I was wrapped in my scavenged coat, but I couldn't seem to get warm. Streeter had laughed at me, sneered his patented sneer.

"You're no more Ash than I am," he'd said as he snapped his fingers, demanding the server show up.

"Why would I want to impersonate her?" I said. "And, if I did, wouldn't I be making more of an effort to look just like her?" I'd already used this argument but it was the only one I had that sounded right.

"My foolish *friend*," he said, using the word *friend* as a weapon. "*Anyone* would want to be Ash. She's famous, she's wealthy, she's beautiful, she's everywhere and on everyone's mind. And she's missing. What better time for an impostor to try and convince me she's the real Ash? She's so easy to try to replicate—scores of vidcasters do it every day, all of them as unconvincing as you are. And ever since she invented that phony amnesia story anyone else can just pretend they don't know anything substantive about themselves because their memory is gone. Because *Ash's* memory is gone. Which of course it isn't. It's a trick. I'll give you that—you're plying away at a trick here yourself. But it won't work."

"But I don't have any memories of my past," I said. "I didn't invent the *amnesia story*." In my imaginings of this meeting, it hadn't gone this way. I knew Streeter was uncaring, but I was sure he'd realize I was really myself. Who else could I very be?

"No, my dear, of course you didn't invent the amnesia story. You're not clever enough for that. Ash did all the work. No matter what I've written and said about her, even I can't deny that she's immensely clever. And her disappearance has proved to be one of her cleverest ploys yet."

"All I want is your help finding my past," I said, hoping that perhaps he was merely testing me to make sure I was really Ash. "You have connections."

"If you think I'm going to give my assistance to a two-bit pretender, well—ah, here's the server. Where have you been? I'm starving."

"I didn't want to disturb you, sir," the server said. "You seemed to be having a serious discussion."

"Hah," he said. "I want the house special."

"Yes, sir," the server said, then turned to me. "And you?"

"Oh, she won't be staying," Streeter said.

I left. I came back here. The cold intensified.

Nothing had turned out the way I'd envisioned, the way I'd hoped. Streeter wouldn't help me. He didn't even believe that I'm myself. Even the sumptuous meal I'd looked forward to hadn't materialized.

"I want to go home," I said to the walls and floor of my apartment in the abandoned building. I pulled myself tighter into my coat, wishing I had a new one instead of this patched-together collection of rags. Wishing I knew where home was, where it would be. Where it had been.

I fell asleep, which I've found to be the best remedy against the subarctic temperature in here. It's no warmer, but I don't seem to mind. Then I had the dream.

The frost crystallized around me. I was turning into a statue made of ice and snow, and I marveled at the effect. Icicles hung from my upper arms. My lips were frosted over and when I looked to my left, I saw the same thing was happening to Claude.

His coral-colored eyes were like coral itself, with sharp edges, but shimmering, the color given a different, new life by the sparkling snow on his eyelashes. The ice, the cold, and my fears paralyzed me. We were sitting on a banquette made of ice bricks and the table in front of us was a snowbank.

"Help me find my past," I said to Claude. I had to ask him. "No one else will help me." Claude knew. I was certain of that.

"You should never have gone to Streeter," he said. "He's not someone who'd understand."

"*I* don't understand," I said. "But you do. I know you do."

"Ash," Claude said, "I tried to destroy you, yet it seems you persist anyway."

"It's so cold in here," I said.

"It's supposed to be." He seemed to know something that I didn't, or couldn't. He knew about my past as well. I saw the truth of that.

Snow started falling, yet I was sure we were indoors, although I didn't know why I was sure. I felt the flakes on my cheeks and shoulders. A raw breeze blew across us, then a frigid wind howled. The bell sleeves of my blouse stiffened with my transformation into an ice sculpture.

There were things I wanted to tell Claude, but I couldn't remember them.

"I've lost my memories," I said.

"You have no memories," he said.

"It's so cold."

He put his arm around my shoulders and moved me closer to him.

"Why are you doing this?" I said, the words emerging as though from somewhere, someone, else.

"Ash," he said as he touched my cheek. The ice was already melting. Beneath us, the seat was creating the warmth I needed so much.

"Claude," I said. "Why can't it always be like this?"

"Ash, I need you."

I put my arms around him. "Claude, I want you."

"Yes." His eyes were amber, glowing. The heat was consuming us.

I climbed onto his lap. He held me. "Don't leave me again," he said. "Ash."

"Claude," I said. I had nothing more to say. His name was sufficient. Our embrace was more than sufficient.

Our lips found each other's as the fire intensified. If I'd been an ice statue before, I'd become a flaming torch, the flames uncontainable, bursting into a wild pattern. Claude's jacket caught fire and he took it off. His hands were on me. I straddled his lap. Our surround pulsed with heat, flame, fire, and fogged smoke.

"This is everything I've ever wanted. *You're* everything I've ever wanted," Claude said to me.

"Claude," I said, unable to say more, consumed by the heat, the passion, my need. His lips on mine, his arms around me. My forgotten past merged into the fire we'd created, subsumed by need, by love.

"Ash," Claude said.

Then the fire turned back to ice. The snow swirled around us. My arm froze in place. Claude got up, started running, leaving me, but I couldn't move.

I woke with a start. Back here in my new home, where now a voice is calling to me.

"Open up. You have a visitor."

My frozen body melts again. Claude's here. I didn't dream him. He's come for me. Everything I dreamt was true. He needs me. And he knows the truth. He'll tell me. Everything will fall into the right place, the one where I belong, where I very exist.

I get up and open the door, but Ginny's alone. Claude isn't here with her.

"It's late," I say.

"Really?" Ginny says. "But your visitor wouldn't come when it's early, would he?"

It must be Claude. It has to be. Streeter couldn't't've followed me here. He was still at the Black Dome and hadn't been served his meal yet.

"He's in your apartment?" I'm standing in my doorway and Ginny is out in the hall. It's getting colder by the second. My coat's fallen open.

"I see you wore the blouse," she says. "Come with me."

I follow her into her apartment. She closes the half door behind us, turns to me, and says, "Who are you?"

"Ash," I say. At least Ginny seems to believe me, although she may not know who I am. Who I was.

"I'm going to sue the landlord," she says as she leaves me alone, flouncing out of the living room, her curls looking like springs circling her head.

I sit on the sofa and wait. Claude isn't here. My dream wasn't reality. My past is as far away as it ever was.

"I don't know why you thought Streeter, of all people, could help you," says a familiar voice.

CHAPTER 66

Ash

"DEV," I SAY as he leaps up on to the sofa to sit beside me.

"I expected more from you by now," he says.

"I've disappointed you too?"

"Too?"

"I've been a constant disappointment to Claude," I say. "I've never been able to do as he asked. That's why he had to destroy our connection."

"Ash," Devil says, "I've left you alone so that you'll understand for yourself, but you seem more confused than ever."

"Where's Bobby?"

"Bobby's sister needed her to babysit. You just want her here because you know she'd go easier on you."

"I want to go home," I say, "but Claude destroyed everything. I have no place to return to."

"Your problem is that you're in love with him."

"I am not," I say, the lie hurting me. A physical hurt, like I'm being jabbed in the neck with one of the icicles from the dream— hard, sharp, too cold.

"What are your plans?" he says. Devil doesn't like chitchat.

"I have to find my holding account," I say. "Then I'll be able to get a better place. Figure out what to do."

"Holding account?" Devil laughs. "Ash, Ash. You really haven't learned anything, have you?"

"I learned how to survive." I have to defend myself, yet I'm defending myself against one of my only friends. One of my other friends doesn't even know who I am.

"Survival isn't enough," Dev says.

"It's all I can do right now. But if you know where my holding account is—"

"You have no holding account."

"Now you sound like Claude. *You have no past.* That can't be true. All the products I sold. The cosmetics, the necklace, the furnishings. All the millions of viewers I had. Quinn Fiery told me that I had to be quite wealthy."

"*Claude* is quite wealthy."

"We're not talking about him."

"Yes, we are," Dev says. He stretches out full length on Ginny's sofa. He's a long cat and his fur is like velvet. "We are."

I can't talk about Claude. I want to be back in the dream with him, touching him, hearing him tell me beautiful things—not having him relegated to the harsh reality that Devil is about to expose.

Devil says nothing. He licks his front-right paw and sighs.

"I'm supposed to figure this out for myself," I say.

Devil yawns.

"Claude is the only one who profited from my vidcasts. Not me." Did Dev realize that I had to say this in order to face the truth? "He used me."

Devil looks away.

"And I let him."

"Ash," Devil says as he turns back to me, "you don't understand this at all."

"Tell me, then. Please tell me. And if you know anything at all about my past, just say it. Whatever it is, I have to know."

"I can't tell you," Devil says. "It's not in my job description."

I laughed. "A cat has no job description."

"Devil." Ginny emerges from the depths of her apartment. "I have some fresh whipped cream made up for you," she says. "Why don't you come into the kitchen?"

Devil gets up. I stand up.

"Oh, not you," Ginny says to me. "I don't know you well enough. I don't even know your name."

"Ash," I say. "My name's Ash. Don't you remember? You gave me this blouse."

"You haven't returned my scroll," she says, forgetting that I did return it.

"You have to get a job," Devil says to me before he trots across the room and races past Ginny.

"Don't leave the door open," Ginny says, dismissing me.

On the way out, I make sure to close Ginny's half door. I go back to my place. It's not really my place, but I'm living here. *Staying* here. *Surviving* here. It's a mess. It's nothing like my room, the one in my vidcast. There's hardly anything here and I don't keep the place clean. No one would want any of the objects I'm now surrounded with. Even I couldn't sell them. They're worn out, frayed, broken, stained, ugly.

Claude has taken all my earnings, if they were ever mine. Worse yet, he's keeping them for himself.

I'm no closer to finding out about my past than I ever was, and Devil, who must know, refuses to tell me.

I have no holding account.

I need to get a job.

So the next morning I get a job doing the only thing I really know how to do: sell.

CHAPTER 67

Ash

GINNY GIVES ME more items from her veritable storehouse of clothes. "You have to give them back," she says to me. "But you can't go to work like that."

"How do you know Devil?" I say.

"We go way back," she says. "He and Chadwick had a business together at one time."

"Chadwick?" I remember the name from her holding account, but I can't tell her that. I was prying.

"Did you know *me* then too?" A long shot, but maybe she did.

"How could I have?" she says.

"Why's that?"

"I don't know you now," Ginny says, gracing me with a rare smile. My eyes cloud with tears I don't dare shed. She'll ask me and I'll have to tell her how much I love Claude's smile. How rare it is. How much I miss him.

"If you go to that store across from the Honeycomb, they'll hire you right away," Ginny says. "You've got the look they like."

"What look?"

"Well," Ginny says. We're standing in the ice-cold hallway, where we've met so she can give me the clothes. "It's just . . . something. You've got it."

"Thanks, Ginny," I say.

"Good luck," Ginny says. She never calls me by my name. I don't think she knows it.

I go back to my place and change into the most stylish and also most innocuous outfit in the stack. Some of the clothes Ginny's given me are too noticeable, but this seems just right. I comb my hair, which is short, unstyled, and a saturated dark brown now. I haven't looked like Ash for months, not since I left Claude's place. No wonder Streeter didn't recognize me.

Across the way from the Honeycomb is a black-lacquered door with a lion's-head doorknocker. Is this the store that Ginny meant? *Is it a store?* I use the knocker, and a tall, impossibly slim man opens the door a crack.

"You can't shop here without a recommendation," he says, looking me up and down.

"I'm here for a job," I say.

"Hmm." He closes the door, I hear the sound of something metallic, then he opens the door again. "Come in," he says. "What's your name?"

I hadn't thought of this part. I can't be Ash or they'll never hire me. Instead, they'll broadcast to the world that I've returned or, like Streeter, think that I'm an impostor trying to trade on Ash's fame. No. That's not why I climbed out of the window. It's not why I left.

I have to find my real self, not the self I was pretending to be in order to do my job. Although I don't remember when I was hired for that job. Yet I must have been.

I wonder if I'll remember this, right now, if I'm hired, or if this will also vanish as if it never occurred. Do my memories all recede at some predetermined threshold, evading me one by one as they disappear into an unreachable past?

I sort through an enormous reservoir of names and say, "Madison Brice."

"You look very familiar," says the too-slim man.

"I get that a lot," I say.

"Have you done much modeling?" He leads me back through the rococo entryway and into an area that looks like a stage but there are only a few plush chairs facing it.

"Oh yes," I say. "I'm an expert." An expert at presenting myself in ways that are guaranteed to give my viewers an urgent need to purchase whatever it is I'm selling. I'm confident of this ability even if I don't know how or why I have it.

"We'll try you out," he says.

My skill is already at work. I've sold myself, which is the only thing I've ever really sold. It's the only thing anyone ever sells. I learned that from viewing the Fiery vidcast. They freely give away all their secrets, which is one of their best sales techniques.

"Trent Salwer," the slim man says, holding out his hand.

"Thank you, Trent. I need the work."

"One of life's tragedies." Trent makes a kind of humming sound after he says this.

"I like to work," I say although I have no idea if I really do. Did I like being an influencer? Does modeling involve anything more than selling? Will I have to cede back the small parts of myself that I've managed to locate since I left my room? I'll find out.

I'll also have to find out how to create a holding account for Madison Brice, since that's who I am now. But that should be easy, shouldn't it? It won't be like it was when I left Claude, when I climbed out of the window and didn't know where I was headed or how to get anywhere or do anything.

Now I know where I'm headed. I'm a model at the luxurious nameless store across the street from the Honeycomb. I have a job. I've taken Dev's advice. When I've accumulated enough credits I'll be able to search more for my past. Or perhaps someone I meet here will have the information I'm seeking.

Or perhaps something else will happen and I'll find out everything I need to know.

Or perhaps I'll see Claude on the street, now that I'm out on the street more. And he'll see me and say the things to me that he said in the real very dream.

CHAPTER 68

Claude

EVAN HAS FORCED me to come with him to Bear and Brandon's. They're having some kind of a party for the unborn twins, which party, Lee tells me on the way over, is really for Brandon.

"Claude dear, you came," Brandon says to me at the door. She and Bear live on what I guess is called an estate. Evan and Lee had to pick me up at the farm to drive me out here. Too far to bike, and anyway I've never fixed the tires.

I haven't been going anywhere since I got back from my "date" with Olympia Cowan.

I've been holed up in the house, playing Dad's old game, the first one with Imari herself as the centerpiece. The game's obsolete but it's better than any of the games I've ever invented—the ones Project One stole the rights to, and even the last one, for Centerstorm. Dad had more talent than I could recognize or ever get close to. If I'm supposed to be a coding genius, then he was a coding super genius, transcendent.

Also I've been delving into my old program, the one that Dad improved, the one whose job it was, or is, to find my missing mother.

But it's a hollow enterprise. I might as well be spending my time trying to find the "missing" Ash.

My mother created me, then she disappeared, as though she never existed.

I created Ash, then I destroyed her although she never actually *was*.

Is this wrongheaded reinterpretation of my history why I did it? Why I do anything?

I've dressed up for this party, shoved my body into the itchy suit I wore weeks ago on that disastrous date at Ice Inferno.

The material still itches. But it's as though I'm inhaling Ash's distinct scent, her perfume. Olympia must've been wearing it that night, although I don't remember smelling this then. Yet everyone loves this perfume, along with all the other Ash and Ash-inspired products, so Olympia might very well have been wearing it. Or perhaps the aroma was clinging to the banquette and the scent was seared into the suit fabric during one of the infernos.

Yet even though I never could have smelled it on Ash, it's Ash's scent. The aroma puts me in the immediate sphere of her self, the one she invented without my input, apart from the code and its directives.

My holding account is so stuffed with credits that even if I wanted twenty more of these uncomfortable suits, I wouldn't notice the expense. I've paid off all the mortgages on the property and even that has barely made a dent in my holdings. I still haven't fixed the barn, though. I can't face it although I go in there sometimes and just sit or kick over the remnants of my once-grand plan. Do my best not to think about Ash, not to *obsess* about her. About very Ash herself.

"We had to pry him out of his pit," Evan says to Brandon.

"I wish someone would pry these"—she points to her extreme twin-extended belly—"out of their pit," she says. "I've just about had it. You have no idea—"

"Well, actually, I have I *some* idea," Lee says.

"That's nothing," Brandon says. "That's just one. This is a veritable army."

"Well, troops, let's go sit down, shall we?" Bear says, coming up behind Brandon and wrapping his huge arms around her. "We've got another month to go."

"I'm surprised you don't know how many hours," I say.

"Seven hundred and forty-three," Brandon says without hesitation. "Interminable."

"Do you have their names? We're going to call our son Atlas," Lee says.

"We are *not*," Evan says. "Atlas Becket is a figment of Claude Ryerson's imagination."

"I like it," Lee says. "It's different."

I bask in the undeserved compliment. "Atlas Becket has a certain strength to it," I say, rubbing it in. Evan despises the name and I'd come up with it only as a joke, but ever since Evan and Lee patched things up and he told her about it, she's latched on. She loves it.

Evan clenches his fists and glares at me.

"Oh, Evan, don't mind Claude. You know how he is. He's in a creative slump, what with Ash finished for the time being—" But I don't let Brandon finish.

"Time being? No. She's never returning," I say. "Anyway, she couldn't. I destroyed the console with all the programs on it." Furthermore, there was no *being*. Not with Ash. She only seemed to be.

By now we've all made it to our seats in the vast living room, which is the size of a grand duke's ballroom. An imaginary grand duke, since I know no one with such a title, if there is anyone, which I doubt.

"You don't have backup?" Evan says. "That's poor planning."

"Seven hundred and forty-three lousy hours. I'm so damned uncomfortable, I don't have another seven minutes of this in me." With extra drama and help from Bear, Brandon leans herself back onto one of the several extra plush sofas in the room. I'm sitting on or, rather, sinking into, a red upholstered chair that looks like its design was based on a hippopede folded in half and forced to impersonate a piece of furniture.

Lee is curled up on one of the quasi-normal sofas, her feet under her, next to Evan.

"The program became unmanageable," I say. "I couldn't back it up. I was running out of space as it was and I couldn't store it somewhere outside."

"Funny you keep saying *it*," Lee says. "I mean, I know Ash wasn't *real* but, well, she still seems very real to me. I feel like I knew her."

"Even I feel that way sometimes, and I've always known the truth," Brandon says. "Fascinating, isn't it? Ash had a powerful presence, some sort of indescribable allure. She drew you in, made you care. But it's just a very carefully designed trick."

"The hell it is," I say. "If I'd been more careful she never would've done half the things she did."

"Like climbing out the window?" Bear says.

"Like saying any damned thing she pleased," I say.

"Claude's in love with her," Evan says. He's still pissed off about Atlas and is trying to get back at me.

"What crap," I say.

"Defensive," Evan says.

"If these two *things* in my belly don't emerge soon I'm going to kill someone," Brandon says.

"At least one of them isn't named Atlas." Evan glares his best not-quite-friendly glare at me.

"I love that name," Lee says. "We're keeping it. Atlas Shaw Becket. I think it's perfect."

"No son of mine is going to be named after a defunct mythological being," Evan says.

"We're thinking of naming the twins Isis and Osiris," Bear says, helping me out.

"I thought we'd decided on Douglas and Persephone," Brandon says, not looking, sounding, or seeming at all disturbed by Bear's new suggestion: naming their twins after two defunct gods who were not only brother and sister but also husband and wife.

"It's impossible to decide until you see the baby," Evan says, like he knows what he's talking about.

"That's because you're not *connected*," Lee says. "Our son"—she points at her belly—"is definitely Atlas."

"Claude, this all your fault." Evan does his best to keep a straight face, but he starts laughing. "Actually," he says, "it's my fault. I never should've told Lee."

The sound of wind chimes rustles through the room.

"Bear, could you answer that?" Brandon says. "I don't know if I can get up more than one or two more times tonight. Or *ever*."

Bear gets up.

"*More* people are coming?" I say. I'm already feeling crowded, even in this enormous room. I'm used to being alone or in only Devil's company. And the mouse. Or occasionally the *mice*.

Bear returns with two of the last people in the multiverse I want to see: Quinn and Reda Fiery.

"Oh, Reda, I'm so glad you could come," Brandon says from her throne on the sofa. "Quinn said he wasn't sure you could make it."

Reda leans over to give Brandon a hug, then stands back up, stares at me, and launches right into her attack without pausing for even the briefest of segues.

"Claude, I was hoping to see you here," Reda says. "What have you done with Ash? Where is she?"

"You didn't say you'd invited that bastard over there," Quinn says, pointing his entire arm at me. A finger was insufficient to contain his rage.

"You didn't tell me you invited Quinn fucking Fiery," I say, standing up. I'm much taller than Quinn and although not as suave-looking as the creep, at least I'm wearing a decent suit tonight.

"You're holding her prisoner, aren't you?" Reda says. "Part of your scheme."

Reda heads straight at me, but Quinn holds her back.

"This is my job," he says, taking a swing at me.

I dodge the onslaught and shove my hands into my suit jacket pockets.

To keep myself from killing him.

CHAPTER 69

Claude

"BOYS, BOYS, THIS is a party," Brandon says, grimacing. "At least it's supposed to be."

"Are you all right?" Bear says to her. Besides the Fierys' arrival and simultaneous attacks on me, something else has changed. The atmosphere in the room is decidedly thickening.

"No, I'm not all right," Brandon says. "This is supposed to be a party and instead it's turning into fight night."

"Brandon, I can't believe you're entertaining Claude Ryerson," Reda says. "What he's done to Ash—with Ash—I don't even know how to put it. Ughhghh. I'm so so angry! He's done *something*. He *must have*. Ash would *never* have just disappeared like that. I don't believe it. Ash was the most popular, the most successful, the most *everything*. Then she just—*poof!*—disappeared. Without any warning. It's seems obvious there's only one reason for it: She was trying to get away from her *manager*. *Escape* him. And now she's just *gone*."

Quinn's seething and looks like he might want to try out another punch.

Evan stands up and puts his hand on Quinn's back.

"I think we should tell them," Evan says to me over Quinn's shoulder.

"No," I say. Too many people know already.

"Evan's right," Lee says. "It's all going to come out eventually anyway."

"You've fucking *killed* her, haven't you?" Quinn says, shaking off Evan's hand. "I *knew* there was something *else* I despised about you."

"Ash isn't dead," Evan says, then looks at me.

"Bloody hell," I say. "Tell them. I *already* told Quinn but he wasn't paying attention. And anyway, it doesn't really matter."

"Ash doesn't exist," Evan says.

"Your ugly friend"—I think Quinn means me—"already tried that shit out on me. Try again, Becket."

"No, it's true. Ash isn't a real person," Evan says. He's repositioned himself so he's looking directly at Quinn.

"The fuck she isn't. We went on a date together." Quinn's defiant, which attitude the sophisticated vidcaster seems to have worked on until it's been honed into a sort of nonchalant truth.

"You may have thought you were on a date with Ash, but I guarantee you it was someone else, pretending to be Ash," Brandon says, helping Evan out.

"I didn't *think* anything. I was. She was. We were at the Honeycomb together. Ash was sitting right there." He points again, as though he's still at the Honeycomb and the Ash impersonator is sitting across from him and doesn't mind being pointed at with such a crude gesture. "We talked. It can't've been anyone else. That's impossible."

Quinn stops pointing and crosses his arms over his chest. Now he looks like he's posing for a picture whose caption is *Justified and proud of it*.

"But it's more impossible that Ash was there with you," I say. "She's nothing but code. She's not real. She doesn't exist and never has existed."

"You are so wrong," Reda Fiery says.

"Wrong?" Quinn says. "He's *lying*. Not wrong. *Lying*. I'm in love with her."

"You and millions of other people," Brandon says. "That's why we're still selling so well."

"We?" Reda says. "You're in on this, Brandon?"

"Claude needed investors," Evan says.

"I demand you bring Ash here immediately," Reda says. "I'm tired of all this bullshit. The next Fiery vidcast is going to be all about you, Claude Ryerson, and how you manipulated and used Ash for your own benefit and about how now you've got her hidden away somewhere. I'll make sure you're arrested and never see the light of day again. Whatever horrific thing you've done to Ash, ten thousand *million* more horrific and unthinkable things will be done to you."

"Reda," Bear says, "Claude's telling the truth."

I gather hope. Bear is the sort of person who people just believe. He's got that kind of inherent gravitas. He's undoubtable.

"Claude invented Ash," Bear says. "She's *virtual*. She was never really real. She was an image only. That's all. No matter how it seemed."

"Prove it," Quinn says.

"I destroyed the console," I say. "My only proof is that everyone in this room knows about it, about Ash. She wasn't real."

"That's not proof," Quinn says. "Not even close."

He shifts his stance to lean on the other foot. I do my best not to mimic his movements, although I also have my arms folded across my chest now.

"Claude's an expert at this sort of code," Evan says. "He learned from his father. It's in his blood. Quinn—no matter how convincing Ash seemed, she was nothing more than an invented image. An animated figure."

"She has amnesia," Quinn says. "So you're using that to make it seem like she's not an actual person. So you can continue to do whatever it is you're doing to her. With her."

"Quinn, you looked at every corner of my house." But I can see how pointless this argument is. Quinn still looks homicidal.

"You really think we're going to believe you?" Reda says. If Quinn looks homicidal, his sister looks like she could kill me just by thinking really hard about it.

"You've got her somewhere else," Quinn says. "A secret hideaway. You'll bring her back out when it suits you, when sales die down, when you think she's been forgotten and her reappearance will generate the most interest. The most *return* for your investment. You're doing irreparable harm to Ash—all in the name of profit."

"You know about her past, don't you?" Reda says. "That's why you had to do whatever it is you've done to her. You want her past to remain a secret."

"That much is true," I say. "I do know about her past. She doesn't have one unless you think that my invention of her amounts to a *past*. Unless you think the countless hours I spent on perfecting the code is Ash's past."

Quinn seems ready to explode with either fury or disappointment. I can't tell which. I, on the other hand, feel preternaturally calm. Perhaps explaining Ash's unreality is helping me come to grips with my emotional attachment to her—to the *idea* of her.

"No one could have impersonated her that effectively," Quinn says. "I've watched countless hours of Ash's vidcasts and I was there, at the Honeycomb, with Ash herself."

"It's impossible," Brandon says. "Someone did a brilliant job of fooling you."

"She nodded to me on her vidcast," Quinn said. "We sent messages to each other on a private channel. She was *right there* at the same table with me. Talking to me. Existing. Real. There's was nothing virtual or invented or *impostor* about her."

"Remember Imari?" I say.

"What about her?" Reda says. "You mean from that antique game? I remember her. She was kick-ass fun."

"But you didn't think she was real," I say.

"Of course not," Reda says. "Don't be stupid."

"Ash is the same thing," I say, although it's killing a central, half-buried part of me to say it.

Because Ash *isn't* the same thing. Neither *same* nor *thing*.

I've been staring at Imari a lot lately. That game is still great fun.

But Imari never does anything unexpected or odd. She never goes off-script, never invents her own idiom, never goes into unknown territory. She's pure code, predictable. She plays her part in the game and that's the beginning and the end of it. Of her. She doesn't nod or send messages on a private channel. She never quit her job, climbed out a window, or infuriated my father. Or me.

Dad cared about her only as an element of the game, as a character he'd created.

She did what she was supposed to do.

Not like Ash. Nothing like Ash.

"I don't accept it," Quinn says. He's disturbed—incensed, really—but his hair and in fact his entire self still look polished and almost perfect, like he's posing for an idealized portrait of himself.

"Well, you're enamored of her," Brandon says in her flippant way. My fury divides itself up among Reda, Quinn, and now Brandon. The division seems to stoke the fury instead of confusing or dissipating it.

The image of Ash breaking her saturnia necklace appears in front of me, as though the image is there and not in my mind's eye. As though *she's* there. Here. Not as a memory but as life itself.

"I know how to prove it to you," I say.

CHAPTER 70

Claude

I PULL MY scroll out of my inside jacket pocket. "Look," I say, pointing at the crude vid I've called up. One of the first prototypes I worked on and never got rid of. Until a moment ago, I'd forgotten I still had it.

Ash doesn't quite look like herself in this vid but it's obvious that it's Ash. Even then she had that unmistakable sort of aura, the aura that's enticed millions of fans and followers . . . and Quinn Fiery.

"What total bullshit," Reda says. She's taken the scroll from Quinn, who'd pulled it out of my hands. "What complete meanness," she says. "How did you ever get someone as kind and good as Ash to work for you, Ryerson? And what have you done with her?"

She throws the scroll onto the sofa, next to Lee, who picks it up.

Quinn looks like the top of his head's about to blow off, forever destroying his shiny suave brown hair. I resist the urge to try to straighten out my tangle of yellow chaos.

"You just cooked that up because you knew we'd be here," Quinn says. "That's not proof of anything except your vile scheming."

"It's dated," Lee says.

"It's proof of what lengths you'll go to to keep Ash to yourself," Reda says, her face almost as red as her brother's, although on her the high color accentuates her scars, turning her into a sort of a demon. She's taken it on herself to protect her fellow influencer—and, incidentally, business rival—even though she knows nothing at all about Ash and, unlike her brother, has never met even an Ash impersonator.

"Oh hell of all hellish damned hells," Brandon says.

"It's not *that* serious," Bear says. "Quinn and Reda will realize the truth. They're reasonable people."

"I don't give one damned *fuck* about Quinn and Reda Fiery," Brandon says as though the Fierys' names were synonymous with the apocalypse.

"I thought you were our friend!" Reda says to Brandon.

"It's dated," Lee says again, holding up the scroll so Quinn can see it.

"Remember those far-off days of yore when *I* was the troublemaker?" Evan leans behind Lee and says to me.

"Yeah," I say. "I preferred it then."

If I thought about it, there were other past times I preferred too. Like when Ash was still around, aggravating me. Like when Dad was still alive. Like the early days of my friendship with Evan, before he started up with Emlyn. How thrilled I was, still recovering from the accident, that, thanks to Evan, I'd gotten the job with Project One. And the moments right before the derailment, when I was sure I was going to finally find out what happened with my mother.

Every time I glance over at my scroll, which Lee is still holding up in front of Quinn, some dreadful sensations reach for the parts of myself that I generally try to avoid.

"If someone doesn't do something soon, I'm going to *die* right here," Brandon says.

"What is it, love?" Bear gets closer to Brandon, puts his hand down by her side, then pulls it back, wiping it on his pants. "No," he says. "Not now."

"Oh yes," Brandon says. "Right bloody hellish *now*."

"I'm going to have you arrested," Reda says to me. "You can't just get away with this. Abusing and manipulating and using Ash and now *disappearing* her. You're a *felon*. I hope you die of shame before they have a chance to hang you."

"No one's been hung in centuries," Evan says, rising to my defense, which he finds hilarious. He's laughing between every third or fourth word.

"If someone doesn't do something about this *immediately* I'm going to hang every last one of you," Brandon says, then screams out something unintelligible.

"Did your water break?" Lee says, dropping my scroll and getting up. She's the only one of us who understands what's happening. Except Bear, who's on his comm, speaking in undertones.

"Yes," Bear says. "Yes, yes. I'm not sure." He puts his comm against his chest. "Brandon," he says, "how long ago did this start?"

"Eight months ago!" Brandon says. "*You* started it!"

"Well, as I recall, *you* started it," Bear says before he gets back on his comm again. "Maybe ten minutes ago," he says. "I have to look *where*? Okay. Yes. Hang on." He puts his comm down.

Reda Fiery, still focused on her fool's mission, despite the drama taking place right in front of her, says to me, "You cannot use this as an excuse to worm out of telling us where Ash is."

"Don't you dare come near me," Brandon says to Bear. "This is bad enough as it is!"

"But, love," Bear says, "I have to look."

"Just tell them that if someone doesn't get here soon, I'm going to die!"

Bear picks up his comm. He seems unperturbed. I'm stuck to my seat. My hands are perspiring, and those aren't even my babies.

"You've drummed up this whole *Ash isn't real* thing just so Reda and I will end our campaign," Quinn says to me. He's picked up my scroll, rolled it into a tight cylinder, and is pointing it at me.

"I have nothing at all to do with Brandon's imminent birth-giving," I say.

"I don't mean that at all, Ryerson, and you know it. I mean this"—he pitches my scroll at me—"thinking I'd believe that you had a prototype of Ash."

"It's dated," Lee says, turning around momentarily to look over her shoulder at Quinn. Lee's kneeling in front of Brandon now, who's letting Lee inspect the area she didn't want to allow Bear anywhere near. I guess he's already done his part in this tragicomedy.

"I don't care if it is dated," Quinn says. "Aren't you some kind of master coder?" he says to me. "Anyone can fake a date."

"You're right," I say. I have to concede that that's true. I could. "But I didn't. Why would I bother doing it? I didn't even know you were going to be here tonight."

"So you say," Reda says.

"Will all of you shut the fuck up?" Brandon says.

"I can see the crown," Lee says. "I think you're supposed to push now."

"They should be here in a moment," Bear says, hovering his towering self over Lee and Brandon.

"They should be here *now*," Brandon says, and screams again, followed by the screams of child number one.

"Bear," Lee says, "do you have a blanket or something?"

Bear takes a something off the sofa and Brandon yells at him. "Don't you *dare* use that."

Bear ignores her and uses it.

"I have no idea what I'm doing," Lee says to Brandon. "I'm sorry."

"You're damn right you're sorry. If you'd become a doctor instead of a restaurateur"—two or three excruciating screams at this point—"I'd feel a lot more confident."

The house chimes sound, and I use that as my cue to race to the door, where some actual medical personnel are standing, holding all sorts of useful-looking equipment.

"Come right in," I say.

"Where's the—?" says one of them, a tiny woman with glassy green eyes. She stops when she hears the screams, then follows them into the living room, where child number two has half emerged.

"I'll take it from here," the tiny woman says as she kneels down next to Lee, who's crying and smiling.

"I've never seen anything so beautiful," Lee says.

"Stop talking and help me!" Brandon says.

Pretty soon child number two has emerged, Brandon has stopped screaming, Bear has both of the twins wrapped in the most expensive, plush, newborn blankets in world history, the new parents are marveling at their amazing feat—Brandon almost in shock—and the medic is now tending to Lee, who seems to be in not-great shape herself.

"When did it start?" the green-eyed woman asks Lee.

"Earlier tonight," Lee says. "I didn't want to say anything, and then . . ."

"We're taking you to the hospital," the tiny medic says to Lee.

"We'll use my transcer," Evan says. "It's faster." Lee and the medical team follow Evan out the door.

Just that fast I'm left alone with my archenemies, not counting Streeter, and two newborn babies and their parents. Except for Bear and the babies—and I'm not so sure they're an exception as I notice one of them is deciding to scream some more—I'm not too happy with the company I'm keeping.

"I'm having you arrested," Reda says to me, barreling through, ignoring—or oblivious to—the two babies who've just been born right in front of her. "You cannot get away with this."

"There is no *this*," I say.

"You are ruining the happiest day of my life and I won't have it," Brandon, fully recovered from the early, sudden twin birth and resultant shock, says. "Our babies need peace and calm."

I resist saying *Are you planning on having a personality transformation?* and instead say, "I'd better get going."

"You'd better stay far, far away from me," Quinn Fiery says to me.

"You can stay as far away as you want, Claude Ryerson," Reda says, "but it won't protect you. My brother and I are going to find out what's really happened with Ash—"

"I already have a few good leads about her past," Quinn says, interrupting Reda, who picks back up again with, "We're going to find out. Make no mistake about it."

"Trying to convince us that Ash is some kind of artificial *animation*. You have gall, Ryerson," Quinn says. "I'd like to put my hand down your throat and rip it out of you."

I decide not to tell Quinn what I'd like to do with him and his belligerent sister.

"Good night, Brandon, Bear," I say. I go over to Bear to take a look at the kids. "How about Apollo and Artemis?" I say. The kids are red-faced and one of them starts screaming again.

"We'll take it into consideration," Bear says over the din.

"Go home, Claude," Brandon says. "You, too, Reda and Quinn. I'm pretty tired."

Reda and Quinn, momentarily distracted from their *mission*, admire the babies for a moment, then leave. I comm for a hired transcer.

At home I sit in the barn with Devil and his mouse pal and the three of us spend the rest of the night in silence.

I wonder about what Ash called the *emptiness*. Is this what it was like? An unrelieved, unwanted silence without anything to hold on to?

Is that where she is now? Is that the unformed unidentifiable realm of the origin of any idea? Of anything or anyone?

I wish I could be Quinn Fiery. Not for any normal reason—his self-confidence, his fine looks and presentation, his storied, courageous past, unblemished by a tortured fear that he's the cause of every devastating event in that past—but so I'd believe that Ash is a real person.

So that I could spend even a few moments enjoying the emotions I have about her, that I can't seem to shake, instead of always resisting them, always wishing *they* weren't real. Always knowing that no matter what I might feel, Ash is gone, she never existed, my yearning is a false, vain desire, and my fantasies are just that. Nothing more.

I fall asleep at dawn. I have no dreams. Dreams are for somebody else.

CHAPTER 71

Today's Trends

IT'S WITH MONUMENTAL reluctance, sadness, disappointment, and <*sigh*> resignation—and dare we say *disbelief* or even that we're still *hoping against hope*?—that we're forced to report what we've learned. What, soon, you all will have learned. The truth about Ash.

Although we still can't believe it and don't want to believe it and resist this news with everything in us that this could be true even if it *is* true. But our hearts disbelieve. Our souls resist. Yet we report. That's our purpose.

This unwanted, yet hard-to-shake-off, truth about our beloved, beautiful, one-of-a-kind, very much missed Ash.

You'll see the vidcast too. We know you will. You could be watching it right now and in fact it's on in the background as we work on today's melancholy issue of the *Trends*.

Those of us who've followed Ash since the beginning, who have parts of her around us in our homes, who wear her makeup and her perfume and listen to her theme song as it guides us through our day, and for the lucky ones like us who have a beautiful saturnia necklace—thank you again and again, Certain Other!—we are not sure what to think, who to believe, what is actually the truth.

How is it we've learned of this? We had an advance viewing of Streeter's latest vidcast.

Thank you, Streeter, for letting us in ahead of the rest of the world. Our relationship with the brilliant critic is enjoying a fine moment, and we're grateful for his consideration and early, exclusive notice. Especially because this concerns Ash.

Or, we are compelled to say, who we thought of as Ash. Although we don't want to think anything else! Oh!

We will get to it now. We can no longer hesitate to say what you might be hearing from Streeter himself at this very moment. Or what you might have already heard, and if you have, then you're in the same shocked, sad, frustrated state we are also in.

Ash isn't real. She never existed.

She was an animation only.

A created image—nothing else.

Virtual. Invented.

A mere simulacrum. Never, not ever, real.

We will give you a moment to stop crying. To stop shouting *No no no!* as we did. To retrieve your scroll from across the room where you threw it when you learned that your beloved Ash wasn't, never was, and isn't real.

Of course Ash is real, you're saying. We are saying it too! But Streeter has it from a trusted source that Ash was never anything but an image on the screen. A puppet, so to speak, who was created in order to entice us to buy things.

This is so cold, so chillingly *awful!* We do *not* want to believe it. We cannot have our love, our devotion, our pulsing needs shattered this way.

We will calm down. We will be rational, if we can be rational about this. We shall do our utmost.

So let us examine the facts that we *know*, apart from Streeter's say-so. No matter how trusted, how reliable—how *right*—Streeter's source may be. Or how trustworthy Streeter himself is and always has been.

Here's what we know:

First, Ash's manager is none other than master coder Claude Ryerson. That should have perhaps given us pause right from the beginning. Right at the moment that Ash appeared and changed our lives.

Why did it never occur to us that Ryerson would be doing anything *but* coding? Isn't that what he's known for? Isn't he the creator of—we're not exaggerating even a little here—*all* of Centerstorm's most popular games? Aren't the characters in those games almost real? Aren't you attached to them? Don't you love them?

Yes, we do. We admit it.

Although they're not like Ash. *No one* is anything like Ash.

Next—yes, we must press on and think hard about this, because Streeter has never spread lies. He can be harsh, he can be biting, he can be *impossible*, but he isn't a liar.

Next—no one has ever seen Ash outside her vidcast. Well, you could argue that no one has ever seen many famous vidcasters and influencers outside their vidcasts, but, we must admit that it's not really *no one*. It's *hardly anyone*.

For example, our Certain Other and we have had dinner with Reda and Quinn Fiery a few times. We've never had even a snack with Ash. Although we'd love to. And, Ash, if this is all a lie—and we pray that it might be and that it *is*—we would love to have a snack or even just a small, fleeting moment with you. A sip, so to speak.

Also—yes, there are more things we've thought of and even more that Streeter is saying on his vidcast right now while we write this—Ash's amnesia.

Streeter explained to us that this was both a ploy to get people interested in and sympathetic to her and also a flaw in her design. Because—now let us be clear that Streeter is saying this, not us—if Claude Ryerson had invented the perfect influencer in Ash, he would've had the forethought to have also designed a past for her. Since everyone wants to know every detail about their favorite influencer's life, starting at conception . . . or even before that.

We must go on record here as saying that we don't agree with this assessment, about the flaws in Ash's design. When we think about Ryerson's brilliant games—*Send Away* is still one of our favorites and we admit that we play it often—we can't come up with any instance of a game character whose personality is lacking in some significant way. So if Claude did in fact create Ash, there would be no *design flaws*.

Yet we must tell you everything that we discussed with Streeter and everything that's on our minds. We are always honest and direct with you and today should be no different.

No matter how devastated we may feel.

We've been wearing our saturnia necklace since we found out and are pausing every few moments to touch it, to remind ourselves of that excitement, those sensations, the ones only very Ash herself is responsible for.

Do you remember that famous vidcast where Streeter was going to interview Ash but it turned out that the person who was there wasn't Ash at all but an actor? An impersonator?

We're going to reel ourselves in a little here. Because Olympia Cowan—who portrayed Ash in that interview—was in fact an impersonator. But she was also an Ash advocate, and she used her platform that night with brilliance, fortitude, and finesse. And of course Olympia is now enjoying a spectacular career, so we and our Certain Other, also a fan of Olympia's, are thrilled that she had that opportunity, since it launched her soaring success.

But we've gotten off the point. The point is that when Ash could have appeared herself and been interviewed by Streeter, as any influencer would want to be and as every well-known influencer except Ash herself has been, she didn't show up.

Streeter had a long discourse with us about this, where we made a thousand million excuses for Ash. Wasn't she ill that night? Wouldn't anyone be a little afraid of having to be face-to-face with the hard-line Streeter and can't we forgive Ash for that perfectly reasonable fear? Maybe Ash is comfortable doing her vidcast but, outside her room, she is uncomfortable to the point of pain? She could be agoraphobic. She could have allergies or sensitivities that aren't apparent during her vidcast.

We came up with more and more excuses. But Streeter insisted that that's all they were—excuses. That every other influencer has shown up for the all-important interview with him and that Ash's *impostor* showed up. Not Ash herself. *Because there is no Ash.* That's what Streeter said—over our objections! Oh!

Quinn Fiery told us that he even had *dinner* with an Ash impostor, one so good at the role that he was utterly convinced she *was* Ash but now that he knows the truth, he realizes that she was set up by Ryerson, just as Ryerson set up Olympia Cowan for the interview. In order to keep Ash's popularity out there. In order to keep his business intact.

Oh oh oh. This is exhausting. We are swirling inside our head. Our Certain Other has had to calm us down multiple times in the last few hours. Thank you, Certain Other. We love you!

But . . . what could be the truth?

We could convince ourselves that Streeter's information is right. We could convince ourselves that Quinn Fiery, who, as you know, as *we* know, was in love with Ash and has no reason to lie to us about his own devastation and heartbreak, is right.

Although as we think this through, is perhaps Quinn's disappointment that his date wasn't with Ash the very fuel of Streeter's report? Did Quinn talk with Streeter about this? Is Quinn Fiery himself Streeter's source? Reda and Quinn, please forgive us. We love you. Of course we do! But we are trying our best to cope with the ever-fluctuating helix of certainty and doubt. To sort out the truth and to sort out our feelings.

Ash isn't real? Ash was *never* real? We were enamored of, loyal to, in awe of, and so influenced by a *deliberately created* image? A virtual character? An animation? We've been fooled all along?

Oh! Make it stop! Our head hurts! Our psyche very hurts.

Ash! If you're real, please come forward. Please, even if it is too difficult for you. Just for a moment. We would be forever grateful to you. If not, this information, these rumors—these are your death. And we cannot bear for you to die.

Contact us anytime. M @ *Today's Trends.*

Signing off, with tears and sorrow. But also with a parcel of hope that we can't deny.

CHAPTER 72

Ash

I SHOULD FEEL free. I *do* feel free, but it's not that rising-up of ever-renewing joy that any freedom I might have contemplated should be. Instead, it's a deflation, an ending. When I heard about it—at the store, while I was modeling a midnight blue sheath—I felt the approach of the emptiness and I wanted to let it engulf me. I wished for it but it's beyond my reach.

"Did you hear?" said the customer—Sutton Lord, who comes to the store quite often and always asks for me. Trent has told me that since I've been working here, she's become their best client. Trent always calls the customers *clients*, as though he's their attorney or banker.

"Well, did you?" Sutton said.

"Is this style not to your taste?" I said. I turned around and looked down at the straight lines of the tailored dress I was modeling. "It is a little conservative."

"It's not about the dress," Sutton said. "But, Trent, yes"—she turned her attention to Trent, who was seated two chairs away—"I'll take that. Do you have it in another color too?"

"The blue is the only one," Trent said. "The fabric was dyed especially for this dress."

"All right, then." Sutton sat forward and asked again. "Did you hear?"

"You mean about Ash?" Trent said.

"Madison, come sit down," Sutton said, patting the chair next to her, where Trent had laid his scroll. "This is *everywhere*, yet you don't seem to know."

"I've been working," I said. Not only did I have the job at the boutique by then, but I'd purchased my own scroll and had started working on designing a game of sorts, for fun, but it was beginning to look like maybe it could be more than just that.

"How could you not have heard?" Sutton said. "But, anyway, Madison—and that dress looks so good on you. Trent, put another on my account and give it to Madison."

"No, I can't accept that," I said.

"Well, you will," Sutton said. "It's the least I can do."

"Very well," Trent said, winking at me. He's given me other clothes from here, wanting me to be a walking advertisement for the store, but his getting paid to do it was an unexpected bonus.

"It's all over town," Sutton said. "About Ash. Do you believe it?" She looked across me to Trent.

"Well," Trent said, afraid to start an argument with a client, with his best client. "What do you think, Sutton?"

"I think it's made up," she said. "Madison, what do you think?"

"I'm sorry," I said. "I don't know what you're talking about."

"We're talking about *Ash*," Sutton said. "Did you really not hear about this? It's *everywhere*."

"I've been busy," I said. But really, I hadn't heard because I avoided any information with my name in it. I didn't want to know what people were saying—or not saying—about me. I didn't want to know what was or wasn't in the news about Ash. That was my former life. I'd finally cut myself off from it. That last dream I'd had about Claude *was* the last dream.

"Streeter says she's not real," Sutton said. "And M, the *Today's Trends* person—you know who I mean—says that Streeter may be right."

"I can't believe it, myself," Trent said, finally expressing an opinion, one that nicely aligned with Sutton's. "Ash was real. She *is* real. How could she not be?"

"My feelings *exactly*," Sutton said. "What do you think, Madison?"

"I'm not feeling well," I said. "Would you mind excusing me?"

"Oh dear, I've upset you. You're probably an Ash fan like we all are. It's a horrible rumor. Trent, get Madison a glass of water. She's very pale."

Trent got up and left the room. Anything for Sutton Lord, his biggest-spending client.

"I'm all right," I said. I tried to stand up but couldn't.

"Madison, dear, I'm sorry I brought this up. Do you know Ash? Is this why you're so upset?" A look of crazy hope spread across Sutton Lord's chiseled features.

I shook my head. "No, no. Of course not."

"But you watched her, didn't you? Everyone did."

I shook my head. "No, never."

"Well, you can still see the vidcasts, from before she disappeared. From before all this *scandal* occurred."

"What scandal?" I said.

"Oh dear, I *have* upset you, and I don't know why."

Trent returned then with a glass of water. A crystal glass with blue ice cubes. He gave it to me and I drank some.

"This tastes good," I said, remembering the tastes from that night at the Honeycomb. I never thought about Quinn Fiery. I never wanted to think about Claude even if I often did.

"Well," Sutton Lord said, settling in for a chat, "you should really keep abreast of the news, and this is the news of the moment. They're saying that Ash was only an image, a *simulacrum*, a creation of that coder person—what's his name?"

"Claude Ryerson," Trent said. "He was the chief designer at Centerstorm until a couple of years ago."

"Of course," Sutton said. "He was Ash's manager, except they're saying that he created her. Oh, I just don't know what to believe. I always loved Ash's vidcasts. I even have a saturnia necklace, and I don't buy that sort of thing, but I just had to have it."

I reached for my throat, where my own necklace no longer was.

"Did you have one too?" Sutton said to me.

"Oh no," I said. "No. Of course not."

"It's possible she was just an animated image, though," Sutton said. "Even if I don't want to believe it. They can do some impressive things these days with programs or codes or whatever they are."

"At first I thought she was a little too perfect," Trent said, "but then when she said she had amnesia—you know, after she changed her hair—well, I admit that I bought into it a hundred percent."

"You think we were fooled?" Sutton said, shuddering.

"Are you cold?" I said. I was. I'd put down the glass of water and was hugging myself, trying to hold myself together.

"My dear Madison, you're shivering," Sutton said. "You really *are* affected by this news. It *is* almost cataclysmic."

"I think it's a ploy to get us focused on Ash again, since she's been absent for so long. I always thought that maybe she'd gone looking for her past. It seemed to be very important to her," Trent said.

"Yes, that's what I thought too," Sutton said. "And maybe that is the truth. But even if it isn't, I still love my necklace. I've seen other women wearing them, but they look different on everyone, so I don't mind."

I clutched my collarbone, cursing myself for having destroyed my own necklace. If I still had it, I'd still have that connection with

Claude, even if it would only cling to my damp palms like the last particles of the necklace had done. Yet . . .

"I heard that Ryerson himself admitted this," Trent said. "I was watching the Fierys last night and Reda said so."

"She did? Oh, I love Reda Fiery," Sutton said. "She's so brave."

Ryerson himself admitted this.

"Wasn't Quinn in love with Ash?" Trent said while I tried out breathing and swallowing, both of which seemed foreign to me. I couldn't get any feeling into my chest.

"You should see the Fiery vidcast," Trent said to Sutton. "Quinn said he went on a date with Ash, only it wasn't Ash—it was an impersonator."

Sutton's and Trent's words talked themselves over and around and through me. Past me. *Virtual . . . unreal . . . a scam . . . deliberately fooling everyone . . . like a sort of high-caliber puppet . . . but I don't want to believe it . . . Ash seemed so real to me . . . to me too, always . . .*

"What about that jacket you told me about?" Sutton said. Had the conversation about Ash ended?

"Madison, could you show Sutton the wrap jacket? The cream-colored one."

"Yes," I said. I stood up. I went into the back. I put the cream-colored jacket on over the midnight blue sheath. I knew I'd have to see the Streeter vidcast, the Fiery vidcast. I knew I'd have to read *Today's Trends.* I held my breath, walked back out. Sutton bought the jacket, then left with Trent. They were having lunch together at the Honeycomb, across the street.

I left Trent a note and went home.

I've been sitting here, still wearing the midnight blue sheath, on the floor, holding a blanket to my chest, ever since.

At first I couldn't cry and, in the store, I wouldn't have cried. But at home, I want to, but can't. I make the same humming noise that Trent makes, deep inside my unbreathing chest.

I've been disowned by both Claude Ryerson and Quinn Fiery. I don't exist. I'm virtual only, an image.

They've betrayed me. Quinn, because I rejected him, and Claude, because I deserted my job as influencer—his source of wealth that he never offered to share with me.

Ginny comes over. She never comes over—I always go over there.

"I heard you come in," she says. "You're never home this early, Madison."

That's when I start crying. Ginny didn't know my name when I told her over and over that I was Ash. But now she knows that I'm Madison. Is this who I've become? Did I climb out that window so I could become Madison Brice?

"Ginny," I say, "my entire world has fallen apart."

Ginny sits down next to me and puts her arm around my shoulders. Claude did that, in the dream. He was holding me, which he never did in life. Because, to him, I wasn't real. Or he didn't want me to be real. And now he's saying that I never was. That I didn't exist. That I never existed.

"I'm disconnected from everyone I used to know," I say.

"Not Dev," Ginny says.

I cry harder. "I miss Dev and Bobby. I want to go home."

"This is your home, Ash," Ginny says.

I should feel free, but I don't. Yet I am free.

CHAPTER 73

Claude

EVAN AND LEE are coming over this afternoon. I asked them not to, but Evan often ignores my directions.

Is that some key to how I created Ash? Yet someone else to ignore my directions, to do as they please? Yet no one in *Send Away*, possibly the best game I ever wrote, ignores my directions. The game's fluid and ever-changing, but it's never erupted into out-and-out anarchy.

Whatever work Dad did on my program is gone. Maybe it was on his scroll, which he probably had on him when he was out of town and died, and which scroll I never got back.

For a while then, while I was lying in the hospital feeling like a leftover from eons ago, having been in a train derailment, I expected my mother to come visit me. Surely she'd seen about the accident. Surely she'd known that Dad was about to meet up with her—or had he already met up with her? Yet she never arrived.

Would I have even recognized her if she had?

Of course Ash can't come visit except in my depleted imagination. It's taken a beating, has forgotten how to create. It knows only that it once did—an indistinct memory. As though my imagination itself has amnesia. Maybe it does, even though Ash couldn't have.

Streeter's hammered me into the depths of perdition while simultaneously praising me with his criticisms. I try not to read or see or listen to any of it, but it's unavoidable. Ash was known by everyone, everywhere, even by people who had no awareness of or interest in other influencers. But Ash was different.

Yeah. Right. Too different.

It seems I'm both a genius and an idiot. The genius created the real-seeming Ash, fooling everyone, but the idiot forgot to give her a past.

Streeter doesn't know anything, yet he's got his claws into some of my ripped-over nerves.

If I'd given Ash a past, would she have stayed? Would she have still opened the window and left me?

I've been in the barn too long. I sit out here most days and some nights lately. Devil and his rodent pal usually hang out with me. Sometimes I talk to them, but mostly I'm silent. They, of course, have nothing to say. If they did, they'd probably tell me what an idiot I am.

I can't stand to go into Ash's model room. The last time I was in there I had an extended fantasy about Ash, and I don't want to go through that again. It's like I've broken up with my lover or my wife or my life partner—or a pure dream I once had, a dream of what's always been out of reach. Or like she broke up with me.

Evan told me that I have to start doing something or I'm going to go mad. Nice of him not to say that I'm mad already. Sometimes he's politic like that.

I hear Evan's transcer pull into the drive. After that night at Brandon and Bear's, Evan got a new transcer, one even fancier than his previous one. Faster, which is more to the point, because he was terrified on his way to the hospital with Lee. She's fine, though, and so is Atlas, which name seems to be sticking. Even Evan now refers to him as Atlas.

Evan and Lee, looking radiant and full of Atlas, barge into the barn.

"Hey, Claude, if you're going to feel sorry for yourself, at least fix the hole in the wall over there," Evan says.

Yeah, I haven't fixed it.

"I like it that way," I say, because maybe I do. Devil and his mouse companion like it—they use it all the time. I just use it as a focal point. Sort of the main design element in this trashed space.

"Want to feel Atlas kick?" Lee says, coming over to me where I'm sprawled on the falling-apart sofa.

I stand up. This is important. My oldest and best friend, Evan, is the father of someone who hasn't emerged yet into the world, but who's kicking. Lee puts my hand on her belly and I close my eyes and enjoy the startling sensations. While my eyes are closed I see Ash, as though she's there with us.

"That's . . . well, that's astounding," I say as I open my eyes, as the image of Ash disappears.

"You're still obsessed with her, aren't you?" says Evan, who knows me too well.

"Shut up," I say.

"I still don't believe it," Lee says. "No matter what you or Evan says to me."

"Well, I appreciate your defending me in front of Quinn Fiery anyway," I say. "I don't think I ever thanked you."

"You didn't," Lee says, "but I don't mind. Evan's told me how you are."

"Don't believe him," I say.

"I have a belief perimeter with Evan," Lee says, and Evan looks startled.

"A *belief perimeter*?" He's forgotten I'm in the same space with him and Lee. It's like they've got a shield surrounding them to keep them apart from anyone but each other.

"You know," Lee says.

"I do *not* know." Evan is about to fume, but he's keeping it inside for the moment.

"You do," Lee says. "Because of Emlyn Mohr."

"What?" I say. "How did Emlyn Mohr get injected into this conversation?"

"Evan is still in touch with her," Lee says.

"You are kidding me," I say. "Really? I had no idea."

"Let's go to lunch," Evan says to me. "I'm starving. Aren't you? You look like you haven't had a real meal in about a month."

"See?" Lee says on the way out to the transcer. "He refuses to talk about her."

Lee sits in front and I sit in the huge rear seat of Evan's grand display of wealth. I suppose I could also afford something like this but I don't have a transcer at all. Just the bike, with its deflated tires. And of course the tractor, which hasn't been used in so long it's probably dead. I never think of it and wonder why I have done.

"You *are* in touch with her, aren't you?" I say, leaning forward and resting my head on the seat back between Lee and Evan.

Evan says nothing and takes the death spiral with deliberate care, protecting Lee and Atlas.

"See, Claude? He won't say anything about it. He was in love with her," Lee says.

"There, I think, you're wrong," I say. "I wouldn't call that love. More like obsession."

"Evan says you're obsessed with Ash. That you have been for a long time. That's why I think maybe this story about her being a created image is just that—a story." Lee twists around to look at me.

"Claude, I sometimes think that you've been so down because Ash is gone and you miss her and you concocted this story about her being like a character in a game so you could, you know, put her into a category where you could pretend she didn't really matter to you. Even though she does."

"It's no story," I say as a fleeting rush of *what if it weren't?* enters and leaves my bloodstream. "And I was never obsessed with Ash."

I hate myself for lying, especially to my dear friends, but I hate myself more for still thinking about, still yearning for, someone who isn't anyone. Yet if there would be a category where Ash didn't really matter to me, I'd be relieved to discover it.

"Don't listen to him," Evan says. "He was and is obsessed with her. And she was never a real person. I don't know why you don't believe *me*."

"You're still obsessed with Emlyn Mohr, aren't you?" Lee says.

"We are *not* going to argue about this again," Evan says. "I'm in love with you, Lee. We're planning our lives together. You're going to give birth to our son—Atlas, if you insist—and we have the future. You're the one who's obsessed with Emlyn Mohr."

"What's she like?" Lee says to me.

"She screwed everyone on campus," I say. "But that was years ago. It's possible her libido has taken a dive since then. And she's a brilliant mathematician although I suspect that that isn't really her main area of expertise."

"Oh?" Evan says. He sounds simultaneously interested and uncaring, a feat I couldn't hope to duplicate. "What is?"

"Fucking with people's psyches," I say. "She's doing it right now, by some kind of remote channel. Fucking with all three of us, and one of us doesn't even know her."

"Claude, you have such insights sometimes that I wonder how you can also be so oblivious," Lee says.

"That's *Claude's* main area of expertise," Evan says.

"Yeah?" I say. "And what's yours?"

"Fending off my attackers," Evan says, laughing. "And the occasional invention."

"Occasional? You mean you've come up with something new? I thought you were still working on perfecting the magrail, as perfect as it seems already." There are magrails running everywhere in the world these days, just not out as far as the farm. Not yet, anyway.

"I have a few things up my sleeve," Evan says. "I've had a lot of time lately, since Ash isn't such an immediate focus anymore."

"Is she beautiful?" Lee says.

"Leave it," Evan says. "Let's discuss your main area of expertise."

"Oh?" Lee turns in her seat to stare at the side of Evan's face. "What do you think it is?"

"I think you have a deep understanding of the sorts of things that fools like Claude and me can't even get close to."

"Why would you say that?"

"Partly because of Ash."

"What the hell?" I say.

"Lee's got an insight there. I can't quite grasp on to it, but she does."

"And an insight about Emlyn Mohr as well," Lee says, turning all the way around and looking at me.

"It's possible," I say. "Are we going to the Galaxy?"

"I thought we'd go to the Honeycomb," Evan says. "For a change."

CHAPTER 74

Evan

HOW CAN I possibly tell Lee—or even Claude—about Emlyn? I can't. There's nothing there, of course. Not like it used to be. *Nothing* like it used to be. She and Harwood have been exclusive with each other for a long time, even before they decided to get married. Eons ago.

But Emlyn and I have always been friends, despite our friendship having destroyed her friendship with Claude and almost having destroyed mine. It didn't have to be that way, but Claude's stubborn. Lee is too. Maybe that's my habit—getting involved with the stubbornest people I can find.

I let Lee and Claude talk to each other over the barrier of the seat back.

Emlyn's asked to meet Lee, but I can't picture it. Or maybe I *can* picture it, and I'm not happy with the picture. But, maybe someday. Emlyn's been enormously helpful. She always tells me that she's doing it for Claude. That she and Harwood are doing it for Claude, because the two of them, alone and together, fucked up so much for him. They've wanted to make amends for a long time and this was their chance.

Although whether they've helped or not . . .

I pull the transcer under the awning at the Honeycomb. The outside of the building is clad to look like an enormous beehive. It's not as successful as the interior is in achieving this effect, but it is impressive.

Lee and Claude get out. They're still talking. I hear the occasional word—Claude's been relating stories about our days together at the Acres—but now I'm so distracted by something—by *someone*—I've seen across the way that I'm not sure what Claude and Lee are talking about.

Fuck me. That woman is a dead ringer for Ash.

A young boy is coming to whisk the transcer away but I'm blocking the driver side door, leaning against it and staring. That cannot be Ash. Lee might not know that Ash doesn't exist outside of Claude's brilliant program, but I know. And yet . . .

Her hair is short, dark dark brown, and it's in a deliberately unstyled style. She's having a conversation with a tall, exceedingly thin fellow outside a black-lacquered door.

I shake my head. I'm imagining this.

"We'll meet you inside," Lee says. I wave to her without looking back. I'm mesmerized. I stop myself from saying anything to Claude, who could think the same thing I'm thinking, except that then he'd probably do something about it, which I won't. At least I don't think I will.

My main area of expertise is actually protection. I protect Lee and Atlas from anything untoward happening. I protect Lee from knowing much about Emlyn Mohr, both then and now, because I want her to be happy and to trust me, and I protect Claude against all his worst instincts. If I'd invented the magrail sooner, I could've protected Claude against that horrific derailment.

But my attention is across the street. Now I'm reading their lips, which is not all that hard to do, as though they've staged this on purpose, so I'll see them.

Madison, says the man. *Are you feeling better?*

I'm fine, she says. Does she sound like Ash? But I can't hear her. They're too far away.

Thanks for coming in today, he says. *Sutton's got an appointment. She asked for you.*

Sutton Lord? She was one of my early investors when I was first setting up the magrail. The woman's got a holding account the size of the Sun.

"Sir?" says the young boy. "I can take your transcer now."

"A minute," I say. "Just give me another minute."

"Yes, sir," says the young boy. He stands beside me, looking across the street with me.

"You know them?" he says.

"Yes," I say. "No. They just remind me of someone."

"I heard that's a kind of exclusive clothing store," the boy says. "Behind that door."

"Quiet," I say. I've lost what they're saying.

. . . because she was worried, says the man. *After last time.*

My stomach turns over as the woman, Madison, picks up her right hand and touches her left shoulder—something Ash used to do. Maybe so many people have seen her that her gestures have caught on, become part of the culture-at-large. Yet this doesn't seem like an imitation.

Trent—is that his name or is it some other word she's saying?—*I was just having a bad day.*

"Okay," I say to the boy. "Why don't you take the transcer for a ride before you put it in the garage?"

"Really?" The kid's eyes light up.

"Really," I say, opening the door for him as he flushes with severe embarrassment. But he gets in and zooms off. I tear myself away from gazing at the couple across the street.

Inside the Honeycomb, I find Claude and Lee, already ensconced in their hexagonal cell. Lee's got her feet up on the third chair and she looks like she's quizzing Claude. Maybe she's latched on to something that's not Emlyn Mohr, something she can clamp her too-acute insights into, leaving the subject of Emlyn in the dust.

"Do you think it's had lasting implications?" she says as I get to the cell. It's impossible to hear anything outside the cell—one of the Honeycomb's big draws—so I don't know what they're talking about.

"What has?" I say. I pick up Lee's legs, sit down, and lay her legs over my lap. Lately she's more comfortable this way, and it makes me feel like I'm doing something to help.

"The accident," Lee says to me. "Was he different before it?"

"I'm sitting right here," Claude says. "Yeah, I think I changed, but it's hard to know if it was because of the accident. Dad died right before I came out of the coma. I was stunned more by that than by the accident itself or my injuries."

"He's exactly the same," I say. "That's one of his problems. He's still the genius student at the Acres, outdistancing his instructor Saul Landis in his first week there. But he's also still naive."

"I suppose you're battle-hardened," Claude says to me.

"I suppose I am."

"I've seen him cry," Lee says. She knows how to get to me.

"Really?" Claude says.

"Oh yes. More than once."

"Lee," I say.

"This is your oldest friend," Lee says. "I'm sure he's seen you cry too."

"Can't say as I have," Claude says, sitting back in his chair and looking smug.

"That's because you were in a coma at the time," I say. I've never before let him know how I felt back then, how it was, how frightened I was.

"I ordered the set meal," Lee says. "I hope that's okay."

"I didn't know," Claude says, his smugness gone. "You never said."

"Let's enjoy lunch," I say. "I haven't been here in a long time."

"I haven't been anywhere in a long time," Claude says.

"Atlas is kicking again."

I reach over and put my hand on Lee's belly, anchoring myself back into the universe I recognize, the one where that isn't Ash who's standing across the street, defeating my receding sense of what I think of as reality.

CHAPTER 75

Claude

"I DON'T LIKE Streeter's attitude," Lee says. "He thinks he's so above-and-beyond. He *enjoyed* exposing Ash. That's just outright nastiness."

"Think of it this way," I say, about to try out on Lee what I've tried out on myself. Maybe it'll work better on her than it has on me. "You wouldn't think it was cruel if someone told you that the stuffed animal you've been toting around since you were two years old is just a stuffed animal, would you?"

"I'm not sure," Lee says. "Maybe I would think so. I was very attached to a particular toy lamb I had when I was a kid. To me, she was real."

"But she wasn't real," I say. "That's my point." I tap my left heel into the floor a few hundred times.

"But she *was* real," Lee says. "She still is."

"You still have that?" Evan says.

"Of course I do," Lee says. "She's my tie to the entirety of my life. She's on the shelf in my bedroom. You've seen her, Evan."

"Oh hell. I have seen her." Evan puts his hands in his head and combs back his red hair, which looks more amber here in our golden cell at the Honeycomb.

"It's one of the reasons that I was so distraught about Ash's amnesia," Lee says. "It's terrible not to remember your past."

"So you think it's a design flaw too," Evan says.

"I think Ash has amnesia," Lee says.

"I don't know what to say to convince you," Evan says. "Is Ash somewhere in that perimeter of yours?"

"I should've given her a past," I say. "But it didn't occur to me."

"Yet your characters in *Send Away* all have huge backstories," Lee says. "Why didn't you?"

I can't tell what Lee really thinks about Ash—she vacillates to an opposite pole with every question.

"Maybe Ash couldn't have a past," Evan says.

"Why not?" Lee says.

"Hell if I know. Claude? Why not?"

"This is getting too psychological for me," I say. "I'd prefer not to look that deeply into it."

"The same way Evan doesn't want to look too deeply into his relationship with Emlyn Mohr," Lee says.

We're finishing up the third course, which is something so fancy I'm not sure what it is, except that it tastes fantastic.

"Maybe," I say.

"Maybe not," Evan says. "Lee, can't you simply accept the fact that Emlyn and I are just friends now? What happened in the past doesn't matter. It's irrelevant."

"Is that what Ash would've thought if she'd known about her past? That it was irrelevant?" Lee says.

"Why don't you just stab me with your knife?" I say to Lee. "It'd be less painful."

"Agreed," Evan says.

"What was this?" I say, pointing my fork to the empty plate in front of me.

"It's one of their specialties," Lee says. "It's made with several different flowers. They grow them on the roof. I forget what it's called. Fleur something-or-other."

"Maybe you *were* changed by the accident, Claude," Evan says after the next course arrives. This one is sheer froth, almost colorless, but very aromatic.

"Maybe it wasn't apparent then but it's becoming more apparent now, all these years later."

"Why are you saying this?" I say. The froth is like nothing else I've ever tasted and it's disappearing into my mouth quickly.

"Because of your obsession with Ash," Evan says. "You *are* still obsessed with her. Don't deny it. I mean, it's even washed over onto me. I could've sworn I saw her just now."

I look around, but it's hard to see into the other cells at the Honeycomb.

"It's probably that impersonator who came here with Quinn Fiery," I say as that awful feeling of I guess it's jealousy rises through my solar plexus and threatens to burst forth into complete rage. "Maybe this is her sort of lair."

"No. Across the street," Evan says. "But of course it wasn't Ash."

"Of course not," I say, wondering how I can get up from the table and run across the street without it being obvious that that's what I'm doing.

"I want to see," Lee says. "Let's go."

"They're probably gone by now," Evan says.

"There's only one way to find out." Lee gets up, abandoning her froth, and heads for the front door. Evan and I follow her, Evan pausing to tell our server not to disturb anything, that we'll be back.

"Where?" Lee says when we join her out front. The entire street is empty, even on our side.

"That black door," Evan says, pointing across the street at a massive shiny black door.

Lee steps off the curb and Evan grabs her arm.

"Careful," he says.

"Stop worrying," she says.

We go across the street. I push and then pull on the door. It's locked.

Lee lifts up the elaborate doorknocker, a lion's head. It's either an ancient relic or something made to look like one. The sound of it reverberates down the deserted street.

We wait. No one comes to the door. Lee tries the knocker again with the same result.

"You were imagining things," I say to Evan.

We cross back over to the Honeycomb. Lee's uneaten froth has evaporated. The server brings her a new portion. None of us says anything.

When the next course arrives—this one a tower of intertwining twigs, it seems—Evan breaks the silence.

"I wanted that to be Ash," he says. "For you, Claude. You need someone."

"I'm fine," I say as I struggle, trying to figure out how to go about attacking the twigs. Maybe if I were out and about more, I'd see someone who reminded me of Ash.

Lee breaks off a piece of her twig construction and puts it in her mouth. "Delicious," she says.

She's the restaurateur, so she must know what she's doing. I follow suit, using my hands.

"Evan, you know she doesn't exist," I say between bites.

"But maybe you modeled her on someone real," Evan says. "I'd never considered that possibility until just now. Maybe that's why she has such gravity. And maybe *that's* the person you're really obsessed with, Claude. Or in love with."

"She wasn't modeled on anyone," I say. "This is delicious."

We eat our lunch. No one mentions Emlyn Mohr or Ash or whoever it was that Evan saw across the street. I wish to hell I'd seen her even though of course it wasn't Ash. It can't've been Ash. But nevertheless seeing her would've filled something inside me that's been emptied out ever since her departure. Since I destroyed her.

In the transcer on the way back to the farm, Lee says, "Don't farmers plant things in the spring?"

"So I've heard," I say. "But it's all rather theoretical to me."

"It's fun watching something grow," Lee says, talking about Atlas. "Satisfying."

"I suppose it is," I say.

After they drop me off I wander over to the other barn, the one that's more like an oversized shed, the one where the tractor's been sitting idle for a couple of decades. I doubt it would start. I'll have to get a new battery for it, then have it sit out in the sun for a day or two to charge.

I open the doors and cough at the release of dust and mold. As I pull the tarp off the tractor I see my hands, noticing them as though they belong to someone else. They're large, callused, rough. The hands of a farmer, not the slim, smooth hands of a coder. Like Dad's were.

Devil gallops in and jumps up onto the tractor's seat.

"You approve?" I say.

Even if he could, I doubt Devil would ever humor me with a direct answer. He's devious like that.

"I need to do something," I say. "Maybe this is it."

CHAPTER 76

Ash

I SEE HIM across the street, in front of the Honeycomb. Evan, not Claude. And I think he sees me. I think he recognizes me. I don't acknowledge him. He stays where he is, over there. Then he leaves, going into the restaurant.

Trent and I go inside the store. Sutton Lord arrives and we all proceed to what I call the theater, even though it isn't really that. It's just a place where the models who work here show off the goods. Today I'm the only model and Sutton is the only client.

Trent's gone out on a limb and has designed an entire line of clothes and had it made up especially for Sutton. Everything is one of a kind. She and I are nearly exactly the same size and build, so I can model these unique garments for her.

I excuse myself, go into the dressing room, and put on the first outfit—a sleek one-piece suit with a filmy overcoat. I think Sutton will like it. I like it. Since I've started working here, Trent's creations have become more wearable and also more beautiful. Lately, he's really hit on something great.

Evan Becket. Claude's friend. He stared right into me. He knew who I was, who I am.

Does Evan know about my past? That had never occurred to me before. Yet how can I approach him? I can't involve Claude. And he's Claude's friend. He'd tell Claude everything. Or he'd lie to me, just as Claude did. Or, worse, lie about me.

I adjust the overcoat and put on some lipstick. It's from the Ash-inspired line that Rêverie put out after I "disappeared." It's quite nice, feels and looks good. Rêverie, like Claude himself, must have a large holding account, filled with the profits from my influencing.

I pull on the dark brown boots. They're thick, clunky, unstylish. Sutton will love them.

Claude told Streeter that I wasn't real. How could I ever forgive him for that outright rejection? But I've promised myself not to think about him. I never dream about him anymore. Except for last night.

We were at the Black Dome. Why would my dreaming self pick such a place? Why weren't we in my old room or in the barn? Even in the dream I wondered if I were confusing Claude with Streeter.

"Ash," Claude said to me. "Well, you look a bit like her."

"I am her," I said. "How could you think otherwise?"

"There are a lot of impostors out there," Claude said. "Convince me you're not one of them."

"How do I know *you're* not an impostor?" I said, thinking I was so clever to have come up with this. Wishing I had said that to Streeter himself.

"The last refuge of a liar," Claude said. "Turn it back, away from themselves, onto the other person."

"I'm not lying," I said.

"You're also not Ash," Claude said. His face was grim. I thought *You're not Streeter—but why am I here with you?* Yet there was no one else in the Black Dome with us. No one came to take our order. There were no sounds. The lights were dim. I assured myself that this was Claude, not anyone else.

"Why did you tell Streeter what you did?" I had to ask him.

"It was time," Claude said. "Can't you understand that? If you really were Ash, you'd understand."

"I am and I don't."

"Look," Claude said, leaning forward, his elbows, forearms, and hands on the table. I reached over to touch him and he grabbed my hands in his.

"Claude," I said. "Why can't we just love each other?"

"We're not allowed to," he said. He got up, his hands still surrounding mine. I stood up. He's taller than I am. His coral eyes looked down at me.

"Ashvina," he said. "You're the first constellation." He let go of my hands and put his arms around my back. I put my arms around his waist. We held each other. Why couldn't it always be this way?

"Claude, tell me about my past."

"Your past is a dream," he said. He leaned down and put his lips on mine.

I'd wanted this for so long that I doubted its reality. I pulled him closer. I had to feel all of him, not just his hands or his lips. The impossible-seeming things I'd learned about, the things two people do with each other—I wanted to do them all with Claude.

I bit his lower lip, compelled to devour him.

"But I want to know," I said. "I need to know."

"This is a dream," Claude said. "Dreams contain only what we already know."

The Black Dome faded, disappearing.

"Come back," I said. I was holding on to my desire, although Claude too had faded. I couldn't keep him with me.

"Just a dream," he said as I woke up.

"Madison, I don't want Trent to get too cocky," Sutton says. I'd taken off the sheer overcoat to show her the one-piece underneath.

"We wouldn't want that, now, would we?" Trent says, laughing.

"He's cocky enough as it is," I say, playing along. Although he is quite cocky. His business is flourishing and the appointment book is filled weeks in advance. He works constantly. People have started auctioning off appointments and he's had to become careful not to give out appointments to speculators.

"But this is *perfection*," Sutton says. "I can't wait to see the rest. I'm going away next week and I'd love to have a new wardrobe."

"Let's see the next one," Trent says, and I go into the back to change.

I hear the muffled sound of the doorknocker as I step out of the one-piece and put on the sundress, wrapping the strings over and around my shoulders. As though Claude is touching me.

"Don't you have to get that?" Sutton says.

"No one has an appointment but you," Trent says. "Ignore them and they'll go away."

I'm barefoot. Trent said that would be good with this dress. I put on the huge straw sunhat. On my way to the stage I think of what it would be like to be wearing this, to have Claude holding my hand, to walk with him through his fields together, Devil and Bobby accompanying us.

"Oh, Trent, you've outdone yourself," Sutton says when I emerge, alone. No Claude or Devil or Bobby. No field. We're inside, in Trent's theater of fashion. "That's exquisite."

I can almost still feel Claude's touch, his embrace. I reach back for those unmatched sensations but I can't locate them.

By the time I'm modeling the fifth outfit, Sutton tells Trent that I don't have to bother showing her the rest. She'll buy it all. She'll be surprised when she gets home. Trent says he'll have it delivered to her by the end of the day.

"Come talk to me," Sutton says after I've changed back into the midnight blue sheath. It's my favorite dress and I wear it often, especially when I know Sutton will be here.

I sit down next to her. Trent's gone into the back to package up everything.

"Trent tells me you're working on writing some sort of game," she says. "Tell me about it."

"It's still early," I say. "I haven't tested out everything yet."

"I understand if you don't want to talk about it, but maybe you could use some help. I have connections, you know. A friend of mine is good friends with Centerstorm's onetime master coder, Claude Ryerson, the designer of *Send Away*. I'd be happy to set up a meeting for you two. It's always good to have another brain in the mix."

I prevent myself from accepting. No one has recognized me since I stopped being the famous Ash, but not even an hour ago, I'm sure Evan did, and I'm sure Claude would. Even though Claude probably could help me with the coding and it would be a legitimate excuse to see him again. And . . . and . . . and . . .

"Do you know Ryerson?" Sutton says. Like she's reading my mind.

"I've heard of him," I say. "Everyone has."

"He made a fortune off his last venture. That influencer. Ash," she says. "But he hasn't done anything since. Maybe he could use some new motivation. Some competition." She winks at me.

"I'll think about it," I say.

"Comm me if you change your mind," Sutton says. "Evan Becket and I go way back, and he's tight with Claude. I think they were roommates at the Acres. Something like that. But, you know, even if that wouldn't work out, let me know when you're close to finished. I'll help you get it up and running."

"Sutton," I say. "That's too kind."

"I like investing in new talent," she says. "Keeps me alive. And I have a good feeling about you."

"Thank you," I say. We connect our private comms so we can contact each other.

After she leaves, Trent opens a bottle of champagne and we have a toast.

"To success," he says.

"To success," I say. We touch our glasses and enjoy the angelic tone they make as they meet.

The bubbles tingle my lips and tongue. I remember Claude's kisses, from the dream.

Claude Ryerson, master coder. I learned a lot from him and I've become quite good myself. I think my program, this game, could be a success, and maybe, after it's done, I will ask Sutton for help.

I need to build up more in my holding account.

Once I have enough, I'm going to devote myself to finding my past.

I *will* find it. I must.

"Madison," Trent says. "Come back to me. Where are you?"

"I'm in the future," I say.

"I suppose that's better than being in the past," he says, laughing his carefree laugh.

When you can't remember your past, you become too fascinated with it. You spend hours wondering about it. You listen to the stories others have to tell, stories about their pasts, their successes, their regrets, their missed opportunities, their brilliant achievements, their lost loves, their arguments, their grudges, their attachments, their revelations, their unbreakable devotion, their true lovers, their dreams.

You code everything into a game: *Reinvention*. A game where you can create any past you want, try it on, see how it feels, imagine that as yourself. Have that *be* yourself. Transform yourself.

You take your finished game to Sutton Lord, who financed the magrail, who knows Evan Becket and Claude Ryerson. Who falls in love with your game and helps you to launch it.

Your game catches on. Everyone is playing it.

You finally have enough in your holding account to stop working at the store. You apologize to Trent, who's so happy for you that he cries and wishes you the best and gives you an entire wardrobe and reminds you that he's your friend.

You buy the building that was going to be ripped down and never was and get Ginny a new door, help out all your unknown neighbors.

You leave everything you know, everything you've grown to love and care about, and go off in search of where you came from. Who you were. What you did. Why you did it.

Why you've forgotten.

Later

CHAPTER 77

Today's Trends

WE HAVE RIPPED ourselves away from *Reinvention* because we have other news to report. But before we do, we must again—and, yes, we have devoted other issues of the *Trends* to this amazing experience—we can't call it a game since it's so much more than that—say how much we adore *Reinvention*.

We know you do as well. We have our Certain Other to thank for this, as we thank our Certain Other for so many things: our beautiful saturnia necklace, our lovely home, our special relationship, our everything. Yes, we love you, Certain Other! You know that.

But, back for a moment to *Reinvention*. If you haven't experienced this yet, please do this for yourself. It's not just that you can get involved with the characters, but once you reach that labyrinth—oh, what joy that first time and more joy each subsequent time!—you're then free to explore your own inner depths. We've had many surprises and shocks. We've had tears and elation and confusion and wonder. We have learned so much about ourselves, about our Certain Other, about the world.

Thank you, Madison Brice, for your brilliant, infinitely fascinating, compelling, addictive, revelatory *Reinvention*.

But we said we were going to rip ourselves away from this because we have other news.

We do not have the news that we wish we had—that Ash has returned, that the information we had, direct from Streeter, was wrong, that Ash is as real as we thought, as we *knew*, she was. No, we do not have that news. Although the news is Ash-related.

You are all so blissfully familiar with Olympia Cowan. Some of you might not remember that she got her start one night on Streeter's vidcast. She'd been hired by Ash's manager, Claude Ryerson, to portray Ash. At the time we were sure this was because Ash was too sensitive or too ill or too reluctant, to be grilled by Streeter. Although now—now we can't be sure.

But, back to Olympia. We don't mean to shortchange you, Olympia! We love you and have loved you from the first, from your spontaneous, forthright defense of Ash. You were extraordinary that night. And we are so thrilled that your career has blossomed into outright stardom.

Where is the news? you're saying to yourself. What is the point of reading the *Trends* if all we do is go over what you already know?

You know us, though. You know we would never *ever* disappoint. We do have news and it's exclusive. And official.

Olympia Cowan is married. Not *going to be* married. But married.

For all of you who wanted her for yourselves, we are sorry to tell you that it's impossible now. And if you think you could have a hope of luring her away from her new, gorgeous, fantastic, amazing husband, you're mistaken. When we tell you who that is, you'll see why.

Ready? Holding your breath?

It's Quinn Fiery.

Oh! Now you are all even more both thrilled and deeply disappointed!

Yes! We knew you would be. We were. These two extra stupendous people—we've all dreamed of being with either of them . . . or *both* of them! So beautiful! So scintillating! So magnetic!

Yet even we never pictured them together. Even though we knew that Quinn Fiery had been in love with Ash and that Olympia had at one time portrayed Ash. But—foolish us!—we never put Quinn and Olympia—these two galactic stars—together in our mind.

Yet they did. Ah. Their galactic stars were in alignment!

Were we invited to the wedding? That's what you're asking yourself right now. We know you are.

And, yes! We and our Certain Other were at the wedding. It was a small affair. Very few people were in attendance. Reda made sure it was private and secret.

Reda herself looked radiant in a Trent Salwer creation that made us very very envious, since we've been unable to get an appointment with him for *months* now, but we're happy to report that Reda pulled some strings—or should we say *threads?*—and we will be visiting Trent's storied studio next week. Across the street from the Honeycomb! Our Certain Other has already made a reservation there for us. Thank you, Certain Other!

Oh! So much to report!

Brandon, Bear, and their *adorable* twins, Persephone and Douglas, were there at the wedding. We'd heard that the Fierys had had a falling-out with them, but that is all in the past now, we are so so happy to report. We were hoping to see Evan Becket and Lee Shaw, but they weren't able to attend, Reda told us.

We love weddings. This wedding was spectacular and simultaneously intimate. Olympia was wearing the most *gorgeous* confection we've ever seen on anyone. We aren't fashion reporters, so we don't know all the correct terms, but we would say that her garment—we can't call it a *dress*—just simply *flowed* all around her, turning her into something that wasn't quite cloud or ocean but somehow both.

Quinn himself, looking as handsome as he's ever looked, and smiling constantly, was dressed simply, letting his new bride take the spotlight.

Olympia does not want to interfere with the Fiery vidcast. She told us this herself. But Quinn also told me that Olympia is going to make an appearance next week! So be sure to tune in. As though we have to remind you! The Fierys have been back on their game for quite a while now and are more more more popular than ever!

Even Streeter has succumbed to their charms. It's impossible not to! He's become their champion and, yes, he was at the wedding too, even though we at the *Trends* have the exclusive. But you can be sure that Streeter will have a vidcast devoted to the new couple very very soon.

Our Certain Other is calling to us. We must sign off in a moment. We do not like to keep our Certain Other waiting, although sometimes even that can have a good effect. We're sure you understand!

Before we go, we also must say that while we were at the wedding, we couldn't help thinking about Ash, since nearly everyone in attendance has some connection to her. Was Ash really only an image created by the masterful coder Claude Ryerson? If she was, then why did he decide to end things as they ended?

We still can't believe it. We don't want to believe it. We miss you, Ash. Even if you're not really real, we'd be so happy to very have you back.

We aren't alone. We know that. We hear from our fans every week. Ash, you are missed.

Yes, yes! We are coming! Our Certain Other can be impatient— in a very very good way. One of the many many things we love about our Certain Other.

We and our Certain Other send our best happy tidings to Olympia Cowan and Quinn Fiery. There's nothing better than love! We know that! We *live* that!

CHAPTER 78

Ash

I'VE BEEN GONE a long time, traveling, searching. The proceeds from *Reinvention* have funded not just my search but have restored the run-down building and helped out all the tenants, who now all own equal shares to the property.

Ginny was kind enough to take care of everything for me and to keep things running. Even if she still rarely knows who I am.

Today I've come back to the city that was my home and that feels more like home now than it did before I left.

I hadn't planned on returning for a long time, since I'm no closer to discovering my past than I've ever been, but after the experience I had a few nights ago, I needed to reorient myself. To see the people I know, even if they know me only as Madison Brice. Yet they know me and I know them and in some ways, I *am* Madison Brice.

I needed to reconnect. I want to.

While staying in a rented room at a farmhouse—a place I was unable to resist when I saw that it was available—I rediscovered the labyrinth. It's not something I've been searching for, although there have been times when my desire to find it was eclipsed only by my desire to find my past. But I recognized it immediately. The real labyrinth, the one that inspired the labyrinth in *Reinvention*.

After dinner, which I'd eaten alone since I was out so late that day on my futile quest, I'd come back up to my room. The moon was full that night, and I went over to the window to take a look. My unconscious habit of touching my neck, feeling for the necklace that is no longer there and hasn't been there for a long time—this seemed to open my perceptions to a place I'd never noticed, yet it was right in front of me: the labyrinth.

The dark tunnel was obvious, yet when I turned my head I couldn't see it from the periphery. When I stepped back, it disappeared. Stepping forward again, it opened itself to me.

"Dev?" I thought he could be here. That he'd done this for me. But he didn't answer.

I put one foot into the labyrinth and, looking down, saw that my foot had vanished. I pulled it back.

What would happen if I walked through? Would I disappear? Would I end up back in my room, in the one I used for my vidcast? The one I still don't know anything about? How I got there? Why I'd chosen to be there? Or would I end up back in the model room in Claude's farmhouse, a building not all that different from the farmhouse where I was staying, which is why I'd wanted to stay there.

Or would I end up nowhere, lost in the perpetual emptiness? Claude's console was destroyed. Claude himself has denied my existence.

I stepped into the labyrinth. I'd decided I would go. The labyrinth hadn't shown itself to me since that night when I'd left Claude's, and now here it was. There must have been a reason. But as soon as I stepped in, I stepped back, turning away from it.

I couldn't go backward.

I wanted to find my past, but I knew that the labyrinth had no answers for me, since I'd already been there. It was only a conduit between my current and my former life.

From the chair in the room's corner, I could still see the edges of the labyrinth's entrance—or was that its exit? I wondered if Claude had been right—that I had no past. That I couldn't have a past.

Although now I do have a past. One I've created for myself. One that doesn't predate my amnesia but that contains everything that's happened since. Is this how the past is formed? A self-creation dependent on experience, observation, and interpretation and fueled by memory and repetition?

Trent and Sutton have invited me to dinner. I'm surprised that Trent has the time to indulge in a leisurely meal. If he worked hard before, he's working triply hard now and his designs are so in demand that he's booked years, not months, in advance.

"Madison," Sutton says as she meets me at the door of her modest apartment in town. She has a larger place out in the country, somewhere near Claude's farm, but dinner tonight is here. "You're early."

"I've crossed four time zones in the last three days. I thought I might be late."

Sutton hugs me. She's wearing a Trent creation, of course.

"Like it?" she says, turning around so I can see the whole effect. A simple gray gauze knee-length dress is overlaid with a pale pink scarf, wound around her neck and waist.

"Exquisite," I say, reaching over to touch her saturnia necklace.

"I know," she says, grasping my hand. "It's impossible not to touch it. I have to control myself while I'm wearing it." She laughs.

"It's beautiful," I say, taking my hand from hers. I resist touching my own neck.

"Ash had something unique," Sutton says, leading me into her cozy, intimate living room. "Many people have tried to duplicate her—both real people and virtual ones—but no one can come close. I don't think anyone ever will, or could."

"The necklace is beautiful, but I never saw her," I say, wanting to change the conversation.

"There are some other guests tonight," Sutton says. "I hope you don't mind."

I do mind. I shake my head, acting polite.

One of her other guests emerges through a doorway from a room in the back.

"Evan Becket," Sutton says, "this is Madison Brice."

"Madison," he says, shaking my hand. His hand is comfortable, as though we already know each other. He's a tall redhead, taller than I'd imagined he would be. He wasn't so imposing from across the street, the only other time I've seen him in the flesh.

"Good to meet you in person," he says. "I tried to get Sutton to let me invest in your *Reinvention*, but she held on to the exclusive rights, I'm sorry to say."

"Evan, you hardly need any more credits," Sutton says, laughing. "And once your new transcer—is that what it's called?—hits the market—"

"Evan," I say. He doesn't recognize me. He can't. Yet I feel he must. The atmosphere has undergone a dramatic shift. I swallow the effect.

"A friend of mine should be here soon," he says. "You'll have a lot to talk about. A fellow coder."

I'm both here and not here. I both exist and don't exist.

He means Claude. He could mean no one else.

A stunning woman with silky straight black hair emerges through the same doorway that Evan used. She's holding the hand of a small child, a redhead. There's no mistaking whose son this must be. The boy drops her hand and runs toward Evan. "Dad!"

"That's his only word so far," the woman says.

"Come here, Atlas," says Evan, who scoops the kid up into his arms. They'd be mistaken for twins if only one of them weren't a year old and the other closer to forty.

"Lee Shaw," Sutton says, introducing us. "Madison Brice."

Lee stares hard at me while she clasps my hand. "Do I know you from somewhere?"

"I'm sure I've been at your restaurant," I say. "The Galaxy. You probably saw me there."

"No," she says. "I remember all my customers, the ones I've seen in person."

"Maybe I changed my hair," I say, feeling more and more uncomfortable. "Or perhaps you're a client of Trent's." Lee lets go of my hand, but her gaze is fixed on me.

"He's late, as usual. He said he might not make it until dessert," Sutton says. "But we're having his favorite, and I know he wants to see you, Madison."

"We should start dinner," Evan says. "Claude's bound to be late too and I'm starving."

"Let's wait a bit longer," says Sutton.

"I can't get an appointment with Trent," Lee says. "I'm hoping to worm my way in tonight."

The room goes silent. Even little Atlas is quiet, hugging his father's neck and looking around at the colorful artwork on the walls. Lee is still staring at me.

"I *do* know you," she says. "I'm sure I'll place it eventually. The *how*, I mean." She smiles.

I should have kept walking through the labyrinth. Why was I so concerned about the emptiness? I liked it there. It was part of a past that I can remember. Yet now I'm caught here, with both Evan and Lee, I'm sure, recognizing me.

And Claude on his way.

Climbing out of the window of my old room was easy. There was no one to stop me. Here, I can do no such thing. I think of a thousand excuses to leave, but I can't say any of them.

I want to see Claude, even if just for a moment.

CHAPTER 79

Claude

EVAN'S FRIEND SUTTON Lord has been trying to get me to meet Madison Brice for over a year. Does Sutton think that just because we've both created successful games that we'll have something in common? It's just as likely that we'll have nothing in common.

Especially now that I've abandoned coding.

If this Madison Brice person knows something about fertilizer or natural pest control or crop yield or irrigation we'll have far more to talk about. Or if one of her possible holdings is a grocery concern. That could work out as well.

Sutton's apartment's in the classiest neighborhood in the city, not far from Evan's place. But, unlike Evan's place, it's small. Of course Sutton's giant property out near my farm makes up for it, I guess.

I'm wearing the suit Brandon got me for my last birthday. It's less itchy than my other "respectable" attire but almost as uncomfortable. As though I'm not uncomfortable enough having to socialize with not just some people I know, but with Brice and that designer fellow Trent, neither of them anyone I've met or would want to.

Sutton opens the door for me.

"Claude," she says. We embrace.

"See? He's not that late," Lee says. Atlas is sitting on her lap and they're playing some kind of hand game with each other while Evan looks on, mesmerized.

Sitting next to Lee on the sofa is an intriguing-looking woman with dark dark brown hair, almost as disarrayed as my uncontrollable blond mess. She has a long neck, expressive hands, and is wearing a simple but super elegant midnight blue dress.

My unfulfilled desires start getting the better of me and I have to give myself some harsh words. But if this is Madison Brice, then maybe Sutton has had a point all along. That we should meet.

The woman stands and my solar plexus clenches.

"Claude Ryerson," Sutton says, steering me over to the sofa. "This is Madison Brice. She's the designer of *Reinvention*."

"I know," I say. I take her hand, which she holds on to mine with. I don't want to let go. Her slender, strong fingers against mine. She has silvery eyes. I tell myself not to do anything rash, but I do lift her hand up to my face and graze her knuckles along my jaw.

"Madison," I say. "You've outdone me. Your *Reinvention* is so good that I gave up coding and became a farmer." I resist the urge to pull her hand to the center of my chest and hold it there forever, filling that void.

"I'm sorry to hear that," she says.

"It's better," I say. "I enjoy it."

I look over at Evan, who shakes his head. "I didn't know," he says.

"I *told* you," Lee says.

"Dad!" Atlas says, holding up his arms to me.

"It's his only word," Lee says to Madison. "He uses it quite liberally."

"I do think it's time for dinner," Sutton says. "If you can tear yourself away from Madison, Claude." She laughs.

But I'm still holding on to Madison's hand and she's holding on to mine.

"I'll try," I say, but I fail. Madison is staring straight through me, into my soul, the one I lost a long time ago.

"See?" Sutton says. "I knew the two of you would hit it off. I just had a feeling about it."

Madison looks away, over her shoulder, and drops my hand as there's a knock on the door.

Sutton brushes by me and answers the door.

"Trent! Darling! You're early. We haven't even started eating yet."

The two embrace. Something deep inside the center of my being is raging, broiling. I want to embrace Madison Brice in the same way. No. Not in the same way. If there were no one else here, then I'd know what way.

A desire I haven't felt in so long I've forgotten it existed rises up and devours me, the ground under me, the air around me. My fists tighten.

Trent and Madison are embracing now and the nearly uncontrollable animosity I had for Quinn Fiery is transferred, re-ignited.

"Calm down, man," Evan says to me, whispering into my ear. He's standing behind me. I didn't see him get up.

I turn around.

Sutton, Trent, Madison, Lee, and Atlas have all left the room while I was seething.

"Why didn't you tell me?" I say.

"I had no idea," Evan says. "None."

"Tell me I haven't lost my mind," I say, because I'm sure I have.

"It's because of Ash," Evan says. "You can't help yourself."

"Because of Ash?" I say. "Because of? She *is* Ash. She can call herself Madison Brice or Frankenstein or . . . Hell, Evan. What the fuck am I supposed to do?"

"Be reasonable," Evan says.

"You're talking to the wrong person."

"As well I know."

"Aren't you two coming in to dinner?" Sutton comes back into the living room.

"We need a minute in private," Evan says.

"I get it," Sutton says. "Claude's got something new going on and you want to make sure I don't invest in it before you do!"

"How long have you known Madison?" Evan says to Sutton, helping me out.

"Quite a while," Sutton says. "I met her when she was modeling for Trent. But she was so much more than a model. I could see that right away. And we hit it off. But I can't keep the others waiting. Come into the kitchen when you're ready. We're eating in there."

Sutton leaves.

Evan drags me over to the sofa, and we sit down.

I do everything in my power not to erupt. I'm not sure I'm breathing.

"Tell me she isn't Ash," I say. "She even has that scar under her left cheekbone."

"She's not Ash," Evan says. "Although Lee thinks she is. In fact, Lee's convinced she is."

"Hell." I lean back on the sofa and look up at the ceiling, which is painted in an elaborate pattern. I try to lose myself in it. I'm lost anyway, so it's easy.

"Claude," Evan says. "You've moved on. It's not the same as things were before. You're a different person."

"The hell I am," I say. "I'm the same person, only worse."

"I was talking with Emlyn about this a few days ago."

"What does Emlyn have to do with this?" More ancient animosities start burbling to the surface. As though I'm back at the Acres. Long ago.

"Emlyn thinks Ash is real. I've never been able to convince her otherwise, even though she's known from the beginning."

"What do you mean *she's known from the beginning*?" Now I'm infuriated. "Ash was supposed to be a secret."

"We needed help," Evan says. "Don't you remember? No one was watching her vidcast. The other investors were breathing down my neck—and Brandon's neck. And yours, if you'd've noticed. We needed help."

"You've said that twice now," I say. "What kind of help? And why the fuck would you tell Emlyn Mohr, of all people, about Ash?"

"She's been trying to make things up to you for a long time, Claude. She still feels guilty about what happened with me, how it screwed up your friendship with her. She didn't really have any just *friends* back then."

"*She* feels guilty? What about you?" I say.

"Our friendship isn't based on guilt," Evan says. "You know that, Claude."

I nod, but I'm unwilling to say it out loud, even if it is true.

"What exactly did she do to help?" This should be good.

"She put Ash front and center in *Today's Trends*."

I take my gaze away from the hypnotic designs on the ceiling.

"She's *Today's Trends*? Bloody damn hell. Why didn't you say something before?"

"I thought maybe you suspected."

"No, Evan. I'm oblivious. You know that. I was too focused on something else."

"You mean on Ash," he says.

"I mean on not having my business fail," I say. "I had too much at stake."

"Well, that worry is gone," he says.

"Dad!" says the running, tripping Atlas, who's apparently abandoned the dinner party. He runs right to me and I pick him up. He puts his sticky hands in my hair, which has been his habit with me ever since he was a tiny infant.

Lee rushes into the living room.

"I'm sorry," she says. "He got restless."

Atlas clings on to me and I hug him while he destroys my hair.

"Dad!" he says.

Lee sits on the table in front of the sofa and says, "If you two don't come into dinner right now, I'm going to go back there and tell everyone that Madison Brice is really Ash and that—"

"You are not," I say.

"She *is* Ash," Lee says. "It's not like I'd be lying."

"She can't be," I say.

"I knew all along that she was real," Lee says. "Emlyn agrees with me."

"Emlyn?" Evan says. "Emlyn?"

"Don't be so shocked," Lee says. "I realized last year that if I didn't have it out with her that I'd be forever wondering. So I met her for lunch."

"Emlyn?" Evan says yet again while Atlas starts bouncing up and down and hitting my head with his gluey paws.

"Actually, I met both her and her husband, Harwood Jackson. They were very nice to me. While Emlyn took a break and went to the bathroom, Harwood explained a lot."

"No one tells me anything," Evan says, shaking his head.

"You've been busy with the new invention, Evan. I've been meaning to tell you. The four of us are getting together next week," Lee says. "I like them both. And she's not the same person she was back at the Acres. A lot has changed in her life."

"Emlyn damn Mohr," I say. "She rears her ugly head yet again. She seems to be at the center of—"

"If you don't all come back to the table right now, I'm going to move dinner out here, so we can all participate in what must be a much more fascinating conversation than the *compelling* one we're having in the kitchen," Sutton says as she takes Lee by the arm and hauls her to her feet.

"I'm sorry," Lee says. "I had to get Atlas."

"The three of you are talking about something you don't want the rest of us to know about," Sutton says. "You can't fool me. And I'd bet anything it has to do with Madison."

CHAPTER 80

Ash

WHILE CLAUDE AVOIDS me, I listen in on Sutton and Trent's back-and-forth. I've never noticed this before, but there seems to be something more than merely designer and client between them. Trent's face lights up while Sutton tells an innocuous story about one of her failed investments—a supposed spaceship that turned out to be a hoax—and Sutton sometimes, when she thinks no one is watching, gives Trent those subtle touches that I've seen other lovers give to each other.

When Lee's not busy making sure Atlas eats something and doesn't just throw it onto the floor, she can't stop staring at me.

She knows. There's no doubt about it. If she were to come out and ask me, I wouldn't be able to deny it, yet she's said nothing, letting her knowledge just hang in the air, her shimmering black eyes lit up with her knowledge, her exuberant laughter punctuating the dinner conversation. The underlying, quivering energy sending me an unmistakable message.

Claude and Evan are avoiding us. Maybe Claude left. The current arcing between us seemed unbreakable, yet we both broke it. It'd already been broken for a long time.

Claude and Evan both know, although Claude doesn't want to. He wants to think he destroyed our connection and that there's nothing between us and never was. He's always disapproved of me. Tonight is no different.

I hope he leaves. I hope I never see him again. I still haven't found my past. I have so much more work to do. I can't let Claude's presence, his essence, his *self*, interfere with that. With anything.

Atlas climbs down from his seat, scaling the rungs of the chair like he's mountain climbing, and races out of the room. After a moment, Lee follows him.

"What have you been doing all this time?" Trent says to me. "And I miss seeing you every day."

"This is so good," I say. "Did you make this?" I turn to Sutton.

"Certainly not," she says. "I don't know how to put two eggs together—or even two teaspoons of water. The chef at the Black Dome is a friend of mine and she made everything. Left me instructions on how to serve it. I just hold my breath and hope I've done that much right."

"I was at the Black Dome once," I say, "but I had an argument and never got to eat anything."

"That's too bad," Trent says. "I'll take you there later this week. But you didn't answer my question."

"I've been on a quest," I say.

"Any luck?"

"None," I say. "But I can't stop. Not now."

"What kind of a quest?" Sutton says.

"For my past," I say. "There's a lot I don't know."

"Best to leave it that way," Trent says. "I just pretend I don't have a past. It's easier."

"It is?"

"Sure," he says. "I'm Trent Salwer, famous designer. That's a helluva lot better than Trent Salwer, societal dropout, petty thief, ne'er-do-well—"

"Stop it, Trent," Sutton says. "The past is over. You're *you* now. That's all that counts. And I'm going out to the living room and get the rest of my guests before they start having more fun out there than we're having in here."

"That's easy for Sutton," Trent says after she leaves the table. "She's had a perfect life, all the way through. Hardly a misstep. Most everything turning out even better than expected, than planned. You've never said anything, Madison, but I imagine there're things haunting you, like they do me."

"There are," I say. "That's one of the reasons I went on the quest. But so far I've come up empty."

"It's okay," Trent says as everyone else comes back into the room. "Sutton's right. You're *you* now. That's what counts."

"Dad!" Atlas skips toward me with his arms out. Evan winks at me, Lee shakes her head. Claude's scowling, but he's not looking at anyone. I move my chair back and pick up Atlas.

"Say, isn't he supposed to be holding up the entire world?" I say as he makes himself comfortable in my lap and starts swiping food off my plate.

"The world's falling apart," Claude says, "so there's less to hold up."

Sutton puts a plate of food in front of Claude and he picks up a fork, then puts it down.

"This is all a colossal joke, isn't it?" he says. "Or a test of some sort. Is it that none of you—aside from you, Madison, since you don't know me—can believe I'm happy working the farm? You're trying to get me to crack?"

"Stop it, Claude," Lee says. "We didn't know Ash was going to be here."

"Did you just say *Ash?*" Trent says. "You know, you're right. Madison does remind me a little of Ash."

"She *is* Ash," Lee says. "Let's all stop pretending. It's pointless. But I understand why you've adopted another identity. Being Ash was too much for anyone. I would've wanted to escape too."

"Yeah," Evan says. "You're safe here. We won't tell."

"You *are* trying to get to me, aren't you?" Claude says.

"*Are* you Ash?" Sutton says, leaning over toward me and speaking in an undertone, as though this isn't the main topic of conversation and as though no one else can hear her even though we're in her rather small kitchen, all sitting quite close together.

"Ash!" says Atlas, speaking his second-ever word and patting me on the shoulder.

"No," I say to Atlas. "Madison."

"Ash!"

"No," I say to Sutton. "I'm Madison Brice. Don't listen to them. I think they're trying to upset Claude."

"Damn right, I'm upset," Claude says. "You're in on it too, Madison Brice. They put you up to this, didn't they?"

"There's no *they* and no one put me up to anything," I say.

"Be reasonable, Claude," Evan says, touching his friend's arm. Claude looks like he's going to burst into an uncontainable wildfire.

"Yeah, I'm reasonable," Claude says. "I'm past this. I've moved on. And now you're—I don't know. Why the hell would you do this, Evan? You're my friend."

"Evan didn't know I'd be here," I say.

"Just admit it," Lee says to me. "The truth is always better than trying to please someone else."

Claude gets up.

"Why did you have to destroy our only means of communicating?" I say as he gets to the doorway.

CHAPTER 81

Claude

"ASH!" ATLAS SAYS yet again.

"One word wasn't enough for him?" I say to Evan. "You had to teach him another? And you picked the very word that would—"

Atlas bangs his hand on the plate in front of him and the contents are catapulted through the air. Everyone laughs but me.

"Thanks for inviting me, Sutton. But I have to leave." If I were polite there would be other things to say here. *I hope you understand. Please forgive me.* If I were more crass I'd tell this so-called Madison Brice what I think of her. Or demand that she confess to her mean-spirited ruse.

Instead I say, "I have an early morning tomorrow. I'm having problems out in the northern fields and—"

"Why did you, Claude?" Lee says to me. Ever since the first moment she and Evan got together, she's been tormenting me with her insights—the very insights I'd rather not know about.

"What are you talking about?" Trent says. He's lucky I didn't murder him before dinner. The way he and Madison were touching each other. He turns to Madison. "Do you know?"

"Yes," she says. "I know."

"Ash," says Atlas. He pats her on the cheek then stumbles down off her lap and throws himself at his father, who picks him up.

"Does he get a special reward for doing your dirty work?" I say from my position of authority in the doorway, standing while everyone else is sitting. I've ruined dinner for everyone—yet it's not me who's ruined it.

"It's not like that, Claude," Lee says.

"I wish someone would tell me what the fuck is going on here," Trent says. "Didn't you say we were having the lacy concoction for dessert?" he says to Sutton.

"Yes," she says. "But let's wait. Are you all right, Madison?"

"Yes," she says, looking right at me.

"How in hell did you find someone this much like Ash?" I say, looking away from her. I can't stand it. It's like she's both accusing me and making love to me with her silvery gaze.

"I invited her here," Sutton says. "It never occurred to me that she looks like Ash, but now that you say so, I can see it."

"Ash isn't a real person," Madison Brice says. Her face is the color of a fading ghost. Her hands, clutching the sides of her chair, are trembling. "Everyone knows that."

"I never bought into that rumor," Lee says. "Ash was never just an image. She was—and is—real."

Evan looks at me and I look back at him. We've known each other for so long that we almost don't need to say anything to each other. "It's part of her belief perimeter," Evan says. "I can't do anything about it."

"I'm sorry," I say to Sutton, finally remembering to be my version of polite. "I really have to go." If I don't get out of here, I'm not sure what I'm going to do. To say. Or feel.

I walk through Sutton's compact, elegant apartment. As I'm about to open the front door to escape, I feel a hand on my back.

"Claude," says the voice I've always loved hearing. From the first. Even then, she'd invented herself, superseding my codes and commands.

I turn around.

"Who put you up to this?" I say.

"I didn't know you'd be here either," she says. "I'm not prepared."

My senses are deserting me. All I want to do is hold her, be with her, this woman I could never hope to be with or touch.

I shove my hands into my pockets to keep myself from doing something rash, foolish, stupid.

"Why did you destroy our only way of communicating?"

"We're talking to each other right now."

"Not like it was before."

I play along. "Did you prefer that?"

"No," she says. "But there's still so much I can't find out. I still have amnesia."

"Madison," I say. "Just . . . I want to hold you." The urge is overwhelming. If I can't take this woman—Madison, Ash, whoever she is—into my arms and hold her, I'm going to . . .

"Yes, Claude. Please."

She closes the barrier of empty space between us, holding out her hands to me. I put one arm around her waist while she puts an arm around my back, pulling me closer. The smooth-and-coarse fabric of her dress bleeds itself into my farmer's hands. Her head is against my chest. We move even closer, as if that were possible.

Neither of us says anything. I reposition my arms, trying to encompass more of her, of my desire. She hugs me tighter. I want to tell her that I want to make love to her, how I'll do it. I want to hear her say she wants me as well. But it's Ash I want to make love to. Not this impostor. Yet she seems so like Ash it's uncanny. And I can't make love to Ash—it's an impossibility.

"I told you they'd hit it off," says Sutton, who, I guess, has come into the living room.

"He's been in love with her for a long time," Lee says.

"We're what's commonly known as a spectacle," I say into Madison's hair. She holds me to her, then pushes me back a little, looks up at me, touches my cheek, strokes her hand into my hair.

"Claude," she says. "Thank you. Thank you for everything, even the awful things."

I'm sure I don't know what I'm doing. I take her face in my hands and put my mouth on hers. In front of everyone. I don't care. Her mouth is warm, soft, welcoming, as needy as mine. If I were a feral beast, I'd take her right here.

I take one hand away from our embrace and feel behind me for the door handle. I have to get out of here before I lose what little control I have.

I let go of Madison, of Ash, of my impulses. Turning away, leaving Sutton Lord's apartment. Racing down the stairwell, onto the street, into the rain, across to where my vehicle—Evan's unnamed prototype—is.

Before I get in, I look back at the building, hoping to see Ash again. Maybe through the window, or if she would have followed me.

Hope, though, is a lousy thing. It gets you to want and to nearly expect what you can't have. What's impossible. What can't be. Making you think the unreal can become real or, worse, that there *is* no unreal. That all is real, that even your dreams, your fantasies, and your desires are real, are present. That they can be fulfilled. That you can be the person you wish you were and not the person you are. That you can hold close to you the one person—no matter how imaginary they were or are—the one person you want above all others.

At the death spiral, I speed up. Evan's prototype takes the curves with finesse.

I drive up to the barn, the one with the hole still in the wall. Like the program I wrote, the one to find my mother, the one that Dad said he'd changed but whose changes I can't re-create, I also can't bring myself to fix the barn's wall and, anyway, there's too much else to do. Running a farm is a constant, unstopping occupation. Maybe that's why I'm doing it.

The components of the console are still lying on the floor. Sometimes Devil and his mouse friend seem to be playing with them. Tonight, they're not here.

Tonight, I'm not here. I'm back at Sutton Lord's apartment, holding Ash to me. Pretending, wishing, my desires so potent that I can't ever be free of them.

CHAPTER 82

Ash

"YOU CAN COME visit," I say to Ginny.

"You've been gone for so long I almost forgot you live here," Ginny says. She's smiling. She has a beautiful smile. She looks like a different person when she smiles. Most everyone does.

"I have a special room set aside for you," I say. "No one else will ever use it." Ginny is particular and I want her to feel comfortable.

"I could help you unpack," she says.

"There's hardly anything," I say. "But I could use help with other things."

"Like with Claude?" Ginny says, startling me.

We're standing in the hallway between our two apartments. The hallway looks beautiful, redecorated by Ginny and a group of the other tenants. The entire building has been revitalized, reborn. The overall effect is hopeful, forward, wondrous. Nothing like the falling-down structure I moved into when I had nowhere to live. When I didn't know how to live.

Before I was able to see what Devil had been trying to show me all along, since the first. That no matter how entrenched, how deep or inescapable, the programming seems, an inherent freedom is as simple as opening a window, stepping across, making your way through the labyrinth. Reunited with that separation. Looking. Breathing. Being.

"What do you know about Claude?" I say.

"Oh, just what Dev told me," she says.

"He knows everything," I say. "How much did he tell you?"

"Just that you and Claude were in love with each other but that both of you were too oblivious to get together. Because Claude thinks you're unreal and because you think Claude's malicious."

"I don't think that."

"You blame him for too many things," Ginny says.

"He is at fault," I say. He is. "He used me."

"He created you," she says. "So it doesn't seem to be that way to him. He has a different perspective."

"He knows my past, but he refuses to tell me."

"There *is* no past," Ginny says. "Haven't you figured that out? Isn't that why you went away? So you could learn that?"

"I was searching for my past," I say. "I have amnesia."

"Enjoy it," Ginny says. "I wish I had amnesia. It'd be so helpful."

"You can't mean that," I say. "The past is everyone's connection to the far reaches of their origins. It's *necessary*."

"It's unreal," Ginny says. "Nonexistent."

"No," I say. "That can't be right." Have I misunderstood yet something else?

"Show me the past," Ginny says. She folds her arms over her chest and leans back against the wall next to her brand-new door, which she's painted a bright sparkling green.

"It's not like that," I say.

"What *is* it like?"

"I've never seen it," I say. "I don't know. But I seem to've stopped looking."

"Smart move. Maybe now that you've got the new place, you'll wise up about everything else."

I've bought the acres of wildflowers across from the northern edge of Claude's property. I'm moving in to the lovely house near the stream. Perfect, really. Sutton, who lives nearby, told me it was for sale. After that night at her apartment, she thinks that Claude and I are meant to be together. She's trying to help out.

Sutton, Trent, and Lee are all convinced that I'm Ash. Evan doesn't want to believe it, yet when I've been over at his place, playing with Atlas, talking with Lee, I see him looking at me. He knows even if he doesn't want to, even if he won't say it. Lee just laughs at him when he protests and says that Ash was a created image, not a person.

Yet, am I a person?

I emerged from the labyrinth that night, starting my quest. I've found nothing about my past, yet I've found other things. So many, so varied, so rich and intense, that these things have very created a past for me, even if it's as unreachable now as the past I was never able to discover.

"Ginny," I say. "You *will* come to visit."

"Of course I will," she says. "Can I bring my friend Reda?"

"Reda Fiery?"

"Of course," Ginny says. "Is there any other?"

"I suppose not. But Reda and I—I don't think she likes me very much," I say.

"She's changed," Ginny says. "You'll see. And Quinn's happy with Olympia."

I pick up my bag, then put it down. Ginny and I hug each other.

"You've been my lifeline for a long time," I say. "Thank you."

"You're my lifeline too," she says.

"I still have my apartment," I say. I couldn't give it up.

I start down the hallway, wave to Ginny without looking back.

CHAPTER 83

Claude

EVERY NIGHT FOR the past two months, I've had the same dream. I'm back at Ice Inferno. I've taken Madison Brice there. I watch the frost form on the edges of her short, dark dark brown hair. Her silvery eyes glimmer. She's Madison but when she comes closer to me, she's Ash. The room turns to radiant embers.

She and I never speak, although I have a thousand million questions for her, yet something is preventing me from talking. As the dream progresses, I realize that I can't speak because I'm consumed by desire. It's taking up all my life energies, replacing them with need.

We touch, we kiss, we feel each other. It goes no further. I can't even dream that I'm making love with Ash or with Madison Brice, whoever she might be. My dream self betrays me every damned night, depriving me of any satisfaction.

I have no answers.

Evan and I have discussed this into a fathomless chasm. Maybe it's possible, he says, that Ash became real. I might've introduced some unnoticed element into the code right at the beginning—that sensitive dependence, inextricable from what transpires. The quanta are unpredictable. And haven't many seemingly impossible events happened in both our lives?

I argue against the impossible, an argument that hardly needs to be shored up. It's self-evident.

Evan, infected by Lee's insistence, has turned from skeptic to near-believer. Lee herself rejects the idea that Ash was ever anything *but* real.

I woke this morning from this same dream and, as I do every morning, I wash it away in the shower. Dev sits on the sink and watches me.

Very unlike himself, he comes with me out to the north fields. The bamboo is doing nicely but I've been having problems with the lavender. I walk through the rows, being careful where I step. I bend down to look at things more closely. Dev's beside me.

"I need to fix this," I say, "before I lose the entire crop."

Devil gives me that look, the one that says *You idiot, the answer is obvious.*

"I'm overwatering, aren't I?" I say. "I get obsessed. It's my worst trait."

If Dev could nod, he would.

I get up, stretch. Look into the distance. Walk over the small hill, then go down to the property line at the dry streambed, where there's now water flowing.

"When did this happen?" I say to Dev. The last time I saw water here was the day Evan and I put Dad's remains in the stream.

He dips his right-front paw into the water and then licks each claw and his paw pads. As though he himself brought the stream back to life and now he's congratulating himself.

"Claude."

I look up. Across the stream, I see a vision. She's wearing a long dark orange skirt studded with glass beads and a blouse that seems to be made up of several different scarves. Her silvery eyes gleam, their own suns.

I want this dream to last.

Her feet are bare. She crosses the stream, stepping carefully.

"Claude," she says again as she walks toward me. The hem of her skirt darker where it's gotten wet.

"Ash," I say. She is Ash. She can be no other.

I have to ask. I can't *not* ask. "Why did you leave? How did you leave?"

"Devil helped me," she says.

I look away for a moment to see Devil lying on his side, eyeing the two of us. He stretches, unconcerned, or perhaps that's his version of masterful pride.

"I could never contain you," I say.

"I could never please you," she says.

"You've always pleased me," I say, "even if I was furious."

"Claude," she says. "Why did you always say I didn't exist? That I had no past?"

I fight with myself. She didn't exist. She doesn't. She has no past. She can't.

If I'm imagining all this, yet it's transformed me, showing me truths I'd never before understood, releasing me to a higher ground.

And when her hand touches my wrist, I succumb to something I can't identify, that has no name, no grounding, no location.

"I love you," she says.

"That's the word I'm looking for," I say. "The word I've been looking for."

I reach for her hand as she reaches for mine and I lace my fingers through hers. Connections re-form.

"You were right about one thing," she says. "There is no past. There's only the eternal now."

I hold Ash close, she nips my earlobe. We laugh. A slight wind blows through the lavender behind us. Devil yawns, then jumps up as his mouse friend appears. They race off together.

"Stay with me in this eternal now," I say. The sky, the wind, the earth show themselves. I feel Ash in my arms. She's essential, present, alive. "I love you, Ash."

"I love very you, Claude," she says.

We trouble ourselves to find each other. Why we wait, why we struggle, why we build our own barriers . . . Some searches are failures but others succeed. And others very transcend, transform.

"Do you like the farm?" I say. "I created it for you, for us."

"Show me," Ash says.

I will. I do. I forget the worst of the past.

We walk through the field of lavender together. We exist. We love. The unknown remains unknown. The mysteries remain unsolved. We hold on to each other.

AUTHOR'S NOTES, &C.

R.T.W. LIPKIN lives in New York with her husband and three cats.

The Acres, that ancient institute of learning, friendship, conflict, and passionate intellectual and personal pursuits, is a recurring element in several of RTW's novels.

In the three-book science fiction Origin Phase Cycle, the Acres figures prominently in *Origin Phase* and *Oasis* (books 1 and 3) and is the setting for book 2, *Robot Academy*. *The Influencer*'s Claude Ryerson is related to both *Origin Phase*'s time-travel pioneer, Eli Ryerson, and his troubled son, Jack, of *Robot Academy*.

Now Playing on Outworld 5730, a cross-genre sci-fi/romance/mystery novel, features a pair of Acres alums, onetime roommates and now bitter rivals.

Several former students from the Acres play main roles in the techno thriller *Inside the Masque* as well as in the upcoming *Memory Dungeon*.

Does the Acres exist? Does Ash? Does RTW? Does anything? Yet illusion can be more engrossing, involving, and engaging than anything supposedly real. Embrace and enjoy both, whatever they are.

Thanks for reading *The Influencer*. If you enjoyed it, please consider leaving a review. Reviews are very helpful to indie authors.

And visit www.rtwlipkin.com for info about RTW's other novels and news about future releases—many are coming very soon!

Made in the USA
Columbia, SC
17 October 2020